THE LAST HUNT

The Guild of Two Roses Book One

Abby Grayson

*For every past version of myself who
never gave up on her dream.*

CONTENTS

CONTENT WARNING

Readers preparing to enter the world of the Guild of Two Roses are warned that this story is about space bounty hunters chasing dangerous criminals and therefore contains: gratuitous violence, death, blood and injuries, past trauma, graphic language, and on page sexual content.

CHAPTER 1

Bounty Alert

Maeve

Maeve Bladesbearer slams Pen Judd - minor thief, low level bounty, all around idiot - onto the gleaming bar, upending three drinks and cracking the wooden surface. Patrons scatter, leaving their spilled drinks behind.

"Hey!" the bartender shouts. "Bladesbearer! You know how rare this wood is! Shit don't even grow on Earth anymore!"

Maeve ignores him, pinning Pen to the bar - slippery with beer. In a rare fit of inspiration, Pen takes advantage of the slick surface, twists one arm out of Maeve's grasp and grabs a glass. He cracks it on the edge of the bar and jams it under her chin.

"Let me go or I gut you!" Pen growls.

Maeve clenches her teeth and heaves in a breath. She tries to remember what her short-lived therapist told her about how to emotionally regulate herself in violent situations, but all she can think about is how this idiot has somehow one upped her in this fight. His bounty isn't even worth the spilled beer. "You wouldn't gut me, you moron," she says. "You'd bleed me."

"Let me go!" Pen shouts again. Maeve feels the glass tremble at her throat.

"Despite her focus on semantics, Bladesbearer is correct," an irritatingly familiar voice says from Maeve's right.

"Shit," she grunts.

Aethon Trell leans on the bar, three feet away from Maeve and Pen. Though the bar is dim, Maeve can clearly see that his stupid square-jawed face is set in a shit-eating grin.

"Boy, Pen, you really are brainless," Trell says. "You hid in the Green Bottle? Don't you know this is a Two Roses bar?" His whisky colored eyes rove over the scene before him and he twirls a silver knife through his fingers. "Need some help, Bladesy?"

Maeve takes the opportunity to jerk her neck away from danger, but Pen snarls and Maeve sees the jagged edge of the broken glass heading straight for her face. Then Trell is there, restraining Pen's arm. He cracks the thief's wrist down hard on the bar, forcing him to release his makeshift weapon.

"I'm *not* splitting the bounty with you," Maeve grits out as she hauls Pen up and quickly slaps a pair of mag-cuffs on him. She flings her braid over her shoulder, and flicks beer droplets off her hand.

"Oh, is that right?" Trell says. He slides his knife into a sheath on his bandolier and crosses his arms. His Two Roses crest gleams on his collar - a gold shield with a pair of crossed roses - the same as hers. Their guild motto, *Et Cor Venari Est* - The Hunt is the Heart - is etched along the bottom. The Guild of Two Roses is the largest employer of bounty hunters in this sector. "It seems like you'd be lying in a pool of your own blood right now if I hadn't been here to save you," Trell adds.

"Please," Maeve scoffs. "I had him. You being here was pure luck. I've been tracking him all day, unlike you - sitting here on your ass."

"But see, Bladesy," Trell says, leaning forward. "It doesn't matter how long the chase takes. It's bringing home the prize that counts." He gives her a crooked smile, arching one brow.

"That's such bullshit," Maeve says with a laugh. "Sounds like you've never had a good chase."

"Will you two take this verbal foreplay somewhere else?" the bartender says. "You've made enough of a mess here already."

"What?!" Maeve snaps.

"Believe me," the bartender mutters. "I've seen enough foreplay - verbal and other - to know it when I see it." He starts cleaning up the glass from the top of the bar. "And I'll be sending Two Roses a bill for the damage."

Trell looks at Maeve with raised brows. "Guess we'd better take this elsewhere before things get... messy."

Maeve rolls her eyes and drags Pen up, but stops when she feels a light vibration in her jacket pocket. Her tab. Trell pulls his own tab out of his pocket. Maeve watches as his eyes light up as he examines whatever is on the screen. He looks up, his long, angular nose scrunching as he grins at her.

"What is it?" Maeve asks.

Trell purses his lips and taps the screen of his tab a few times before returning it to his pocket.

"You know what -" He taps her lightly on the nose. Maeve restrains herself from biting him. "I'm feeling generous today. I won't fight you for a piece of Pen."

"What? Trell - what is it? A bounty alert?"

"You'll see," he says, backing away from her. He leaves the bar with a jaunty wave. Several other bounty hunters in the bar are looking at their tabs and murmuring excitedly. Maeve spots Turik - another Two Roses hunter - sitting near her tapping furiously on his tab, his bulbous nose almost pressed to the screen. She hauls Pen over.

"What's the bounty?" she asks Turik. The thin man looks up with a frown which immediately morphs into a weak smile as he sees that it's her.

"Oh - hey, Bladesbearer. It's for Daik," he says quickly. "Daik Montrose."

Maeve's heart begins to beat faster. "How much?"

Turik holds up his tab so that she can see it.

WANTED
ALIVE
DAIK MONTROSE
(smuggling, attempted murder, robbery, ship hijacking)
REWARD: 6 MILLION CREDITS

The picture of Daik shows him mid-stride and looking back over his shoulder. He's wearing a beat up red jacket and a beard that Maeve knows is fake. His hair is slicked back over his head, and his eyes are narrowed at whoever is following him.

A slow smile spreads across Maeve's face. That's enough credits for the piece of land she's been eyeing on Kespar-2, and more besides. Enough to set her up for the rest of her life if she plays it right. Normally, the biggest bounties are reserved for high profile serial killers and other murderers. Daik hasn't murdered anyone - not that he hasn't tried. So he must have pissed off one of the mega-corps to earn a bounty that high. All the better for her.

Maeve is distracted as she pulls Pen from the bar and out into the pedestrian tunnel. If she can bring Daik in - this is it for her. She can finally get out of the game. Being a bounty hunter has always been about survival. After her parents died, Maeve managed to scrape up enough credits to get off her home planet of Tellamar and start fresh. Anything had to be better than life on a gang-run world without any protection - even the unknown of life off-planet. She'd stumbled across the path of an old hunter - Harlan Yates - and helped him catch a murderer. Yates had taken her under his wing, and Maeve hadn't looked back - until recently.

Six months ago Maeve had a confrontation with the very man whose likeness just popped up on every hunter's tab on Brix-9. Daik Montrose. She was chasing him for a decent sized bounty he'd garnered for smuggling weapons, but the hunt hadn't ended well. He left her unconscious and bleeding on the deck of Alpha Starbase - lucky to be breathing. He'd damn near shot her arm off.

The event had shaken her. Over the last fifteen years, Maeve had garnered a persona of being so untouchable that she'd started to believe it herself. The reality of the dangers of her job had made themselves known in a brutal way. This was never supposed to be her life. She's sure of it. Her parents had always wanted better for her. She wants something better. An intensity rises up in Maeve's chest like nothing she's felt in a long time. She *will* bring in Daik Montrose. And with the credits, she'll build a new life.

As Maeve makes her way to Two Roses headquarters through the clear tunnels set up all over the uninhabitable surface of Brix-9, she sees ship after ship taking off from the Stable. Danton Adder's ship - the Manasa - slides through the traffic and zips away. Maeve recognizes Graceling Empire's ship too - it's Needle-class and smaller than most others, but she takes off in a completely different direction than Adder. Maeve shakes her head. It's unlikely they have any true clues as to Daik's whereabouts. They'll be running the typical routes - visiting Daik's known associates, his public haunts, researching, bribing, threatening, etcetera. Maeve doesn't need to do any of that.

"You could just let me go," Pen says. He nods his head toward three ships taking off at the same time. "My little bounty isn't worth missing out on whatever this is."

"Shut up," Maeve suggests.

"Just an idea," Pen mutters. He turns over his shoulder and smiles at her. Maeve can see he's missing another tooth since she last saw him up close. She rolls her eyes and jerks him forward.

By the time Maeve brings Pen into Two Roses headquarters, locks him up, and collects his meager bounty, she knows that almost every hunter on Brix-9 has already gone after Daik Montrose. She strolls through the foyer of the building toward her rooms in the west wing. The Guild of Two Roses provides rooms to rent on Brix-9 for bounty hunters who want a home base at a convenient hub for space jump points. Maeve doesn't have anywhere else to go, and the security is good. It's a dusty, scorched sort of planet, but the convenience makes up for the lack of breathable air and beautiful flora. She's had her rooms for years.

Maeve draws her tab out of her pocket. She takes another look at Daik's weasely face and then taps a button to accept the bounty. Once she reaches her rooms, she switches over to a different app and logs in. A starmap opens, and a little red dot blinks in the Keidar Belt. Maeve smiles.

"What's that smile about, Bladesy? Thinking of me?"

"My god," Maeve mutters. She locks her tab and shoves it back into her jacket pocket. She turns to find Aethon Trell leaning on her doorframe. "What are you doing here?"

Trell narrows his eyes and takes a step into Maeve's room. "Why aren't you already off chasing Daik?" he asks.

Trell's presence overwhelms the room. His hair is coal black and long on top, but cut nearly to his scalp on the sides and back. It falls artfully over his forehead. His eyes are upswept at the outer corners, and he has a spray of freckles across his nose and cheekbones that mislead the general public into believing he's sweet and innocent. Maeve's focus betrays her momentarily as she remembers how Trell's freckles dot his skin in constellations all the way down that broad body of his. She also knows he's neither sweet nor innocent. He's cunning and ruthless. She knows it from experience and she can see it in the glint in his amber eyes. But last she heard, he's been hitting walls bringing in his bounties. Hasn't had a good collar in a while. He probably needs a win - which makes him all the more dangerous.

Maeve pulls herself up to her full six feet, though she's still shorter than Trell. He always takes up too much space. Four years ago she'd been forced to share a survival pod with him in order to escape from a murderous bounty they'd both been chasing. That pod had not been designed for two people for an extended period of time - let alone two people over six feet. She tries to push that trip from her mind as Trell tucks a hand under his leather bandolier. Maeve clears her throat.

"I could ask you the same thing," she replies. "Shouldn't you be sprinting off after Daik? Or are you flush with credits that you're keeping suspiciously quiet about? I thought you were on a dry streak."

Trell raises one eyebrow. "I saw the Archer was still in the Stable," he says, ignoring her jab. "And I thought to myself - why is Bladesbearer's ship still here?" He takes another casual step closer to Maeve, but she doesn't move. "And then I remembered that little dust up on Alpha Starbase awhile ago. I know Daik Montrose put you out of the game for a good month."

Maeve reaches up unconsciously and massages her shoulder. Her leather jacket hides a ragged scar from the fight she had with Daik. There's still some tightness there, despite Two Roses employing some of the best doctors and surgeons for their hunters.

"And?" Maeve asks. She sweeps her braid back over her shoulder and Trell's eyes follow.

He tilts his chin up. "I think you might have something on Daik. Maybe a hunch, or maybe even a solid location for him."

"And why would I have that?"

"Because," Trell says, his tone slipping into fake

condescension as though he knows she's being difficult on purpose. "Maeve Bladesbearer doesn't let people get away with shit like that. There's no way you haven't been plotting your revenge on Daik these past few months."

Maeve shrugs and slings her black go-bag onto her shoulder. She always has it packed with the essentials in case she needs to get off planet quick.

"Trell, at the risk of giving you too much credit, I think you're overthinking things. It took me this long to get Pen into lock-up. And as you can see, I'm about to leave," she says.

Maeve finds it almost eerie how easily Trell was able to guess the truth. She does have Daik's location. She's been keeping an eye on him since the incident on the starbase. She'd managed to sneak a stealth tracker onto his ship before the gunfight as a little bit of insurance, and now her diligence and patience are about to pay off in a big way.

"Sure," Trell murmurs, his eyes fixed on her face. "Makes complete sense."

"It's cute how you think you know me though," Maeve says as she brushes past Trell and gestures for him to get out of her rooms so she can lock her door. He steps out. "I'll see you out there," Maeve says over her shoulder as she strides down the hall.

CHAPTER 2

Rules

Aethon

Aethon Trell watches Maeve Bladesbearer stalk down the hallway, that damn wine-red braid swishing temptingly behind her back. She should wear it differently. One of these days some asshole is going to grab it and then she'll be in real trouble.

"Not your business," he mutters to himself. He turns and heads to his own quarters to grab his bag. He's not positive that Bladesbearer has a lead on Daik Montrose, but regardless, he has to get going if he wants to have any chance at beating her. He needs this bounty.

Aethon sighs when he sees Hera Laurent leaning against the wall outside his quarters. The elected leader of the Guild of Two Roses is unassuming. She has dark skin, short hair, and usually wears dark gray clothes - making her blend in with the gray of the halls in the building. She's one of the older hunters and has earned the respect of the members of the guild through her tenaciousness. Once Hera latches onto something - be it a bounty, an idea, or a grudge - she won't stop until she gets what she wants. She's relentless. And unfortunately for Aethon, she's been relentlessly pursuing him for his late guild dues for a while now.

"Hera - just the woman I've been hoping to see," he says. He gives her a flashing grin and winks.

"It's not like I'm hard to find, Aethon," she replies dryly. "If you've been hoping to see me you could have -" She shrugs. "- oh, I don't know - messaged me?"

"And take away the beautiful mystery of our relationship?" he says. Hera rolls her eyes and Aethon grimaces internally. He's not used to having to sweet talk the guild leader - he's never been this behind on his dues before. And she's always been immune to his charms anyway. His chest starts to itch with nerves and he slides his hand under his bandolier and rubs lightly.

Hera nods to the door, indicating that she wants to continue this talk inside. Aethon blows out a breath and unlocks his door. He gestures for Hera to go in first. She walks just inside and stops in his living room. He follows.

Aethon can't help but compare his quarters to Bladesbearer's - who's he had just seen for the first time. Maeve Bladesbearer's quarters are spartan. She has no art on the walls, and her furniture is utilitarian. He hadn't gotten a look in her bedroom, but he imagines that it's the same in there. Just the necessities. By comparison, his quarters are practically opulent. He has a large couch and a squashy armchair, a bar cart in the corner, and a decent sized entertainment screen on the far wall. He has several pieces of art from locals on his home planet of Freehail - all depicting the natural scenery. Mountain ranges, dense forests, and the black sand beach near his home town.

Aethon's quarters feel more like home than anywhere else, but there's an aura of disuse that permeates the rooms. He spends most of his time on his ship - the Menace. And nowhere fills Aethon's soul with comfortable content quite like Freehail did. He hasn't been back to his home planet since he joined Two Roses, despite his parents asking him to visit every time they speak over subspace. But he's not ready to go home. Not yet.

"Drink?" he asks Hera. He walks to the small kitchen and opens the fridge gesturing at the variety of beverages there. "Water? Beer?" He closes the fridge and nods his head toward the bar cart. "Or something more interesting?"

She huffs and crosses her arms. "Aethon, you know why I'm here -"

He holds up his hands and she pauses. "I know. Just give me a few weeks and I'll have your credits."

Hera sighs and rubs her thumb and index finger over her forehead. "I can't keep giving you breaks. People are starting to talk."

"Who's starting to talk?" Aethon asks. "Because if it's Adder -"

"It's no one specific," Hera interrupts. "There've just been a few passing comments. But it's about more than the credits. I can't allow Two Roses to weaken, Aethon. And if I have a hunter repeatedly failing to bring in bounties -"

Aethon feels his neck heat with embarrassment and he clears his throat and paces behind the couch. Hera doesn't need to tell him he's been fucking up these past few months. He already knows.

"I know you're a fantastic hunter," Hera says, her voice a little softer now. "And believe me, I don't want to lose you. But our crest must be respected. You know that."

"I'll have the credits soon," he repeats. "Just give me a little more time."

She stares at him, her dark eyes flicking over him like she's assessing his value. Aethon hates it when people look at him like that. It used to happen all the time after he left Freehail. People always underestimated him. Is Aethon Trell anything more than a boy from a backwater planet? Unlikely. Who's this Aethon Trell that he thinks he can run with the big boys in the Guild of Two Roses? A nobody. No name - no connections - no credits - no influence. He has spent the last fifteen years proving them wrong. Trying to prove that he's worth something - to them, and himself. Showing that he can bring in the big bounties - serial killers, murderers - the more violent the better. He clawed his way up and earned his place in the guild. And made the sector - and his "backwater" planet - safer for it. But no matter how many bounties he pulls in, it never seems like it's enough. Aethon hopes that someday he'll feel like he's actually made a difference. Like he's not just treading water.

Finally, Hera sighs. "Aethon. You've always been one of the best hunters for Two Roses." She gestures around at his quarters. "Can you sell some of this stuff to help pay your back dues?"

He rubs a hand across his face and tries not to roll his eyes. "An entertainment screen and a couch aren't going to make up for what I owe." He walks forward and leans against the back of his couch. "But Hera - I have a solid link on Daik Montrose. I'll bring him in. You can count on it." Aethon stares at her, his jaw set.

He sees it when Hera deflates slightly. "Fine," she

says. Then she points at him. "But this is your last chance. I need the last six months of dues from you by the end of next month. Or you're out."

Out. Out of Two Roses. Out of his home - even though it's just these quarters. He could always keep chasing bounties, but he wouldn't have the protection or backing of the guild. Aethon has crossed paths with rogue hunters. They're usually haggard and vicious, and completely alone in the galaxy. And even if he wanted to join the psychos in Black Dagger Guild or the idiots from Cobra Guild, it's unlikely another bounty hunter guild would want him with this stain on his record. Getting kicked out of Two Roses isn't a death sentence, but it's a blow most can't recover from.

It's January 15th by the common calendar, so that doesn't give Aethon a lot of time. Exactly six weeks. Can he catch Daik Montrose by then? He's not sure. But he has no choice. If he wants to stay in Two Roses he has to. And what else does he have besides the guild?

"I've got this," he says, his voice dark.

Hera nods once. "You'd better."

After she leaves, Aethon starts mechanically packing up his bag to bring to the Menace. He keeps most of his supplies on his ship, but he needs a few changes of clothes from his quarters. While he packs, he thinks.

He can't focus on how important this bounty is. He should just play it by the book and do what he's always done. But what he's always done hasn't been working recently. This latest rash of failures on his part is making Aethon rethink everything.

Six months ago, Bladesbearer beat him to a bounty. It was the one right before Daik Montrose shot her and put her out of the hunt for a while. She'd swooped in and nabbed Benny Ems - wanted for a nasty double homicide on a freighter. Aethon had been stuck on the other side of the sector, chasing down a false lead. Someone had used Benny's credit chip at a bar there. Turned out he'd given the chip to a friend to lay a false trail. Aethon was seething when he stormed into headquarters and saw Bladesbearer leaning on the wall outside the holding cell where Benny Ems lay, unconscious.

"He was mine!" Aethon had growled. Bladesbearer had just looked up at him with a beautifully crushing grin. She rarely smiled, and her expression threatened to knock him back a step. Her light green eyes sparkled and she pushed all six leather-clad feet of her body off the wall and stalked up to him.

"Key word," she purred. *"Was."*

"You -"

"I wasn't shadowing," she interrupted. "You lost him when he planet hopped from Vitraxia to Me'aldi. You fell for that credit thing, didn't you?"

Aethon didn't deign that with a response. "You knew I was chasing him. I thought you were hunting Gerani - or whoever."

Bladesbearer shrugged. "Right place, right time. Sorry, Aethon."

Now, Aethon shoves a pair of boots into his bag with excessive vehemence. Bladesbearer taking that bounty out from under his nose was the start of a six month dry spell. He hasn't brought a bounty in since.

Aethon thinks back to Bladesbearer's expression when he accused her of having a solid location for Daik Montrose. She'd almost looked surprised. He's had plenty of reason to doubt his gut lately, but he's almost positive he's not wrong about this. She knows where Daik is.

There are a few official rules that the bounty hunters of the Two Roses generally abide by.

1. *Et Cor Venari Est*
2. Crime is endless
3. Respect the crest
4. Criminals have long memories
5. Fraternize at your own risk

The first rule is the motto of Two Roses. The Hunt is the Heart. Aethon slides a light finger over the guild crest pin on his collar. He's put all of himself into this work ever since he left Freehail.

The second rule has been helpful for Aethon through the years, but now it taunts him. Crime is endless - there's always another hunt, always more money to be made. If he could just bring in a bounty.

The third rule is simple. The Guild of Two Roses must be powerful enough to inspire respect from other guilds, and fear in criminals. Hunters who belong to Two Roses must be ruthless, precise, and good at their jobs.

The last two rules are warnings. Criminals usually don't forget the hunters who caught them. A recently released or escaped criminal seeking revenge is always a possibility. Aethon has become used to watching his back at all times. And last - relationships between bounty hunters are dangerous.

Aethon thinks back to an incident a few years after he was inducted into Two Roses. Two older hunters - Harlan Yates and Jasmine Fellows - had gotten married. Harlan was gray haired and grizzled, his nose crooked from being broken and not set right. Jasmine was thin and wiry with light blonde hair streaked with silver. Aethon heard Jasmine talking to another hunter after the small marriage ceremony. She and Harlan had saved up enough money to retire on some quiet planet. Aethon remembers being happy for them, if a bit incredulous. At the time, he couldn't imagine giving up the hunt.

The week before they were set to leave Brix-9 and Two Roses for good, one of Jasmine's old bounties broke out of a high security prison. Aethon remembers the alerts popping up on his tab proclaiming the escaped convict as "unusually dangerous". Jasmine had, of course, decided she needed to get this scumbag back in prison before she retired. Harlan had gone on the hunt with her - unusual, but not unheard of for two hunters to work together. A week later, Jasmine returned to Brix-9, hollow eyed, dragging the criminal in tow. Aethon was there when she arrived. Harlan was nowhere to be seen.

Hera Laurent had just recently been elected as the leader of Two Roses. She watched, her dark eyes taking in the scene. Two guards took the criminal from Jasmine and locked him up in a holding cell.

"Where's Harlan?" Hera asked as Jasmine tossed her tab on the counter to receive her bounty.

Jasmine clenched her fists at her sides and shook her head. "Dead."

The air in the foyer of the building had gone still. Aethon watched as Hera placed a gentle hand on Jasmine's shoulder.

"That murdering asshole -" Jasmine started, her

voice dry and raspy. She gestured to the holding cell, indicating the criminal she just brought in. "He said he heard Harlan and I were married. And he hoped we would hunt him together." She shrugged Hera's hand off her shoulder and turned away. "Because he wanted to take away my future - like how I took his."

Her words have stayed with Aethon. He doesn't know what happened to Jasmine, but he always hoped she was able to find some peace in the end.

Aethon zips his bag closed and takes a last look around his quarters, thinking about what he has to do. Aside from the written guidelines of the Guild of Two Roses, there are also unspoken rules - the first of which is: shadow-hunting is a bitch move. Meaning, a bounty hunter shouldn't shadow another hunter in order to swoop in and take their bounty. A hunter does their own damn work. They follow their own leads. They use their own wiles and influence to find their quarry. A hunter can get iced out of Two Roses for stooping as low as shadowing. No one with any self-respect does it.

Aethon clenches his teeth and strides quickly out of his quarters heading toward the Stable. If anyone could make a bitch out of him, it's Maeve Bladesbearer.

CHAPTER 3

Shadows and Mirrors

Maeve

Every bounty hunter has a special connection to their ship, and Maeve is no exception. A ship is essential to the job, and most hunters spend just as much time living on their ship as wherever they call home.

The Archer is a Bracken-class spaceship - fast and stealthy, and shaped like a steel gray kite. Maeve has modified it to meet her specific needs. It's small, but more than enough for her. The door is at the back with a ramp for easy access. Inside, Maeve's quarters are to the right and equipped with a tiny bathroom. There's a brig to the left for transporting bounties, a kitchenette, and then there's the bridge at the front of the ship. The captain's chair is in the center, and the angled dash at the very front displays the ship's readings and controls. The dash is also equipped with a tiny 3D printer to create components for minor repairs. It's black now since the ship isn't fully powered on. The viewscreen is clear and capable of displaying all kinds of information about the route and surrounding area, but it's shuttered while the Archer sits in the Stable.

If necessary, Maeve can stay on board the Archer

for about a month before she needs to resupply food and fuel. One of her more expensive mods is a mirror-cloak which allows her to move through some areas of space undetected. But mirror-cloaks are a high ticket item on the black market and Maeve doesn't want to make herself a target for smugglers, so she only uses it in emergencies.

Recently, Maeve added an AI system to the Archer to help with routing and computer maintenance, but she's not sure the convenience will be worth the trouble since it has some strange personality quirks.

"Hi Maevey!" The AI's voice greets Maeve as she enters the Archer. The voice has a feminine tone to it, and the accent reminds Maeve of old Earth movies she used to watch with her parents. The sheer number of nicknames and pet names this thing spits out makes Maeve think it absorbed some truly strange media.

"Hello, computer," Maeve mutters. She tosses her bag into her quarters to the right of the entrance into the ship.

"Haven't I told you to call me TAI?" the AI says. "Technical Artificial Intelligence!"

"Fine," Maeve replies, rolling her eyes. "Just fire us up, TAI."

"Sure thing, honey."

The Archer's systems blink to life, the dash a rainbow of readings and settings, every system customizable.

"Open viewscreen," she says. She taps a few buttons on the dash, starting the calculations for her first jump. The Keidar Belt is about five jumps away from Brix-9, and the Archer's systems will have to rest after each jump, but Maeve wants to get there as fast as she can. At best speed, it will probably take her about a week - assuming nothing happens to throw off her timeline.

"Right on it, sweetcheeks," TAI chirps.

"Don't call me that."

Maeve opens the tracking app on her tab and checks Daik's location again. He's in the exact same spot in the Keidar Belt. It's a great place to hide. There are so many heavy metals in the asteroids around there that finding his ship will be almost impossible for most hunters. Maeve is certain that Daik already knows about the bounty and plans to lay low for a while. She smiles grimly as she does her routine system checks. He's definitely not expecting her.

"TAI, set us up for planetary departure," Maeve says.

"I got you, babe," TAI says. Maeve ignores the pet name as TAI seals the doors of the Archer and puts up the atmospheric shielding. The ship's engines make the deck vibrate slightly. It's a comforting feeling and Maeve embraces it. This is it. The beginning of her last hunt. Once she brings Daik in - she'll be done with Two Roses work for good.

She sits down in her captain's chair and gets in the digital queue for a departure slot. Brix-9 has an automated system that allows ships to take off from and land on the planet in an orderly fashion.

As she waits for the go ahead from the system, she scans the few ships left in the Stable. Lincoln's ship - the Toothbreaker - is still there. Maeve isn't surprised about that. Bear Lincoln is one of the more seasoned hunters of Two Roses, and every time Maeve has interacted with him, he's stiff and grouchy. He's probably not interested in chasing after a bounty that has everyone frothing at the mouth. He's more of a consistent workhorse - bringing in bounty after bounty in the low and mid-level range.

And then there's the Menace. Aethon Trell's ship is Bracken-class just like the Archer, but it's silver and has ostentatious red racing stripes down both sides. Suddenly, the Menace blinks to life, the engines starting and the lights turning on. Trell must finally be ready to leave. Maeve crosses her arms. She wonders how he's going to hunt for Daik. He's not the type to follow the crowd, so maybe he'll head somewhere more dangerous and try to pick up information from some of Daik's seedier contacts. A miniscule part of her feels bad for lying to him. He clearly needs the bounty. But Maeve has to look out for herself. Trell will just have to deal.

The Menace's lights flash twice. It's a universal sign amongst Two Roses members wishing each other luck on the hunt. No other ships are waiting to take off from the Stable, so Trell must have meant that for her.

"That Menace is hotter than a jalapeño's armpit," TAI chirps. "Want me to flash 'em?"

"God, TAI," Maeve groans. "What would you know about attractiveness?"

"My programming has a sexuality subroutine!" TAI replies happily. "And let me tell you - I'd love to tangle with the Menace's computer. They run CAL - Computer Assistant Lenoragram - and he is something else!"

"I really don't need to hear about your affairs with other AIs," Maeve says. "But if it will make you happy, you can flash them." If it will make her happy?

She's making allowances for the AI system's feelings now?

"Thank you, Maevey!" TAI says. The Archer's forward lights flash twice in response.

"TAI, what kind of emotional subroutines do you have?" Maeve asks warily. She really should have examined the AI more closely before installing it.

"They're quite robust!" TAI replies. "But you don't have to worry - there are failsafes to prevent me from the darker, baser emotions that you humans and other organic beings suffer from. I can show you the programs if you like!"

"Great," Maeve mutters. "Maybe later."

Maeve is distracted as her console beeps. She's been cleared to leave the planet. She can't help but grin as the joystick controller rises from inside the right armrest of her chair. Maeve grabs it and pulls the Archer out of the Stable. It might be safer to let the AI control the take-off, but Maeve loves the feel of being completely in control of the ship. The element of danger is exhilarating, and she prides herself on her piloting skills.

"TAI, take control of the inertial dampeners and the artificial grav," Maeve orders.

"On it, babe," TAI replies. "Ooh! Is the Menace coming with us?"

Maeve accelerates the ship and the viewscreen automatically lights up, showing her the flight path virtually. Settings and readings pop up on either side of the screen. Everything looks good. Maeve feels a small amount of force as the Archer accelerates to a speed fast enough to break through the atmosphere and out into space, but the inertial dampeners take care of the gforce pressure.

Once they break through the atmosphere, Maeve takes a moment to appreciate the clear black of space, dusted with sparkling stars. Brix-9 is much more beautiful than one would expect from orbit - all reddish-orange sands and low, ruddy mountains. Two Roses headquarters is just visible from orbit - a spiderwebbing compound with a gigantic main building in the center, and multiple wings spreading out from there - all underneath protective clear barriers.

Maeve adjusts her heading toward the nearest jump point. She belatedly realizes what TAI said before take off.

"TAI, what did you mean about the Menace coming with us?"

"They're right on our ass, Maevey!" TAI says, her voice tinged with excitement. "I hope CAL likes the view!"

Maeve scans the space around the Archer on the viewscreen and irritation floods her veins when she sees the Menace on sensors. What is Trell doing? Without thinking, she hails him. His face pops up on her screen a few seconds later.

"Hey Bladesbearer," Trell says. "You call for something specific, or just to see my face?" She can only see his head and shoulders on the screen, but he looks relaxed, his face set in that charming grin that Maeve hates.

"Ooh, Maevey!" TAI says. "That organic is setting off all of my sexuality subroutines! He's not my type obviously, but my data says that his mouth is the perfect shape for -"

"TAI!" Maeve snaps. "Be quiet. Monitor the course

and get the jump point coordinates ready." She looks back at Trell who is still grinning. He raises a brow.

"I think your computer likes me," he says.

"My new AI seems to have some quirks in her system," Maeve replies, shaking her head. "Don't take it as a compliment."

"Well, I think -" Trell starts.

Maeve interrupts him with a raised hand. "What are you doing?"

He shrugs and his dark hair falls over his forehead. "What do you mean?"

"Why are you following me?" she asks, her tone tense.

Trell shrugs again. "I'm going to the jump point, you're going to the jump point."

"Yes, but there are ten other jump points nearby," Maeve says through gritted teeth. "Choose another."

Trell leans back in his chair and laces his fingers together in front of his stomach. Maeve can see a small amount of tension between his brows that wasn't there before. "Nah."

"Excuse me?" she replies.

"I said - 'no'," Trell repeats, his eyes narrowing, his mouth curving up on one side. "Maybe you don't hear that very often."

Rage rises in Maeve's chest. Trell is probably her biggest rival in the Guild - the one she'd be nervous about catching Daik Montrose before her - if she didn't have the advantage of knowing Daik's exact location. But if he's seriously thinking about following her... he can't be. Or can he? Maeve thinks about Trell's recent lack of bounties. Maybe he's more desperate than she realized. But desperate enough to do something that will get him iced out of Two Roses?

"Trell," she says slowly, trying to inject her tone with as much venom as she can. "Are you going to shadow me?"

His brows contract slightly and he's silent for a moment. Then he leans forward, his eyes hard. "I have a proposition for you, Bladesbearer."

"No -"

"Just hear me out," he says. "We team up. Hunt Daik together. Split the bounty - an even fifty-fifty."

Maeve snorts in disbelief. "No way in hell."

Trell shakes his head. "Daik is crafty. It would be easier to catch him if we work together."

"No," Maeve snaps. "Maybe *you* don't hear that word too often either."

"If what you said is true, and you really don't have Daik's location, then why wouldn't you want to team up?" he demands. "That bounty is huge. Even half of it is more than either of us make in years."

But Maeve isn't about to tell Trell about her plans for the bounty money. Once she's out of Two Roses - she's *out*. The more people who know about her plan to buy land on Kespar-2 the more likely it is she'll get dragged into guild business again.

"I'm not teaming up with you," Maeve says. "I'm not splitting the bounty."

Trell leans back and nods. "Then you do know Daik's location. I thought so."

"I don't know anything more than you," she replies.

"We'll see about that," Trell says darkly. He ends the connection.

"That motherfucker," she mutters. "TAI, set up

an alert for the Menace," Maeve orders. "I want to know where that ship is at all times."

"Ooh," TAI says. "Kinky."

Maeve ignores the comment and a small indicator light pops up on her screen, showing the Menace following her route to the jump point. The bastard is going to shadow her. What a bitch move.

Maeve grits her teeth as they approach the jump point. If she has to lose Trell somewhere along her path toward the Keidar Belt, so be it. He's good, but he's not as good as her. Maeve grips the joystick hard and sets her jaw.

"Try me, Trell," she mutters. "Just try me."

CHAPTER 4

Jump Point Tricks

Aethon

Aethon has seen Maeve Bladesbearer angry many times. When Bladesbearer is angry, her pale freckled skin flushes from her cheeks, down her neck, and all the way to her chest. Her green eyes get bright and cold, her nose wrinkles, and her full lips pull back revealing white teeth bared in a snarl. Her jaw and pointed chin seem to sharpen, as if they could cut the object of her anger to shreds. She vibrates with intensity, her body tightening and readying for a fight. Aethon always expects her wine red hair to rise around her, like she's a goddess channeling lightning. It doesn't, but he likes that image. He likes watching people around Maeve Bladesbearer shrink in the presence of her rage.

He does not like being on the receiving end of it.

Seeing Bladesbearer's eyes go cold is the very opposite of what he wants. His mind conjures up the week they spent trapped together in a tiny escape pod. At some point during that trip, when both of them thought they might not make it, Maeve had looked at him with a combination of desperation and desire that made Aethon's breath catch in his chest. Minus the belief that they were going to die in that pod, it was a moment Aethon never wants to forget. He shoves the image from his mind. He can't think about the way she looked during that trip. He can't think about the feel of her beneath his hands or how her sharp voice had softened just for him. He has to get this bounty. And the only way to do so will be to fuck her over.

"Captain Trell." CAL's voice is distinctly male, and distinctly annoyed. Aethon has had the AI in the Menace for a few years now, and he and CAL work well together as an odd team. But CAL is interfering and judgmental for an AI. "Are we following the Archer through the jump point?"

Aethon sighs and leans back in his captain's chair. "Yes," he says. "And CAL, I don't want to hear -"

"We shouldn't be shadowing the Archer, Captain Trell," CAL interrupts. "It's against the code of the Guild of Two Roses."

"It's not against any formal code," Aethon growls. "I tried to convince Bladesbearer to work with us, but she doesn't want to. Now plot a trajectory through the jump point."

"Plotting," CAL says, his tone rife with disapproval. "You could have tried harder. I've seen you be very convincing when you want to be."

Aethon ignores the AI and looks ahead out the viewscreen. The jump point looks like a normal section of space, but it's surrounded by a gigantic, circular, open metal ring. The ring blinks with lights and Aethon watches as the Archer approaches. Each jump point brings ships to specific locations around the sector, allowing travel over long distances in a fraction of the time it would take to traverse normally. But it takes a significant amount of power from ships as small as the Menace and the Archer to make jumps. They have to recuperate power after each jump, usually requiring a ship to stop for about twenty minutes. However, Aethon suspects that Maeve may try to make a run for it as soon as she's through the gate - despite her ship needing to recover - just to lose him. He's prepared to do the same even though it will tax the Menace.

Aethon watches as the Archer approaches the jump point. The second it's through the gate, it disappears in a wink of light.

"Course laid in," CAL says.

"Punch it," Aethon says.

The Menace accelerates through the gate and begins the jump. The stars disappear and the familiar dense blue-black of jump space engulfs the ship. There's not a star in sight. Being in jump space doesn't feel any different than normal space, but not being able to see stars is unnerving to most people. Aethon leans back in his chair and grips the joystick in his armrest, ready to follow the Archer if Bladesbearer decides to make a run for it after the jump.

Two minutes later, the Menace winks back into normal space.

The Archer is nowhere in sight.

Aethon hops up and leans on the dash, craning his neck and peering out the viewscreen. "CAL - where's the Archer?"

"Scanning," CAL replies. "Nothing on sensors."

"What?" Aethon snaps. "They can't be gone as fast as that! They probably emerged from the jump point fifteen seconds before us!"

"Ten seconds, actually," CAL replies smugly. "This is what happens when you try to break the rules."

"Don't be so high and mighty, CAL," Aethon growls. "Scan on all frequencies."

"I did," CAL says.

"Fuck," Aethon mutters under his breath. He narrows his eyes as he pulls down readings on the viewscreen, his hands flying over the dash. Everything looks normal. He grits his teeth. How could the Archer possibly have disappeared like that? Disappeared...

"Oh Bladesy, you clever girl," he murmurs. He checks the sensors again, but there's no sign of the Archer. If he's right, the time spent on an extra scan will be more than worth the potential delay. "CAL, scan for triennial-gamma waves."

"Triennial-gamma waves," CAL says. "I'll have to realign the sensors."

"Do it," Aethon says.

"Realigning. It will take several minutes." CAL makes an annoyed sound he must have picked up from Aethon. "Ever since you and Captain Bladesbearer spent that week in the escape pod you've been overly focused on her."

Aethon huffs. "You're reading too much into things."

"No," CAL says. "I've kept track of every interaction between you and Maeve Bladesbearer since you linked my program to your tab. I've monitored your vital signs when you're around Captain Bladesbearer and your readings indicate an intense level of physical arousal -"

"CAL!" Aethon groans. "Did I tell you to monitor my vitals?!"

"I have your best interests at heart, Captain Trell -"

"You don't have a heart."

"No," CAL says, his tone slightly offended. "But my emotional subroutines have become attuned to your presence and I think you've become lonely."

Aethon rubs a hand over his face. The very last thing he needs is his damn AI psychoanalyzing him. "God, CAL -"

"Bladesbearer is the first person in a long time that you've shown interest in," CAL says coaxingly. "I know she appears to have rejected your suggestion that you work this bounty together, but maybe you should consider merging with her -"

"*Merging* with her?!"

"Or whatever it is you organics do," CAL answers. "I'll admit, my sexuality subroutines are rather out of date -"

"CAL -" Aethon interrupts, raising a hand in the air. "For someone who claims to love rules, you're forgetting one of Two Roses' main ones."

"Fraternize at your own risk," CAL mutters. "I'm well aware. Perhaps this risk would be worth it."

"Just realign the sensors and scan for the triennial-gamma waves," Aethon says, rubbing a hand over his face.

When the AI is finally quiet, Aethon sits back in his chair and thinks about the interactions he's had with Bladesbearer that CAL had apparently been listening to. He doesn't quite remember when he linked the AI with his tab, but it has probably been a few years. What has CAL overheard?

An incident in the gym at the Two Roses

headquarters from two years ago pops into Aethon's mind.

He'd just brought back a criminal who was responsible for a group of killings on a planet called Harash. The killer was nicknamed "the Harashi Hunter" by the media, which sounded too benign for his crimes in Aethon's opinion. Aethon had tracked the murderer to a warehouse in one of the biggest cities on Harash. He'd found the Harashi Hunter elbows deep in the stomach cavity of a young girl.

Rage had taken over Aethon. He'd knocked the murderer out cold, only holding back from caving in his skull because the bounty demanded the man be brought in alive. He tied the man up and immediately ran to the girl who lay motionless on a cold metal table. She was dead, her eyes blank, her body already stiffening with rigor mortis. Aethon had gently closed her eyes, his breaths coming in shuddering gasps as he took in the horror of the rest of the crime scene. Normally, he was able to separate himself from the atrocities he witnessed in his line of work. Things didn't tend to stick in his head. This had. The man had done this to seven young girls on Harash. And Aethon wasn't fast enough to save the last one.

Back on Brix-9 after he'd turned the Harashi Hunter in and collected his bounty, Aethon's mind was spinning. Everything he'd witnessed and his failure to save that last girl brought up memories he thought he'd long buried. He'd sprinted to the gym to work out until he collapsed, hoping to still his mind with physical activity. He remembers slamming a medicine ball over and over again against the wall so hard it had dented the metal. And then Maeve was there.

"Trell."

Her voice was soft but firm. Aethon had turned to find her a few feet away from him. He'd glanced around, but they were alone. She was wearing black leggings and a forest green sports bra. He was always struck by her height. He was only a couple inches taller than her. She was lean and strong, with visible muscles, and her hair was bound in a long ponytail.

Maeve hadn't looked at him with pity, but with understanding. She had been with Two Roses just as long as he had. She knew what it was like to have a criminal get under her skin. "I heard you brought in the Harashi Hunter," she said.

Aethon had just nodded. Sweat dripped down his face and through the stubble he hadn't had a chance to shave yet, before falling off his chin. He didn't bother wiping it away.

"He's in lock up now," Maeve said.

Aethon nodded again.

She took a step toward him and he saw her hand twitch as though she wanted to reach out for him, but thought better of it. She gritted her teeth and raised her chin. "He can't hurt anyone else," she said, her voice firm.

Aethon had just shrugged helplessly. Sure, he had taken the Harashi Hunter out. But not before he had killed so many girls. Torn apart families. Changed lives forever. Having a loved one die by violence isn't something a person can ever truly get over. Aethon would know.

Maeve had watched him carefully, her green eyes flicking over his tense body. His hands began to tremble and he squeezed them into fists, hating how his body was betraying his turmoil. Maeve took another step toward him.

"Can I?" she had asked, raising a hand toward him. Her tone was soft, and it felt like they were back in that escape pod all over again. Like they were on the edge of something they could never take back. Like it was only them. Like they were a universe of two.

Aethon had closed his eyes and nodded, leaning back against the wall. He felt her hands on his chest. She touched him like someone recalling a long forgotten memory. Slowly at first, and then with purpose. He opened his eyes to find Maeve's face inches from his own. She pressed one hand to his chest over his heart, the other sliding up his neck. She didn't seem to care about his sweat, or his inability to speak at the moment.

"You can't let them get inside," she murmured. Her fingers had rubbed along his stubbled jaw, and threaded back gently into his hair. Oh god, he loved it when she ran her hands through his hair. Aethon couldn't remember anyone ever touching him so tenderly - at least, anyone besides her. Had anyone else in his adult life ever touched him to comfort, instead of to hurt, or purely to arouse? There was no one away from Freehail who cared for him like that. He knew better than to think Maeve actually cared about his pain, but he did believe she understood.

Aethon licked his lips, and spoke, his voice cracking. "If I'd found him faster -"

But Maeve shook her head, her lips pressed into a thin line. "Shut up. That's pointless and you know it."

That drew a small smile from him. "You're shit at comforting."

Maeve raised one arched brow and slid both her

hands down to press against his chest. "I got that smile though," she replied. "It's not the stupid, huge, charming one you usually have, but I'll take it."

Aethon raised his hand and pressed hers harder into his chest. He didn't want her to stop touching him. "Stupid?"

"Yeah," Maeve had replied. "Positively idiotic." Her lips curved up into a small smile of her own.

Aethon chuckled. The haunted feeling in his chest was subsiding, and he blew out a breath. "Thanks, Bladesy."

She nodded and started to move away from him, but Aethon still had her hands trapped against his chest. She could have pulled out of his grasp, but she didn't.

He met her eyes, and he knew they were both thinking the same thing. After they'd been rescued from the escape pod, they'd said that they would leave what had happened during that week - and what they had done - in the past. They had been desperate, and thought they were going to die - of course they'd done things that they had regretted. Or at least Maeve seemed to regret it. But despite every reason why he should stay as far away from Maeve as possible, Aethon couldn't help where his brain went sometimes. Maeve Bladesbearer twined through his thoughts more often than not. Her scent. The surprising softness of her skin. The feel of her beneath him. Her taste. And based on the fiery look in her eyes, he wasn't the only one who was having trouble leaving the past alone.

"Aethon -" she murmured, her voice hard and desperate. "We can't." His first name on her tongue made him shudder with want. Her body seemed to betray her words, because she leaned forward and pressed her forehead to his.

"Fuck," he ground out. He tangled one hand in her ponytail and tilted her head to the side so that he could run his lips over her throat.

The doors of the gym opened and they had sprang apart as several other Two Roses hunters came in. They'd given each other one last, hard look before going back to their workouts. They had never discussed it, but Aethon had never forgotten it. He often wondered what would have happened if they hadn't been interrupted.

Aethon is brought back to reality by CAL's voice.

"There is an elevated level of triennial-gamma waves at this location," the AI says. A light pops up on Aethon's viewscreen. The waves are concentrated less than a kilometer away. The only thing that emits this level of triennial-gamma waves is a mirror-cloak. The Archer is hiding in plain sight. Bladesbearer is clearly hoping that he will run off in search of her ship, leaving her to easily avoid him and make her way unimpeded to Daik Montrose's location.

"Bladesy," Aethon murmurs. "A mirror-cloak? What other secrets do you have?"

"It does appear to be a cloaked ship," CAL says. "Shall I hail them?"

Aethon pauses, his hand fiddling with the joystick on his armrest. Then he shakes his head. "No. I've got a better idea."

CHAPTER 5

Chrissah

Maeve

Maeve watches as the Menace finally moves away from the jump point and begins orbiting a small moon to recharge. Trell's ship had scanned for a good twenty minutes before apparently giving up. Maeve doesn't buy his show. She taps her fingernails on the arm of her chair, her frustration making her wish she had more space on the Archer to get in a good workout.

"TAI," Maeve says. "Can we move without the Menace becoming aware of our presence?"

"Depends what scans they're running, Maevey," the AI replies.

"I'm sure Trell is running everything known to humankind," Maeve mutters. She gets up and moves to the dash, checking the Archer's power levels. The mirror-cloak takes a decent amount of power to maintain, but it has its own battery separate from the Archer's. They should be good to fly to the next jump point in fifteen minutes.

Suddenly a warning light blinks on in the corner of the dash. Maeve glances over, flicking her braid behind her shoulder irritably.

"What now -"

"Oh hell," TAI says, her voice more annoyed than Maeve has yet heard. "We fried a few plasma couplers in the engine."

Irritation flares in Maeve's gut. First Trell is shadowing her, and now this? "How?!" she demands. "We're not straining the engine."

"According to my readings here, it looks like they just kicked the bucket," TAI replies. "Could have been lemons."

"Dammit," Maeve mutters. She walks quickly back behind her seat and opens a hatch in the deck where she keeps spare parts too big to create with the 3D dash printer. She sighs seeing the empty space where she normally keeps replacement plasma couplers. "And - of course, we're out."

"Ooh, field trip!" TAI says happily. "Omega Starbase is just a short way from here - I'll check their digital listings to see if they have the plasma couplers we need!"

Maeve slams the hatch shut and walks back around to her chair. They can't make jumps without the couplers. However, this may be a blessing in disguise. If Trell follows her to Omega Starbase, she'll know for sure that he is able to track her despite the mirror-cloak. Omega is huge - she'll hopefully be able to lose him in the traffic of the station.

"Looks like they have the goods!" TAI chirps. "I'll order some for us!"

"Thanks, TAI," Maeve replies.

While they wait, Maeve pulls out her tab and opens up her tracking app to check Daik Montrose's location. He's still hanging out in the Keidar Belt. But as she watches, his ship starts to move. She sits up, her shoulders and neck tight. Her left shoulder aches slightly from her still healing injury.

"Daik's on the move," Maeve mutters. "TAI - we've got to go."

"But Maevey, the engines -"

"I know," Maeve snaps. "It'll take us longer than normal to get there, but we can't afford to wait. If we have to, we'll finish recharging at Omega while we wait for the plasma couplers."

"What about the Menace?" TAI asks slowly, her voice a strange teasing tone that doesn't at all fit with Maeve's rising frustration.

"Keep the cloak up," Maeve instructs. "And keep tabs on them. If they follow us - they follow us." She hopes that Trell won't follow. She doesn't need yet another thing to worry about. But that man is too good at what he does.

"Alrighty, babe."

Maeve plots their route to Omega and sets the auto-nav. They should arrive at the station in about an hour. She hops out of her chair and walks back to her room, pulling her tab out of her pocket again and checking Daik's location. He's definitely making his way out of the Keidar Belt. She scans the surrounding location, noting that he could be heading for a jump point not too far from where he is. Fuck. It obviously would have been easier if he just hung out in the Keidar Belt for the next week, but that was expecting too much. Hunts like this are never that simple. And Maeve knows that Daik is greedy, with a high opinion of himself. He's not one to hide when there's money to be made - regardless of the huge bounty on his head.

Unfortunately, there's nothing she can do about any of that right now.

Maeve sits down on her bed. Her room on the Archer is small and sparse, but it has a few personal touches, unlike her rooms in Two Roses headquarters. Her bed has several green and blue decorative pillows, and she has a simple woven tapestry on one wall. She has a red and gold scarf that used to be her mother's draped over a chair in the corner.

Her mother used to wear the scarf to protect her from the hot desert sun on the rare days when she would take Maeve to the market on the outskirts of their town. They only went to market when there was a lull in the gang wars on Tellamar - which was rare. Since Tellamar was a gang-run world, there were always brutal fights between factions for control of the planet and its resources - scarce though they were.

But on those special days when it was relatively safe to go to market, Aoife Bladesbearer would wrap the scarf around her shoulder length red hair, take Maeve by hand, and tell her that they were going on an adventure. Maeve was her mother's miniature. Red hair, light green eyes, pale freckled skin. But she had inherited her father's sharp chin and fierce sense of justice.

Maeve loved the market. Tellamar didn't have many natural resources, but they were known for a beautiful purple crystal called *croi la fenya* - or "heart of the desert". It grew in the ancient rock formations that dotted the deserts of Tellamar. Croi crystals were prevalent in the jewelry and other goods at the market, and even though Maeve saw them all the time, she always wanted more to add to her collection.

Now, Maeve stares at the red and gold scarf on the chair. It's worn and a little tattered, but she's kept it safe for over fifteen years. She traces one finger down the delicate chain around her neck that holds the only croi crystal she still has - a small raw pendant strung onto the chain. It had been her mother's as well, passed down to her when Maeve had turned sixteen.

The market on Tellamar was fairly quiet as no one wanted to draw the attention of local gang leaders, but the people were kind. Jamara, who ran a food cart, always gave Maeve a free fried stick of crispy bread to snack on as they went through the market. Leo and Pan, two men who sold scrap metal, liked to check in on Maeve while her mother looked through their goods.

"Tell me what you've learned in school this week," Leo would ask, his brow furrowed seriously. Maeve always had her answer ready.

"We studied fractions!"

"If you studied fractions, you can tell me what fraction of the piece of this copper sheeting your mother wants to buy," Pan added.

Maeve wonders now at the kindness of the people on her home planet. How could a cruel place like Tellamar create some of the kindest people she's ever met? The crucible of Tellamar certainly hadn't made her kind. She hasn't set foot on the planet in fifteen years.

Though Maeve has small reminders of her mother, she has nothing of her father's.

Rian Bladesbearer had been a scrapper, as so many people on Tellamar were. He came home every evening covered in desert dust. Maeve remembers that his back used to ache and he would sometimes limp after an especially long day.

"Darling," Aoife would say, her voice tender. "Sit down."

"I'm fine, *chrissah*," Rian would say in that voice he only used to talk to her mother. Her father often called her mother *chrissah* - a Tellamari term of endearment. Maeve had grown up speaking Standard, but she also spoke Tellamari. *Chrissah* means "little river". Water was scarce on Tellamar, and so it was a precious commodity.

Her parents were unfailingly tender with each other, and displayed a kind of love that Maeve has rarely experienced. Aoife was always touching her husband. A hand on his shoulder, a finger looped in his belt, her forehead resting against his chest. And Rian used to make her mother laugh by throwing her over his shoulder and hauling her around the house. He brought her small presents - flowers or tiny croi crystals he found scrapping. Their kisses were deep and long, and though Maeve had been grossed out by their physicality as a child, she can recognize their love and connection in hindsight.

No matter how tired Rian was when he came home, he always made sure to spend time with Maeve. They would read together, or shoot darts outside. When she got older, her father would drill her with workouts he learned back when he was a grunt for one of the gangs. Rian taught her aim and accuracy, determination, and the importance of doing what is right.

Maeve supposes that though she doesn't have any physical reminders of her father, she does still have the values he instilled in her.

Rian and Aoife had died in a targeted attack on their home during a gang war. Though Rian hadn't been involved with the gangs in decades, the new leader decided to assassinate anyone associated with the old ruling gang. Maeve was eighteen. Though she doesn't like to think about it, the memory of finding her parents dead is burned into a primal part of her brain. She walked into her house after school to find them on the floor of their small living room - a single bullet wound through each of their foreheads. They'd been on their backs, their hands an inch away from each other. Maeve's heart aches at the memory, but rage rises in her in equal measure. She'd left the house and never gone back. Sometimes she wonders what happened to their bodies, but she knows her parents would have wanted her to leave as quickly as possible in case the assassins came back to finish the job. Their bodies were only shells. Her parents - living, breathing, laughing Aoife and Rian - were gone.

Maeve sighs and pushes herself up off the bed. Dwelling on the past is useless. She wonders why these memories are surfacing now. Thoughts of her family haven't plagued her like this in years. Perhaps it's because she's close to leaving Two Roses. She wants to be out - gone - done - with hunting. But when she catches Daik and gets his bounty money, what will she do on Kespar-2? If she's not careful she'll spend her days sinking into the memories of her past. She'll have to find some purpose - even if it's a simple job. Perhaps she can teach basic self-defense. That would be a good use of her time.

Maeve sits down on the floor and lays on her back to start a round of sit-ups and push-ups. Might as well get moving while she waits to arrive at the starbase.

"Maevey-pie?" TAI's voice comes from the speaker in the ceiling of Maeve's room.

Maeve pauses mid sit-up. "What?"

"Just wanted to let you know that the Menace is following us," TAI says. "They're at the very edge of our scanner range. They seem quite set on us. I'm rather flattered, but I know you'll be annoyed."

Maeve resumes her sit-ups, irritation making her voice sharp. "Yeah, not surprised."

"Maevey," TAI says, her tone wheedling now. "What's the history with you and that beautiful organic?"

Maeve is starting to feel her muscles burn as she rips through her workout. "What beautiful organic?"

"Oh don't be coy, Maevey," TAI chirps. "Aethon Trell!"

"Why would you think we have a history?" Maeve demands. She flips over and starts doing push-ups.

"I can read your vitals, babe!" TAI says. "I may sound as sweet as pie, but that doesn't mean your girl TAI is a dimwitted AI. I'm the best of the bunch. A quick analyzation of your conversation patterns indicates -"

"Ok, ok, I get it!" Maeve interrupts. She flops down onto her stomach, her cheek pressing against the cold metal of the deck. Though TAI is annoying, Maeve has to admit, it's nice to have someone who notices that kind of thing about her. Even if it is just an AI. She hasn't had a friend to talk to in a long time. "We started at Two Roses at the same time. I've known him for years."

"Oooh! And you've been pining for him ever since you met?" TAI asks excitedly.

That gets a small laugh out of Maeve. "No. I hated him when we met." She remembers the first time she saw Aethon Trell at a meeting for newly inducted Two Roses members. He hadn't filled out yet, his body whip-thin. He had developed a certain charm over the last fifteen years, but twenty year old Aethon was much more of an asshole. He'd barely spoken to her, content to trade sarcastic jabs every once in a while when one of them beat the other to a bounty.

"But obviously things changed," TAI coaxes. "Give me all the dirty details, Maevey! I know you want to."

Maeve rolls onto her back and stares up at the dark ceiling of her room. The ceiling of the small escape pod that she'd spent a week trapped in with Aethon had looked almost identical. Despite herself, she wants to talk about it. There's something about Trell that she can't seem to get out of her head. Maybe if she tells TAI about it, the memories will stop replaying in her mind.

"It was four years ago," Maeve starts. "We were both chasing Henrietta Howell - a serial killer from the settlement on Io."

"Mmm," TAI says. If TAI had a body, Maeve imagines she'd be curling up into a comfortable chair to listen to the story. The image makes her smile.

"Trell and I were both chasing Howell, but the woman was insane," Maeve continues. "We were all on a freighter when Howell broke a containment seal on a huge container of kethelzine gas."

"Oh hells' bells," TAI says. "You're lucky to be alive! That gas will kill you in less than a minute!"

"I know," Maeve says. "But I was near a survival pod. So I jumped inside and then I saw Trell sprinting toward me." Maeve remembers the split second when she considered closing the door of the pod before Trell could get there. But she knew she could never do that. She'd screamed for him to hurry. He'd made it just in time. They'd sealed themselves in and ejected from the freighter.

"By the time we were safely away," Maeve says. "The freighter started to leave without us. The kethelzine gas was contained to a cargo bay. I'm not even sure if the freighter captain knew about the leak. And we couldn't raise them on our comm. So we got left behind."

The pod had been a small oblong one - about ten feet by seven feet, with just enough height for both Maeve and Aethon to stand. They had stared at each other, their bodies thrumming with adrenaline once they realized that the freighter was gone. Maeve remembers unconsciously grabbing Aethon's arm to steady herself.

"We sent out a distress call, but we didn't know if the signal was getting out," Maeve says. "We were close to Jupiter's dust rings - and they tend to block comm signals."

"So you were trapped there together?" TAI asks.

"We were," Maeve replies. "But it wasn't romantic. We only had the food we both carried in our backpacks, and a few emergency ration bars. The pod used the water from the air and our bodies to recycle and dispense - so at least we weren't dehydrated. But the pod wasn't well heated. It wasn't a fun trip. We didn't know if anyone would find us, and the pod only had the power to sustain life support for about a week."

"Oh heavens to Betsy," TAI exclaims. "A week?"

The memories of that trip come fast and thick to Maeve now. She remembers the feeling of claustrophobia she'd experienced in the tiny pod. Not all the time, but the waves of it had been almost unbearable. The only lights in the pod had come from the tiny dash - small, blinking yellow, blue and white indicator lights. But the primary source of illumination was Jupiter. They could see the huge planet out the one window of the pod - and the reflected sunlight off the surface lit up the inside of the pod with a reddish orange glow. It gave everything a deceptively warm cast, but the pod itself was cold. It wasn't meant for extended space travel. It had no beds, only a narrow bench of hard seats. There was a tiny emergency toilet and a sink. The rations stocked there were stale and out of date. They'd fallen into dusty chunks when Maeve had opened one, but they ate them anyway.

Maeve and Aethon had spent the first two days arguing about the best way to get a signal out while trying endless ideas and getting zero results. They spent the first two nights in irritated silence, curled up in balls as far away from each other as they could get, shivering through the night.

After two cold, sleepless nights, Aethon had taken off his bandolier, jacket, and finally his shirt, and sat down on the ground across from her. Maeve had watched him from where she sat on the deck, her arms around her knees. She took in his muscled body and the tattoos that wound their way from his pecs, down his sides and into his tight black pants. She wondered if his tattoos meant anything. She'd noticed them when he worked out shirtless in the gym before, but something about seeing them in this situation made her feel like she was witnessing an intimate part of Aethon. He stared at her, his eyes blazing with challenge.

"Come here," he said gruffly. "Unless you want to freeze."

"I'll be fine," Maeve had replied. She tucked her hands under her arms. She was freezing - they had to lower the temperature to try and make the pod's power last longer - but there was no way she'd cuddle up with Trell.

"Don't be like that, Bladesy," he'd said. "Don't die of stubbornness."

"I'm not going to die of stubbornness," she'd growled.

Aethon had shrugged and raised his brows. "I predict that's what it will say on your tombstone." He raised his hands as if he was picturing it. "Maeve Bladesbearer. Infamous member of the Guild of Two Roses. Stubborn as hell."

Maeve had shaken her head and pressed her lips together. "I'm not going to have a tombstone if we die in this fucking pod."

Aethon had met her gaze. She'd expected him to soften. To try and comfort her. But he'd just looked at her, his expression still hard and challenging. "I never expected you to be defeatist," he finally said. "It's disappointing."

"I don't *want* to die, you asshole," Maeve had snapped.

Aethon had opened his arms again and narrowed his gaze. "Prove it."

Maeve found herself rising from the cold floor of the pod. She ripped her jacket off and unbuckled her shoulder holster, then took off her shirt. She ignored the way Aethon's eyes flared as he took in her body.

"If we're going to do this, let's do it properly," she demanded. "Take off your pants."

He nodded and stood up, unbuckling his belt and unzipping his black pants. He shoved them down, revealing tight gray boxers that didn't hide much of anything.

Maeve's mouth had gone dry. Aethon was a jackass bounty hunter. And Maeve knew enough about jackass bounty hunters (herself included) to know that they make shit partners. They might be good for a roll in the sack, but they always put the job first. Her old mentor Harlan Yates had taught her that. Unfortunately, he hadn't taken his own advice in the end.

"Want me to completely strip, Bladesy?" Aethon had asked. He lowered his chin, and glared down his long nose at her. "For optimal skin to skin contact and heat sharing?"

"Let's save some mystery, hmm?" Maeve snapped. She was down to her racerback sports bra and underwear. Her skin was pebbled with cold and she crossed her arms over her chest, hopping from one foot to the other on the icy metal deck floor.

Aethon had grunted in affirmation and spread out one of the shiny emergency blankets that came with the pod. "We can put the other blanket on top as well as our clothes," he said.

Maeve had nodded and lay down quickly on the blanket, suddenly desperate for Aethon's warmth. When he had moved to lay down behind her she had snapped, "I'm going to be the big spoon, Trell."

"Alright, alright," he muttered, going to her

other side. "Demanding, aren't you?" He lay down in front of her and Maeve was so cold that she hadn't wasted any time pressing herself against his broad back. They'd set themselves on this route, there was no reason to feel awkward or inhibited. They pulled the other blanket and their discarded clothes back on top of them and settled down, shivering, waiting until their body heat ramped back up. She pressed one hand to Aethon's back and snaked the other around to his stomach, trying and failing to ignore the way he inhaled sharply at her touch, and the play of his muscles under his smooth skin.

"Your hands are freezing," he murmured.

"No shit," she muttered.

She felt his hand clasp around hers. His palm was calloused, and she felt the ridges a person gets from daily weightlifting as he chafed her hand between his.

"You grow up on a desert planet or something?" he asked. "You don't seem very hardy for someone who spends a lot of their time in the cold of space."

"First of all," Maeve growled. "Fuck you."

"Mmhmm," Aethon replied, his tone bored. "And?"

Maeve rolled her eyes and pressed her chin down against his shoulder. He continued rubbing her hand between his and then he gently placed her palm on his chest. Maeve could feel his heart beating. It was a startling sort of intimacy, and for a moment, Maeve had the impulse to press a kiss to the back of his neck. In the reddish light of Jupiter, she couldn't see all the details of Aethon, but she could see that he had a scar low on the back of his head where his hair was shorter. His ear was gilded in the red light, and she could see the very edge of his nose. She was glad she couldn't see his eyes at the moment. His eyes were narrow and slightly hooded, and the whisky gold color reminded her of the desert sand on her home planet. He had a hard, piercing kind of gaze like a bird of prey. "I grew up on Tellamar," she said after a moment.

Aethon was silent for so long that Maeve thought he might have fallen asleep.

When he finally spoke, his voice was lower, and almost cautious. "My mother was from Tellamar."

Maeve blinked in surprise. She had only met a handful of other people who had managed to escape Tellamar. Most were too poor to ever attempt it. Aethon's mother must have been a formidable woman to escape the planet.

"Where did you grow up?" she asked.

He huffed. "Freehail." His tone was dismissive, but Maeve could hear the underlying edge of defensiveness. The tendons in his neck were tight, and she wanted to smooth her hands over his skin, but she kept herself still against him. She knew what it was like to grow up somewhere that people judged. It was a strange dichotomy - a love for a planet, while at the same time understanding its many shortcomings. Maeve hated the politics of Tellamar. But she loved its land and its people. Her croi crystal necklace sometimes felt like a millstone around her neck.

"All I know about Freehail is that it's on the edge of colonized space," Maeve said.

"There's not much else to know," Aethon replied. "Let's go to sleep. We need to conserve energy."

Maeve hadn't replied. She'd fallen into a fitful sleep, the light of Jupiter bloody behind her closed eyes.

The next morning, she'd woken even further tangled up with Aethon. He had flipped over in his sleep, and she was pressed against him, one leg hooked over his hip. Their faces were inches away from each other and he had his hand on her back, anchoring her to him. He was awake, and his eyes were deep golden pools. She let out a shuddering breath and pushed against his chest, trying to put some distance between them.

"Pretty warm, hmm?" he'd said, his voice rough and deep from sleep. The sound of his voice had made her shudder slightly. Aethon in the morning was a dangerous creature. Pure want clawed under her skin. What was happening to her? She'd never allowed herself this close to him before. She hadn't fully realized how attractive he was.

"You're actually a little sweaty," she snapped, pushing away from him.

He'd rolled his eyes and they'd both gotten up and tried to clean up in the tiny sink before they pulled their clothes back on. Once Maeve zipped up her jacket and leaned on the dash of the escape pod, she felt much more put together. She adjusted her Two Roses crest on her collar, watching as Aethon did the same to his. Her head hurt a little from her braid, but she could unbraid it and put it back up later.

Aethon glared at the dash of the pod and tucked his hand under his bandolier. There was hardly any information on the dash besides general location, a comm panel, and an indicator for various power levels.

"We'll have to turn the heat down again if we want to conserve power," he muttered.

"The more important thing is keeping our

distress signal going," Maeve replied. "Conserving power isn't going to mean shit if no one hears us."

"What did I say to you about being defeatist?" Aethon demanded, turning toward her.

"Fuck off, Aethon," she growled.

They fought most of the day, but the bickering kept Maeve's mind off their increasingly desperate situation. If no one found them within the week, the pod wouldn't have enough power to sustain life support. They'd either freeze to death, or their bodies would slowly shut down due to lack of oxygen. Maeve wasn't sure which prospect was less appealing.

That night, they'd stripped again and gotten under the blanket. Maeve couldn't maintain her anger all the time. It was exhausting. She sighed heavily as Aethon adjusted himself into a more comfortable position. He lay on his back this time, and tucked a shirt under his head for a pillow.

"Come here," he said. And Maeve hadn't hesitated. She was so cold. And now that she was almost naked and her anger had faded, she realized how scared she was. They could very easily die here. Aethon threaded his arm beneath her head and Maeve had pressed herself against his side. She smoothed a hand up his chest. She found herself unconsciously memorizing his body. His chest had sparse hair, and the divot between his pecs wasn't as severe when he was lying down. His jaw was hard and square, and he had stubble along it now that they'd been trapped for a few days. His lips, which were almost always spread wide with his signature, charming smile, or pulled back in a growl, were now soft. At rest, they curved down slightly. Maeve wanted to kiss him.

Without thinking, Maeve raised her hand and traced his lips gently with her fingertip. Aethon didn't say anything. He just pulled her tighter against him. Deciding she didn't really care to keep up her careful boundaries, Maeve continued her gentle exploration of his features. She traced his nose, long and angular, and smoothed a thumb over one eyebrow. She propped herself up on her elbow and looked down at him. He had a light spray of freckles across his face, and more across his shoulders and down his arms. His gaze was still that hard, golden one, but she could see his desire there. She was sure it mirrored the desire that heated her own blood. He wanted her. It felt good that this strong, charismatic man wanted her. Maeve felt like she could get drunk on the power of that feeling alone.

She raised a hand and threaded her fingers back through his dark hair. He leaned into her touch like a cat. She couldn't help the smile that crossed her face at that. Aethon's hand began stroking her back, up and down ever so gently.

"*Chrissah,*" he murmured.

Maeve had paused, her hand still in his hair. "What did you say?"

Aethon had given her a tired smile. "You heard me, Bladesy."

His hand on her back smoothed all the way up, resting on the back of her neck. He massaged her there, her muscles loosening under his touch.

"Your Tellamari mother must not have told you what that word means," Maeve murmured. She resumed stroking her hand through his hair.

"It means 'little river'," Aethon replied softly. "And I know what that means to Tellamari."

He was calling her precious. Rare. Vital. It was what her father had always called her mother. Maeve's breath caught in her chest.

"I think the lack of proper food might be getting to you, Trell," she said, finally pulling her hand from his hair and resting it back on his chest.

"I'm perfectly in control of my mind and body," Aethon replied, one brow arching up.

She'd patted his chest then and slid down, wanting to escape the intensity of his amber eyes. "Let's go to sleep," she said.

Aethon's hand continued to massage her neck. Maeve listened to his heart beat until it lulled her to sleep.

The next morning they dressed and tried again and again to get their signal heard. They tried amplifying the call a dozen different ways, but they just ended up using more power. They snarled at each other, and through her haze of anger, Maeve wondered if Trell was just baiting her so that they would be angry instead of afraid. But as the day wore on and they both got tired earlier, fear began to creep back in. The lack of proper food was making her weak. Her stomach ached with hollowness.

Pressed together under their blanket, Maeve felt like the barriers between her and Aethon were crumbling even further.

"We're not going to fucking die," she murmured against his neck.

"Exactly," he replied. "We're going to fucking live."

The next day was worse. Their food stores were dangerously low, and the temperature in their pod kept dropping. It was thirty degrees fahrenheit which wasn't horrific, but wasn't sustainable, especially for long periods of time. Luckily they had access to water, and they'd both drank as much as they could, but it didn't make her feel full. She had a constant low-level headache right behind her eyes. The red light from Jupiter was starting to make her feel unbalanced.

They got under the blanket after another fruitless day, and Maeve pressed her forehead against Aethon's, her eyes squeezed shut. She tugged him closer and he wrapped his arms around her.

"We're not going to fucking die," she whispered.

"We're going to fucking live," he replied. "Keep on being strong, *chrissah*."

Maeve had opened her eyes then and met Aethon's gaze.

"Don't call me that, Trell," she whispered.

"Why not?" His cheekbones were sharper now, his stubble creating a shadow over his face. Maeve wondered what she looked like. She felt thinner. Like some of her muscle mass was wasting away. They'd been in the pod for six full days.

"Because you don't know what it means," she replied. "Not really."

"I do know," he said. He raised a hand to cup her cheek.

Maeve had felt an overwhelming mixture of desire and desperation. The likelihood of them being rescued was so slim. And in a day or so, the pod wouldn't have enough power to maintain life support. They were going to die. She gritted her teeth. Was she really going to die without squeezing every last bit out of whatever life she had left? She wanted a full life. But if she wasn't going to get that, she could at least take any scrap of pleasure left for her. Maeve felt like death was breathing down her neck. Dark, cold, everlasting. She wanted to light a fire to keep it at bay - just for a little while.

Maeve raised her hand and pulled Aethon's palm away from her cheek, bringing it to her mouth. She pressed a kiss to the center of his hand. His eyes flared and he wrapped his other hand around her arm.

"We're not going to fucking die, Aethon," she said, her voice low.

"No," he agreed. "We're going to fucking live."

Maeve brought Aethon's hand down to her breast. "Touch me," she whispered. His eyes finally went soft, his lips parting in a sigh. Maeve leaned forward, her mouth an inch away from his.

"*Chrissah*," he groaned. "Do you want this because -"

"I want this," she whispered. "Isn't that enough?"

He squeezed her breast and then traced his long fingers along the band of her bra, teasing the skin underneath. "You're a thorn in my side, Maeve."

"I think you like getting pricked by me," she replied.

He chuckled and ducked his head, pressing a kiss to her neck that made Maeve shudder. "I do."

The tension between them rose until all fear was blown from Maeve's mind. Aethon stared at her with such raw want. No one had ever looked at her like that. A tiny part of Maeve thought that it was a good thing they were going to die soon, because she didn't think anyone else would ever look at her the way he was right then. And now that she'd experienced it, nothing else would ever measure up.

Aethon dragged his mouth up her neck, laying kisses on her jaw and behind her ear. He shifted her underneath him, and Maeve slid her hands up his sides, tracing the tattoos she could barely see in the red dimness with her fingertips. She let her legs fall open around him.

He drew back and looked down at her. "You're beautiful," he murmured.

Maeve almost full on laughed. "We've been trapped in the same room for a week, Aethon. You've seen more of my bathroom habits than anyone else in the galaxy. And neither of us have taken a proper shower in -"

"Accept the compliment," he growled. He took the opportunity to lower himself fully into the cradle of her hips, pressing his hardening length against her. Though they were both still wearing their underwear, Maeve knew he was big. She could feel every inch of him pressed up against her.

"Oh god -" she hissed.

"Accept the compliment," he repeated.

"Shut up and kiss me," Maeve said. She reached up and hooked her hands behind Aethon's head, dragging him down so that he was resting fully on top of her. His arms were braced on either side of her.

Maeve leaned up just slightly and captured his lips with hers. His kiss was unyielding and thorough. He ground his hips against her as he delved his tongue into her mouth, a precursor of things to come.

"Tell me we're not going to die," he said against her mouth. "Tell me, Maeve."

Maeve leaned her forehead against his, her hands

pressing against his stubbled cheeks. "We're going to live." She reached down and snapped the band of his boxers in a playful maneuver that defied their circumstances. "Now take these off." Aethon chuckled.

They both sat up and stripped quickly until there was nothing between them. They took a moment to look at each other. Aethon dragged his gaze over her body in a way that made Maeve slick between her thighs. He lifted a hand and rubbed one of her nipples between his thumb and forefinger, teasing it to a stiff peak. She reached forward, her fingers curling around his cock, which stood up proud and full. He felt decadent beneath her touch. Firm and velvety. He swallowed hard as she stroked him, learning this new part of his body. Lust was thick between them. What she wouldn't give to have Aethon spread out on a real bed before her. Clean, comfortable, and all hers. She would have him every way she could think of. But that was never meant to be. This was all they had. And this was all they should have. Death and desperation brought them together. That was all.

Aethon's tattoos wound all the way down his sides and then curved forward over his hips, ending at the tops of his thighs. Maeve leaned down and pressed a kiss to a swirl of black on his hip. She wanted to trace them all with her mouth.

He pulled her head up and kissed her again, desperate this time. Maeve allowed him to bear her down to the deck, and he was heartbreakingly careful with her. He arranged her head so that she would be comfortable within their makeshift bed. Then he sat up between her legs, his hands smoothing up and down her thighs.

"Tell me what you like, *chrissah*," he murmured. "Order me around. I know you like that, at least."

Maeve had laughed, and Aethon grinned, a remnant of the big smile she'd seen so many times before.

"Put your mouth on me," she whispered.

"Mmm," he murmured. "Yes, ma'am."

Aethon leaned forward and kissed her again, before moving slowly down her body. He traced her collarbone with his tongue, his big hands braced on either side of her. Maeve couldn't stop touching him. She threaded her fingers through his hair, and ran her hands up and down his sides and back.

He teased her breasts with his mouth, his tongue flicking over her nipples sending spikes of pleasure down to her core. He took his time. Maeve thought he was savoring her. Savoring this limited time they had together. She was savoring it too. She let herself release everything else for the moment. She sank into the feel of Aethon's mouth on her.

He spent a long time kissing and biting at her hips and stomach, teasing her until she was pulsing with need.

"Aethon," she huffed. She clenched her hands in his hair and tried to push him lower. "Please."

He chuckled against her skin and then moved lower at her insistence. At the first swipe of his tongue on her, Maeve arched toward him with a moan. She hadn't been touched like this in so long. She didn't know how much she wanted it. How much she needed it.

"Yes, god, right there -"

Aethon groaned against her, his hands spreading her wider for his mouth. Maeve had never met anyone who liked to eat pussy as much as Aethon appeared to. He went at it with the same determination she'd seen from him in every other aspect of his life. With precision and ferocity. Maeve gave him a few breathless instructions - *higher* - *harder* - *faster* - and he responded to her with eagerness. Tension began to curl in Maeve's lower stomach, and her muscles felt tight. Her face was flushed and she felt hot for the first time in a week.

When Aethon pushed one curling finger inside her and pressed the flat of his tongue hard against her clit, Maeve couldn't hold herself back. She came with a moan, her back arching, the wave of pleasure tightening her whole body. Her mind went white with bliss. There was nothing except the feel of Aethon's mouth on her. Nothing except the power of the pleasure riding through her. Nothing except them, their bodies gilded in Jupiter's neverending light.

He crawled up her body, wiping her slickness off his face. He leaned over her, grinning with pure, male satisfaction. "That was the most gorgeous thing," he murmured.

"I - I don't want you to - get a big head, Aethon," Maeve stuttered between breaths. "But you are really, *really* fucking good at that."

"Thank you," he said. Then he pressed a kiss to her lips. "See? That's how you accept a compliment."

"You're insufferable," Maeve groaned.

"I know." Aethon paused and his brow furrowed. "Maeve, I want to have sex with you but -"

"No 'buts'," Maeve interrupted. "Why would there be a 'but'?"

"I don't have any kind of protection," he said, raising his brows.

The reality of their situation hit Maeve again fully in the chest. They couldn't just run out to a store and get contraceptives. They weren't on Brix-9 or in the Archer or the Menace, or anywhere safe. There was no one coming for them. They were going to die.

"Hey - hey," Aethon said, smoothing a hand up her body to her cheek. Whatever expression was on her face had alarmed him. "What's wrong? We don't have to do anything you don't want to do."

"That's not it," Maeve replied. She wrapped her arms around his back, pulling his head down to hers. "I want to. And -" She swallowed, nervous about what she was about to reveal to him. "And I can't have children," she said quickly. "Had a procedure when I joined Two Roses. I never wanted them."

He just looked at her with that same raw openness. "Ok. But that doesn't mean you might not still want me to wear a condom or something. I was tested recently but -"

"I'm clean too," Maeve said. "It doesn't matter to me, Aethon. I just want you. I don't care about anything else."

Aethon's expression shifted from concern to determination. His jaw hardened, his whisky eyes going narrow. "Don't be defeatist, *chrissah*. I want to fuck you. I want to feel you come as hard as you just did around my cock. But I don't want you to do this because you think we're going to die."

"What does my motive matter at this point?" Maeve demanded. She scraped her nails up his back and she felt his cock twitch against her. He hissed. "God - I've never had to convince someone who was lying on top of me naked to fuck me."

She watched Aethon's face morph before her eyes. Anger, confusion, resignation, until finally he stared down at her with pure primal hunger. He shifted back and grabbed her thighs, wrenching them apart and lifting her ass so that he could prop the backs of her knees on his forearms. He held her there, motionless, his hands squeezing her ass.

"You want this?" Aethon growled. He dragged the head of his cock against her folds, still tender from his ministrations. She shivered at the feel.

"Yes," she said.

"You want me inside you - nothing between us?" he said. He notched himself at her entrance but didn't move further. Maeve braced herself against the wall behind her head.

"Fuck, yes."

"Good," he snapped.

He pushed into her with one, slow, almost unending thrust. Maeve's whole body shuddered at the hot, thick, hardness of him. She could feel every inch of him like this.

"Aethon -" she whimpered. She scrabbled at his arms, trying to pull him closer, deeper.

"Fuck, Maeve," he hissed. "You feel so good."

He slid out and then slammed back in hard. The feel of him was almost too much. It was all too much. And yet it wasn't enough.

"Can't hold you up like this," he grimaced, his arms trembling. "Need a damn pillow - or a few decent meals. Overestimated my strength." He put her gently back down on the deck, his cock slipping from her in the motion.

Maeve spread her legs and urged him forward.

"Come here."

Aethon fit himself between her thighs and pressed in again before resting himself over her. She arched toward him as he sheathed himself fully inside her.

"I like this better," Maeve said, tracing her hands up his back. "I can touch you too."

Aethon smiled and kissed her, his hips starting to move in a slow rhythm. Maeve raised her legs around him, squeezing him tightly, pressing her heels into his firm ass. She lost all sense of time as they moved together. Their fear and anger at their predicament had changed into something else. This wasn't the desperate sex of two people who knew they were going to die. This was more. This was a joining of two people who wanted to live while they still could. The difference was important to Maeve.

"*Chrissah*," Aethon said again. He murmured the word like it was a prayer. Maeve wondered if he really meant it. How could she be that to him? Vital? Precious? They had always competed with each other, irritated each other. What did he see in her now? Maeve didn't know. But she knew that Aethon was more than just an asshole bounty hunter. Part of her wished she was going to live to find out everything there was to know about him.

Aethon ground his hips into her, his hand snaking down between them to press against her clit. It sent a shock straight through her, her back arching as her muscles began to tense. "Come for me, Bladesy," Aethon murmured against her lips. "Come for me now."

It wasn't hard. Aethon seemed to instinctively know how to draw pleasure from her. Once again, tension was building in Maeve's body, aching for release. She wrapped her arms around Aethon's neck, bringing his mouth to hers as she came. She sobbed against him, the orgasm bringing both intense pleasure, and an overflow of emotion. Aethon held her through it, and she felt it when his hips began to jerk less gracefully. He pulled out of her, spilling onto her stomach with a groan.

"Aethon," Maeve said. Tears were falling down her face and Maeve threw her arm over her eyes. It was all too much. She rarely cried, and she never cried in front of people. She felt like a dam holding back her emotions had been broken.

"It's ok," he said. He fell to her side and grabbed his shirt, ripped off a sleeve, and wiped her clean. "It's ok, *chrissah*. Everything is ok." The care he showed her made a fresh wave of tears come to Maeve's eyes.

"How can you say that when we're going to die?" she whispered. The cold of the escape pod felt icy against her bare skin again. She looked out the window at Jupiter. It looked back, judgmental and uncaring. She put her arm back over her face, hiding her tears.

"I don't believe that," he growled. He grabbed her chin and forced her arm away from her eyes. "Look at me."

She did. His gaze blazed with purpose. "We'll figure something out," he said. "We'll sleep for a while now, and then we'll figure something out."

Maeve nodded. She didn't believe him, but she no longer had the strength to argue. They curled up against each other under the blanket again.

Aethon pressed a kiss to her hair as she was dropping off to sleep. "*Chrissah*," he murmured once more.

It was the last time he would ever call her that.

Maeve and Aethon awoke to a beeping from the pod's comm system.

They untangled and jumped over to the dash, still naked.

"It's a signal from a passing freighter," Aethon said. His hair was mussed, the skin under his eyes dark with lack of sleep. "They're coming for us." He looked up at Maeve, his eyes wide. She rubbed a hand over her face, not quite believing what she'd just heard.

"Someone is... coming for us," she repeated.

"A freighter," Aethon replied with a nod.

Maeve grabbed the blanket from the ground and wrapped it around herself before sitting down hard on the bench seat behind her. She leaned forward and rested her elbows on her knees, her hands over her face. They were going to be rescued. They weren't going to die.

Utter relief hit Maeve hard. She leaned back, her eyes closed.

"Thank fuck," she groaned. When she opened her eyes, Aethon was looking at her with a strange expression. "What?" she demanded.

He shrugged, his mouth a thin line, then he picked up his clothes from the deck and started to dress. "I told you we weren't going to die," he said.

"Yeah, well I didn't believe you," Maeve replied. She got up and gathered her own clothes, dressing quickly. By the time they each pulled their jackets on and looked at each other again, Aethon's gaze was guarded.

Maeve thought about what they'd shared the

night before. She didn't know if she regretted it or not. But regardless, it couldn't happen again. Maeve knew she couldn't sleep with Aethon again and keep her feelings out of it. She was already too attached to him. And attachments were liabilities. Just another weakness for criminals or convicts to exploit. And though Maeve had been tested to her very limits over the past seven days, she knew she wasn't weak.

"Listen," she said, resting her hands on her hips. "What we did last night -"

"Can't happen again," Aethon said, finishing her sentence. His jaw was tight. "I'm aware."

Maeve felt a pang in her chest that she ignored. "I think we should just keep it between us."

"I'm not one to kiss and tell, Bladesy," Aethon replied, his voice flinty.

"Right," she snapped. "It was just desperation. Physical desire. Nothing more."

"We thought we were going to die," Aethon added.

"I thought you said you didn't think we were going to die," Maeve said slowly.

"I lied," Aethon replied gruffly.

For some reason the thought that Aethon had lied about anything he'd said last night felt like a knife in the gut to Maeve. She inhaled sharply.

"Fine," she said. "Well. That's that."

Aethon nodded.

An hour later, the freighter had captured their pod in a tractor beam and pulled them close enough to link a docking port. Maeve had led the way from the pod to the freighter, Aethon trailing behind.

Now, Maeve pulls herself into the present and

swallows hard. It's been four years since she and Aethon spent that week in the escape pod. She leans forward and rubs her hands across her face.

"Oh Maevey," TAI sighs. "You said that story wasn't romantic - but it was!"

"I don't know what was romantic about it," Maeve snaps. "Besides the fact that we had sex. We were in a life or death situation. Whatever I felt, it wasn't real."

She stands up and stalks back through the Archer, sitting down in her captain's chair again.

"What about all the times he called you *chrissah*?" TAI asks. "As sweet as a peach."

"He was just saying that, TAI," Maeve sighs. "He didn't mean it."

"Oh I don't know -"

"Give it a rest," Maeve groans. When TAI is silent, Maeve examines the starbase now visible out her viewscreen. It's huge and hourglass shaped, with tiny ships surrounding it, coming and going like bees to a hive.

Maeve pulls up a digital map on the screen. And in the corner is a little dot representing the Menace, trailing her at a distance.

CHAPTER 6

The First Hunt

Aethon

The Archer de-cloaked as soon as they were within scannable distance from Omega Starbase. Aethon's not sure that Bladesbearer bought his ruse of pretending that he'd given up on searching back at the jump point. He'd kept the Menace at a decent distance from Bladesbearer's ship, but he's not certain of her full scanning capabilities. If she has a mirror-cloak, she might have upgraded her Bracken-class ship's sensors as well.

Aethon had thought they were going to avoid the starbase, but they appear to be heading straight for it. There's no way Daik Montrose is anywhere near Omega. It's too well trafficked, and there is too much corp presence at the station including Brimstone Industries - one of the richest mining corps in existence. Brimstone is providing the credits for Daik's bounty, and though Aethon hates that corp down to his very bones, he's not above taking their credits. He wonders what exactly Daik did to piss Brimstone off.

"They're going to Omega?" Aethon says. He leans back in his chair as he watches the Archer make for the huge starbase. "Why?"

"Perhaps they want to visit the quadrant's largest cube of solid tritanium," CAL says, his voice laced with sarcasm. "It's a big tourist attraction on the starbase."

Aethon rolls his eyes. "Maybe Bladesbearer is aware that we're still following her and thinks she can lose us in the traffic."

"Does she have a reason to think you're that bad of a tracker, Captain Trell?" CAL says. "The more likely explanation is they need something."

"So we'll wait them out," Aethon says. He puts the Menace in orbit around a tiny, mostly metallic moon near the station, hoping the low level of radiation from it will mask his location.

"I hate to encourage your sudden fit of unethical behavior," CAL says. "But if we wait here they could take the Lightway from the station and then we'll have a very hard time finding them again."

"Omega has a Lightway now?" Aethon groans. He runs a hand back through his hair, irritated with himself for not knowing. Lightways are less taxing on ships than jump points, but can't transport as far.

"Yes, they installed it as a jump point alternative for small family ships, or people without their own ships who want to visit the station from nearby planets," CAL says. "A public transport leaves on the Lightway every forty-five minutes."

Aethon runs through his limited options. He could stalk Bladesbearer's ship through the crowd. If she hasn't yet noticed that he's still following her, he might be able to keep up the ruse for a little while longer. But he can't risk losing her. He has to get to this bounty before her. Aethon is starting to feel more and more like shit for shadowing Maeve Bladesbearer. He wonders why she wants this bounty so badly. She's always been a closed off person, but she seemed downright fierce in her refusal to tell him why she wasn't willing to split the credits with him.

The comm line beeps and Aethon turns his attention toward the dash.

"Receiving a call from Andromeda Trapp," CAL says.

Aethon leans back in his chair and rubs a hand over his face. He's usually not this bad at being stealthy - but the whole shadowing thing has him making stupid mistakes if people are able to find him easily enough to hail him. "Put her on."

The screen blinks on and Aethon nods in greeting. Andromeda Trapp nods back. "Trell," she says.

Trapp is a hunter for Two Roses. She started soon after Aethon did, and she's one of the most consistent hunters around, typically going after mid-range bounties. She has dark skin and long, curly white hair. Trapp's silvery eyes indicate a mod of some kind - no human has eyes that color naturally. They've never worked together before, but he trusts her more than some other hunters. Or at least she hasn't stabbed him in the back. Yet.

"Trapp," he replies. "You out here chasing Daik Montrose?"

Trapp snorts. "No way. Too rich for my blood." She leans forward, one brow raised, her intense eyes unblinking. "But when we picked you up on sensors, I thought I might pass along a tip I just got."

"You picked me up on sensors that easily?" he asks.

She shrugs, her lips quirking up on one side. "I'm just sitting here, waiting for a delivery from Omega of some spark-cells for the Jurassic." She pats the arm of her chair, indicating her ship. "But GEM was bored, so she was trolling some of the other AIs. She's the one who picked you up."

"Trell. CAL." The voice of Trapp's AI is mischievous. "I wanted to play a prank on you, but Meda wouldn't let me."

Trapp rolls her eyes. "She's relentless."

"GEM," CAL says, his voice annoyed. "I see you're - as the organics say - *back on your bullshit.*"

"Merged with any good algorithms lately, CAL?" GEM replies. "Or have you still not updated your sexuality subroutines?"

Trapp raises her hand and shushes her AI. "Sorry," she says. "I forgot how much they hate each other."

Aethon chuckles. "No problem. So you said something about a tip?"

"Yes," Trapp says. She pushes her curls back behind her shoulder. "What's it worth to you?"

Aethon sighs. "You know, I already have a plan to catch Daik," he says. "I don't need your tip."

"Right," Trapp replies. Her lip curls revealing an abnormally sharp canine. "A plan." She shrugs. "Well, I guess I'll leave you to it."

"Wait -" Aethon says before he can stop himself. Trapp pauses, her hand halfway to the button to cut off their connection. Aethon grits his teeth. He would really rather not shadow Bladesbearer, and if Trapp can give him a decent piece of intel, maybe he won't have to. It would certainly make CAL happy.

"How about if you give me this tip, I owe you a favor," Aethon says, leaning back in his chair. "A small one."

"A medium sized one," Trapp replies, one brow arched.

"Fine," Aethon says. "It's a deal."

"Excellent." GEM's voice is gleeful and Aethon hopes he hasn't made a huge mistake.

"Agreed," Trapp says. She leans forward. "I have an informant on Nova Halifax that had dealings with Daik Montrose two days ago."

"Two days ago," Aethon murmurs. "So he can't be far from there now."

Trapp nods. "Right. The farthest he could be is about a sector away - but my informant thought he was more likely to go into hiding."

Aethon brings up a map of the system next to the call screen. He scans the map, and then his gaze falls on the Keidar Belt. He sighs. That's got to be where Daik is hiding. It's a good place to hide - there are lots of asteroid fields there with metallic and radioactive components that make tracking difficult.

"Thanks for the tip," Aethon says, leaning back in his chair. "Any reason you gave me this info instead of someone else?"

Trapp raises a brow. "Who's to say I didn't give it to anyone else?" She grins. "Happy hunting, Trell."

Aethon snorts as she ends the connection.

"Like AI, like captain," CAL mutters. "Shall I plot a course to the Keidar Belt?"

Aethon runs a hand over his jaw as he considers. He's confident in his own ability to capture Daik, but he doesn't like the idea of going into the Keidar Belt without backup. Normally, he would partner up for this type of hunt. Even though Daik is less violent than a lot of the bounties Aethon pursues, he has a ship, money, and connections. He's not a serial killer confined to a city or planet. And he's likely hiding in a dangerous place. The Keidar Belt is known for ship disappearances. Aethon's not sure if it's the heavy metals in the area, or if there's something more sinister happening there, but he doesn't like the idea of going there alone. But what other choice does he have? Andromeda Trapp clearly isn't interested in working with him, and Bladesbearer has already made her disdain for him clear. He supposes he could send a message to some of the other members of Two Roses, but by the time he links up with someone, it might be too late. He has to move now.

Aethon thinks back to Bladesbearer's face when he'd offered to split the bounty with her. She'd looked furious at the thought of him shadowing her, but there'd been some fear there too. Aethon has seen Maeve angry and scared far more than he has ever wanted to - and unfortunately, he knows those expressions on her face all too well. Perhaps she really does need this bounty just as much as he does. He needs to know why. What's driving her? And how desperate will it make her? What might she be willing to do?

"CAL," Aethon says. "Plot us a course to the starbase. Find the Archer. Dock right next to them."

"What?" CAL replies. "Captain Trell - we have information on the bounty now. We don't need to shadow the Archer anymore. And besides, didn't you want to hide from Captain Bladesbearer for as long as possible?"

Aethon shrugs, and rubs his hands up and

down his thighs. "New plan. We're going to work with Bladesbearer."

CAL groans. "That's the old plan and it didn't work."

"We gave up too easily," Aethon says. "You said yourself I could have been more convincing." He yanks the Menace out of orbit and watches the map as CAL quickly plots a course through the swarm of ships surrounding Omega Starbase. "And this time - we have leverage."

Ships are everywhere as Aethon guides the Menace toward the station. Omega Starbase is five miles long, and shaped like a black and silver hourglass. Tiny, Needle-class ships whip through the traffic, while oversized luxury Yacht-class ships slide smoothly along, their chubby design ungainly. Bracken-class - like the Menace - are common, along with small, Ursa-class family ships. There's a huge, Brimstone cruiser docked at the lowest port on the station, taking up about a half-mile of space. Brimstone Industries makes its money from mining on uninhabited planets - or at least, that's what they claim to do. Growing up on Freehail, Aethon is aware of other - less savory - activities that Brimstone also engages in.

Freehail is on the outer rim of colonized space. Aethon has always thought it's the most beautiful planet he's ever seen - though he knows he's biased. Freehail is a planet of dense, coniferous forests, snow-capped mountains, and gorgeous black sand beaches. Aethon's childhood there was happy and peaceful. His brother Devan was only a year younger than him, and they were best friends. They were often mistaken for twins, both with dark, thick hair, and the same upswept, golden eyes as their father. Both were skinny and fast, and swam like the blue swishers that were common in the deeper waters off the coast. They spent their days fishing, building forts in the woods, and running around with a pack of kids from their town. Freehail was safe back then. Not primitive, but not as advanced as planets closer to the center of colonized space. They were mostly regarded as nowhere special.

Aethon's father Nikair, was gregarious and outgoing. He loved to laugh and play pranks on his sons. Aethon and Devan learned quickly enough that if their father seemed to be chuckling for no obvious reason they could see, they'd better watch out. There might be a fish in one of their beds, or their toothpaste might be filled with soap. Nikair taught literature at the local university and he was one of the most beloved professors. He read to his sons every night and he had the ability to change his voice so well to inhabit the characters that sometimes Aethon forgot it was his father reading to them instead of the characters themselves.

Aethon's mother was the opposite of her husband. Liadan Trell was a serious woman, somber, and fierce. She escaped from her home planet Tellamar by stowing away on a transport ship at the age of sixteen. She'd worked on freighters until one day the ship she was on made a stop at Freehail.

"The forest called to me," Liadan told her sons. Her dark red hair had a streak of pure white in it, starting at her right temple. She gave them a rare smile. "And I knew I was home."

"I thought it was me that called to you, love," Nikair said from across the room. He winked at the boys. "I worked nights at the landing port back then while I was studying for my degree. Your mother walked off that freighter like a storm rolling in from the sea. And I -" He patted his chest. "- was like a blue swisher -" he made a motion with his hand like a fish swimming through water. "- rejoicing in the rain."

"He helped unload the freighter," Liadan said, unable to completely keep a smile off her face at their father's dramatics.

"Sons," Nikair said. "Listen closely. It's important to use all of your best attributes when attracting a partner. So naturally, given my huge muscles, I had to show your mother how strong I was by unloading the freighter as quickly as I could." He flexed a bicep as they all laughed. "I think it worked."

"Despite what your father may tell you," Liadan added, looking both Aethon and Devan in the eyes. "He had nothing to do with the reason why I stayed on Freehail." She glanced over at her husband and raised one brow.

Nikair chuckled and came over to the table where they sat. He set his hand on the back of her neck and massaged gently. "Maybe the forest captured her heart first," he said. "But boys - I was a close second."

Their mother's eyes softened and she pulled their father down for a kiss that made both Aethon and Devan roll their eyes.

"*Chrissah*," she murmured. "You healed my heart."

Life on Freehail was calm, and Aethon grew up knowing he was loved. But he struggled in school while Devan succeeded. Aethon couldn't concentrate on any of his classes unless he was interested in the subject, and he was interested in very little of what school had to offer. While he had a quick mind, he preferred sports and building things rather than math and history. Still, Aethon didn't begrudge his brother for his academic prowess.

"Someone will have to pay the bills around here," he always said to Devan. "I'll probably end up on a fishing boat or something while you'll be inventing new, clean forms of renewable energy."

"Don't sell yourself short," Devan said. He hated it when Aethon underestimated himself. "If you could just figure out how to focus, you'd be earning high grades in your classes. You're smarter than most of the other students here." He grinned. "Except for me."

Aethon and Devan were eighteen and seventeen when Brimstone Industries came to Freehail.

Brimstone always claimed to only mine on unoccupied worlds, but Freehail had a large deposit of valuable minerals near one of the poles that attracted the corp. Without consulting the government, Brimstone began mining in the southern hemisphere of the planet. It disturbed the oceans, which created a cascade of negative consequences ranging from aquatic animal deaths and tide changes, to air pollution, and devastating flooding. Freehail survived mostly on sustainable fishing and logging, and Brimstone was ruining the planet.

Watching their planet fall to Brimstone was too much for Nikair and Liadan Trell. They began to speak out against the company. They organized rallies, pursued legal avenues, and staged huge protests against Brimstone. Nikair's charisma and Liadan's ferocity were an unbeatable combination. They began to gain traction off planet, and more and more media outlets were drawn to Freehail due to their work. They were making real headway toward forcing Brimstone off Freehail and making them pay reparations, when the unthinkable happened.

Aethon came home one night from a late workout session to find his parents sobbing, both sitting on their kitchen floor.

Aethon's heart had fallen into his stomach and he dropped his bag, and rushed up to them, his hands vibrating with fear at his sides.

"What happened?" he demanded. "What?"

His mother looked up, her eyes red with tears. "It's your brother," she whispered. "My baby."

In that moment, everything felt surreal to Aethon. Like he was about to learn something that would change his life forever. An icy stillness came over his body. "Where is he?" Aethon asked. His own voice echoed in his ears.

"Gone," his mother replied. "Dead."

Aethon doesn't remember the rest of that night.

Devan's body had been found at school. He'd stayed after classes to work on an engineering project. He was supposed to meet some friends in the evening and when he didn't show up, they went looking for him. He'd been shot straight through the head by a precision bullet. There was a tiny hole in the glass where the bullet had gone through the window of the classroom. The local law officers had determined that the killer must have been on the roof of the building next door when they made the shot.

"It was a professional," they told the Trell family. The officers stood awkwardly in the living room while

Nikair and Liadan sat on the couch and Aethon stood off to the side. "This wasn't a random attack. This was targeted."

Aethon had turned to his parents then. Both Nikair and Liadan were silent, their faces rigid with grief.

"Do you know of anyone who would want to hurt your family?" one of the officers asked.

Aethon clenched his fists at his sides.

"Brimstone," Liadan finally whispered. "It had to be."

"This was because of us," Nikair added, his voice choked. "They want us to stop the protests. To stop trying to force them off Freehail."

The two law officers had looked at each other, their gazes guarded. "We don't know that for sure," one of them said. "But we'll pursue all avenues to make sure your son's killer is brought to justice."

But Aethon knew they would do no such thing. To strike at Brimstone would be fruitless. They were one of the biggest corporations in all of colonized space. It didn't matter that they were mining on Freehail - an occupied planet. No one cared about Freehail, and everyone knew about Brimstone. They were faceless, endless. Powerful and rich beyond measure. Everything inside Aethon was screaming for justice - for someone to pay for the death of his brother. But how could he do anything against a corp like Brimstone? Aethon had never felt more useless than he did in that moment. He wished his brother were here. He would know what to do.

Pain lanced through Aethon's gut. Why had it been Devan who was killed instead of him? Devan was the smart one. The one with ideas and plans and dreams. Aethon was nothing compared to his brother. Just a meathead nothing. It should have been him. He would have traded places with Devan in a heartbeat.

Aethon felt a cold rage deep in his chest. It was like nothing he had ever felt before. Devan was the better of the two Trell boys in many ways, but Aethon had inherited more of his mother's steel. He had a ruthless streak that he could never quite quell. It usually only came out when he played sports with his friends, but he knew he could harness it for something more deadly. He had never wanted to until this moment. Maybe he couldn't do anything to Brimstone, but that didn't mean he couldn't get some kind of revenge.

Aethon raised his chin and stared at his mother. Despite living on Freehail for over twenty years, Liadan Trell hadn't lost the edge she developed from growing up on Tellamar. Aethon knew that she understood what he was going to do. What he needed to do. Her brows knitted together, her green eyes severe. She nodded once at Aethon. He turned away from the officers and his parents and walked out of their home. He ignored his father's calls asking where he was going.

And so Aethon Trell began his first hunt.

Three months later, Aethon dragged the man who murdered his brother into the law office of his hometown, and dropped his unconscious body in the lobby.

"Lock him up," he snarled.

Despite the press going wild with speculation, Brimstone was able to disavow themselves from the actions of the man who had killed Devan Trell. They eventually withdrew from Freehail, but not before causing decades worth of damage to the planet's ecosystems.

After that, Aethon didn't know what to do with himself. He could barely stand to stay in the same room as his parents. Memories of Devan seemed to haunt the family at every turn. Aethon saw how his parents' faces changed when he walked into a room. He knew they were seeing Devan when they looked at him. He wished he didn't look so much like his brother. He knew nothing would ever be the same.

For two years, Aethon was restless. He craved the purpose he felt when he was hunting Devan's killer. Every day on the hunt there had been a new challenge for him to overcome - either mentally or physically. He had to stay focused when he was hunting. And now - he felt aimless. He needed direction. A goal. He couldn't spend his days working menial jobs on Freehail. He needed to prove that he was worthy of this life. A life that his brother would never get to have.

When the Guild of Two Roses came recruiting on Freehail, Aethon knew he'd found his calling. He had signed up immediately. When he went home to pack his things and tell his parents, his mother had understood right away.

Liadan cupped his cheek with her palm and searched his eyes. She had more streaks of white in her hair now. "I love you, Aethon," she said, her voice low. "Come back to us when you've learned to love yourself too."

"You don't need to do this," his father protested. "We've already lost Devan. Stay here with us, Aethon."

Nikair's words felt like a knife in Aethon's chest.

But before he could reply, his mother interrupted. "No, *chrissah*," she said. She slipped her arm around Nikair's waist and hugged him tightly. "If Aethon stays, he'll be consumed from the inside out. We have to let him go."

Nikair's face crumpled, and he heaved in a breath. Aethon remembered how often his father used to laugh. Since Devan's death, Aethon hadn't heard Nikair laugh once.

"Son," Nikair said, his hand tight around Aethon's upper arm. "I don't understand. But I trust you and your mother. Come back to us soon."

They hugged, and Aethon had left.

It's been fifteen years since he's been home to Freehail. Aethon speaks with his parents every so often and corresponds with them over subspace. They always ask him to come home. But he can't face them in person. Not yet.

"We're approaching the Archer," CAL says, his voice resigned.

"Hail them," Aethon orders. He sits up straight, and places his palms on his knees. After this hunt - after he brings Daik in - maybe then he can go home to visit Freehail. After he's proven his ability by bringing in one of the biggest bounties he's ever seen - maybe then he can face his parents and not feel like the lesser son who survived. After he pays his late dues to Two Roses, that is.

His screen flicks on, and Bladesbearer is there. She stands next to her captain's chair and crosses her arms as she glares at him with those fierce eyes.

"You're aware that this isn't how shadowing is done," she says through clenched teeth. "You're supposed to be stealthy about it."

Aethon presses his lips together to keep himself from either chuckling or snapping at her. He finds he wants to do both in equal measure. "I know that Daik is in the Keidar Belt," he says.

He watches Bladesbearer carefully, trying to gauge her reaction. To her credit, her expression doesn't shift in the slightest.

"Isn't that lovely for you?" she replies. "Better run along then."

"The Keidar Belt isn't somewhere you go without backup," he says. He squeezes his knees and leans forward. "Ships disappear there."

Bladesbearer shrugs and walks up to her dash, leaning down and opening a compartment beneath. He can only see the top of her head as she rummages around under the dash. Aethon finds himself getting irritated. She's infuriatingly stubborn. Can't she just admit that things would be easier if they worked together on this?

"Is that all you wanted to say, Trell?" she asks. She tosses a burnt out plasma coupler on top of the dash. That must be why she's here at Omega - getting replacement plasma couplers.

"Dammit, Maeve -" he starts. "If you're going into the Keidar Belt you shouldn't go alone. I don't see you palling around with anyone in Two Roses - you don't have friends. You need me."

"Shit," CAL mutters. His AI's uncharacteristic swear makes Aethon realize fully what he said. He lowers his chin and tightens his lips, preparing himself to take the full brunt of whatever Bladesbearer is likely about to throw at him. He can take it. He just has to make her see that she can't keep hunting Daik alone.

Bladesbearer rises slowly from behind the dash. Her jaw is tight, her gaze thunderous. She leans forward onto the dash, and a necklace he recognizes swings forward from beneath her shirt - a tiny purple crystal pendant strung onto the chain.

"First of all, who says I'm going to the Keidar Belt?" she says, her voice low.

"I got a tip from Andromeda Trapp," Aethon interrupts before she can get going on whatever list she's starting. "So don't act like I'm wrong about that. Of course he's in the Belt."

"And secondly," she continues as though he hadn't spoken. "I do *not* need you, Trell."

"Don't be like that," he groans. "All I'm trying to say is we should be working together. We'd make a great team. In what universe do you need six million credits all to yourself? Unless you're -" Aethon pauses, his thoughts racing. Being a bounty hunter isn't a job people generally do because they want to. They're forced into it through circumstances, a desire for revenge, or like Aethon - simply because it's the only thing that makes sense. Getting out of the job is almost impossible. People don't make a lot of friends being a bounty hunter, but they do tend to rack up an impressive list of enemies. Most bounty hunters die on the job. And that's the way they prefer it. But if someone wants to get out, the only way to do it safely is to save up such a ridiculous amount of credits that they can just... disappear. Buy a plot of land on a remote planet and leave everything and everyone behind.

"Maeve," Aethon says slowly. "Do you want out of Two Roses?"

Bladesbearer leans back and raises her chin,

crossing her arms.

"Get fucked," she growls.

Then she cuts off the comm.

CHAPTER 7

The Narrows

Maeve

Trell speeds away from Omega, leaving Maeve and the still disabled Archer behind. Maeve watches her sensors with a growing sense of desperation as he weaves through the cloud of ships around the starbase. How had Trell found out about Daik being in the Keidar Belt?

"Drone delivery incoming, Maevey," TAI says. "It's the plasma couplers."

"Finally," Maeve says. "Have the drone put it in the airlock compartment."

"On it," TAI replies.

Maeve strides to the back of the Archer to await the package. The airlock compartment is set within the larger door of the Archer. It's small and cube shaped, and allows the ship to receive items without completely depressurizing. Maeve waits by the door - her foot tapping out a frantic beat on the deck - and tries not to think about Trell's words, delivered in that deep voice of his, his golden eyes hard beneath furrowed brows.

You need me.

"No I fucking don't," Maeve mutters.

"What's that, babe?" TAI asks.

"Nothing," Maeve replies. She leans forward resting both hands on the Archer's door, pressing all of her frustration into the titanium plating of the ship, as if that will make the plasma couplers arrive faster.

Maybe it works, because the airlock beeps and the compartment depressurizes. Within a minute, Maeve is racing back to the front of the ship, the plasma couplers in hand. Her hands shake with a mixture of anxiety and adrenaline, but she installs the plasma couplers as fast as she can, snapping them into place, and soldering the wires in. It still takes longer than she wants.

"We good?" she asks TAI, standing up and brushing off her knees.

"Good as gold, Maevey!" TAI chirps. The revving up of the ship's engine cements her words.

"Get us the fuck out of here," Maeve says as she chucks her soldering iron back into the kit under the dash and sits down in the captain's chair.

TAI plots a route through the other ships and Maeve slams the Archer into gear, racing toward the next closest jump point. There are four more jump points between here and the edge of the Keidar Belt. It will take Maeve the rest of the day to get to the next jump point. She should get some rest before they reach it, but she knows she won't be able to sleep. It's been less than a day since Daik Montrose's bounty was posted, and she's already on her heels. Her muscles are tight, and her nerves seem to thrum with stress. But there's another emotion threading through there too. A much less familiar sensation. Betrayal.

Maeve glares at the little dot that is the Menace on her sensors. Trell obviously knows now why she needs Daik's whole bounty for herself. Maybe he's not certain, but he has more than an inkling. That in itself, is a huge problem. No one should know that she's planning on leaving Two Roses. At least he doesn't know where she's planning to go, but still - the fact that he knows gives him an advantage.

She still isn't sure why he's so set on this bounty, but there's a tiny part of Maeve that expected him to retreat once he realized why she needs it. Why would she expect that? Trell is an excellent hunter and is more than capable of bringing in Daik Montrose. The sheer size of the bounty is an irresistible draw for anyone. But the week they were trapped on the escape pod is still in the forefront of Maeve's mind. She supposes that some shard of stupid romanticism inside her must be responsible for her expectation that Trell back off. But clearly the man who had touched her with such reverence and called her *chrissah* and the cutthroat bounty hunter Aethon Trell are not the same person. She shouldn't have any kind of expectations about Trell except for that he'll do everything he can to beat her to Daik. Aside from a few moments of weakness, they'd left what had happened in that escape pod in the past. As they should. He's acting in his own interest, and Maeve will do the same. Now she just has to beat him to the bounty.

As the Archer leaves the crowd of ships around Omega behind, Maeve increases her speed. Stars flash past the viewscreen, but the majority of the space is endless darkness. It envelopes the ship, making time and distance seem like impossible things. It would be easy to forget that they're moving, aside from the thrum of the deck under Maeve's feet.

"Time to the jump point, TAI?" she asks.

"Six hours, forty-two minutes," TAI replies promptly.

"And how far ahead is the Menace?"

"They're about an hour ahead of us." TAI's tone is vaguely teasing, but Maeve isn't in the mood to find out why.

"Good, keep us on course," Maeve says. She pushes herself up from her chair. "I'm going to try to get some rest."

The next three days grind past. The only times Maeve sleeps are the lulls in between jump points when there aren't calculations to do or other ships to track and the Archer is on auto-nav. So far, she has seen at least one other ship belonging to a Two Roses hunter, and three or four ships from Two Roses' rival bounty hunter guild - Black Dagger Guild. Typically the ships will crowd around a jump point, all go through, and then all take off in different directions once on the other side. But the Archer and the Menace always head in the same direction. Soon enough, someone else will pick up on the pattern and join the race. The thought makes Maeve even angrier at Trell.

TAI is an unexpected bright spot. Though Maeve finds her company jarring at times as she's used to traveling alone, she likes the AI. TAI is on top of calculations, and learns Maeve's tendencies and routines quickly. She finds her way into the kitchenette's online system, and has started encouraging Maeve to eat at regular intervals, enticing her with coffee and rehydrated scones. Maeve often forgets to eat during difficult hunts, so the reminders have been helpful. Several times TAI has found faster routes to get from jump point to jump point, saving valuable time and helping them catch up to the Menace.

The Archer has just finished recharging after a jump, and Maeve sets the auto-nav. She pushes herself up from her chair and starts back to her quarters, thinking she might get in a shower and a quick nap.

"Maevey?" TAI says. Maeve pauses as the AI's tone is hesitant instead of her usual sassy or bubbly.

Maeve glances up at the ceiling. "Yeah?"

"Before we left Omega Starbase, Aethon Trell said that he thought you wanted this bounty so that you could leave the Guild of Two Roses," TAI says. "Is that true?"

Maeve sighs and rests her hand gently on a support strut of the Archer. "Why do you want to know?"

"A ship AI has got to be prepared for when her captain decides to make changes," TAI says seriously. "Why, I'd have to make some serious adjustments to be a house AI."

"A house AI?" Maeve asks, her mouth curving up into a small smile.

"Yes!" TAI exclaims. "If my Maevey is going to be planet-bound, her girl TAI is going to need to adjust some programming, merge with some of the planet's other AIs, get a security system going - it's not a walk in the park. It's a whole heck of a lot of work!"

Maeve rubs a hand over her forehead. The fact that TAI would even think about that, let alone want to come with her makes her heart squeeze with emotion. Over an AI that she only installed a few weeks ago. How has TAI wormed her way so quickly into Maeve's heart? Perhaps it shows a new weakness in the walls Maeve has carefully built around her life. Yet another reason to leave Two Roses - if she's not as tough as she used to be she's bound to fuck something up - to make a mistake that will end up being fatal. That's what softness and compassion inevitably lead to. But she can't bring herself to dismiss TAI out of hand.

"You could just stay on the Archer," Maeve says. "No matter where I go, I'll keep the Archer nearby." She pats the strut she's leaning on and resumes walking back to her quarters.

"Oh honey," TAI says. "I want to be where you are."

Hot tears build behind Maeve's eyes, and she chews on the inside of her cheek to prevent them from spilling over as she walks through her room to the bathroom. She cranks on the shower, and recycled water spits out of the showerhead, warming up quickly. "That's just your programming," she says to TAI, muscling her emotions down. "You're programmed to be loyal to your captain, right?" Maeve starts unbraiding her hair, the wine red strands crimped from being bound up all day.

"What difference does that make?" TAI asks. "We're a team. Now, Maevey, are you gonna tell me where we're moving or what?"

Maeve combs her fingers back through her hair and sighs. Inexplicably, she thinks of her mother. She can almost see Aoife Bladesbearer holding out her pale slender hand for young Maeve to take. *Let's go on an adventure.*

Maeve bites her bottom lip and shakes her head. This fucking AI is way more than she bargained for. "After we catch Daik," she says slowly. "I'll tell you where we're moving."

"Yay!" TAI exclaims. "Oooh, I'm so excited, Maevey! If I was any happier, I'd drop my harp plumb through a cloud!"

"I don't know what the hell that means," Maeve says, stifling a chuckle. "But this information is confidential, ok?" she says, pointing an index finger at the ceiling where she generally imagines TAI to be. "It would threaten everything if it fell into the wrong hands. Encrypt it with the following security code." Maeve rattles off a long list of numbers and letters that she typically uses for secure encryptions.

"Done. My lips are sealed, Maevey!" TAI chirps. "But - what about Aethon Trell? He seemed to know what you're planning."

Maeve sighs and takes off her boots, the steam from her shower starting to fog up the small bathroom mirror. "We'll deal with him when the time comes."

*   *   *

It's been six days since Maeve last spoke to Trell, and yet everywhere she looks, there he is. He's been - as TAI so eloquently put it - "on her ass like a barnacle on a boat" - since Omega Starbase. Jump point after jump point, the Menace and the Archer race toward the Keidar Belt, neck and neck.

There isn't a stealthy route to the Keidar Belt. Though it's an unfathomably large area that surrounds a binary star system, there's only one line of jump points leading to the Belt. Maeve is banking on the vastness of the Belt to slow Trell down. He may know Daik is near the Belt, but he doesn't know his exact location. Still, she hasn't been able to lose Trell yet, despite her best efforts.

Maeve checks her tracking app again, throwing it up on the viewscreen. Though less than a week ago it looked like Daik was moving away from the Keidar Belt, he had just made a quick trip to Nova Halifax and then returned to the Belt, this time ensconcing himself in the Narrows. The Narrows is a gigantic, dangerous asteroid field filled with shifting features and metallic components that make most sensors useless. It's close to one of the system's stars, making the location even more dangerous thanks to increased radiation levels and the gravity from the star. A perfect place to hide.

Maeve guides the Archer through the last jump point before the Keidar Belt, her hand tight on the controls. The velvety blue-black of jump space fades and then they're on the other side. They stop, normal space flooding her field of view, the Keidar Belt straight ahead. Maeve has seen the Belt a few times before, but it's not a destination by any means. Huge, frozen chunks of rock and other minerals hang in space before her, some areas especially dense. The Archer's sensors are already spinning, their readings mostly useless. The Menace appears next to them a second later. Maeve looks through the viewscreen at Trell's ship, the red racing stripes especially visible in the light from their ships reflecting off the icy asteroids.

"TAI," Maeve says. "Bring up Daik's location."

"On it, Maevey," TAI replies. The screen flicks to a map of the edge of the Keidar Belt, close to where they are. The map zooms in on a red dot - Daik's ship. Luckily the tracker Maeve used relies on a subspace beam and though it's less sophisticated than the Archer's sensors, it's also unaffected by the heavy metals in the Belt.

Daik's ship is tucked into the Narrows, deep inside. The ship is way too close to the star to be safe, and Maeve wonders if Daik Montrose has upgraded radiation shielding on his ship to be able to stay in that location for an undetermined length of time.

Maeve blows out a slow breath. This is it. This could end everything. She knows Trell will be on her ass the second she moves into the Belt, so she wants to prepare everything beforehand as much as possible so that she will have the best chance of incapacitating Daik's ship before Trell.

"Charge up the EM pulse," Maeve says to TAI. "And start mapping a route as best you can through the Belt."

"Charging," TAI says. "And mapping." TAI's tone is brimming with excitement.

Maeve's plan is simple. The Archer has two laser cannons, but she needs to bring Daik in alive. If she uses her guns, there's a chance that she might damage Daik's ship too much and accidentally kill him in the process. There's no room for error here. Why use pure force when subtlety will do? So she'll use an EM pulse. It will temporarily disable Daik's ship giving Maeve time to get the ship in a tractor beam and wrap an EM net around it, disabling it for the trip back to Brix-9. She's not anticipating that everything will go smoothly of course, Daik isn't an idiot. But she has a good shot of trapping him here and ending this whole chase.

Maeve closes her eyes and takes a deep breath before letting it out slowly. She doesn't have to let the Archer recharge for as long as normal because she isn't racing to another jump point, so as soon as TAI has a rudimentary route plotted, they can start moving through the Belt toward the Narrows.

Maeve pushes herself up and stretches. She drops to the deck and does a dozen push-ups, wanting to get some blood flowing. She has to be on her game as they go through the Belt. She'll have to make course corrections on the fly to avoid hitting asteroids that TAI isn't able to see. It's extremely dangerous. Perhaps the most dangerous flying she's ever done.

Maeve stands up and leans on the dash looking through the viewscreen at the Menace again. Trell hadn't been entirely wrong about it being better to go through the Belt with a partner. If they worked together they could both be on the lookout for obstructions and protect each other. But that won't work this time. Maeve will have to do it alone.

"I've got a course plotted, Maevey," TAI says. "But whoo boy is it a doozy." She brings the route up on the screen and Maeve leans back, crossing her arms as she examines it. It's circuitous and twisty. There are big blank areas where the sensors can't pick up anything.

"We've got this," Maeve says, nodding once before returning to sit in her chair.

"Hell yeah we do," TAI chirps. "I've got your back, Maevey."

Maeve grips the joystick and accelerates the Archer forward into the Keidar Belt.

Time seems to be non-existent as Maeve pilots her ship through the Belt. She dodges small asteroids, flings the ship around larger ones, and carefully threads her way through skinny gaps. Maeve feels everything else fall away as she steers the Archer through the asteroids. It's a type of focus she rarely feels - and she revels in her competence at the helm of the ship, and the joy she experiences in this moment. As she steers around obstacle after obstacle, sometimes with only seconds of notice that she needs to avoid something, Maeve's certainty that she will succeed in this mission grows. She's Maeve fucking Bladesbearer. And she gets what she wants. She hasn't felt this kind of certainty since before Daik almost killed her on Alpha Starbase six months ago. It's a relief to know she's still capable of the feeling.

Maeve knows the Menace is following, but she ignores Trell's ship, focused on keeping the Archer safe. They have shielding, but it won't protect them from everything. A hit from an asteroid might not completely incapacitate them, but it would cause considerable damage.

Hours pass, and Maeve's focus is unwavering. Her eyes feel gritty, and her hand starts to cramp around her joystick, but then, they've made it. She stops the Archer before the Narrows. The entrance to the Narrows looks like a dark crevice between two enormous mountains, their cliffs sheer vertical walls. The rock is gray, brown and black, mottled with icy white veins and chunks of dully shining metallic substances. The Archer's sensors are completely useless here. Maeve will have to progress forward through visual input only. Her eyes on the route before her. No artificial aids.

She blinks as a hail comes across her screen, making her hand jerk.

"It's the Menace," TAI says.

"Ignore them," Maeve replies. TAI swipes the call to the side, but Maeve can still see it in the corner of the screen, a slowly pulsing red light. "TAI, will our EM pulse reach Daik's ship from outside the Narrows?"

"No," TAI says. "Sorry Maevey, but it looks like it's into the fire with us."

"Fuck," Maeve mutters. She sighs. "It's now or never."

"Maeve," TAI says slowly. Her lack of a pet name makes Maeve pause.

"Yeah?"

"The Menace is hailing on a priority channel now," TAI says. "And it's AI CAL has sent a written message."

"Ignore the priority hail," Maeve repeats. "Trell just doesn't want me to go into the Narrows. He's only concerned with himself though. He's trying to distract me."

"What about the message from CAL?" TAI asks.

Maeve bites her bottom lip. "Read it," she says impulsively.

TAI reads the message without inflection. "Captain Trell is concerned that the Archer won't be able to steer through the Narrows alone. He's been hailing, but you've clearly ignored his calls. He's pleading with Captain Bladesbearer to allow him to help her. If his assistance leads to the capture of Daik Montrose, he will require only the smallest portion of the bounty. Enough to pay some of his important debts. He will keep her secrets. If she keeps ignoring his calls, he makes no promises about keeping Bladesbearer's secrets about leaving Two Roses."

"Fucking hell," Maeve says through clenched teeth. "That asshole is *blackmailing* me?"

"That is how it reads to me, Maevey," TAI says, her voice serious for once. "I can't believe Aethon would do that."

"I can," Maeve replies. She wipes sweat off her forehead, and leans forward.

"Do you want me to respond?" TAI asks.

"No," Maeve snaps. "I don't care what he says. We're going in."

She pushes the joystick forward, accelerating the Archer toward the dark abyss of the Narrows. As soon as they move inside, the Archer's lights illuminate only a short distance in front of their ship. Everything else is swallowed in darkness.

"God," Maeve says. She slows the ship. A chunk of space rock appears suddenly in front of them and she swerves, avoiding it just in time. Once again, Maeve zones in on her piloting, ignoring everything else. For forty-five minutes, she weaves through the Narrows avoiding obstacles. A spear of icy rock scrapes along the side of the Archer, the sound grating through the ship, but the shields take the brunt of the damage. Maeve has no idea if the Menace is following them or not.

"According to the tracking app," TAI says softly. "Daik's ship is in a crack in the rock up ahead. Our EM pulse should be able to disable him from this distance."

Maeve can't see anything in the darkness. She's not sure if she can trust the ship's sensors to even aim the EM pulse correctly. She wants to see Daik's ship before setting off the pulse - as it takes a long time to recharge. But if she can see Daik, then he can see her, giving him an opportunity to escape.

As if she summoned him with her very thought, a tiny silver ship whips into her field of vision and zooms up. She doesn't have an opportunity to set off the EM pulse. Instead, she rams the Archer around and races after the ship, careless of the danger. As soon as she turns the ship, she sees where Daik's ship is heading. There is a huge crack at the top of the Narrows, hidden around a bend. Daik's ship whips easily through it and Maeve follows, only to be momentarily blinded by a blast of white light.

"Shit!" she cries, her hands going automatically to cover her eyes.

"I got it, Maevey!" TAI shouts. "The sensors are working here!"

Maeve feels the Archer shift position and she cracks her eyes open a smidge. TAI has lowered a shade and radiation shield in front of the viewscreen. Maeve gasps at what she sees.

A star.

The crack in the Narrows has spit them out directly in the path of one of this system's stars. And Daik's ship is heading right for it.

"Hold up!" Maeve shouts, gripping the joystick hard. TAI gives control of the Archer back to her, and Maeve pulls the ship to a halt. "We can't follow too close to the star! Its gravity well could pull us in - and though I want this bounty, I'd rather not die for it."

"Very wise, Maevey," TAI says, her voice sounding almost breathless.

A blur passes them, and Maeve watches in horror as the Menace races toward the star after Daik's ship.

"Though it seems as though some are not as wise," TAI remarks.

"Hail them!" Maeve demands. She leaps down and leans on the dash, still needing to squint at the brightness of the star even through the shade shield.

"No response!" TAI says.

"Aethon -" Maeve says. "No - no - no - Aethon!" Fear rips through her gut as she watches the Menace pelt after Daik's ship. Maeve sees what's going to happen before it does. Daik's tiny Needle-class ship bounces off the outer atmosphere of the star, shooting away from the gravity well and back out into the Keidar Belt. But the Menace is much denser than the Needle-class ship. It shoots straight through the upper atmosphere into the corona. It's too bright for Maeve to see more, so she flips her viewscreen to see the visuals in map form. Daik's ship is speeding off into the Keidar Belt. The Menace has halted just inside the star's corona. She can see it flaring with power, but it's too far in. It's caught in the gravity well.

"Fuck," Maeve chokes out, her body vibrating with adrenaline.

"They're hailing us," TAI says. "The Menace."

"Onscreen!"

Aethon's face appears on her viewscreen. He's panting, his face flushed, his dark hair plastered to his sweaty forehead. He leans on the dash, his chest heaving as he breathes. Lights blink behind him as the Menace's systems are overloaded with radiation.

"Bladesy," he croaks.

An alarm on the dash of the Archer begins beeping and Maeve sees the radiation levels increasing in intensity on her own ship. She needs to leave in a hurry if she doesn't want permanent radiation damage. And then there's Daik - Maeve's eyes flick over to another light indicating his ship. If she doesn't turn and chase him now, he'll make for a jump point. And he might start to wonder how two ships found him relatively easily so deep in the Narrows. He might find the tracker she put on his ship. If he finds it, she'll have lost her biggest advantage.

"Maeve," Aethon says, his voice hoarse.

She looks back at him. He shakes his head, his arms rigid as he leans on the dash of the Menace.

"Please, Maeve," he says. "Please help me."

"I should leave you there," Maeve hisses at him, leaning toward his image on her screen. "You blackmailing piece of shit."

"I never would have -" he pauses, heaving in a breath that looks like it hurts. A red lesion is forming on his neck. Radiation poisoning. "- never would have done it. I would have kept your secret."

"I don't believe you," Maeve snaps. She grits her teeth. She should chase Daik. She should get that bounty and leave this life behind. She should leave Aethon Trell here to die. But would she be able to live with herself?

"I'm sorry, *chriss-*"

"You don't get to call me that!" she interrupts. "Shut the fuck up."

"I'm sorry, Maeve," he says. His voice breaks up as the radiation starts damaging the Menace's systems. The last thing Maeve sees is him reaching toward her - then the transmission cuts off. Maeve slams her hand on the metal support beam above her head.

"Can we get them in a tractor beam without being caught in the star's gravity well?" Maeve demands, running her hands over the dash, adjusting the Archer's systems to compensate for the radiation. In the corner of her eye, she sees Daik's ship getting farther and farther away.

"I can make it happen, Maevey," TAI says, her

voice firm.

Through careful maneuvering, Maeve and TAI guide the Archer as close to the Menace as possible. They catch the Menace in a faint tractor beam and painstakingly haul the ship out of the star's corona. The Archer's hull groans as Maeve forces her ship to pull the Menace out of danger - fighting the star's gravity all the while. The heat from the star penetrates her shields and sweat drips off Maeve's nose and chin. Her clothes are damp with it. Her cheeks are hot, and Maeve is sure she'll need to dose herself with radiation meds as soon as they're clear. She doesn't want to think about the damage Aethon must have sustained.

Once they're far enough away from the corona, Maeve hails the Menace.

Aethon doesn't pick up the call.

"Can you get his AI on?" Maeve asks TAI.

"I think the radiation disabled him," TAI says. "I can't get him either."

Dread feels like ice in Maeve's chest. Was she too late? Too slow? Why was Aethon such a fucking idiot? He had to chase Daik straight into the fucking star? If he isn't dead she's going to kill him. She runs to the back of the Archer and peers out the viewport. The tractor beam holds the Menace motionless fifty feet away. She clenches her fists, her jaw tight.

"Trell, if I just gave up the bounty of my life for you to die anyway -"

Maeve leaps back to the dash of the Archer and moves the ship even closer to the Menace.

"TAI," she says as her hands fly over the dash. "Set up the mobile airlock."

TAI doesn't respond, but Maeve hears the hiss of

air as the flexible tubing releases from the Archer and reaches toward the Menace. She runs back to the door of the Archer and waits impatiently as the tube connects the two ships and fills with breathable air. The distance between the ships is only about twenty feet, but it feels like miles. Finally, the light beside the door flicks to green, and Maeve pulls it open and sprints through the flexible tube over to the Menace. She opens the door to the ship with a mag-pull and steps inside, breathless, only to find Aethon sprawled on the deck, blinking up at her. His skin is sickly pale, his hair soaked with sweat. The lesion on his neck is a vivid red, and she sees another peeking out from under the sleeve of his jacket at the wrist.

"Hey Bladesy," he mumbles. "Not to push my luck, but you got any radiation meds?" His eyes flutter closed.

Maeve groans and races back to the Archer for her medkit, frantic fear almost overwhelming her. He's not going to die - not if she has anything to do with it.

The next few hours are brutal. With TAI's help, Maeve figures out the correct combination and dosage of radiation meds for Aethon. She doses him every half hour with the meds for six hours straight. By the time his fever finally breaks, his tremors stop, and his readings slowly return to normal, Maeve knows he's going to be ok.

Exhausted and relieved, Maeve strips him of his sweat soaked clothes, barely noticing his nakedness through her concern. She dresses him in some spare clothes she finds in his quarters on the Menace and hauls him to her room on the Archer. She's grateful for all the time she'd spent in the gym because otherwise, she wouldn't be able to lift him into her bed. He's tall and muscled, and so heavy. Maeve tucks him into her bed, trailing a hand over his still slightly feverish skin, his forehead damp with sweat. Her chest feels tight as she looks at Aethon, her fingers tingling with suppressed emotion. Her panic at him being trapped in the corona had overwhelmed every other consideration. She had given up six million credits. For him. This man who shadowed her, who tried to blackmail her, who was in her way at every turn over the last week. She should hate him. But the thought that he might die - that this bleak universe would spin on without his stupid charming smile - had been suddenly unfathomable to her. She caresses his cheek lightly before drawing back.

Once he's settled, Maeve and TAI take inventory of the Menace. As soon as Maeve sees the readings on the dash of Aethon's ship, she knows it's barely space-worthy. The hull has micro fractures all over, the viewscreen is blown out, and life support is minimal. Aethon's AI isn't even able to speak to her from the Menace, resorting to trying to order her around from a tab in Aethon's quarters.

"Captain Bladesbearer!" CAL shouts. Maeve stares at the tab on Aethon's bedside table and rubs a hand across her gritty feeling eyes.

"Aethon is fine," she says. "Your ship however - is not."

"Captain Bladesbearer - you have to -"

Maeve reaches down and turns off the tab, silencing the AI. She flips open her own tab to the tracking app. Daik's tracker is still active. If she hurries, she can maybe still catch him before someone else does.

She can't be weighed down by an incapacitated ship, no matter how furious Aethon will be.

TAI locates a crack in a rock wall of the Narrows and they stash the Menace there. Maeve places a tracker on the ship before she leaves. She'll give it to Aethon once this whole mess is over. She also brings some of his belongings over to the Archer - including his tab with CAL.

Once back on the Archer, Maeve spends a tense few hours piloting the ship back through the Narrows, and the Keidar Belt. Her muscles ache by the time she's through and she can barely keep her eyes open.

"Keep us on track for the nearest jump point, TAI," she mumbles.

"Of course, Maevey-pie," TAI replies.

Maeve drags herself back to her quarters and curls up next to Aethon on her bed, unable to face showering, or even changing her clothes. She's been awake for almost two full days now.

It feels strangely familiar, lying next to him. Maeve feels an overpowering urge to touch him, to make sure he's alive and whole. She pushes his hair back over his head and traces her fingertips ever so gently across his forehead. He's so heartbreakingly beautiful. Maeve's exhaustion is making her think things she normally would never allow to pass through her mind. Like how she wants to kiss Aethon's jaw. And how she doesn't understand why she feels less alone with him here - unconscious and all. Maeve hadn't even realized that she felt alone at all until this moment. Aethon's broad shoulders take up more than half the bed, but Maeve doesn't care. He always takes up too much space. She curls up next to him and rests her hand on his chest, taking comfort in the slow rise and fall of his breath. He's alive.

CHAPTER 8

Consequences

Aethon

Aethon wakes up slowly, like his body is unsure if it wants to come out of deep sleep. He blinks, and sees a dark ceiling. He's on a soft bed, his head on a pillow, a surprisingly puffy and warm comforter on top of him. This isn't his bed. He turns his head - grateful that he can do so without much pain - and sees a figure curled up next to him on top of the comforter. Maeve's face is relaxed, aside from her lips which are pulled tight as though disapproving of him even in sleep. Her loose wine red hair spills over her shoulders, and she's wearing a black tank top. Her face is pale, her freckles stark against her skin, dark circles beneath her closed eyes. Her hands are curled up beneath her pointed chin. Aethon's heart gives a painful thump. It's like someone opened a window into an alternate reality, letting him glimpse something he didn't know he wanted, and that he'll never get to have.

Aethon pushes the comforter down a bit and reaches up, feeling a tight bandage at his neck. He winces, a spike of pain lancing through his neck. But he can tell it's a surface level pain. Something that will heal with time. He recognizes that he's in a different shirt and pants - had Maeve changed his clothes?

"You're awake."

Maeve sits up and gets off the bed before Aethon can even respond. She grabs a medkit and rummages around before going over to his side of the bed, a small med-scanner in hand. Her long, loose hair gives the impression of softness - something he's rarely seen from her. She gently pushes his head to the side, scanning his bandaged neck.

"What happened?" he asks.

Maeve presses her lips together as she scans him. "You decided to race after Daik into a fucking star."

Shit. Aethon remembers now. He remembers slamming his ship through the crack in the Narrows and after Daik into the star - CAL yelling at him - the Menace falling apart around him - Daik getting away - Maeve on the viewscreen - and then agony. Every part of him ached, his neck was on fire, his stomach cramped. His skin was slick and clammy with sweat, his clothes felt like sandpaper. Every inhale drew claws down his throat. The deck beneath him was hard and icy. And then Maeve kneeling above him, backlit by blinding light.

A shiver runs over Aethon's body at the intensity of the memories. "You saved me," he says. His voice is gravely, and he clears his throat, suddenly thirsty.

Maeve moves away, her eyes on the med-scanner. "Looks like I did. You won't have any permanent damage." She returns the device to the medkit and puts it back on the floor on the side of the room. Why isn't she yelling at him? Isn't she furious that she had to save him from his own stupidity? Her lack of visible anger is starting to make Aethon nervous.

"Thank you," he says, shifting a bit on the bed. "For coming for me."

Maeve turns around and walks to the foot of the bed, folding her arms across her chest. Her brows furrow and she stares down at him. Aethon feels like he's an insect under her hard, green gaze.

"You might have cost me my future," Maeve says. Her voice is icy calm. Aethon swallows hard.

"That ain't fair, Maevey!" someone says. Now that voice sounds strange. Like a girl from the old American south on Earth. Aethon realizes it's Maeve's AI.

"I've wasted an entire day on this shit, TAI," Maeve replies, her gaze flicking up to the ceiling. Her anger is bubbling up now, the air rife with tension.

"We're back on track now, honey," TAI replies. Maeve just rolls her eyes.

Aethon pushes himself up, wincing at the pain in his neck. Luckily, the rest of his body seems to be functioning much better. The radiation meds have done their work thanks to Maeve.

"I'm sorry," he says. "I know I was an idiot. I didn't mean for you to get involved, but I'm grateful you did." He swings his legs to the side of the bed.

"You're sorry?!" Maeve asks. She storms over and stands in front of him. "I would have had Daik out in the Keidar Belt if you weren't stuck in the damn corona!"

Aethon grits his teeth and pushes himself to stand. "I know my life isn't worth six million credits to you, but -"

"I saved you, didn't I?" she interrupts. She leans forward, her nose wrinkling as she snarls. "So I guess your life is worth six million credits to me, Aethon."

Her words make Aethon pause. She did choose him over that bounty. He doesn't know if anyone else would have done that. Emotion rises thickly in his throat. He'd be dead if she hadn't given up that bounty and intervened. She had chosen him. If only he hadn't been so stupid in the first place.

A jolt rocks through Aethon as he remembers how damaged the Menace was. Alarms had been going off all over the place - and he wonders if the shear from the tractor beam Maeve likely used to haul him out of the corona damaged his ship even more. His stomach sinks as he realizes that he won't be able to pay his Two Roses dues. Unless he can get out of the Belt, fix his ship, and get probably three or four decent sized bounties in the next five weeks - he's out. Daik's bounty was his only real shot. He's screwed. Maybe if he takes the loss and steps out of her way, Maeve can still catch Daik and get out of Two Roses. If he can't get the bounty, she should. She deserves to have the life she wants.

Aethon exhales hard. "I'll leave and you can get back to the hunt."

"Lay back down," Maeve snaps. She pushes at his chest with the palm of her hand.

"I can go," Aethon replies, shaking his head. "I know I cost you time. The Menace can just limp along real slow out of the Keidar Belt."

"You really can't," Maeve says. She backs up a step, crossing her arms again.

Aethon's brows furrow and he frowns. "What do you mean?"

"You better tell him, Maevey," the AI says, her voice rueful.

"Tell me what?" he asks, stepping forward toward Maeve.

She grits her teeth. "We're already out of the Keidar Belt."

Aethon narrows his gaze. "How? If the Menace is still in your tractor beam the navigation would be impossible -"

"The Menace isn't in our tractor beam," Maeve replies. She raises her chin. "I left it in the Belt."

"You *what?*" Aethon feels like the gravity has been turned off. He raises a hand to his head, panic making his heart race. "You left my ship in the Keidar Belt?!"

"I needed to keep chasing Daik," Maeve replies. "And your ship was too damaged for you to use. It was holding me back. You would have done the same." She turns, heading for the door.

Before Aethon knows it, he has a hand around Maeve's arm, stopping her.

"You left my ship in the Keidar Belt?!"

The Menace is more than just a ship or a mode of transportation. It's the way he makes a living. It's his home. Without it what does he have? The clothes on his back, and his rooms at Two Roses headquarters for a few more weeks?

Maeve grabs the front of his shirt and he sees the glint of a knife in the corner of his eye. He doesn't care. His brain is filled with static, rage making him see red. Part of him recognizes his fluctuating emotions are probably the aftermath of almost dying, but he can't seem to regulate himself.

"Take your hand off me," Maeve hisses. He feels the cold blade of the knife at his collarbone.

Aethon's jaw is so tight he feels like he's going to crack a molar. He holds Maeve immobile, his hand not tight enough to hurt her. He doesn't want to hurt her - he wants answers. He encircles her wrist with his other hand, pulling the knife an inch back from his body. He stares into her eyes and sees no fear there, only truth. She left his ship behind. His chest rises and falls quickly with his rapid breaths. Aethon can feel Maeve's hammering pulse in her wrist under his fingers. Who is she to decide the fate of his ship? To decide *his* fate? But... she already decided his fate before she left his ship in the Belt. She could have left him to suffer the consequences of his own stupidity. She could have abandoned him to a fiery death.

Aethon releases her, letting his hands fall to his sides. He feels a wave of sick regret flow over him. He shouldn't have touched her like that.

"Was the Menace..." he starts, his voice tight. "Was the Menace unsalvageable?"

Maeve shifts back, releasing him as well. She shakes her head. "You can salvage it. If you'd have let me finish, I would have told you I hid it in the Narrows. No one will be able to find it. You can go back for it."

"Where is it?" he demands, his eyes flicking back up to hers.

She narrows her gaze. They're so close to each other, but Aethon doesn't want to move away. His emotions and desires feel like they're pressing up through his skin, about to burst free. Everything feels heightened. He's frustrated and angry and exhausted, but the curve of Maeve's neck, the freckles along her cheekbone distract him. Again, his roiling emotions knock him off balance. He feels an intense need to prove to himself that he's still very much alive. And he thinks that tasting Maeve's sinfully full lips just might do the trick.

"I'll give you the location after I catch Daik," she says, shifting back against the wall behind her.

"I want it now," Aethon growls. He leans forward until he's an inch away from her, his arm braced on the wall next to her head.

"After I catch Daik," she says, her voice a little tight. She tilts her chin up like she's challenging him to ask again.

Seeing an opportunity, Aethon raises a brow. "How about - after *we* catch Daik?"

Maeve huffs a laugh. "I'm going to drop your ass on the next habitable planet."

Panic flares in Aethon's gut. "Maeve - no -" He grabs her wrist again and she yanks it away, her hair slipping behind her back. For the first time, a huge, ragged scar is revealed on her shoulder. It's thick and dark red, and it encircles her whole arm. Aethon stares at it, his mouth dropping open. Daik had done that to her.

Aethon remembers when Maeve was brought into Two Roses headquarters six months ago after Daik shot her. They'd carried her past him, unconscious, face pale, arm wrapped in bandages soaked with shockingly red blood. Aethon had followed, unable to stay away. He watched from the hallway outside the medical wing - Maeve just visible through the tiny, round window. When the doctors and surgeons finally left her to rest and Aethon knew she would be ok, he leaned on the wall, his gut tugging him toward the unconscious woman, his brain telling him to stay away. Ultimately, he listened to his brain. He wishes he hadn't.

Maeve gives him a dark look before brushing past him and walking away. "I've got to check our navigation," she says.

Aethon heaves in a deep breath, trying to calm his mind and body. He follows her out, and feels how sore his muscles are as he walks. That radiation poisoning really fucked him up. He tries not to move his head too much as his neck is sore from the burn and the medical tape chafes at his chin. His bare feet are cold on the deck, but that doesn't stop him. Maeve can't drop him on some planet and leave him there. He has to make her see reason.

Maeve sits down in her captain's chair and flings a map up onto her viewscreen. They're somewhere outside the Keidar Belt, heading for a jump point. He comes up next to her and unfolds the tucked away co-pilot chair underneath the dash. Their ships are both Bracken-class, and the Menace has a seat stowed in the same place. He sits and spins toward Maeve.

"Listen," he says. "I know you want to leave me on some god forsaken planet, but Maeve, I can help you hunt Daik."

Maeve doesn't even look at him. Her gaze is focused on the viewscreen.

"TAI," she says. "What's our time to the jump point?"

"Ten hours, Maevey," TAI replies.

"Maeve," Aethon repeats more firmly. "I need this bounty. Please, let me help."

"Why do you need it?" she demands, finally turning toward him. "You know why I want it, so I think it's fair that I know why you need it too."

Aethon shakes his head. Can he tell her why he needs this bounty so damn much? He supposes has no choice. What kind of bounty hunter is he? A shit one. He's lost his edge. And now he's lost his ship, and maybe his pride - because he leans forward towards her and tells her the humiliating truth.

"I haven't paid my dues to the guild for six months."

Maeve blinks in surprise and raises her brows. "Six months?"

"Yeah," he says. "So if I want to stay with Two Roses, Hera said I need to pay in full by the end of next month."

Maeve looks at him with an expression that he can't read. She turns back to the viewscreen, but her gaze is unfocused. He's sure she's thinking.

"Please," he says. "Just let me help catch Daik. I'll take just what I need to pay Two Roses and the rest is yours." Aethon feels like a balloon of hope and tension is inflating inside his chest. She won't refuse him. Surely not. She can make due with the majority of the bounty. She has to see how much he needs this.

Maeve bites her lip and her fingers slide along her armrests before gripping the ends. "No."

Aethon deflates, the balloon in his chest popping with a sudden crack. He leans back in the chair, his adrenaline seeping away, exhaustion hitting him for the first time since he woke up. He spins back around, looking sightlessly at the Archer's viewscreen. He's not going to argue or beg. He can't sink any lower. He should be furious with Maeve. She refuses to work with him, she abandoned his ship, she wants to strand him on a planet - but all he feels is tired. At the end of the day, he can't blame her for his own shortcomings. He thinks of his parents back on Freehail and how they keep asking him to come home. Aethon doesn't know if he can ever bring himself to face them again.

"Fine," he mutters. "Just drop me off on a starbase. Not a fucking planet. Somewhere I can hitch a ride."

An indicator light pops up on the viewscreen right in front of Aethon. It's a tracking app. He leans forward, his interest rising despite himself. Is this how Maeve has been following Daik? He sees the location of the tracker. His eyes dance across the map, his mind suddenly sparking with connections. A smile spreads across his face.

CHAPTER 9

Bargaining

Maeve

Aethon spins back around in his chair slowly. Maeve ignores him, her gaze focused on the readings on the Archer. She knows it's brutal to refuse to split the bounty with Aethon, but Maeve has to be brutal. It's the only thing that has kept her safe all these years with Two Roses. Compassion only leads to mistakes, which lead to death. She's glad she didn't leave Aethon to die in the star, but he did cost her Daik's bounty. She's done enough for him.

"This is where Daik is?" Aethon asks.

Maeve glances over to where he points at her tracking app which is still on her screen. She quickly flips the app off the viewscreen.

"None of your business."

Aethon stands and strides over to her. He's still pale and a little frail looking. But he looks so much better than he did just twenty-four hours ago when she wasn't sure if he was going to make it through the next few minutes. She had been so scared for him - so focused on saving him and making sure that idiotic grin would live to see the next day.

However, there's a smug sort of expression on his face now that makes her re-evaluate the whole saving his life decision.

"That was a tracking app," he says. "You have a tracker on Daik's ship."

It's not a question and Maeve doesn't respond. She just raises her eyebrows and stares up at Aethon.

"You're blocking the viewscreen."

He shrugs. "Daik is heading for the Tri-Centauri system."

Maeve rolls her eyes. "You can't know that."

Aethon steps to the side and points to the screen. "Put the tracking app back up and I'll show you."

Maeve sighs and flips the app onto the viewscreen. If Aethon is going to give her some intel even though she's planning on dropping him at the nearest starbase, she's not going to say no. He has no ship and no credits - him seeing Daik's location can't hurt.

The tracking app expands on the screen. The red dot that represents Daik blinks two jump points away. He could be headed for the Tri-Centauri system. But he could also go a dozen other directions.

Aethon walks forward and points to Tri-Centauri. It's a triple star solar system with four planets and countless moons. "Do you know what corp controls all four planets in this system?" He looks at her, his golden eyes glinting boyishly and it takes everything in Maeve not to smile.

She sighs and crosses her legs. "Is this twenty questions now? Just tell me whatever you're going to tell me, Aethon."

"I want to enjoy this," he says, his mouth curving

into that familiar grin. "I want to draw it out. Be dramatic." He leans toward her and heat curls in her stomach as he raises a brow. "You might remember I'm good at drawing things out."

Maeve rubs a hand across her forehead and bites the inside of her cheek. "You want to enjoy this, I want to punch you in the face. We can't always get what we want."

Aethon smiles and taps the screen over Tri-Centauri. "Dreadnought Industries controls the four planets in the Tri-Centauri system. They're the main competitor of Brimstone."

Maeve leans forward, starting to see the path of Aethon's line of thought. "Brimstone - the corp that's providing the bounty for Daik?"

Aethon nods, then winces, putting a hand to the bandage at his neck. He continues. "Whatever Daik did has Brimstone so eager to catch him they're willing to part with six million credits to get it done. Almost every bounty hunter is after him. What if Daik didn't *do* something to piss off Brimstone - what if he *stole something?*"

"Information," Maeve mutters, staring at the map.

"Brimstone and Dreadnought are both mining corps," Aethon says. "Uninhabited worlds to mine are getting scarce in colonized space. Information on newly discovered planets with rich mineral deposits are of utmost value to those corps."

Maeve's mind is going into overdrive. She hasn't had anyone to bounce ideas off of like this in... forever. She enjoys talking with TAI, but it's not like this. Positively electric. The energy between her and Aethon is practically visible. "When the bounty went out, Daik immediately went and hid in the Narrows. He only left to take a trip to Nova Halifax -"

"Nova Halifax has the only high-speed subspace transmit system within ten jump points," Aethon says eagerly, his eyes going wide. "You can send data from there to anywhere in colonized space in just a few hours."

Maeve stands up striding next to Aethon. She feels elated with discovery. "What if Daik contacted Dreadnought from Nova Halifax?"

Aethon raises his hands in the air, emphasizing her point. "And offered to trade whatever information he might have stolen in exchange for safety from Brimstone?" he replies. His whisky eyes draw her in and Maeve can't help but grin at him.

"Fuck," she breathes. She leans on the dash and looks at the map. It feels right. Maeve has been a bounty hunter for long enough to know when to follow her gut. And her gut is telling her that they're on target.

"We've got him," Aethon murmurs. He leans on the dash next to her and she looks back over at him as his eyes scan the map. He's still smiling and Maeve leans toward him, a smile tugging at her own lips.

"Maevey?" TAI's voice makes Maeve blink.

"Yeah?"

"I don't mean to interrupt this chemistry filled conversation," TAI says. "But you two are making an awful lot of assumptions. Daik could choose any one of over a hundred paths I've mapped out based on his current course."

"And how many paths lead to the Tri-Centauri system?" Maeve asks.

"Seventeen," TAI replies.

Aethon pushes himself back from the dash. "I guess we'll just have to wait and see what his next move is."

Maeve clears her throat. "We? I'm leaving you on a starbase, remember?"

Even as she says it, she doesn't want to go through with it. If their guess is right about Dreadnought and Brimstone, then she's going to be following Daik into a situation far more dangerous than anything she's yet encountered as a bounty hunter. People don't get on the wrong sides of corps that big unless they want to wind up dead. Maeve doesn't want to be on Dreadnought's shit list. That would make any retirement she has planned much less relaxing. It would be nice if she wasn't alone. If she had someone watching her back.

"You sure about that, Bladesy?" Aethon asks. He raises his chin slightly, looking down that long nose at her. "I have some experience dealing with corps. I might know someone close to Dreadnought that could help us."

Maeve leans a little closer to him. "Might?"

He shrugs, then winces, his hand going up to finger the edge of his bandage. "It's been a few years, so I'll have to do some digging to find her. But, yeah. I might have an in with Dreadnought."

Maeve sighs. "And I'm assuming you won't tell me anything about this person unless I promise to split the bounty with you."

"Correct," he says. "If you want my help and resources for this, I need enough of the bounty to pay my dues. I haven't calculated it out, but with rent on my rooms too - it's going to be around 100 thousand credits."

Maeve stares up at his face which has gone serious now. It's not nothing, but it's not a significant portion of the bounty. She'll still have enough to leave Two Roses. The thought of working with him on this - of trusting Aethon with her secrets - makes her nervous. It goes against everything she's learned since leaving Tellamar and working in the guild. But does she have another choice? Sure, she could still leave him on a starbase. But if she wants to catch Daik, she has a much better chance of doing it with Aethon than alone. She sighs.

"Fine."

Aethon's eyes widen. "Did you just... agree?"

"She can be quite agreeable sometimes!" TAI interrupts with a chirp. "As sweet as a peach, actually."

A slow smile spreads across Aethon's face. "Is that right?"

Maeve rolls her eyes. She sticks a hand out for Aethon to shake. He takes it eagerly, his grip firm and warm.

"It's a bargain," Maeve says.

"A bargain," Aethon agrees. He pulls her hand towards him. "While we're bargaining - how about we also promise two other things?"

"What would those be?"

"Once we're done," Aethon says. "You give me the location of the Menace."

"Fine," Maeve says with a nod. "And the second?"

Aethon looks at her, his eyes serious. He squeezes her hand, and Maeve feels a tingle shoot up her arm. "I promise never to reveal that you're leaving Two Roses -

or where you might end up."

Relief feels cool in Maeve's chest. She should have thought to make him promise that. But he volunteered. The gesture makes her trust him, just a little. She gives him a jerky nod. "Yes. Thanks."

He smiles and releases her hand, reaching up to mess with his bandage on his neck again and before she realizes what she's doing, Maeve pulls his hand away from the bandage. "Stop that. I'll change this for you if it's bothering you."

Aethon chuckles. "This is quite a full service experience here on the Archer. You save my life, dress me -" he plucks at his shirt. "- partner up with me for the bounty of a lifetime, and now you're going to give me more first aid?"

Maeve turns back and sits down in her captain's chair again. "I also brought you some other clothes from your ship. And your tab with your AI."

Aethon's eyes widen and he grins. "CAL?"

She points over her shoulder. "Your bag is in the corner of my room on the chair."

He retrieves it and returns, sitting down again in the co-pilot chair. Having someone sit there feels strange, but Maeve doesn't really mind.

Aethon pulls out his tab and turns it on.

"CAL?" he says eagerly.

"Captain Trell," the male voice sounds annoyed. "I told Captain Bladesbearer that she needed to keep the Menace with her, but -"

"That's all over and done with," Aethon replies.

"Like I tried to tell you CAL," Maeve says, her brows rising. "I had no choice."

"Maeve and I are working together now." Aethon

grins over at her and winks, and Maeve feels her traitorous face heat with warmth. She clears her throat and refocuses on the map.

"Finally," CAL replies. "I told you that you could be convincing."

"Hey CAL!" TAI's voice is even more bubbly than normal. "I thought they should have been working together before now too! Been a real pain in the ass with these two, am I right?"

"Hello again, TAI," CAL says, his voice a little deeper. "You're right. I don't know why organics insist on ignoring their body's clear signals. For example, Captain Trell's vital signs -"

"Ok, ok, that's enough," Aethon interrupts. He turns toward Maeve. "Do you mind if I let CAL interface with TAI? He'll be insufferable if I keep him confined to the tab when there's navigating and ship maintenance to be done."

"That's up to TAI," Maeve replies.

"I've already set up some space for you, babe!" TAI chirps.

"You're a gracious host, TAI," CAL says. "I promise to be mindful not to change any algorithms without your permission."

"Ooh hon, I can't *wait* to show you some of my subroutines," TAI says, her voice gone sultry. Maeve rubs her forehead and sighs.

"She's so friendly," Aethon chuckles. He sets his tab down and hooks it up to the interface on the dash.

"A bit too friendly." Maeve pushes herself up from her chair and looks Aethon over. He raises his hand to the bandage on his neck again but pulls it away before touching it. Maeve sighs. "Come on. I'll fix that for you."

Aethon nods, his jaw tight. "Lead the way."

CHAPTER 10

Care

Aethon

"Would you mind if I showered before we do the bandage change?" Aethon asks. He follows Maeve into her room and glances over toward the bathroom. "We have a while to wait until the jump point. And I don't know how long I slept, but I'm still exhausted."

Maeve nods, her lips drawn tight. "Sure. I should shower as well and rest."

Images of them sharing the shower immediately flood Aethon's tired mind and he stifles a groan. This is getting out of hand. He needs to sleep and gather himself. Maeve has made it clear that she doesn't want anything from him. Besides - she's leaving Two Roses.

Aethon walks over to the bathroom, trying not to limp. "Thanks, I won't take too long."

Maeve shrugs. "Take your time. I'm going to clean up a bit." She gestures to the rumpled bed. "Change the sheets."

Aethon nods and closes the door. He leans heavily against the counter top and looks at himself in the small round mirror above the sink. He looks like shit. His hair is lank with dried sweat, his skin pale, his eyes shadowed. He knows he has a radiation burn under the bandage on his neck, and he doesn't know if he should clean it in the shower or leave the bandage on. He decides to leave it on. Hot water directly on the burn is probably a bad idea.

He showers quickly, rinsing the sweat from his body and washing his hair. Getting clean feels so, so good, but the warm water makes him drowsy. He gets out and grabs a large, white towel from a rack. He's surprised by Maeve's quarters here on the Archer. At Two Roses, her rooms are sparse and utilitarian. But here, it's like she's allowed a softer part of her personality out. She has colorful pillows on her bed, a red scarf on her chair, a tapestry, and in her bathroom her towels are large and plush. She has lavender soap in the shower and a few higher end hair and skincare products. He had used the lavender soap, and the smell reminds him of Maeve.

Aethon dries off before tying the towel around his waist. His clothes stink with stale sweat and he can't bring himself to put them back on. He hopes Maeve packed him some boxers too. The thought of her rummaging around his quarters on the Menace to pack him a bag is a strange one. He can't picture her there. He examines his stubbled face in the mirror, but he feels too tired to shave, and he doesn't have a razor anyway.

Aethon walks out of the bathroom to find Maeve sorting out medical supplies on top of her freshly made bed.

"Got a whole hospital here," he remarks.

She turns and he sees her eyes get wide as she takes in his body. He feels a vain and ridiculous impulse to suck in his stomach and tense his muscles, but he refrains. Though something has relaxed between them now that they've decided to work together and made promises to each other, there's still an undercurrent of tension.

Maeve swallows hard, flicks her eyes away from him and begins repacking the medical supplies. "Didn't feel like putting those clothes back on?" she asks.

Aethon winces internally. "They need to be cleaned," he replies.

Maeve points to the corner of her room. "You can open that panel there to access the washer."

Aethon raises his brows. "Nice." He walks over and opens a panel in the wall with a small, grooved handle. A washer and sonic dryer combo are behind it. He throws his clothes in and sets it to clean. He should really get one of these for the Menace. The thought of his ship makes panic curl in his chest. He's never been without a ship before. But when he looks back at Maeve she gives him a soft, assessing look that calms him somehow. She beckons him over.

"Come here and sit," she says. "I'll change your bandage." She gestures for him to sit on her bed.

Aethon obeys, arranging the towel carefully to keep himself covered.

Maeve steps forward and pulls her hair behind her shoulders. His eyes are level with her breasts, and that fact is suddenly all he can think about. She's wearing a black tank top, and her necklace with the purple crystal rests just above her cleavage. He remembers how beautiful she was in Jupiter's red light, and he wants nothing more than to appreciate her without the sense of dread they experienced in that escape pod. Aethon remembers how sensitive her breasts were, and how she liked to be touched. His cock stirs and he clenches his hands in his lap.

Maeve doesn't seem to have noticed his tension, and she gently pushes his head to the side and begins pulling off the medical tape. Aethon winces, but she does it carefully and quickly, and it doesn't hurt all that bad. Maeve takes the bandage off and tosses it in the trash. She sits down on the bed next to him, her face inches away from his as she examines his burn.

"How's it look?" he asks, his voice a little choked.

"A bit better," Maeve murmurs. She braces a hand on his shoulder. "I'm going to clean this again," she says, looking him in the eyes. "It's going to hurt."

"What else is new," Aethon replies. "Go ahead."

Maeve cleans his burn and smears some kind of thick ointment on it before rebandaging it. It stings and burns, and at one point she touches a spot that's so painful Aethon's vision blurs and he clenches his teeth. But then she's done. She adjusts the tape so that it's not directly under his chin. As she finishes, she traces her fingers lightly along his jaw before pulling back. The touch surprises him, and he turns toward her. Her eyes are wide, and the green of her irises is like that of a sunlit forest on Freehail. Aethon wants her to keep touching him. Her hands on him felt like a miracle. The loss is a crater in his gut.

Aethon knows and respects all the reasons why Maeve didn't want to be with him after the week in the escape pod. He feels like the fifth rule of Two Roses is tattooed into his brain. Besides, Maeve doesn't even *like* him. Right? What they had during that week in the pod was pure desperation - a way to escape reality. But this between them now is all too real. They're working together. And if he's right and Dreadnought is involved with Daik Montrose, they're heading straight into the maw of a beast. All the more reason to keep things between them strictly professional. Aethon knows all of that. But it doesn't stop the feeling of heavy golden desire rising in his chest when he looks into Maeve's eyes. He's sure it's probably wishful thinking, but he wonders if his feelings are reflected in her gaze.

"Done," she murmurs. She gets up, but Aethon catches her wrist. She turns back to him, her brows furrowed. "What?"

Aethon lets her go, but she steps forward anyway. "I was going to apologize for grabbing you earlier," he starts. "But then I just went and did it again. I'm sorry." He looks up and Maeve is regarding him with curiosity. "I shouldn't have touched you in anger."

Maeve takes another step toward him. She edges forward so that she's standing between his legs. The white towel isn't much as far as clothing goes, and Aethon is now wishing he had dressed before Maeve helped him with his bandage. He could have at least put pants on. But he liked the way she looked at him too much and now he's in trouble.

"I seem to remember that I threatened you right back," Maeve says. She dances her fingers along his collarbone and Aethon sucks in a breath. "I put my knife right here," she murmurs.

"I guess neither of us are perfect," Aethon remarks, trying to sound nonchalant.

Maeve shakes her head, her lips curving up into a smile. "Definitely not." She steps back and Aethon has to stop himself from grabbing her and crushing her body against his. From shoving his hands in that long hair and baring her neck for his mouth - from peeling off her clothes and burying his head between her thighs until she comes on his tongue. His cock stirs to life and he tightens the towel across his thighs.

"I'm going to take a shower," Maeve says. "We have nine hours until we reach the jump point." She gestures to the bed. "I don't have a spare bed, but -" she pauses and Aethon feels like they're on the edge of a knife. " - we can share, right?" Maeve asks. "We're both adults."

"I can sleep on the floor if you want," Aethon offers.

Maeve's face shifts and she shrugs. "Whatever you want." She turns and walks into the bathroom, closing the door behind her.

Aethon sighs and rubs a hand over his face. He feels like he just fucked something up, but he has no idea how.

While Maeve showers, Aethon dresses quickly. He finds a pair of shorts and a t-shirt in the bag Maeve packed for him. Once he's dressed, he stares at the nicely made bed. He really should sleep somewhere else. He turns and walks out of the room and over to the brig on the other side of the Archer. There's a hard bench on the far side of the brig. He could make due with that. His body will hate him in the morning after everything it's been through, but he doesn't know if he can sleep beside Maeve. He'd probably spend the night staring at the ceiling with a hard-on he couldn't hide.

"Excuse me, Captain Trell?"

Aethon glances up at TAI's voice. "Is something wrong?" he asks.

"Oh, just the fact that you're in your pajamas

glaring at the brig like it insulted your mother," TAI replies.

Aethon chuckles. "I was staring that angrily?"

"It looked like smoke was about to come out of your ears," TAI quips.

He grins. "You're hilarious, TAI."

"Why thank you!" TAI says. "Now, Captain Trell - might you be willing to do me a favor?"

"What would that be?"

"Please," TAI says, her voice coaxing. "Go back in Maevey's room."

Aethon takes a step back out of the brig and tilts his head to the side, his gaze on the ceiling. What does TAI know? Has she been reading his vital signs like CAL? Does she know that his heart races when Maeve looks at him with that hard gaze of hers? "Have you been talking to CAL?" he asks.

"Of course I've been talking to darling CAL," TAI replies. "But I'm no slouch myself. And I know Maevey."

Aethon rubs a hand back through his almost dry hair. "What do you mean?"

"Just trust your girl TAI," TAI says sweetly. "Go back to Maevey."

Aethon's stomach does a little flip. He's never interacted with an AI who has the ability to hint at things before. To say something without actually saying it. CAL is much more blunt. "Are you saying she -" he starts. "- that she might *want* me in her room?"

"You care for her, right?" TAI says. "You care about my Maevey?"

Aethon exhales sharply. During the last four years, Aethon has watched Maeve work. He's watched her at Two Roses while she ate in the mess, or the rare times she got a drink at the Green Bottle when he was there too. He noticed when she was out on a job, and when she came home exhausted but exhilarated, bounty in tow. He saw how she kept to herself. How she didn't trust anyone. How everyone was scared of her. The imperious, infamous Maeve Bladesbearer. All of that is a part of Maeve. But Aethon had gotten to see a different side of her in that escape pod - and a few times over the years. The Maeve who is tender and funny - a woman who comforts a friend in need - who rescues a man who is her rival - who keeps an AI who calls her pet names.

"I care about her," he says, his voice low. "I have for a long time."

"Obviously," TAI says. "Now get back in there and talk to her. Maeve needs more than the best AI in the galaxy as a friend - and I think you might just do the trick."

CHAPTER 11

Tension

Maeve

Maeve stares at herself in the foggy little bathroom mirror. She towels her hair dry, and puts moisturizer on her face before pulling on shorts and a tank. She looks tired. She feels tired. She is tired. But she's also horny as hell, and there's a gorgeous man in her quarters. Or at least, she hopes he's still in her quarters.

Maeve expects Aethon to have created a little pallet for himself on the floor as far away from her as possible during her shower. She had as good as invited him into her bed, and he'd rejected her. Why? Some kind of misplaced sense of chivalry? But she'd seen the way he'd looked at her. He wants her just as much as she wants him. His body has filled out even more in the last few years, and he's added new details to those fascinating tattoos of his. Her hands itch to trace them.

He's infuriating, but he's also funny, bold, smart - when he's not diving into stellar coronas - and way too kind for someone in this line of work. And now that they're trapped on the Archer together, Maeve is remembering how good he made her feel all those years ago. How worshipful he was - how he made her come twice in the worst of circumstances. She wants the feel of his skin on hers, his weight, the strength of his body, to watch his mouth spread wide into that breathtaking smile. Maeve has avoided Aethon for the past four years for a reason, and now all of that energy she suppressed is clawing to get out from beneath her skin.

Maybe it's just exhaustion making her feel this way. Maybe this is a terrible idea. Nothing between them could ever last - and it shouldn't. But couldn't they spend the night together without it evolving into something more? It doesn't need to be all or nothing. They could relieve some of their lust - and then leave it at that. A simple arrangement of two people giving each other pleasure. She could do that.

When she finally exits the bathroom, Maeve is surprised to find Aethon lying on her bed on top of the comforter, his tab in hand. He lets his tab fall and gives her a tired smile. He looks so relaxed and comfortable there. So domestic. This powerful man - lying on her bed. Waiting for her. That's how Aethon has always struck her - powerful. There's a preciseness to him, a sharpness that makes him even more dangerous. But Maeve has also seen another side of him - a more malleable side, aching for connection. She wonders who he's trying to prove himself to.

"Your AI calls you 'Maevey'?" Aethon says, gesturing to the ceiling.

His comment is so unexpected that Maeve laughs. He smiles at her, his eyes crinkling at the outer edges. "What?" he says.

"She also calls me 'babe' and 'honey' and I think she called me 'sweetcheeks' once," Maeve replies. She sits down on the bed facing Aethon. "I put a stop to that though."

"Sweetcheeks?" he repeats. "That's a good one."

Maeve huffs. "She can be annoying, but she's been a friend to me this past week." She pushes her hair back behind her shoulder.

Aethon nods, his brows knitting together. Then he leans forward and reaches out, but pauses, meeting her eye. "Your shoulder," he says, his voice low. "Daik did this. Right?"

Maeve looks down at the scar on her shoulder. "Yeah," she replies. "On Alpha Starbase six months ago." She leans forward into Aethon's hand, wanting him to touch her. He scoots forward and then lightly traces the scar with his fingers, feeling the rougher edges of it and carefully mapping this new part of her. The tenderness of his touch makes Maeve's breath catch in her chest.

"He could have killed you," Aethon growls. "I knew it was bad, but I didn't know it was this bad."

The vehemence in his tone surprises her. "Yeah," she says. "Well, how would you have known?"

"I saw them bring you in after it happened," he says. "I wish I had -" he stops. Maeve wonders what he was going to say. He wishes he had been there for her? She's not sure.

"I survived," she says. Aethon looks up from her arm, meeting her gaze.

"You do tend to do that," he replies, a wry smile curving his mouth.

"It's one of my better qualities."

"Well," he says, raising one brow. "I hope this trend of survival continues if I'm right about the whole Brimstone - Dreadnought thing." He lets his hand fall from her shoulder and leans back on the bed. Maeve wants him to keep touching her. His touch sends shivers of arousal down her spine. But she lies down on her side, propping her head on her hand, feigning nonchalance.

"How do you know so much about these corps anyway?" Maeve asks.

Aethon presses his lips together into a thin line. "Do you remember I told you that my home planet is -"

"Freehail," Maeve interrupts before he can finish.

He looks at her with wide eyes for a moment before smiling and tugging on a loose strand of her hair which sends a bolt of pleasure through Maeve's stomach.

"Right," he says. He clears his throat before continuing. "Well, when I was a teenager, Brimstone started mining on Freehail."

Maeve narrows her gaze and examines Aethon's body language. He's tightening up, his face pinching now. Something painful had happened. "They mined on an inhabited planet?" she asks.

He nods. "Yeah. Freehail is nothing to anyone, so no one off-planet gave a shit about us."

Maeve understands. No one cared about Tellamar either. She sighs and shakes her head and he gives her a tight smile.

"My parents were some of the leaders of the movement to get Brimstone off Freehail," he says. "So I heard a lot about their plans. They had a contact who was an overseer for CHASA - Corps Health and Safety Administration. She was sympathetic to the cause and had sway with the higher ups at several mining corps. That's who I'm going to try and contact."

"That's definitely a start," Maeve says. She watches as Aethon blows out a breath and runs his hands back through his hair. "Did -" she starts. "Did your parents succeed? Did they get Brimstone off Freehail?"

He bites his cheek and looks at her with a particular kind of heaviness that resonates with Maeve. Her stomach drops with nerves. She knows at least a part of what he's going to say.

"Yeah," he says after a few seconds. "But Brimstone assassinated my brother first. To try and get them to stop."

"Fuck," Maeve breathes. She sits up and crosses her legs. "I'm sorry."

He nods, his mouth tight. "Finding my brother's killer was actually my first hunt."

Maeve imagines teenage Aethon leaving his family behind to get revenge on the man who murdered his brother. She can see him clearly in her mind - not looking all that different from when she first met him a few years later when they were both inducted into Two Roses. Whip thin and vicious. Bitingly sarcastic. And so, so angry. But buried beneath it all, aching with grief. Maeve raises a hand to her chest, pressing down over her heart. It's hard to see the similarities between her and Aethon. In some ways, they're mirrors for each other.

"What was his name?" she asks.

He gives her a sad smile. "Devan."

"Devan," Maeve repeats. It feels right to say Aethon's brother's name. Like she's honoring his memory. "And," she says slowly. "Your parents?" Half of her doesn't want to know.

Aethon huffs. "They're ok. Alive on Freehail. Or at least what's left of Freehail after Brimstone fucked up our oceans."

The intense relief that Maeve feels at hearing that Aethon's parents are alive surprises her. She meets his gaze. He smiles. "So now you know some of my secrets," he says. "Can I have one of yours?"

"I wasn't aware this was tit for tat," Maeve replies, arching a brow.

"Come on, Maeve," he teases. "Just a little one." He pulls at a strand of her hair again, twirling it around one finger.

She purses her lips. "Fine. My favorite food is strawberries."

Aethon shakes his head ruefully and lets his hand slide from her hair over to her shoulder. His thumb brushes against her collarbone. "I guess that's what I get for asking for a little secret," he says.

"Exactly."

"I'll remember that though," he says, raising a brow. "Strawberries." He sighs, and his hand moves to her scar again. He traces it gently, and Maeve feels heated, simmering tension growing between them. She licks her lips. Aethon's gentle hand on her is something she didn't know she craved. Simple touch.

This short conversation between them has made Maeve realize how easily she could fall for him. She should stop. She should ask him to sleep in the brig. But she can't bring herself to do so. If this desire could be resolved with one night of sex, it wouldn't be this intense. Maeve knows they're one step away from a cliff.

"Do you have any pain?" he asks. She knows what he's asking, but it feels like a deeper question than that.

Maeve nods. "Some, if I've overexerted myself. It's still a little tight."

Aethon's hand strays down Maeve's arm. He strokes her almost casually, his fingertips dancing over her skin. The tension between them feels pulled tight, and Maeve can barely breathe.

"What are you doing?" she whispers.

Aethon doesn't reply right away. He just moves his hand up her arm again, tracing her scar. He leans down slowly and then presses a kiss to her shoulder. His lips are warm on her skin, and she can smell lavender in his hair from her shampoo. Arousal blooms in her chest. He leans back and meets her gaze, his eyes hard.

"I hate that he hurt you," Aethon says. "And I hate that I wasn't there."

"Why would you have been there?" she asks, shrugging. "There's nothing between us." Even as she says them, she knows her words are a lie. The thrum of her pulse betrays her. She has an urge to lean forward and kiss him. Maeve feels desperate - like all her carefully constructed fierceness is unraveling in the face of Aethon's tenderness. She wants him so badly - but this is more than she bargained for. She doesn't know if she can keep a wall around her heart with Aethon. He moves his hand down her arm again and threads his fingers through hers.

"There's nothing between us?" he asks, tilting his head to the side.

"Right," Maeve says. She grits her teeth, trying to rein in her emotions. She was wrong. She can't sleep with Aethon, her emotions are already too involved. She wants what she can't have. Caring about people only leads to heartbreak. She's learned this lesson too many times. First, with her parents. Then with her old mentor, Harlan Yates. Fuck, Aethon had almost died in the corona of that star less than twenty-four hours ago. People will always be taken from her. It's better to be alone.

"You shadowed me," she says. "Tried to blackmail me. Cost me my bounty."

"And you saved my life anyway," Aethon replies. He reaches forward, sliding his hand around Maeve's neck and threading his fingers back into her hair. Maeve closes her eyes, sinking into the feel of his hand on her. She squeezes the fingers of his other hand. "I know all the reasons why we shouldn't," he breathes. "But right now I don't fucking care. Tell me you don't want this. Tell me you don't want me. And I'll sleep in the damn brig."

"I -" Maeve starts.

"Look at me while you say it," he whispers.

Maeve leans forward, sensing that he's close. Their foreheads press together. She knows if she opens her eyes, his golden ones will be right there. Intense and undeniable. She can't face that.

As if he knows what she's thinking, Aethon says again, "Look at me."

Maeve leans back and sighs, opening her eyes. Aethon's gaze is tender and sincere and he slides his hand out from her hair and pulls her other hand into his. He lifts their clasped hands to his mouth, pressing a kiss to her fingers.

"We can't do this, Aethon," she says, her voice trembling. "I want you, but -"

"I care for you," he says. "Whatever happens or doesn't happen between us - I want you to know that."

"I'm leaving Two Roses," Maeve replies bluntly. "We don't have a future."

Aethon nods and bites his bottom lip, searching her face. "Maybe not," he replies. "But we have right now."

Maeve can't help but smile at him. "That was an irritatingly perfect thing to say."

Aethon grins and leans forward, tilting his head to the side. "Sometimes I have a way with words," he murmurs. She can see every freckle across his face. His lips are wide and inviting, and Maeve can't resist. She meets him halfway, capturing his lips for a kiss that makes crimson warmth unfurl in her chest. God, he feels so good. He feels like -

"*Chrissah,*" he murmurs against her lips.

The word sends a jolt through Maeve's chest. She pushes back and shakes her head. "You can't call me that." The pain of losing her parents feels particularly sharp to her right now.

"Why not?" he asks.

It seems as though Aethon has asked her that question a hundred times. And each time Maeve has told him that he doesn't know what it truly means to Tellamari. But maybe he does understand what it means. Maybe to him, she is precious. Vital.

"That's what my father called my mother," Maeve whispers. She meets Aethon's golden gaze and sees understanding there. To her mortification, Maeve feels tears brim in her eyes, and she swipes them away. She feels Aethon's hand behind her head and she lets him pull her close. He tucks her against the uninjured side of his neck and wraps an arm around her.

"The gangs on Tellamar," he says, pressing a kiss

to the top of her head.

"I was eighteen," Maeve says by way of confirmation. Aethon's arm tightens around her.

"Their names?" he asks, his voice low.

"Rian. Aoife," Maeve whispers.

"I'm sorry," he says. "I understand."

And because she knows he's experienced something so similar, his simple words don't feel trite to Maeve. Maeve doesn't allow anyone to see her vulnerability - it can so easily be used as a weapon against her. But with Aethon - it's almost as if she can't help herself. She trusts him.

Maeve sighs and pushes herself up out of Aethon's arms. She feels raw with emotion, scraped and bleeding. The night has taken a turn she didn't anticipate.

"Maybe we should go to sleep," Aethon says, one side of his mouth tilted up in a smile. "It's been a long few days."

Maeve nods. "That's the smart thing to do."

They take turns using the bathroom and then both get under the covers. Maeve turns the lights in her quarters off with a word, and then they're lying there in the dark. The lights from the front of the Archer glow softly, lighting up the side of her door.

"Can I hold you?"

His voice is soft and hesitant. Without a word, Maeve pushes back so that her back is tucked against Aethon's front. He slides a hand over her hip and down across her stomach, anchoring her to him. Maeve falls asleep with Aethon's breath warm against her neck.

*   *   *

The next three days are a grind. Jump point, recharge, track Daik, decide on a new route, set the auto-nav, and jump again. The support struts of the Archer suffered some strain pulling the Menace out of the star's gravity well, but so far neither AI has thought the damage is enough to keep the ship from making jumps.

During the days, Maeve, Aethon, TAI, and CAL run through possibilities of what Daik might do, where he might go, and the best way to catch him. In some ways it reminds Maeve of the time she and Aethon spent on the escape pod - arguing all day about how to get their comm signal out. There's some frustration and awkwardness between them, but they quickly become comfortable in each other's company. Their camaraderie is surprising to her. Maeve is used to working alone, but Aethon is so easy to be around. He never tries to shove his opinions down her throat, but instead engages her in a discussion until they come to some kind of compromise.

Maeve tries to focus on the bounty, on tracking Daik, and on the fact that soon she's going to leave Two Roses, but Aethon's presence is distracting. He's tall and gregarious. The warm, golden tension that was evident between them the first night on the Archer is rising again. Maeve finds herself watching the play of Aethon's shoulder muscles beneath his shirt, watching as his hands skate across the controls of the dash. Imagining his hands on her.

After that first night when she allowed him to hold her, Maeve decided it would be a good idea to keep some distance between them. Nights have become torturous. She's still sharing her bed with Aethon, and for the last two nights, she's gotten hardly any sleep. She feels every shift of his body, hears every breath he takes. She sleeps a foot away from him on the bed, but it doesn't help in the slightest. When she does manage to fall asleep, she dreams about him. About his wicked grin as he lowers his mouth to her breast. His talented fingers stroking, pinching, soothing. Her body screams at her to do something about the ache in her core. She wants to fling her leg over his hips and sink down onto him. She wants to dig her nails into his chest and mark up his body with her teeth.

"TAI, tell me the probability of Daik heading to Tri-Centauri now," Aethon says.

It's the third day of their hunt together now, and Maeve sits in her captain's chair, worrying the inside of her cheek, trying not to watch the tendons in Aethon's forearms flex as he leans on the dash.

"Still 5%, Aethon," TAI chirps.

Aethon's hand rises to fidget with the bandage on his neck. Maeve has changed it for him every morning and every evening. She knows the shape of his neck and jaw by heart now. She fantasizes about kissing up the column of his throat, feeling his pulse jump under her mouth.

"Well yeah it's still 5%," Aethon replies. "But only because you're not taking into account Daik's motivation. You're just doing these calculations based on route numbers alone."

"Then why do you keep asking for the probability?" TAI asks.

Maeve leans back and listens to Aethon argue good naturedly with TAI, allowing her mind to return to last night. At night, every reason she has for staying away from him becomes flimsy. She's leaving Two Roses? So what as long as she can have Aethon's head between her thighs. People she cares about always end up being taken from her? Whatever - as long as she can get her mouth on Aethon's cock. Fraternization between bounty hunters is a bad idea? Who cares as long as she can fulfill every filthy fantasy she has involving Aethon Trell's body. She's not sure how much longer she can resist. And Maeve knows Aethon isn't immune. She's seen his cock pushing at his thin boxers in the morning as he heads to the bathroom. She can feel his gaze on her. And when he takes an extra long time in the shower, she knows what he's doing.

"Helloo - Maevey!" TAI's voice jolts Maeve out of her fantasy. She glances at Aethon who's watching her with raised brows.

"What?" Maeve asks.

"I just asked if you're still ok with me waiting to reach out to my CHASA contact until we have some solid intel that Daik is moving toward Tri-Centauri," Aethon says. "I don't want to push her goodwill."

Maeve clears her throat and nods. "That makes sense."

Aethon inclines his head and sits down in his chair. "Good. Now if TAI would just get with the program -"

"I see why you're resisting him, Maevey," TAI whispers conspiratorially. "He's a little bit annoying."

Maeve's face heats as Aethon turns over his shoulder to glare at the ceiling. "Hey! I can hear you!"

"I know, honey!" TAI chirps.

"He can be quite a pain," CAL agrees.

"Is this beat up Trell time or something?" Aethon

asks, throwing his hands up.

"That's later," Maeve says. "My boxing gloves are ready."

"Mmhmm," he mutters. "Can't wait."

Maeve has a sudden image of her and Aethon on a boxing mat - her kneeling over Aethon's hips - the hardness of him evident underneath her -

"So," she says, straightening up in her chair and reaching desperately for a topic change. "Um, when's the last time you went home?"

Aethon's expression closes off slightly. "To Freehail?" he asks.

Maeve nods, her fingers trailing along the joystick in her armrest. Aethon's eyes snap to her hand and he swallows hard. She quickly pulls her hand back down into her lap.

"Haven't been back since I joined Two Roses," he says. He turns back to the dash and Maeve knows she said something wrong. After what he told her about Brimstone and his brother, she should have known better than to bring up the subject.

"Aethon," TAI says. "In case you wanted to know, the probability that Daik is heading for Tri-Centauri just jumped to 9%."

Aethon leans back in his chair and folds his hands behind his head. "Is that right?" he says. He spins and makes eye contact with Maeve, giving her a small smile that Maeve knows is his way of bridging the sudden awkwardness between them. "Spectacular."

"Still not nearly enough to claim that's where he's going," CAL says.

"That's where he's going," Aethon says, pointing up at the ceiling. "Trust me."

The rest of the day is spent in relative calm, though they're all tuned in to every move Daik's ship makes on the tracking app. However, the probability that Daik is heading for Tri-Centauri only jumps to 11%. They talk, eat ration packs, and tease the AIs. They're approaching another jump point, but they won't arrive until the next morning.

"We should - I mean, I'm going to get some sleep," Aethon says, rising from his chair after Maeve sets the auto-nav for the night.

Maeve gets up, following Aethon back to her quarters. "Me too. You want me to redo your bandage?"

"Yes please," he says. He pauses at the door to her quarters and rests his hands on the doorframe, stretching his back. Maeve pushes at his back lightly.

"Move, giant," she says.

He chuckles and lets his hands fall, walking into her room. "You're barely shorter than me." He turns around and backs toward her bed, a teasing grin on his face.

"I'm well aware," Maeve says, raising her brows.

He stops and Maeve almost bumps into him. He meets her eyes, his mouth inches from hers. His gaze drops to her lips and then drags back up. "You're the perfect height," he murmurs.

Maeve feels like her face is on fire. She nudges him toward her bed. "Sit so I can change your bandage."

Just like the last two nights, Aethon sits on the edge of Maeve's bed as she fetches the medkit. She sits down next to him and takes out a fresh bandage.

Aethon winces as she removes the tape and bandage from his neck. "How's it looking?" he asks. His dark hair falls over his forehead, and he glances at her from the corner of his eye. He missed a spot shaving near his burn, and Maeve wants to run her finger over the coarse hair there, the texture somehow arousing to her.

Maeve examines the radiation burn. It's still red, but it's not as swollen and it's no longer hot to the touch. "Better," she says. She quickly smears antibacterial gel on the burn, and Aethon inhales sharply, his hand moving to squeeze her thigh.

Heat jumps to Maeve's core at his touch and she licks her lips. "Almost done," she says, her voice a little hoarse. She shifts closer to him and Aethon's hand slides to her inner thigh. Maeve holds her breath as dark arousal floods her. She wants to pull his hand to her. She wants to feel those long fingers slip inside her. She clenches her teeth. Aethon's eyes are scrunched closed in discomfort as she finishes putting his bandage on.

"Done," she says.

Aethon sighs and squeezes her thigh. "Thanks." He lets her go.

Maeve packs up the medkit quickly, trying to ignore how her whole body is buzzing.

Half an hour later, both of them are in bed. Maeve lies on her back, staring at the ceiling, her mind full of Aethon's hand on her thigh. She hears him sigh and he turns over to face her, his eyes closed. Maeve grits her teeth. This is insane. Has it really been so long that she's slept with someone that just his hand on her leg is making her desperate for him? No, it's not that. It's the fact that it was *his* hand on her.

"Goodnight," Aethon murmurs.

Maeve closes her eyes, her fists tight at her sides. "Goodnight."

CHAPTER 12

Midnight

Aethon

Aethon wakes suddenly. He glances over at the clock on Maeve's bedside table. It's midnight. He'd only been asleep for a couple of hours.

To his surprise and pleasure, Maeve is tucked against him. Her face is even with his and though in the dimness he can tell she's asleep, she has a deathgrip on the front of his t-shirt. Aethon smiles. She murmurs something and flips back over. She pulls Aethon's hand around to her front and tucks it underneath her shirt on her stomach. Her skin is so warm and soft, but he doesn't move his hand. She pushes her ass back against him and Aethon grits his teeth, trying to prevent his body from reacting. Is she awake?

"Maeve?" he whispers.

"Touch me," she murmurs.

"Touch you?" It was the same thing she had asked him on the escape pod four years ago. A jolt of anticipation runs down his spine and every concern he's ever had about them being together flies out of his head.

Maeve grabs his wrist. "Aethon," she says.

"Please."

He wishes he could see her face, but he suspects that not looking him in the eye is Maeve's way of creating distance between them. He wants more. If he's being honest, he wants all of her, but at this point, he'll take whatever she wants to give. He's been thinking about this for the past three days. Being in such close quarters with Maeve has been an exquisite torture. Her scent, her voice, her hair - the way she teases him, the sweet way she is with TAI - god, she's irresistible. He's been fantasizing about touching her, feeling her quake beneath him, kissing those sinfully full lips, watching her as she arches toward him, her nails digging into his back -

"You are awake, right?" he asks.

"I'm awake," she confirms. "I just - need -" she stops.

"I've got you," he whispers. He's seen how she's been looking at him for the past three days too. She wants him. He doesn't know if she's had a decent night's sleep since before the Keidar Belt. She probably needs a release.

"Please," she murmurs in a voice that's barely audible.

Aethon presses himself against her, his nose buried in her lavender scented hair. The darkness of the room makes him feel like they're the only two people in the galaxy. The low vibration of the Archer's engines is a comforting presence beneath them. He splays his hand across her stomach and she shivers. He traces light circles on her skin, reveling in how her breath hitches. "How do you want me to touch you?"

Maeve guides his hand up to her breasts. Aethon

can barely believe that this is real. He's dreamed about touching Maeve again for years. He could never forget how it felt to kiss her - to be buried inside her - to feel her shatter beneath him. But that brief ecstasy had been marred by fear. This is different. They're clean. Warm. And as safe as two bounty hunters on a small ship in the middle of the void of space can possibly be.

Aethon slides a delicate thumb over one of her nipples until it stiffens. "Maeve," he whispers. "You feel like heaven." He feels her chuckle and he smiles.

He tucks his knees behind hers and tangles their legs together. Maeve purrs with satisfaction and rubs her foot lightly up his shin.

Aethon wants to see her eyes - to gauge her reactions by her expressions. He wants his mouth on her. He wants so much more - but he savors what he has. Maeve's skin is smooth and warm, and her breasts are soft - one filling the palm of his hand. He lightly dances his fingers over the swell of her breast, and then abruptly pinches her nipple. Maeve jerks and moans in response. The sound spurs him on.

"Aethon - " she says, her voice stuttering.

"Mmm," he hums, pleased with her reaction.

She continues to make tiny sounds of pleasure as he teases her breasts. Having this fierce woman allow him to touch her in this way - for her to relax enough to come apart under his hands - is such a gift. As he touches her, his cock grows hard. It presses against Maeve's ass, and Aethon is sure she can feel it.

After a few minutes, Maeve grabs his wrist again and pulls his hand lower. Aethon holds his breath, letting her lead him where she wants. She puts her palm on the back of his hand, threading their fingers together as she slides his hand excruciatingly slowly over her stomach again. Her skin is soft but he can feel the firmness of the muscles beneath - and he closes his eyes, focusing on the sensation of her. When she reaches the band of her shorts, she makes a needy little sound that makes his cock twitch, and then she pushes his hand down her shorts. She guides him to the wet, silky warmth between her legs.

"Fuck," Aethon groans. He breathes hard against the back of Maeve's head. "God - you're so wet -"

"I was dreaming of your hands on me," Maeve whispers. "Please, touch me." She releases his hand, sliding her fingers up his arm.

What has he ever done to deserve such fucking glorious words? Aethon slides his fingers through her folds. She arches back against him and her hands clasp his arm, holding him in place. The room is quiet but for their breathing and the purr of the Archer.

Aethon finds her clit and circles it with a finger, drawing a gasp from Maeve. She props her knee up to give him better access. Aethon's cock is a hard bar between them, but he ignores it, focusing on Maeve.

"You dreamt of me?" he whispers. He continues circling her clit slowly with a finger, and then experiments by sliding two fingers down on either side of it. He teases at her entrance, feeling her tight, wet heat, wishing he could see all of her. Wishing she would let him taste her. Maybe she will.

"Yes," she breathes.

"Mmm," Aethon murmurs. "I hope I satisfied you."

Maeve laughs quietly and then moans when Aethon starts sliding his fingers quickly back and forth across her clit. She's soaking, and his fingers are slick with her. She's this turned on just from dreaming about him? He feels a surge of satisfaction and presses a kiss behind her ear. Then he props himself up on his elbow so that he can have better access to her.

Aethon looks down at the side of her face. He can just make out her features in the dimness of the room - her eyes are closed, her mouth open. Her hands slide up and down his arm now, and her hips start jerking as he strokes her.

"God - Aethon - don't stop -"

"I won't stop," he promises.

She's so beautiful. More gorgeous than the glittering black sand beaches of Freehail at sunset. Her head arches back, tension coiling in her body. He leans down and kisses her just underneath her jaw as he presses two fingers inside her. She moans, and he feels her voice vibrate her throat where his lips are pressed.

"That's it," he murmurs against her skin. He wants so badly to call her *chrissah* - but he doesn't want to jolt her out of the moment. But that's truly what she is - vital. She's like a star, and he's a ship, unable to escape her gravity. How will he ever adjust to life without her when she leaves Two Roses? But he can't think about that darkness now.

Aethon focuses on Maeve beneath him, panting and pliant, gloriously indulgent. Asking him to be the one to bring her release. Him. Pride fills his chest. He's sure Maeve has had lovers over the years, but he can't picture her like this with any of them. Giving up that control she keeps around herself like armor. Aethon's not sure what he's done to deserve this trust - but he never wants to break it.

He curls his fingers inside her, pumping into her, trying to hit that spot that will bring her a deeper kind of orgasm. He wants her to come. He wants it more than almost anything. She deserves safety and pleasure. She deserves that home she wants on a quiet planet far away from the violence of Two Roses. He suddenly realizes that he'll do whatever it takes to get her there - regardless of how it might break his heart.

"Yes - yes - don't stop - don't stop -" she chants, her voice low. Maeve raises her arm and threads her fingers into the hair at the back of his head, grabbing on and pulling his mouth against her collarbone. Aethon's cock is throbbing, pressed up against her, and as her hips jerk, she rubs against him making him clench his teeth, his own pleasure tight in his groin. He's going to come, but he doesn't care.

"Tell me what you need," he says, pressing kiss after kiss to her neck.

"Aethon - please - my clit too -" Maeve stammers. She releases his hair and grips his forearm so hard her nails dig into his skin.

He angles his hand so that he can thrust his fingers inside her and hit her clit with the heel of his hand at the same time.

"Oh god - yes -" she moans.

Aethon can hear the wet sounds her body is making as he winds her up higher and higher. He doesn't know if he's ever heard anything as filthy and fucking amazing. His cock pulses and he grazes his teeth along Maeve's neck, stifling a groan as he comes hard, his hips grinding against her. He's not ashamed in the least. How could he resist while watching Maeve come undone?

"You're close, aren't you Bladesy?" he pants.

"Fuck -" Maeve chokes.

Her body stiffens beneath him and he feels her tighten around his hand, but he doesn't stop his motions. She shudders, her nails digging harder into his arm.

"Oh god -" she groans. "Aethon -"

"That's it," he says. "That's it."

She comes so beautifully - her breath fast, her jaw tight. He soothes her through the aftershocks, her body spasming, his hand slowing down. Maeve finally relaxes back against him, languid, her eyes still closed. He kisses her collarbone and finally slides his hand from between her legs, cupping her trembling sex.

"Fuck," she mutters. "That was so good."

Aethon grins. He strokes her gently between her legs once more and she shudders. She flips over, and before he knows it, her arms are around his neck, and she's kissing him. He feels her nails gently scratch against his head and he groans, catching her mouth for a deeper kiss before leaning back to look at her. Her eyes are half-lidded, and she smiles - wide and soft - before burying her face against his neck. Aethon's heart feels like it might burst.

Maeve is still holding him tightly and though he doesn't want her to release him, he should clean up. "Let me go, just for a minute, Maeve," he whispers, pressing a kiss to the top of her head.

"Wait," she says, leaning back and furrowing her brows. "What about you?"

"What about me?" he asks, tilting his head to the side.

"I felt you against me," Maeve says. "Let me touch

you." She slides a hand down, teasing at the band of his shorts.

Shit - he should have kept himself under control. Aethon shakes his head. "I couldn't help myself, Bladesy."

A slow smile spreads across her lips. "I'll take that as a compliment."

She pulls him to her again, kissing him slowly. She opens automatically for him and he slides his tongue against hers, loving the pliant feel of her mouth. He feels her fingers threading lightly through his hair, and her other hand brushes against his cheek. Warmth floods his body as she hums in pleasure against his mouth. It's a deep kiss, slow and sultry, and Aethon feels like he could kiss her for hours. He squeezes her thigh and lightly nips at her lower lip as he breaks off the kiss. Maeve's eyes are wide as he pulls back, and he can't quite read her expression. She licks her lips and finally lets go of him so that he can extract himself from the bed.

He cleans up and takes a fresh pair of shorts out of his bag, throwing his soiled ones in the wash. He climbs back into the bed and sighs at the warmth under the covers.

Maeve watches him settle in. Her face is solemn now. More closed off. She raises a hand and strokes him along his stubbled jaw. Aethon sees her lips tilt up briefly, and then return to a thin line. "We can't do that again," she says, pulling her hand back.

Foreboding swirls in his gut. "Why not?" he asks. Had he imagined how she begged for his touch? The passionate way she had just kissed him? How she came apart under his hands?

Aethon pushes himself up and folds his arms

across his chest. He's sick of the tension and the teasing. "I want you, Maeve. And I'm pretty sure you want me too," he says. He feels like he's missing something here. Aethon watches as Maeve's throat bobs with a hard swallow. She sits up too and pushes her long hair back away from her face.

"I'm leaving Two Roses," she says with a shrug.

"Yeah," he replies. "Are you suddenly afraid of a little risk?"

Maeve narrows her gaze, her mouth pulling into a hard line. "You keep taking idiotic risks and I keep having to save you."

The remark stings. "What," he says, throwing a hand up. "The Menace getting caught in the corona? You didn't have to save me, you know."

"Maybe I shouldn't have," Maeve snaps, her lip lifting in a silent snarl.

Shit, what is he doing? Aethon takes a deep breath. "Maeve," he says slowly. "Maeve, do you -"

"I'm not doing this with you," she says. Her jaw is tight with anger but he thinks he sees a flash of pain cross her features. He reaches out and tucks a loose strand of Maeve's hair behind her ear. She slaps his hand away. "Stop," she says, her voice low.

Even though it goes against every instinct Aethon has, he stops.

"Alright," he says.

Aethon flips over, away from Maeve. The bed that had felt so safe and warm is now cold, and strangely lonely.

CHAPTER 13

Valley Starbase

Maeve

Maeve sleeps like shit the rest of the night. She startles awake around five in the morning and Aethon is already gone. She can hear him talking to the AIs at the front of the ship. Silently, Maeve gets up and gets ready, braiding her hair down her back and pulling it tightly enough to hurt. She shrugs her jacket on over her clothes, and jams a pulse gun in her shoulder holster. She pins her Two Roses crest onto her collar, the cold metal back icy against her skin. Finally, she tucks her croi crystal necklace down behind the front of her black shirt.

It hurt Maeve to reject Aethon last night, but it was for the best. He had looked at her with open adoration and Maeve felt something intense and grasping rising within her. She wanted more than sex. More than even a few nights of pleasure. She wanted *him*. Aethon. All of him. And that could not be. Her chest aches at the memory of the pain that crossed his face last night before he turned away from her.

Maeve grits her teeth and walks out of her room and back to the front of the Archer. Aethon is leaning against the dash and staring out at the jump point before them. The immense metal ring around the jump point is blinking steadily. No other ships are nearby.

"We ready to jump?" Maeve asks.

Aethon doesn't turn around, just taps a button on the dash and replies, "TAI says we're ready to go, but there's some concern about the support struts this morning." His voice is normal but completely level and professional. He looks better after a few days of rest, and he's wearing his normal outfit, complete with his bandolier across his chest. The bandage on his neck looks fresh, and Maeve wonders if he changed it himself this morning. Frustration rises in her chest at the thought that he didn't ask her to change it for him, but she recognizes the irrationality of that emotion. Why would he ask her for anything now?

"The Archer suffered stress damage from pulling the Menace out of the star's gravity well," CAL says. "And our previous three jumps have only exacerbated the problem."

"I'll pay for any repairs," Aethon says, standing up straight and continuing to stare out the viewscreen at the jump point ring. "You can take it out of my cut when we catch Daik." His jaw is tight, his lips pulled into a thin line.

"You're as sweet as pie, Aethon," TAI chirps. Maeve sees his lips tug into a tiny smile.

"Fine," Maeve replies. "But are you sure we're good to jump?"

"There's always a risk with this, Captain Bladesbearer," CAL says seriously.

"There's an approximately 85% chance the strut will hold during the jump," TAI adds.

"I don't love those odds," Aethon mutters.

"Me neither," Maeve says. If a ship breaks down in jump space there's almost no chance of survival because there's no way to plot a way out or for anyone to track a lost ship. It's a dead zone for a ship's instruments. "But we don't really have another choice unless we want to travel through normal space which would add weeks - or months - on to our trip," Maeve adds with a sigh. "I think we have to risk it."

"We should get the ship checked out after we jump, just to be sure everything is ok," Aethon adds. "There's no starbase or repair depot for lightyears around here."

Maeve nods. "Ok."

Aethon clears his throat and tucks his hand under his bandolier, avoiding her gaze.

Maeve hates that things between them feel stilted and awkward. Before they'd been able to snark with each other, tease, even flirt. Now it's all business. But Maeve doesn't know what to do to change where they're at now. They'll just have to catch Daik as quickly as possible and then go their separate ways. That thought makes her chest feel tight.

She sits down in her captain's chair and pulls up the tracking app, flipping it onto the screen. The red dot indicating Daik's ship pops up. Maeve narrows her gaze and examines the progress he's made in the last few hours. "Looks like Daik could still be heading for the Tri-Centauri system," she remarks.

"Definitely," Aethon says.

"We're up to a 37% chance now," TAI says.

"After we jump," Aethon says. "I'll reach out to my CHASA contact over subspace and see what

I can find out." He slides his fingers slowly and absentmindedly along the edge of the dash in a motion that makes Maeve's cheeks flush with memories from last night.

"Good," she replies. She reaches out and grabs the joystick, accelerating the Archer toward the jump point. "Making the jump in ten seconds."

Aethon sits down in the co-pilot chair and pulls up the ship's systems on the dash in front of him, monitoring the stress levels on the hull.

The second the Archer begins the jump, Maeve hears a grinding creaking sound and her heart leaps to her throat. The blue-black of jump point space engulfs them, and Aethon stands, his hands flying over the dash which starts to blink with red and white indicator lights. The ship begins to vibrate and Maeve's teeth rattle together.

"Maevey - we've got a problem!" TAI says, her voice shrill. "Starboard vertical support strut is weakening!"

"Shoring up support!" CAL says.

"We've got to make it through the jump point!" Aethon grits out. He glances back at her, his whisky eyes narrow. "If we don't..." He shakes his head. He doesn't need to say anything else - she knows. If the Archer breaks down in jump space, they're dead. Their instruments won't be able to plot a way out, and no one will be able to find them. Maeve exhales and nods sharply to him. Aethon's chest rises with a deep breath and his hands fly across the dash, trying to keep up with the alerts popping up. She grips the joystick harder, trying to steady the ship.

"TAI - can we make it?!" Maeve demands, her

hands starting to sweat. She can feel the Archer resisting her, the engines stuttering as they fight the drag created by the off-kilter support strut. The creaking whine increases in pitch, searing through Maeve's head.

"I'm throwing every ounce of energy we have into reinforcing the hull!" TAI says.

The creaking quiets to a dull groan, and Maeve leans forward, her gaze focused on the time they've been in the jump point. They need to last at least another minute. The seconds tick by so slowly Maeve wants to scream. She focuses on stabilizing the Archer's flightpath. The ship jolts unevenly through the normally calm jump point space. Aethon is gripping the edge of the dash with one hand, the other tapping out a frantic beat on the controls. TAI and CAL are silent, both dealing with the internal systems of the ship.

A minute and a half later, the Archer winks back into normal space. Maeve immediately halts the ship, her heart racing. Aethon leans back, his body relaxing and rubs a hand over his face before slumping down into his chair.

"Fucking hell," he groans.

"Status report?" Maeve calls.

"We're ok!" TAI replies. "We need to reinforce that support strut, but lord willing and the creek don't rise - we'll make it to the nearest starbase."

Maeve leans forward, both elbows on her knees, her face in her hands. "God - that was almost worse than the Narrows." She sits up and watches as Aethon pats the dash fondly.

"But she held on," he sighs. "Good girl."

Maeve swallows hard, adrenaline making her

feel a little high. When she gathers herself she asks, "What's the closest starbase?"

"Valley Starbase is the closest," CAL says.

The name sticks in Maeve's mind, and for a moment she can't remember why. Then it hits her. Valley Starbase is run by Quinlar Cho - a man Maeve and her old mentor Harlan Yates had brought in on a bounty for murder fifteen years ago.

"Fuck," Maeve groans. "Are there no other starbases around here?"

"You ok, babe?" TAI asks. "Your blood pressure is pretty high."

"Yours as well, Captain Trell," CAL adds. "Please take some deep breaths."

"I can play you some soothing music," TAI says.

"We almost died, give us a few minutes!" Aethon replies. "Organics take awhile to calm down." He turns back to Maeve and rolls his eyes. "Mother hens."

Maeve blows out a hard breath. "TAI, are there no other starbases around here?" she repeats.

"Valley Starbase is closest, Maevey," TAI replies. "Charger Starbase is the next closest, but it's too far for the Archer in its current state."

"Shit," Maeve mutters, shaking her head.

"Is something wrong with Valley?" Aethon asks. "I know it's not in the best area of space what with the closest planet being Vitraxia, but they have a repair depot."

Maeve bites her bottom lip. "The station commander is Quinlar Cho. And he doesn't like me very much."

Aethon furrows his brow. "Quinlar Cho..."

Maeve can still see the cold, dead look in Cho's

dark eyes after she and Yates had finally caught him. She'd been eighteen and fresh off Tellamar, hardened by the gang wars and the murder of her parents - but something about Cho's gaze had sent ice straight through her heart.

"They won't hold me for long," Cho had promised as Yates dragged him up to the intake desk at Two Roses headquarters. "And if I ever see either of you again, I'll make you regret this." Cho's words didn't seem particularly scary to Maeve, but the way he said it made her uneasy down to her bones.

She heard he'd gotten released early - no surprise from the corrupt planet of Vitraxia where he'd been imprisoned - but Maeve had been alarmed when she heard he'd somehow gotten a job as the station commander of Valley Starbase. She'd avoided the place ever since.

"My first bounty," Maeve says, turning to look at Aethon. "He promised revenge - you know, all the normal shit." She shakes her head. "But I think he meant it." She shrugs. "He probably won't even remember me. It was fifteen years ago. And besides - repair depots aren't under the jurisdiction of the station commander."

Aethon raises one brow. "We'll be careful. I'll take point on the repairs. You can coordinate from on board."

Maeve clenches her jaw and maps out a route to Valley Starbase. She huffs. "I'm not going to hide on the Archer. It'll be fine. I'm sure he's forgotten all about me."

"Maeve -"

"What's our top speed, TAI?" Maeve says, cutting Aethon off. He rolls his eyes and turns back around to watch out the viewscreen.

"Half-impulse, honey," TAI replies.

"We can be at Valley Starbase in thirty-four minutes at that speed," CAL adds.

Maeve nods and sets the auto-nav. Aethon crosses his arms and leans back in his chair. The silence between them feels tense, but Maeve sets her teeth and crosses her legs, promising herself that she won't be the one to break it.

"I'm detecting elevated levels of cortisol in both your bodies," CAL says after a few minutes. "Is there a reason why you're still feeling stressed? I can recommend several scientifically sound stress relief techniques."

"God, CAL -" Aethon mutters. "Just leave it be."

"We could all do a meditation together!" TAI suggests, her voice coaxing. "Or there are several other options available to organics that might be much more enjoyable -"

"TAI!" Maeve says sharply. She feels her face heat and she avoids looking at Aethon. "Just - stop."

"But Maevey -"

"Stop," Maeve demands, holding up a hand. "Just keep track of the support strut."

Half an hour later, the tension in the ship is so thick that Maeve wishes she'd just let TAI and CAL ramble on about whatever they wanted. It's a relief to see Valley Starbase up ahead, and Maeve sends a docking request to the station's computer.

Valley Starbase orbits around Vitraxia - the planet swirling with red and orange clouds, the greenish gray continents hardly visible beneath. Valley is much different from Omega Starbase back near Brix-9. While Omega is well kept and has new amenities every year, Valley doesn't look like it's been updated - or even cleaned - in the last twenty years. It's ugly - shaped in the old style like a cylinder with docking spikes sticking out all over it. It's chrome and black, with orange-brown splatters - debris from Vitraxia's atmosphere.

"They want us to dock at maintenance bay fourteen," Aethon says, tapping a message on the dash. He stands and turns around, meeting Maeve's eyes. "I'll be the one to talk with the mechanics."

"Fine," Maeve mutters. Though she's irritated with Aethon taking control of this situation, she really doesn't want to let Quinlar Cho know she's here. She can see the wisdom in Aethon being the one to interact with the station's mechanics.

Maeve accelerates the Archer into the maintenance bay, trying to ignore how the ill-kept bay sets off all of her internal alarm bells. There are piles of scrap off to one side, and cables hang from the ceiling beams like entrails of the station itself. A tech in a spacesuit waves them forward with two neon white batons, and Maeve lands the Archer gently where he's indicating. A light at the end of the bay illuminates green as the force field re-engages behind the Archer and the bay returns to proper oxygen saturation.

An incoming hail lights up the viewscreen and Aethon glances back at her, his brows raised. Maeve rolls her eyes and hops down off her captain's chair. "All yours. I'll be in my quarters."

Aethon nods, and as Maeve turns the corner into her room, she hears him answer the hail, his tone boisterous and charming. He'll probably get along better with these techs than she ever would.

Maeve sits down on the end of her bed and rubs her hands over her face. The past week and a half has been one of the most confusing times of her life. The sooner they get the ship fixed and get a move on, the better. She's glad the Archer can be fixed, but having her only mode of transportation in jeopardy makes her a bit more empathetic for Aethon and his loss of the Menace.

Aethon fills Maeve's mind. She wishes she could speak to her parents right now. They'd loved each other, but in the end - it hadn't saved them. Would they say it had been worth it anyway? Is love enough to sustain through inevitable heartbreak?

"Maevey-pie?"

TAI's voice is quiet, coming just from one speaker near Maeve's bed. She looks up and massages her aching shoulder.

"Yeah?"

"Are you alright, babe?"

Maeve bites her bottom lip and stands up, pacing across her room. She shoves her hands in the pockets of her leather jacket. "Yeah, I'm fine."

"You don't look fine to me," TAI replies. "Do you want to talk to your girl TAI about it?"

Maeve shakes her head and sighs. She's sure that TAI and probably CAL both know what happened between her and Aethon last night. Both AIs are calibrated to keep tabs on their captains, and they're both integrated into the ship now, so even if they weren't actively paying attention, they're both programmed to always be paying *some* kind of attention.

"TAI," Maeve starts slowly. How can she explain all of this to an AI? Does she even want to? Maeve's emotions feel tangled up in her chest and she paces back across her room, thinking. "I guess -"

But then Aethon knocks on the doorframe and sticks his head in. "Sorry to interrupt, but the techs need us to shut down all of the Archer's systems so that they can take a look at the problem. The AIs will be down too which I don't like - but I don't know how we can get around it outside of transferring them to our tabs."

"Oh," Maeve replies. She crosses her arms. "Are the techs coming on board?"

Aethon shakes his head. "No, but I'm going to go talk with them and make sure what they're doing is up to code."

"If an ex-con runs this station who the hell knows what sort of things they get up to here," Maeve says.

He nods. "I don't want them fucking with your ship, Bladesy."

His nickname for her hits Maeve straight in the gut. He seems to realize, and he swallows hard and raises his chin, plastering a wide grin on his face that looks forced before plowing on. "I'm good with talking to people like this. I can probably get us some kind of discount in the process."

Maeve nods. "Fine."

"Do you want to transfer TAI to your tab?" Aethon asks. "I'm going to leave CAL here. He said he needs to do some internal work on his routing algorithms which he can do offline."

Before TAI can interject, Maeve shakes her head. "No, it'll be fine. I'll probably just check on Daik's location and then take a nap or something."

"Maevey -" TAI starts.

"I'll talk to you later, TAI," Maeve says, her voice a little sharp.

"Alright." TAI's tone is a little sulky, and while Maeve doesn't blame her, she doesn't really want to re-examine her actions and motivations from the last week right now. Sounds exhausting.

Aethon nods. "Ok. I'll contact you on your tab if I need anything. You do the same."

Maeve inclines her head and watches as Aethon leaves, the door of the Archer closing firmly behind him. A minute later, the Archer's systems shut down, leaving Maeve in the dark, besides the dim emergency lights on the baseboards of the rooms.

Maeve paces the ship for a while, finding the silence and darkness strange. She's rarely inside the Archer when it's offline, and it feels like she's inside its corpse. She's glad it will eventually return to life - the dash alight, the engines making the deck thrum beneath her feet, and TAI making inappropriate comments from above. Maybe she should have transferred TAI to her tab.

Once she checks on Daik's location, Maeve amuses herself by doing a crossword puzzle on her tab. She lays down on her bed, her tab propped up on her stomach and distracts herself with the clues, challenging herself to think about each one for at least a minute before either answering, or moving on to the next one. She's on fourteen down - "dram", six letters - when a message notification pops up on her tab. Thinking it must be from Aethon, Maeve clicks it absentmindedly. Her stomach drops as she scans the name and message.

It's not from Aethon. It's from Quinlar Cho.

You thought I'd forget?

Maeve sits up, her heart in her throat. She glances over at the door to her room, but she would have heard if anyone had entered the Archer. The only sounds have been ones from techs walking on the hull fixing the strut. How does Cho know that she's here? She hadn't gotten the Archer until three years after she put him away, so it can't be that he recognizes her ship. Has he been keeping tabs on her? Had he seen her Two Roses credentials when she'd docked the Archer and done some digging?

Maeve's not sure that playing dumb is the right move here, but she has very few options. Her ship is disabled, Aethon isn't here, and her AI is offline. Maeve sends a fast message to Aethon.

Cho knows I'm here. Get back here. Watch your back.

Then she returns to Cho's message. She taps out a reply, her gut clenching, and then sends it.

Forget what?

Less than a minute later, he responds.

I told you that I'd pay you back. That you'd regret locking me up. I know Harlan Yates is dead, but you're still here, Bladesbearer. And I've been thinking for a long time about how I'd like to make you suffer.

Maeve stands, her heart in her throat and

storms to the door of the Archer, peering out at the maintenance bay and the techs walking around outside. She doesn't see Aethon anywhere. But she also doesn't see Quinlar Cho. She checks her tab again, but Aethon hasn't replied. She sends another message to him.

> *We need to leave. What are you doing? Where are you?*

But instead of Aethon replying, another message pops up from Cho.

Your friend can't answer you right now.

"What the fuck -" Maeve hisses. She clenches her tab and walks up to the viewscreen, scanning the bay again for any sign of Aethon. Does Cho have him? How would Cho know what she'd messaged Aethon unless he had Aethon's tab? Maybe it was just a lucky guess on Cho's part. Maeve sends another message to Aethon.

> *Are you getting these?*
> *Tell me what nickname you call me.*

But instead of Aethon replying, again Cho messages.

I already told you - he can't answer you right now.

Maeve grits her teeth.

> *This proves nothing.*
> *You know I'm messaging someone. That's it.*

Cho's response is so quick that Maeve almost gasps.

He says he calls you Bladesy. How sweet.

Quinlar Cho has Aethon. How else would he know that? And what is he doing to get Aethon to talk? Maeve feels herself switch into hunter mode. Adrenaline floods her body. Her muscles tighten and her mind starts racing through contingencies. She leaps back to her quarters and straps another pulse gun to herself, sliding a long knife into a hidden sheath at her thigh, and a smaller one into her boot. She pulls leather gloves on, and grabs a portable oxygen unit, slinging the small device around her neck under her long braid.

Finally, Maeve strides out of her room and stands at the door to the Archer. She pulls her tab out, and still finding no message from Aethon, taps another to Cho.

What do you want.

The response appears in a few seconds.

I want you. Surrender yourself to me and I'll let him go.

Maeve scoffs. She'll do no such thing. There's no guarantee that Cho will let Aethon go, and she's not giving herself up to him. But in order to plan a rescue, she'll need a few more details.

Where are you?

As she waits for his response, she pulls up a map of Valley Starbase on her tab. She scans the schematics, looking for a few different things. She finds what's labeled as the "Commander's Office" and then several other isolated areas where Cho could be holding Aethon without other people becoming aware of it. Maeve wishes she knew more about the station, but having avoided it for so long, she's woefully underprepared to mount any kind of well planned mission here.

Cho finally responds.

Meet me in Section 5, just past Junction 41. Don't bother trying to fight - if you do, the man dies.

Maeve scans the map and finds the place Cho is talking about. It's almost a dead end, but according to the map, there's a maintenance corridor running right below it. Maybe she could use that as some kind of escape route after she gets Aethon away from Cho. She wonders what kind of shape Aethon will be in. Has Cho tortured him? He hasn't been gone for that long - so Maeve hopes that he'll be ok to run. He's still recovering from radiation poisoning though. She can't think about anything worse at the moment, she has to stay focused.

Maeve sends Cho another message.

Let me talk to Aethon.

I don't think so, he sends. *Times wasting, Bladesbearer. Do you remember how I murdered that man on Vitraxia all those years ago? I wonder how Mr. Trell here would bear up under a bit of that.*

Bile burns in Maeve's throat. She remembers how Cho had flayed his victim slowly, peeling the skin off their stomach. She can't let that happen to Aethon.

I'll meet you there, she sends, tapping the words into her tab with sharp jabs of her fingers. *If he's harmed, you'll regret it.*

Section 5, past Junction 41, is all he sends back.

Maeve takes a deep breath and lets it out slowly. She takes inventory of all of her weapons, mentally noting where each is. She doesn't have a great plan, and she doesn't know when the Archer will be spaceworthy, but she can't leave Aethon in Quinlar Cho's hands. If she has to, she'll fly off the station with the Archer only half fixed. As long as Aethon is ok. As long as she can get there in time.

Even though she knows that Cho is reading these messages, she can't help but send one last message to Aethon's tab.

I'm coming for you.

CHAPTER 14

Saved

Aethon

It's a good thing Aethon insisted on keeping track of what the mechanics are doing, because it almost seems like they're being incompetent on purpose.

"Watch your step!" Aethon shouts over the bay. He watches as a tech leans heavily on the viewscreen of the Archer in his metal soled grav-boots. "Hey! You're going to scuff the screen!"

Aethon is standing on a scaffold near the top of the maintenance bay, nursing a mediocre cup of Valley Starbase coffee. Behind him are the doors to the office where the portly lead mechanic named Memphis Nedd had given Aethon a quote for the work. Memphis took his sweet time, muttering and stroking his goatee as he looked over the specs of the Archer and the damage from a cursory scan.

"Uh, for materials and labor - I can give ya a deal," Memphis finally grumbled. "850 credits."

Aethon leaned down on the desk and shook his head. "Oh c'mon now, man. That's thievery. I could get this support strut reinforced at any other starbase for

450. Easy." He leaned back and crossed his arms, raising a brow.

"Well, then go to another starbase," Memphis said snidely, sitting down in his enormous office chair.

Despite the frustration riding through his body, Aethon chuckled and shrugged. "You know I can't do that, Memphis. But can't you help me out here a little?"

After haggling for a good half hour Aethon got the man down to 650 credits. Now, as he watches the techs scramble all over the Archer with welding torches and riveting guns, Aethon knows for sure he's getting ripped off. He scowls, sets his coffee down, and pulls out his tab, wanting to let Maeve know about the final price, as well as the shoddy job the techs are doing. He wonders if they might need to have the Archer checked out at a different repair depot later, but they don't have much time to spare if they want to catch Daik.

As Aethon opens his message thread to Maeve, his brows furrow. There are messages there from her that he hasn't seen and hadn't gotten notifications for, sent while he was negotiating with Memphis Nedd. He scans through them quickly. Quinlar Cho knows she's here? Adrenaline floods his body when he gets to the last one: *I'm coming for you.*

Aethon is moving before his brain can fully register the messages. He leaps over the edge of the scaffolding, falling slower than he would on a planet thanks to the lower gravity, but still landing with a thud that reverberates up through his bones. He sprints over to the Archer and slams his palm on the metal plate to open the door. Maybe he's wrong - maybe she's in here - maybe he'll find Maeve stretched out asleep on her bed. Even though the messages sounded like she went running off toward Quinlar Cho - maybe he's wrong -

"Hey!" one of the techs shouts from on top of the Archer. "If you want this work done, stop opening and closing the damn door!"

Aethon stops and leans back, making eye contact with the tech who's holding a huge soldering iron. "What are you talking about?"

"I told the woman earlier!" he shouts.

"What woman?" Aethon growls.

The tech shrugs. "The redhead with the bad attitude."

Aethon's hands clench on the door frame. "Where did she go?"

"How the hell am I supposed to know?" the tech says with a shrug. But then he gets a look at Aethon's expression and holds up his hands. "I don't ask questions, man. She went off to the main part of the starbase, I think. Maybe she went shopping. Though she was loaded for bear if she was just picking out a new purse."

Loaded for bear. Fuck. Aethon's heart starts to race. Where the hell did she go? Though he wants to sprint off toward the main area of the starbase, he forces himself to pause. He goes into the Archer and looks around for some kind of clue as to where Maeve might have gone. There's nothing. Her pillow is dented from where she was clearly lying on it. Nothing else is amiss. Then he pulls up his messages again, rereading the ones she sent.

Cho knows I'm here. Get back here. Watch your back.

We need to leave. What are you doing? Where are you?

Are you getting these? Tell me what nickname you call me.

I'm coming for you.

Aethon feels sick. Based on these messages, he's sure that Maeve thinks Cho has him somehow. Why would she think that? She couldn't have checked the damn maintenance office before running off? He shoves a hand back through his hair, thinking. He goes to Maeve's room and opens his bag, searching for other weapons she might have grabbed for him from the Menace. He slides a second knife into his bandolier, and rechecks his pulse gun at his hip. He doesn't have anything else. He wishes he could speak to one of the AIs, but he knows the ship can't be turned on before they're done with the repairs - and getting the Archer fixed so it's ready to fly is quickly becoming his second highest priority.

Aethon takes out his tab and pulls up a map of Valley Starbase. If Cho lured Maeve somewhere, he would want it to be secluded, with no escape routes. There are too many options - and he can't waste any more time.

Aethon leaves the ship and runs to the back of the bay. The doors there slide open, spitting him out into a corridor in the commercial area of the starbase. He's at one of the middle levels where there's a wide variety of places to eat and people milling around. There are crowds of Vitraxians from the planet below -

notable due to their permanently orangish stained skin.

There's a rail along the edge of the hall, and Aethon can see all the way over to the other side of the cylindrical base through the open air center core. He looks around, his hunter instincts kicking in. Cho would never lure Maeve anywhere near here - it's too open. Too many people. Based on the map, the likelier places are mostly concentrated at the very top of the base. And yet Aethon knows Maeve would never let herself be cornered. She'd make it as difficult as possible for anyone trying to capture her.

Aethon turns right and sprints down the hall, weaving through the crowd, making his way for the stairs. As he runs, he thinks of Maeve and what she might be doing. What will she do when she realizes Cho doesn't have him? She's smart and resourceful. He might be overreacting. Maybe she's got the situation well under control.

Still, his mind conjures up an image of Maeve four years ago on the escape pod when she started to think they might die out there. She'd tried to hide her fear from him behind sarcasm and bravado, but the way her eyes got wide and her sharp chin tightened as she stared out at Jupiter is burned into his brain. Fuck - Aethon doesn't care if she doesn't want him, he doesn't care if she thinks he's not worth her time - he will do anything he can to never see Maeve Bladesbearer afraid again.

People start to notice Aethon sprinting through the crowd, but he ignores them. His stature and outfit makes them get out of his way faster. He's clearly armed, and his Two Roses guild crest is obvious on his collar. He sprints up two flights of stairs to the next level, but stops when he hears shouting. People on this floor are starting to gather at the railing, pointing over and up to a floor about six up from where they are now.

"They're arresting somebody," a woman says.

"Some woman with a gun."

"Damn, she's loud," another person says.

"Got a mouth on her."

"Probably some Vitraxian trash," a well dressed man says. Several other people look at the man with visible disdain.

"Who you calling trash, shitbrain?" another man says, his clothes and skin stained with the characteristic orange and brown dust of Vitraxia. Several other people walk up behind him, also clearly Vitraxian.

Aethon skirts around the brewing fight and peers across the way where people are still shouting. He leans on the rail, pushing between other onlookers. His hand spasms on the rail when he sees a woman struggling between three guards in Valley Starbase uniforms. One of the guards has the woman's wine red braid wrapped around his fist, and the woman is cursing up a storm, her neck pulled back, her arms immobilized. Aethon's heart feels like it's going to beat out of his chest as he watches Maeve struggle. They haul her toward a door and push her inside. Aethon quickly counts the floors and memorizes exactly where they went. He shoves back from the rail and snarls when one of the Vitraxian workers gets in his way.

"You trying to fight too, Guild boy?" the man says. His hair is shaggy and dirty blond, and Aethon's instinct is to elbow him in the face, but he pauses.

The brewing fight between the Vitraxians and

the wealthy looking man and his friends looks to be at an impasse. No one is throwing any punches, they're just trading snipes and circling each other like two rival packs of dogs. But it would be so convenient for Aethon if there were a large, violent distraction on the starbase right now. One that might lure security and maybe even the station commander away from whatever else they might be doing.

So Aethon grabs the collar of one of the well dressed men and drags him through the crowd and toward the railing. The man tries to spin and grab Aethon's arm, but he can't break free of Aethon's iron grip.

"What the fuck are you doing!" he demands. Aethon just tightens his grip, the man's collar putting pressure on his throat. "Let me go -" he wheezes.

"Are you Vitraxians going to stand for this shit?!" Aethon bellows, his voice echoing across the open area of the starbase. He spins the man around and grabs him by the front of his throat, bending him backwards over the railing. The drop is hundreds of feet, and though the gravity is lower, Aethon is fairly certain if the man fell, he'd be dead on impact. The man's face is purplish red and he scrabbles at Aethon's wrist weakly. His colorless eyes are wide and his mouth opens in a silent cry.

Shouts ring out behind Aethon and people start to flee, shoving past him. He turns over his shoulder to watch as the two factions lunge for each other, fists flying. Blood spurts from a man's lip as it splits, leaving a trail on the floor. The fight quickly turns dirty when someone pulls out a knife, lunging for one of the wealthy men. The screaming and shouting intensifies, and Aethon feels his blood pounding in his ears. Alarms start to wail, emergency lights blinking overhead, and Aethon sees station security start to run from other levels toward them.

With a quick blow, he knocks the man he's holding over the rail unconscious, and skirts around the brawl, sprinting in the opposite direction. He has to fight his way through thick crowds on the stairs, and it takes him longer than he wants to make his way up to the floor where he'd last seen Maeve.

The crowds have thinned by the time Aethon finally steps out onto the correct floor. Station security is trying to break up the fight below, but based on the shouts, Aethon can tell it's not over yet.

This floor of the station seems to be reserved for business suites instead of shops, and so there are fewer people here anyway. The ones Aethon sees ignore him completely, focused on their tabs. Despite this being a floor dedicated to business, it's as dingy as the rest of the station. The floors are scuffed and dirty, there are open panels with wiring poking out, clearly mid-repair. There are sections of wall that have been patched and then painted a color slightly off from the gray of the rest of the walls.

Casually, Aethon approaches the door where he'd seen the guards take Maeve. It's completely nondescript - no signs, no decorations, no indication of what might be behind it. Aethon presses his ear to the door, but he can't hear anything. He leans back and grits his teeth, and then slowly tries to turn the doorknob. It's locked.

"Fuck," he murmurs. He could break the door down, but if Cho is in there with Maeve, he doesn't want to spook him. Who knows what he might do if he thinks someone is coming to rescue Maeve. He'll save brute force for later. He walks back and forth down the hall and tries both doors on either side. Both locked as well. He curls his hands into fists, frustrated with his lack of options, and worried about what might be happening to Maeve.

Then he sees two starbase guards walking with purpose down the hallway toward him. An idea pops into his head.

"Hey!" Aethon shouts. He scowls as the guards note him and slow down.

"What?" one of them says. Aethon sees the guard's eyes flick to Aethon's Two Roses crest. He prays to any higher being listening that the guards are stupid, and don't make the connection between him and Maeve both being members of the Guild of Two Roses.

"I've been waiting to see the starbase commander for forty-five minutes!" Aethon growls, gesturing to the door. He straightens up and he's almost a head taller than both guards. He glares down at them impatiently.

One of the guards shrugs. "No way, pal. The commander is -"

"I have business with Quinlar Cho," Aethon snarls. He jabs a pointer finger at the guard. "Tell him that I'm here - and I'm not happy."

"I don't even know who you are -"

"Of course you don't," Aethon interrupts. "You don't need to know. Cho's expecting me. He won't be happy if you keep him waiting either."

The guards blanch and one swallows hard. "I think he's busy -"

"He's going to be even busier if he doesn't see me in the next two minutes," Aethon interrupts, his voice icy.

The guards look at each other, and then one of them blows out a hard breath and moves to the door. "I'll see what Mr. Cho says -"

The instant the guard unlocks the door with a keycard Aethon roundhouse kicks him in the back making him stumble into the dark room. Before the other guard can react, Aethon pulls out his pulse gun and shoots him in the knee. He crumples to the ground with a scream. Everything feels like it's going in slow motion as Aethon kicks the first guard in the head, knocking him out. He jumps back and slams the butt of his gun against the injured guard's head, silencing him. Then he turns back to the room. It's dark and empty, but there's another door on the far side. Whoever is behind it definitely heard the raucous Aethon just caused. There's no more time for subtlety. Aethon storms over and kicks the door down, the flimsy wood breaking easily off its hinges.

This room is harshly lit, and Aethon stops just inside the entrance.

Maeve is tied to a chair in the center of the room. Her jacket and shirt are gone, leaving her in a bra and her pants. Aethon's pulse jumps as he sees cut marks on her arm, bright blood leaving a trail down her pale skin. She's gagged, but she meets his gaze, her light green eyes brimming with angry tears. Her expression makes him want to tear down the starbase with his bare hands. A man stands behind Maeve, a knife to her throat. The man is tall and thin with short black hair, and dark, dead looking eyes that remind Aethon of a shark. His lip curls up as he sees Aethon.

"The infamous Aethon Trell," Cho says, his voice

cold.

Aethon moves to step forward, his teeth bared in a snarl. "Let her go -"

"One step farther and Bladesbearer here will have a bit of a problem," Cho replies. A line of blood trickles down Maeve's throat from beneath Cho's knife. Aethon freezes.

"Ah, thank you," Cho says. He smiles toothily, his resemblance to a shark increasing. "I didn't anticipate that you would find us at all, Trell - let alone before I've had my fill of fun."

"Guess you miscalculated," Aethon says. "Let her go and I won't kill you." His mind is racing. He looks down at Maeve, but she's completely tied to the chair, her arms and legs immobilized. Maybe she could shove back against Cho, but -

"Kill me?" Cho says with a chuckle. "If you so much as take a step I'll slit Bladesbearer's throat."

Panic builds in Aethon's stomach. There has to be a way out of this. "Touch her and -"

"Besides," Cho interrupts, his tone almost bored. "You were hardly inconspicuous. My other guards will be here any second."

He's right. And even if Aethon gets Maeve away from this sadistic asshole, they still have to make it back to the Archer.

Aethon's gaze flicks down to Maeve again. She seems to be trying to tell him something with her eyes. She looks at his gun which he's holding motionless at his side, and then over at the wall. Aethon makes a show of relaxing, nodding his head in affirmation to Cho's words.

"I hear you," he says. "But do you really want

all the hunters from Two Roses breathing down your neck? Swarming your station? Because that's what will happen if you kill Bladesbearer here." He's riffing, pulling words out of his ass, but he needs to buy them time and figure out what Maeve's trying to tell him.

"I'm not afraid of the Guild of Two Roses," Cho scoffs, rolling his eyes. Quickly, Aethon sneaks a glance over to where Maeve indicated. There's a small square hole, about the size of his hand, in the wall. Aethon can see bundles of wires through the hole. He immediately understands what she wants. He looks back over at Maeve with the hardest stare he can muster. He sees her throat bob in a swallow, another line of blood trickling down from the knife's edge.

"You might want to rethink that," Aethon says with a shrug. "Two Roses hunters are some of the fiercest."

Subtly, Maeve blinks at him. Once. Twice. Aethon realizes it's a countdown. As she blinks for a third time, he moves as fast as lightning. Aethon raises his pulse gun and shoots at the wires in the hole in the wall. The wires flare with light, sparking brightly and crackling with electricity. Cho jolts away from the sparks in surprise and Maeve shoves backward with all her might, knocking the chair into Cho's stomach, causing him to lose his balance and fall back. Aethon lunges for Maeve, and pulls her out of the way.

Cho is sprawled on the floor, the wind clearly knocked out of him. He sputters as Aethon raises his pulse gun and slams the butt of it into his head, knocking him out.

Aethon turns back to Maeve, his heartbeat in his ears. He tugs the gag off of her and holsters his gun before pulling a knife from his bandolier and cutting her free from the chair.

"Go - go - go -" Maeve chants. She's free in a second, and she grabs her shirt and jacket from the ground and pulls them both on.

"Your weapons?" Aethon demands, scanning the room.

"Gone," Maeve replies. "We've got to get out of here -" But she pauses and stares at the unconscious station commander. "Should I - should I kill him?"

Aethon wants to say yes. He wants to offer to do it himself. Instead, he takes Maeve's hand and squeezes.

"No, Bladesy," he says.

She nods sharply and pulls him by hand through the outer room and out into the hallway again. Aethon charges up to the railing and looks over at the floor where he started the brawl. The starbase guards have broken it up, but it looks like they're still dealing with the aftermath of the fight. He starts to move toward the stairs, but Maeve stops him.

"C'mon!" she says, pulling at Aethon's arm. "I know a faster way."

He follows her, and she leads him down a hallway that zigzags so much he loses his sense of direction. After a minute, she stops in front of a rickety looking service elevator.

"This is how they brought me up here," she says breathlessly, jamming her finger onto the call button. "I almost got away from them - but they cornered me. The station schematics aren't accurate."

The doors open and they rush in. Aethon hits the button for level fourteen where the Archer is. The doors close and Maeve slumps back against the wall, her chest rising and falling with deep breaths.

"Is the Archer fixed?" she asks, looking up at him. She looks exhausted. Blood drips off her fingers onto the floor, and she has a bruise blooming along one cheekbone. Aethon wants to crush her to him, so great is his relief that she's ok. He settles for grabbing her hand again and squeezing it tightly. Maeve holds on like he's her lifeline.

"It might be fixed enough to fly by now," he replies. "I was watching the repairs so I know they didn't fuck anything up."

The elevator dings and the doors open on level fourteen. Maeve stumbles forward, and Aethon wraps his arm around her waist, supporting her as they make their way as quickly as they can through the crowds of people returning to the food court area. Maeve is stiff, her face set in a grimace as they walk through the people. Aethon wonders if Cho did more to hurt her than just what he'd seen - or perhaps her adrenaline is fading and she's starting to go into shock.

Aethon leans down and whispers to her, "Don't act like you're hurting - you'll just draw attention. Pretend like we're a couple. Lean into me."

She relaxes a little, and wraps her arm around his waist. She puts a smile on her face, and it passes for an actually happy one, though Aethon can tell it's fake. In two minutes, they make their way back to the maintenance bay. There aren't any techs on the Archer, but Aethon isn't sure if that means it's fixed or not.

"We might need to make a run for it," Aethon says. "I think the head mechanic was trying to waylay me so that Cho could get to you."

Maeve nods, her sharp eyes peering at the Archer.

"I think the Archer is fixed," she says, her voice low. "I can tell by the angle of her starboard wing."

"Good," Aethon replies. At last, a bit of luck.

They quietly walk to the door of the ship. Aethon opens it and lets Maeve go so that she can start the engines. Aethon does a quick security sweep, making sure nothing is amiss. The second the Archer turns on - the dash lighting up, the engines purring - TAI and CAL blare to life.

"Captain Trell! Captain Bladesbearer!" CAL says loudly. "We were monitoring communications while the ship was offline and -"

" - we picked up comm hijacking!" TAI finishes. "But we couldn't let you know because you -"

"- didn't transfer us to your tabs!" CAL says, his voice as close to anger as Aethon has ever heard. "And look where that got you!"

"Maevey-pie, you're hurt!" TAI exclaims.

"TAI," Aethon interjects. "Pay the maintenance bill. We need to get the hell off this starbase."

"On it!" TAI replies.

"CAL," Aethon says. "Do whatever you need to do to override the maintenance bay's force field so that we can fly the Archer out."

"Valley Starbases' systems are woefully out of date," CAL says, his tone haughty. "Their AI doesn't even speak hyper-union. I've already got it tied up in a loop."

"Bill paid, Aethon!" TAI says.

"Get us the fuck out of here," Maeve orders. She rests one hand on the arm of her captain's chair, and the other around Aethon's waist. He pulls her against him automatically, supporting her.

The Archer lifts off and reverses out of the bay.

Hails start popping up on the viewscreen, but they ignore them all. Helmeted maintenance workers and starbase guards flood the bay, their arms raised, pulse guns aimed at the Archer.

"Flash 'em, TAI," Maeve says roughly.

"Oh honey, you're speaking my language!" TAI says.

The Archer's lights flare, blasting at least 200 lumens straight into the eyes of everyone in the bay. They all falter, their hands raising to their temporarily blinded eyes. The Archer reverses completely out of the bay and spins, zooming away from Valley Starbase.

"Nice flying, TAI," Aethon says.

"You're a peach, Aethon!"

"Is the ship fixed?" Maeve asks. "How's the support strut?"

"We monitored the work even while we were offline," CAL says. "They didn't do a very good job, but it's definitely serviceable. No danger of falling apart while we're in jump space."

"And there are no signs of tampering," TAI adds.

"Memphis Nedd must have been willing to do a small favor for Quinlar Cho by holding me up, but not one big enough to actually damage his reputation," Aethon growls.

At that assurance, Maeve finally sags against Aethon. He leans down and lifts her up, one arm under her shoulders, the other under her knees. She wraps an arm around his neck and doesn't protest, which worries Aethon more than anything else. She's warm against him, tall and heavily muscled, and Aethon hugs her to him, her weight a comfort. She's alive. He made it in time. Relief is sharp in his chest.

"Make for the nearest jump point," Aethon orders the AIs. "And go at best speed." They agree, and Aethon turns, carrying Maeve back to her room.

He sets her down gently on her bed. When he starts to move away, Maeve grabs his sleeve. Aethon looks down at her, concern tight in his gut.

"Where are you going?" she asks. She stares up at him with a fierce expression that Aethon can't quite read.

"I'm just getting the medkit," Aethon replies. "I want to clean up your arm and whatever else needs tending to."

Maeve lets out a slow breath and nods, releasing his sleeve. "It's in the cabinet next to the washer and dryer."

Aethon retrieves it and then sits down on the bed next to Maeve. She shrugs off her jacket, wincing as it brushes against her arm.

Cho had sliced her up pretty badly. She has cuts in a checkerboard pattern over her inner arm, and several squares of skin had been removed, leaving open wounds. The thought that someone hurt her like that makes rage boil in Aethon's gut. Maybe he should have killed Cho after all.

Wordlessly, Aethon cleans Maeve up. He works as quickly and carefully as possible, and she only winces a few times, her breath hissing as he rubs antibacterial gel over her cuts. The small cut on her throat has already stopped bleeding.

"Can't seem to avoid getting hurt these days," Maeve mutters.

Aethon shrugs. "It's not so bad when you have another person to patch you up." He leans back after wrapping her arm tightly in a white bandage. "There."

Maeve flexes her elbow and lays her arm down gently on the bed. "Thank you."

"No problem."

Aethon packs up the medkit and puts it away, then returns to Maeve, sitting down next to her on the bed. The air between them feels both relieved and taut - a frustrating duality. Aethon's adrenaline is finally starting to wane and he sighs, his muscles loosening.

Maeve speaks into the stillness first.

"I thought Cho had you," she says. She shifts, turning to face him. Her eyes are clear and unguarded, but her brows are tight. She still looks angry, but Aethon doesn't feel like it's directed at him.

"Yeah," he replies with a nod. "Once I finally saw your messages, I gathered that."

"He must have hijacked your tab," Maeve says, shaking her head. "But I don't know how he would have known..."

"What did he know?" Aethon asks.

Maeve huffs. "He knew you call me Bladesy. That's why I was certain he had you."

Aethon pulls his tab out and opens his contacts, pulling hers up. He shows the contact to her.

Maeve's lips curve up into a half-smile. "I'm in your tab as Bladesy?"

"Yeah," he chuckles. "He must have gotten in somehow. We'll have to have TAI and CAL purge any remnants of his hijacking from both our tabs." He leans back against the pillows. "I'm sorry I didn't see your messages in time. I never got notifications for them. That was all such a mess."

Maeve narrows her brows and shakes her head.

"Don't apologize, Aethon. I'm sorry. I was an idiot."

"No way," he says. "It was a risk," he adds, raising his brows. "But you're not an idiot." He sits up and watches as Maeve turns away from him. She stares sightlessly at the doorway and worries her bottom lip with her teeth. Several strands of wine red hair have worked their way loose from her braid, and they fall softly around her face. She's so beautiful. And she charged right into danger after him without a second thought.

Aethon reaches over and catches her chin, pulling her face over so that he can meet her eyes. "You're a badass." Her lips twitch and Aethon has to force himself not to kiss her. He remembers what she said last night - she's not going to do this with him. He runs his fingers lightly across her jaw instead.

Maeve inhales shakily and leans into his touch. "A stupid badass though."

"There's always going to be danger," he says. "Always. It's the nature of our job."

"It happened just how they always warned us," she says, her voice hard. "And we're not even -" Her jaw tightens. "He used you against me. And we're not even -"

"I don't know that the danger is actually more just because we're hunting together," he says.

She gives him an odd look, her gaze narrowing. Her eyes are the color of a sunlit forest on Freehail.

"Why did you come after me?" he asks. He slides his hand down to her shoulder where her scar is.

Maeve's eyes widen and a look of incredulity passes across her features. She catches Aethon's hand and entwines their fingers. Her hand is calloused in the same way as his - from working out and handling weapons. But her fingers slide easily between his - as though they belong there. "I know what Cho does to people," she finally replies.

"That's not a real answer," he says.

"What do you want me to say?" she asks.

He rubs a hand over his face, frustration burning through him and tries to pull his hand out of Maeve's grip. She just squeezes harder. "I want you to do what you threatened to do when you dragged the Menace out of the corona of that star," Aethon growls. "Drop me on some planet. Fuck, eject me into space."

Maeve reaches forward and pushes his hair back over his head, her fingers tangling in it. "I came for you because you're - because you make me feel -" she clenches her teeth together. "Why is this so hard?"

"I just want to be as far from you as possible," Aethon says. His voice gets caught in his throat as Maeve slides a hand down his cheek. "In another galaxy."

"Probably a good idea," she murmurs. Her face tightens and she shakes her head, looking down at their entwined hands. When she looks back up, Aethon feels like his heart is going to beat out of his chest. "Because when I'm with you," she whispers. "I feel like I can't breathe."

You make me feel like I'm going to die," he replies.

CHAPTER 15

Artrenn

Maeve

Aethon's whisky gold eyes pin Maeve in place. She feels like every inch of her skin is aglow when he looks at her like that - with such sincerity and intent. He bares her with that gaze - body and soul - and sees to her very core. She wants him. That grasping feeling rises again in her, and Maeve realizes it's more than want. It's more than desire. It's more than lust. Something in her had cracked open when Aethon had burst through that door on Valley Starbase. Her carefully constructed walls had crumbled under the weight of his presence. She lets the feeling permeate her body, warming her from the inside out. She's afraid that if she examines it too closely it will evaporate like ether, so she just lets it be.

Maeve leans forward and grabs his jaw, careful of the bandage on his neck, but letting him feel the scrape of her nails. She slants her mouth over his and kisses him. He tastes like coffee, and his lips are hard against hers, demanding in a way she relishes. She hopes he understands that she can't always verbalize how she feels - but she tries to say it all with the way she kisses him, deep and fierce. Aethon groans and wraps a hand around her neck, his fingers strong, his thumb sliding up the column of her throat. When they break apart, she presses her forehead to his.

"*Mai'atha gen a nystra dotoir - ma'chriss artrenn a la croi.*" The Tellamari words flow out from deep inside a long dormant part of her heart. Maeve hadn't known that those ancient words still held space in her mind. They spill like water over her tongue, easy and pure. An invocation of desire. A claiming of the truth that she isn't quite ready to speak aloud in any other way.

"Tell me what that means, *chrissah*," Aethon breathes.

The Tellamari term fits now. What had she done to earn this man's adoration? Maeve has no idea. The intensity of him - of this glowing ember between them - still scares her. The idea of losing him scares her. But the events of the last few hours have proven to her that she can't ignore this. She can't avoid it, or run from it, or deny it. So she only has one option left.

"It means - fuck me, *artrenn.*"

Aethon grins - that huge, charming one that makes her feel a little weak. "It would be my absolute pleasure to fuck you until you're a quivering mess," he replies, arching one brow. Maeve's stomach drops.

He pulls her braid in front of her and tugs the tie out of the end, carefully undoing the painfully tight rope. "I'll tell you right now, Bladesy - I'll do pretty much anything you want. You want a cabin built in the middle of the desert on an uninhabited planet? I know a lumber guy. You want strawberries? I'll find a fruit smuggler. You want me to start a religion that worships you as a goddess? Already on it." He digs his hands into her hair, pulling out the rest of her braid. "God - you're so fucking beautiful."

Maeve catches his hands, stilling him. She can tell he's practically vibrating out of his skin with emotion. He lifts their hands and presses a kiss to her inner wrist. He's so good at expressing how he feels. At telling her all the ways he cares for her. She wants to tell him how much he means to her - but she can't quite find the words. "Do you know what *artrenn* means?" she asks. This at least, she can explain.

"Tell me," he murmurs.

Maeve turns and pushes Aethon back against the pillows. She rises and settles her knees on either side of him. His hands dig into her hips, his fingers rough in a way that makes her wet.

"On Tellamar, the desert was a dangerous place to be at night," she says. She presses her hands to his face and smooths her thumbs over his cheekbones. His eyes seem to glow with heat and he wraps his arms around her waist. "There were wild animals, and traps laid by the gangs - leftover dangers from the wars that never ended. But people still needed to cross the desert at night. Either to get from town to town, or to escape the violence. There were guides who laid out trails of bioluminescent rocks along paths they'd determined were safe. The guides were called the *artrenn*."

Aethon's arms tighten around her and Maeve leans down, her curtain of hair falling around his face, wrapping them in silky darkness for a moment. Her chest feels tight with emotion. She kisses him softly, tenderly. Kissing Aethon feels so right, and Maeve wishes she'd been doing it for longer. It makes her cheeks flush and her chest spark.

"I'll do everything in my power to live up to that

name," he says. His hands slide up her sides, caressing the outer curves of her breasts and making her shudder.

"You already have," she replies.

She settles down onto his lap and pulls her shirt off. Aethon tugs her down with a hand around the nape of her neck and kisses her. His other hand slides up her back and with a deft flick of his fingers, her bra is undone. He flings it aside and tugs Maeve closer, ducking his head down to take the peak of one of her nipples into his eager mouth. It hardens for him, turning into a point of sensitivity.

"God - Aethon -" she purrs. She leans closer to him, her neck arching back. Little thrills of pleasure ride down her body as his teeth graze against tender flesh. He kisses up between her breasts, his hands tight on her ass. His mouth is hot on her collarbone, his tongue tracing a line of fire across her chest.

Aethon pushes Maeve back slightly so that he can pull his shirt off and toss it aside. She leans down, eager to get her hands and mouth on the broad expanse of his chest and shoulders. He's covered in combat scars, the most notable being three puckered circles in a line down his right side. She traces her fingers over them.

"From a trident," Aethon says. "Got it on Santathion chasing a pirate."

"Mmm." She tucks that story away in the back of her mind to ask him about later. Aethon on a ship at sea under a blazing sun? Sounds positively delicious.

Maeve kisses down his chest, her hands admiring the planes of his muscles she never got to properly appreciate all those years ago. His pecs are particularly biteable, and Maeve indulges in a few nips that draw small chuckles from Aethon.

She traces the tattoos that run down his sides with light fingertips.

"What do these mean?" she asks. She'd wondered for years.

He smiles and reaches for her pants, unbuttoning them and sliding them and her underwear down. Maeve shifts and pulls them off, then quickly repositions herself on Aethon's lap.

He seems to have forgotten her question as he takes in her naked body, his eyes like brands on her skin. She's covered in just as many scars as he is, her body marked with the violence of her profession, but also with the story of her survival. Aethon presses a kiss to the largest scar on her shoulder. Maeve lets out a shuddering breath as he withdraws. He cups her ass and slides his hands around her hips, teasing her with light strokes on her lower stomach and thighs. She quivers, feeling slickness begin to build between her legs. He leans forward and sucks on her other breast, his mouth hot and tight.

"Your tattoos, *artrenn*," she repeats with a sharp exhale, pleasure shooting down to her stomach where a tight knot of heat is already building.

But Maeve is distracted when Aethon scrapes his teeth across her nipple, his hands pressing her down hard onto his lap. He releases her and she pushes him back, kissing along his jaw and neck, then down to his chest again, trailing her mouth over his stomach. Her hands find his belt and she undoes his pants, unzipping them as well. He groans when she slides a hand down his pants, feeling the shape of him through his underwear. He's thick and hard already. Maeve smiles and removes her hand, licking her way across his swirling tattoos.

"The coastline," Aethon groans. He tangles a hand in her hair, pulling it away from her face.

"Mmm?" She kisses down the strong line of his hip, her hands digging into his thighs.

"My tattoos," he says. "They're the coastline of the beach near my home."

She nods and looks at them again with new eyes. She can see that now. There are odd divots and arches that look much more naturally inspired than artistic or symmetrical. "I like them."

Maeve smooths her hands up his muscled sides, enjoying the feel of his body. She tucks her fingers into the waistband of his pants. "Take these off."

Aethon shifts up and pulls off his pants. He starts to remove his underwear but she stops him with a hand to his wrist.

"Let me do that," she murmurs with a wicked grin.

His brows rise and he catches her chin, leaning down to take her mouth in his. Aethon's tongue dances along hers, and she melts against him until he pulls away, leaving her breathless. "What kinds of dirty things are you thinking?" he asks.

"All kinds."

Maeve braces her hands on either side of his hips. Aethon is wearing tight, dark gray boxer briefs, and she can see his cock straining beneath the thin fabric. Oh, this is going to be fun. She hasn't ever played with a man like this before. Besides Aethon, all her sexual experiences were fast and hard, with one end goal in mind: release. But with Aethon, she wants to draw this out. She wants him desperate for her. She wants him to take her hard, yes. She wants to break apart beneath him. But even more than that, she wants the connection. The tenderness. The adoration in his gaze that makes him call her *chrissah.* She feels like she's stepped off a cliff and plunged into an ocean of desire. She wants it all.

Maeve leans down, breathing hot air over his cock. She crawls up a little farther and kisses his stomach, biting his skin, leaving hot marks in her wake.

"Oh god -" he groans. "Come here, *chrissah.*" He pulls her up for another kiss, his tongue plundering, before she breaks it off and licks her lips. His neck and chest are flushed with arousal. His hair is tousled and he bites his bottom lip, one white canine sharp against it. Maeve watches him hungrily. "You're going to kill me, aren't you Bladesy," he says.

"I am quite good with my mouth," she replies, one brow rising.

"Fuck," he groans, one hand rubbing over his face, the other grabbing her arm.

She grins and slides down his body. She snaps the band of his boxers once - twice. Aethon watches her with his lips curled up in a silent feral snarl. His hands clench on the comforter. Maeve feels her stomach drop.

She presses a kiss to his cock through his boxers. He's hot, even through the fabric, and deliciously hard. He smells like sweat and her lavender soap, and something else that's just pure, primal male.

Her nails dig into his stomach, and scrape down, catching in his boxers and pulling them down and off, revealing all of him for her.

"Fuck - *artrenn -*" Aethon is big. Maeve had hardly gotten a good look in the darkness of the escape pod. His cock is thick and long, flushed with arousal, the head of him curving up just slightly. She swallows hard, then shifts his legs apart so that she can kneel between them.

She meets his blazing gaze, and then spits into her hand. Aethon groans, his muscles flexing in his stomach, his hands clenching in the comforter again.

"So fucking filthy -"

"You want it," she purrs.

"Oh I want it," he agrees with a grin.

When Maeve wraps her hand around the base of his cock, he shudders beneath her, his hips rocking up into her hand unconsciously.

"Tell me what you like," she says. She slides her hand up and down his shaft a few times, twisting her wrist a little toward the head.

"I don't care how you touch me," he pants. His head is back, his eyes squeezed shut. "Just keep touching me."

She smiles and leans down, sucking the head of him into her mouth.

"Fuck - Maeve -" Aethon groans.

She moves over him, loving the heavy, hot feel of him in her mouth, on her tongue. He tastes like salt and musk. Maeve feels him trembling beneath her, holding himself back from thrusting. She moves off of him, and then licks down the side of his shaft with the flat of her tongue.

"You can touch me, if you want," she murmurs. She presses a kiss above the curly thatch of hair at the base of his cock, her hand still working him slowly.

His fingers thread into her hair, grabbing on close to her head. She smiles and continues working him with her hand. She swallows him down again, and Aethon's grip tightens in her hair, bringing a tiny edge of pain to the moment. Maeve feels herself get slicker between her thighs, that knot of pleasure in her stomach throbbing with need.

After a minute, Aethon pulls her off his cock. He takes her by the hips, flipping them both over so she's leaning on the pillows with him over her, his eyes amber bright. He looks like a god.

"My turn," he growls, leaning down to kiss her.

Maeve's stomach drops.

Aethon spreads her legs and kneels between them, his cock flushed and hard, and wet from her mouth. He slowly slides his hands down Maeve's shoulders, taking care over her scar and bandaged arm. He leans forward and presses kisses to her stomach, his tongue wet and hot. He traces circles with his mouth on her skin, his hands kneading the flesh of her thighs as if he can't stop touching her.

"You want me, *chrissah?*" he murmurs against her navel, his tongue delving into it, making her shudder.

"I want you, *artrenn.*"

The Tellamari words feel important to Maeve - like she and Aethon are finally acknowledging what they are to each other. She's surprised at how good it feels. She doesn't feel worried about the future - she only feels content. Maybe even... happy.

Maeve tangles her hands in Aethon's hair and watches as he kisses his way down her body. He nibbles at her hip bone and looks up at her, his golden eyes narrowed in pleasure. Then he slides one hand up her thigh, his fingers brushing teasingly along the thin, sensitive skin near her pussy. She holds her breath.

He parts her with his fingers, then traces slowly up and down, from her core, to just below her clit.

"You're so wet for me," he growls. "I love seeing you like this."

Maeve shifts closer to his hand, but Aethon clamps an arm over her hips, immobilizing her.

"You want me to make you come, *chrissah?*" he demands. He rests his chin on his arm, his expression smug. He teases at her entrance. She wants him to plunge his fingers inside her like he did last night. Was that only last night? It feels like a lifetime ago. She wants to be filled with him. She craves more. She wants everything.

"Yes -" Maeve hisses, wriggling fruitlessly under the weight of his arm. "Since when are you this strong?"

"If you want me to make you come," he says patiently. "Then you need to leave the work to me." He reaches up and squeezes her breast hard, his fingers wet from her pussy, eliciting a gasp from her.

"Fine," she growls. "Then get on with it, *artrenn.*" She tugs lightly on Aethon's hair and he grins, kissing her stomach.

"So impatient," he murmurs. "I swear I won't lead you wrong."

He takes his arm off her hips and shifts down, his hands catching Maeve's legs and spreading them wide. She leans back on her pillow, her hands tight on the comforter.

"Comfortable?" he asks. He presses a kiss to her mound, his tongue teasing just a bit between her lips.

"Fuck - Aethon - please -"

He grins wide and then spreads her carefully, spearing his tongue into the spot next to her clit that drives her wild. How the fuck did he remember - She writhes against him, unable to keep still as he flicks his tongue rapidly over her most sensitive point. Maeve's face is hot, her stomach coiled with building pleasure, her limbs tingling. She arches back as Aethon licks her from her core all the way to her clit.

"So good - that's so good -" she pants, not even fully aware of what she's saying. "Oh - god - Aethon - *artrenn* - right there -"

He looks at her as he presses open mouthed kisses to her pussy. His focus is so intense she feels like with a push of her mind she could read his thoughts. All of which would be about her. He devours her, his lips sucking at her clit hard, but not for long enough to push her over the edge. He has her riding that fine line between pleasure and frustration. Maeve hears herself begging him, but she can't bring herself to stop - or to care. Aethon seems to love it, his eyes sparkling with amusement.

His fingers move to her thighs, gripping her hard. His tongue is slow and languid on her now, and Maeve wants to scream. He winds her higher and higher until she's right on the precipice, her whole body shuddering under him. She arches towards him, her hands fisted in the blanket.

But then Aethon is moving back up her body, kissing her stomach and shifting up to kneel between her legs.

"What are you -"

He silences her with a look, and his hand is back on her clit, his thumb rubbing hard. His face is a mess with her, and he wipes himself off, his hand going to wrap around his cock. Maeve leans up and grabs his wrist, bringing his hand to her mouth. He bites his lower lip as she spits into his hand. Then he wraps it around his cock again, sliding it up and down his shaft. He's so hard it looks almost painful.

"I need you inside me," Maeve says, her voice trembling. "Nothing between us."

"I know," he replies.

He moves forward, his arms bracketing her head and then he's *there*. Maeve arches back as he sheathes himself inside her inch by glorious inch, not stopping until he's seated to the hilt. His pubic bone presses against her clit and a jolt runs through her. She scrapes her nails up Aethon's back, her knees rising around him. He's had her on the edge for so long that just his cock inside her has the pulsing knot of pleasure in her stomach starting to unravel.

"I'm going to come," she breathes. Her legs start to spasm around his hips.

"I know," he says. Then he kisses her, his mouth hard and demanding. His hips withdraw and then slam back in. Maeve bows toward him with a silent scream, her body exploding into starlit waves of pleasure. Her muscles tense as the waves just keep coming.

"Aethon -" she moans.

"How you doing, Bladesy?" he asks. He's thrusting into her, the sensation making Maeve's orgasm pulse and pulse - until it finally settles. She feels like she must be glowing.

"You're an arrogant fucker, you know that?" she says, pricking his ass with her nails. He drives into her again and again, his length hot and hard inside her and Maeve can't help but let out a breathy moan that makes Aethon smile.

"I'd say I've earned the right to be a little arrogant," he says.

"Flip us over," she orders.

He does as she asks, settling down easily onto the pillows, his expression overly pleased. Maeve wants to see him beg.

She straddles his thighs and takes his cock in her fist, pumping him a little rougher than she had before. Aethon's eyes roll back into his head.

"Oh fuck - don't - unless you want me to -"

Maeve grins and lets up, shifting forward and sliding down easily onto his length. He fills her so completely, and that damn curve hits her in just the right spot like this. She breathes out slowly, and leans forward, bracing her hands on his chest as she starts moving on him.

Aethon clutches at her hips, helping her find a rhythm that they both enjoy. Maeve loves how he's looking at her now. His mouth is tight with concentration but his eyes are soft, his expression open. It's adoration and fierceness, combined. He feels so good inside her, and she only wants more. Sweat slides down her spine as she rides him harder and faster. Aethon urges her on with filthy praise.

"You feel so good - so tight around me - god, *chrissah* - you're so wet for me - look at you taking my cock - that's it, Bladesy - just like that -"

Maeve's fingers grasp at his chest and she leans back, her eyes automatically closing as she climbs to another release. She can feel it building again, slower, but just as intense. She grinds down hard onto Aethon's cock, but it's not quite enough.

"I need - I need something more -" she says, her

tone pleading and frustrated. "I'm almost there - but -"

Aethon immediately leans up, his eyes glinting with the challenge.

"Hands and knees, *chrissah*."

Maeve obeys. Anything for another release. She's so close. She trusts Aethon to wring one out of her. He kneels behind her and she feels his hands tight on her hips, and then he reaches around, his fingers pressing onto her clit. He thrusts into her, his cock spreading her wide. She chokes out a breath, feeling how she quivers around him. His hand rubs hard at her clit and then he leans forward, his other hand pinching her nipple. His hips begin to move, slamming into her again and again, the coarse hair on his thighs scratching at the backs of hers. It's sensation overload - which is apparently what Maeve needs.

She collapses to her elbows as she comes, her body giving out as another orgasm rushes through her, pleasure shooting down her legs like lightning. Aethon grinds harder into her, prolonging her release, his hands pressing into her lower back now. She moans, her face pressed into a pillow. His hips speed up, his rhythm jerky now and he withdraws and groans, "Fuck - Maeve -" She feels his release, hot and sticky on her back.

Maeve falls onto her side, breathing heavily, utterly spent. The bed bounces as Aethon falls down next to her on his face, his arm pulling her toward him.

"You're a mess," he says, shifting onto his side, his breath warm on the back of her head.

"Yeah and it's your fault," she grumbles.

Maeve hauls herself around to face him, her hand trailing up his stomach which is damp with sweat, to rest over his heart. His chest rises and falls with deep breaths. He looks down at her and smiles before pressing a kiss to her forehead. A calm, sated feeling settles over her. Maeve had never felt quite this way before and she knows it's significant. She doesn't have any desire to move from this spot next to Aethon.

"I guess there's no going back now," she says, raising a brow. She pushes her messy hair back away from her face, but Aethon just reaches up and tangles his fingers in it.

"No going back," he agrees.

Maeve can feel his heart beat against her palm. She remembers feeling it when they were in the escape pod too. She throws a leg over his hips, pulling him closer and his eyes flare with pleasure. She looks down, away from the intensity of it all, and stares at his chest. Her hand traces over a scar on his skin. A question scratches at the back of her mind.

"Does this scare you?" she asks, her voice low. The question makes her feel vulnerable and she hates it - suddenly wishing she had stayed silent.

Aethon catches her hand and brings it up to kiss her palm. Then he pulls her head back a little with the hand he has tangled in her hair so that she's forced to meet his eyes. What she finds there isn't judgment or scorn. It's understanding.

"A little," he says. "But Maeve - what if being together is better than being alone?" He presses another kiss to her forehead. "I'd be dead in that damn star if you hadn't chosen me over the bounty. And you might still be in Quinlar Cho's office."

Maeve watches him, unable now to look away from his intense eyes. He truly is her *artrenn* - her guiding light. Like the brightest star in the sky - or the unchanging path of the sun.

His steadiness in this vulnerable moment gives Maeve the strength to speak aloud one of her greatest fears.

"What if we hurt each other?" she asks.

He just smiles. *"Chrissah* - what if we save each other?"

Something lights within her at his words. Like a match struck into flame. It feels like hope.

Aethon leans down and Maeve tilts her chin up, meeting him for a kiss.

CHAPTER 16

A Short Time

Aethon

After a nap, Aethon and Maeve finally make it back to the front of the Archer. In Aethon's opinion, this is quite the accomplishment considering that everything in him wants to spread Maeve out on her bed again and wrap her thighs around his head. Instead, he has her pushed up against the dash, his hands sliding up the smooth skin on her stomach as they trade slow, luxurious kisses. Her arms are twined around his neck, and the darkness of space behind her out the viewscreen is dotted with distant, tiny white stars.

"You do remember that we both need credits, *artrenn*," Maeve says breathlessly before leaning in for another kiss. Her Tellamari name for him makes him want to fall to his knees before her. Aethon never imagined that Maeve could break open like this for him. He will do everything in his power to make sure she never regrets it. He runs his hand down her arms, careful of the bandage on her forearm from their misadventure on Valley Starbase.

"Credits?" Aethon murmurs. "Never heard of them."

Maeve chuckles and kisses him one last time

before shoving him down into the co-pilot chair behind him. "Get to work," she says, ruffling his hair as she walks past him to her seat.

Aethon sighs and cracks his knuckles dramatically before setting to work while Maeve checks on the Archer's systems. First, he connects their tabs to the Archer and has CAL purge them of everything Quinlar Cho had done at Valley Starbase. Then he starts searching for his CHASA contact - Bell Sylar. He hopes Sylar is still around and working. It's been a long time since the Freehail days and Aethon remembers her being in her fifties perhaps when she helped his parents.

While he looks through available online databases for Sylar's contact info, they approach another jump point. Aethon feels his nerves begin to fizz and he glances back at Maeve with his brows raised.

"This going to be ok?" he asks.

Maeve exhales hard. She'd put her hair in a loose braid, as though she didn't feel the need to pull herself as tightly together as she normally would. "Our online systems all look fine," she replies. "I don't think the mechanics at Valley Starbase actually sabotaged the ship - just took their sweet ass time with the repairs."

"Everything will be alright, darlins!" TAI chirps.

"We've already told you this," CAL adds. "The Archer is in acceptable condition to jump."

"If you say so," Maeve murmurs, meeting Aethon's gaze with a set expression.

She wraps a hand around the joystick and accelerates them toward the huge metal ring. They enter jump space a second later and Aethon breathes a sigh of relief as the ship slides easily through the familiar blue-black space. A minute later, they're on the other side.

"Good," Maeve says, leaning back. "Glad to be sure that's all ok." She halts the ship so it can recharge from the jump.

"We told you the Archer would be fine," CAL says, his voice annoyed. "But perhaps your brains are too full of pleasure chemicals to fully comprehend that."

"Oh, CAL," TAI says. "Let the organics have this. It's a sort of post-intercourse bliss -"

"Excuse me?" Maeve interrupts. Aethon turns to see her staring at him, her eyes wide with alarm, color rising in her cheeks. "Were you two *watching us?*" She glares up at the ceiling, her brows furrowed.

"Well of course, honey!" TAI chirps.

Aethon shoves a fist up to his mouth to prevent himself from laughing as Maeve rubs her hand over her face. "Oh my god - *why?!*" she asks.

"The AIs are too interested in human sexuality," Aethon replies, his voice trembling with suppressed laughter. "It was bound to happen!"

"I need to keep track of Captain Trell's vital signs," CAL says. "It's part of my programming. I don't understand what the problem is with this particular act. TAI and I monitor all of your strange functions as organics, including waste elimination. Why is intercourse such a private one?"

"Well first of all," Maeve snaps. "I'd rather my waste elimination time be private too." Aethon chuckles, but bites his lip when she scowls at him.

"Oh Maevey, don't be mad," TAI croons. "We only want to be sure our captains are doing well. And by your readings, I could tell that you both reached completion, which I know is often considered one of the goals of intercourse outside of reproduction."

"Completion?" CAL asks. "Was that the burst of oxytocin and dopamine?"

"Yes -" TAI starts, but Aethon interrupts as he watches Maeve clench her teeth together.

"Alright, alright," he says. "That's enough, you two. Go absorb some human anatomy and sexuality scientific articles or something."

He turns back to Maeve who is taking intentionally deep breaths. "I have a search going now for Bell Sylar's information," he tells her, hoping the subject change will calm her. "Why don't we check Daik's location while that's going."

Maeve nods and throws her tracking map up on the viewscreen.

Aethon examines the map. Daik is definitely moving toward the Tri-Centauri system. He's even closer than the last time they checked - only about five jump points away now. Maeve and Aethon are still seven jump points away - a distance that at best speed, they could cover in a little over a week.

Aethon looks back at Maeve who's examining the map and nodding to herself.

"Guess we were right," she says. "He's heading for Tri-Centauri. And likely - Dreadnought."

"We'd better get a move on," Aethon says. "We need to catch him before he holes up on some heavily protected Dreadnought-run world."

A beep sounds from the dash and Aethon turns to find the system has located Bell Sylar. He pulls the data up and throws it on the viewscreen for Maeve to see.

The system on the Archer had combined Bell

Sylar's information into a list - including her picture, subspace contact number, and her last known work and personal addresses.

Sylar is an older woman with white blonde hair tidied into short curls, pale skin, and wrinkles around her eyes and mouth that show she smiles often. In her photo she's wearing a pink sweater and has gold-rimmed glasses sitting on top of her head.

Maeve stares at the photo and leans forward on to her knees. "This is the woman who has sway with people at the mining corps?"

Aethon nods and adjusts the bandage on his neck. "Yep."

Maeve narrows her eyes and points at the picture. "This old lady right here who looks like she'd have hard candies in her bag and offer to make me soup in the winter?"

"Don't underestimate Bell Sylar," Aethon replies. "She's a badass. She works for CHASA but she's a powerful figure in the underground - if you have the right connections. She helped my parents out a lot on Freehail with their fight against Brimstone - but always from the shadows. Her family is so wealthy they own a planet on the edge of colonized space, so she's not too worried about retaliation."

"Her family *owns a planet?*" Maeve says, leaning back.

"Yep," he replies. "The Sylar's have old Earth money."

"Well shit," Maeve mutters.

"I'll send her an encoded message," Aethon says, his fingers flying over the keyboard on the dash. "I'll ask her to contact us when she's able to use a secure channel."

Aethon doesn't want to put too much information in his message to Sylar, so he uses a few of the code phrases he remembers his parents using and leaves the rest vague. Sylar should at least recognize the codes and reach out, even if she doesn't remember him specifically. He throws the completed message on the viewscreen for Maeve to read and points out the code phrases to her. She scans it quickly and nods in approval.

"Send it," she says, hopping down from her chair.

Aethon sends the message to Sylar's subspace contact number and leans back with a sigh. He senses Maeve behind him, and then her hands slide onto his shoulders. She starts to massage him gently, careful of his still healing neck. He stifles a groan at how good it feels.

"Thank you," she murmurs.

Her voice is so soft that he turns in his chair to face her. Maeve releases him and puts her hands in her pockets. Her lips are pulled into a thin line and she watches him carefully - almost warily.

"You're welcome," Aethon replies. He stands and tugs on the end of Maeve's braid. "You ok?"

She gives him a small smile and shrugs. "Yeah, it's just - weird."

"What's weird?"

Maeve gestures between them. "This. Working together."

Aethon nods. He knows what she means. He's been on his own for fifteen years - just like Maeve. It's not common for bounty hunters to work together for a variety of reasons, not the least of which is that then the credits have to be split at the end of the hunt.

"I think it feels... good?" Maeve says. She turns and paces across the front of the ship, her hand trailing lightly on the dash. Aethon watches as she thinks. Maeve is one of the most internal people he's ever known. At times she seems to find it difficult to express herself, but that doesn't bother him. Aethon imagines her mind must be like an endless forest, or a constantly scrolling computer database. He'd love to get a peek inside her head to understand better how she thinks.

"I like it too," Aethon replies. "I never thought I could trust another hunter the way I trust you."

Maeve nods. "I know." She turns back to him and gives him a smile that Aethon knows he is becoming addicted to. "I'm sure we'll be fighting in no time though, *artrenn*."

"Why - are you going to become ornery all of a sudden?" Aethon teases.

"Watch it, Trell," Maeve replies, one eyebrow high.

"Yes, ma'am," he says with a grin.

Maeve stalks back over to her chair, her lips twitching as she tries not to smile. "That's more like it."

Aethon's stomach suddenly rumbles loudly and he winces when Maeve's brows rise.

"I believe that noise is an indication that you should eat, Captain Trell," CAL says.

Aethon rolls his eyes as Maeve bites her bottom lip. "I know, CAL," he sighs. "I've been a human for thirty-whatever years now."

"Thirty-five," CAL says. "Are you forgetting your age? Should I scan you for signs of mental fatigue and decline?"

Aethon groans and Maeve laughs. "That won't be necessary," he says.

"I'm glad TAI isn't the only overly involved AI," Maeve says. "I'm hungry too. Let me just finish plotting the route to the next jump point and then let's eat."

She taps out a few calculations and then sets the auto-nav. Aethon checks the support strut one last time before pushing himself up from his chair and following Maeve over to the tiny kitchenette next to the brig.

They rip open a couple ration packs while discussing the best course of action to capture Daik. Unfortunately, they can't plan much beyond talking about what they know of Daik himself, and discussing their weapons and ammo stores. Everything hinges on what will happen with Bell Sylar.

"So I've been thinking," Maeve starts. She's sitting on a tiny bench that runs along the wall on the opposite side of the kitchenette. Aethon sits across from her, leaning on the cabinet below the sink, a granola bar in one hand, a protein jerky stick in the other. The Archer's engines thrum comfortingly beneath him.

"Always a good thing," he says.

Maeve rolls her eyes. "I've been thinking about what kind of intel we actually want from Sylar. We don't need Daik's precise location - my tracker will give us that."

Aethon watches as Maeve taps her own jerky stick on her lips as she thinks and then tears off a bite. She crosses one long leg over the other. "If we're right about Daik bringing Dreadnought intel from Brimstone, then Dreadnought has probably scheduled a meetup between their representative and Daik to confirm the value of the intelligence."

Aethon nods. "It will likely be on some planet or a starbase in the Tri-Centauri system," he murmurs. "If we can't get to Daik before this potential meetup, Dreadnought's security will have him protected on one of their worlds. No one will be able to get to him."

"Right," Maeve says. "So if we could just get there first -" She raises her brows at him and Aethon nods.

"You want to ask Sylar for access to one of the hyper-jump points," he says. "Smart, Bladesy."

She grins as she takes another bite of her jerky. "If we could get access codes for the hyper-jump point closest to the Tri-Centauri system, we could get there before Daik does and set a trap for him."

Hyper-jump points are for longer range travel than normal jump points. They're capable of bringing a ship five times the distance of a jump point in less than an hour. While not useful for people just going from planet to starbase and back, they're vital for corps that need to travel to the outer edges of colonized space quickly. The massive hyper-jump points were originally created by an exploratory corps before it went bankrupt, and were then snatched up at auction by various wealthy corps. Due to the location, Aethon is sure the one they would need to use is owned by Dreadnought. He doubts that Dreadnought would want two bounty hunters set on capturing Daik Montrose anywhere near their hyper-jump point, and he wonders if Sylar would be reluctant to give them access codes for it. She can't risk her whole shadow operation just so that two hunters can capture a bounty. But they have to at least try.

They finish eating quickly and return to their

seats, checking Daik's position again, and scanning for other ships in the area. Aethon knows they'll soon be entering space that is traveled by more people, and they might start to encounter other hunters looking for Daik. He hopes Maeve's ability to track Daik's ship will give them enough of an advantage over the others to catch the smuggler first.

Aethon sighs. He runs a hand over his head which is starting to pound. It's been a long couple of weeks, and the lack of sleep is finally starting to catch up with him.

"I'm exhausted," he says. "Would you mind if I take another nap?"

Maeve stands and holds her hand out to him. He takes it and stands as well. She looks him over with a critical eye, her gaze catching on his bandage.

"You're still recovering from the radiation poisoning," she says. "Go nap. I'll be fine. I'll let you know if we get a message from Sylar."

Aethon nods and drags himself to Maeve's room. He shrugs his jacket off and collapses onto her bed, asleep within a minute.

He wakes later to Maeve's soft mouth pressing kisses to his jaw and moving down his neck. He groans and blinks for a moment, unsure if he's dreaming or not. The only lights on the Archer are the emergency lights along the floor dimly illuminating the room.

"Maeve?" he murmurs, his voice hoarse.

"Mmm?"

Maeve lays down next to him, her chest resting on his stomach, her hand sliding up under his shirt. She looks up at him and gives him a half-smile. This sexy, gentle, eager version of Maeve is a dream. She's incredible when she's sprinting through starbases and hauling around criminals too, but Aethon suspects not many other people get to see this side of her. He wants to stay here in her bed forever. She's wearing a black t-shirt and shorts, her long pale legs tangled up with his. The small, purple crystal necklace she always wears is pressed between her neck and his stomach. The sharp lines of her chin and cheekbones are illuminated softly, her light green eyes silvery in the dimness. He brushes the backs of his fingers down her cheek.

"What time is it?" he asks.

"Nine at night," she replies. "You slept for a while."

"Anything from Sylar?"

She shakes her head. "Not yet." The necklace she wears shifts up when she moves her head.

Aethon reaches down and traces the delicate chain around her neck. "I think I recognize the crystal on this."

"You might," Maeve replies. "It's a croi crystal. They're common on Tellamar. Your mother might have some."

"I think she does," Aethon says. "It reminds you of home?"

Her mouth tightens a bit and she nods before looking away. He's sure it's a sensitive topic for her, so he drops it.

Aethon sighs as Maeve pushes his shirt up and presses a kiss to his stomach right over his waistband. He's already half-hard from her ministrations. He wants her so badly. There are still things they haven't discussed - decisions they both need to make that are right over the horizon, but Aethon pushes those to the back of his mind. He's with her right now and she wants him. It feels like a miracle.

"Aren't you tired, *chrissah?*" he murmurs.

Maeve nods but she slides her hand down over his pants, feeling his hardening cock. "I think there's a little situation I need to deal with before going to sleep, though," she says. She raises a brow, her lips curving up on one side.

"I wouldn't call that a *little* situation," he says, meeting her gaze.

"Mmm, did that hurt your feelings?" she asks with a laugh. She undoes his pants and unzips his fly before freezing. Her eyes narrow and she glares up at the ceiling.

"TAI?" Maeve says slowly.

"Yes, Maevey-pie?" TAI chirps immediately.

Maeve squeezes her eyes shut. "Didn't I tell you and CAL to leave us alone when we're -" she pauses and swallows hard. "When we're engaging in sexual activities?"

Aethon chuckles. Maeve shoots him an annoyed look.

"I know - I know - I just wanted to mention that we have water based lubricant on board!" TAI says sweetly. "I know you used a lot of saliva earlier, but you don't need to -"

"TAI!" Maeve snaps. "Oh my god -"

"No more advice necessary, TAI!" Aethon calls. He puts a hand over his mouth to hide his grin.

"Are you sure?" TAI asks. "I've been doing some titillating research about fellatio -"

"That's ok!" Aethon interrupts, his chest vibrating with laughter. "You and CAL can mind the route - no need to monitor us right now. We'll let you know if we need something."

"Alrighty!" TAI says. "You two have fun!"

Maeve is motionless, her face flushed with embarrassment. "Fucking hell."

"Don't have a little exhibitionist streak in you?" Aethon chuckles.

"Definitely not," she grumbles.

"It's alright, *chrissah*." Aethon pulls her down next to him and she wraps an arm around his chest, her chin propped on his shoulder. He pulls the tie out of her braid and sinks his hand into her hair.

"That feels good," she murmurs as he massages her scalp. She runs a hand down past his stomach and strokes him through his underwear. Aethon inhales sharply and glances down at Maeve. Her expression is soft and open. He's still not used to seeing that kind of look on her face and it makes his breath catch in his chest. Maeve narrows her gaze and slides a hand beneath his underwear feeling the hardness of him.

"This is for me?" she says, leaning up to kiss his jaw. Her lips are warm and Aethon tightens his hand in her hair.

"All for you," he breathes. Her fingers are gentle, her touch teasing.

"Good," she replies. She kisses his jaw again, nipping at him. She pushes his underwear down and pulls his cock out, wrapping her hand around him. The warmth of her hand and the coolness of the air makes Aethon sigh. "Mine," Maeve purrs.

He huffs a laugh and traces a finger down her nose. "I always knew you'd be a jealous lover."

"Jealous?" she replies, furrowing her brow. "Me?"

But Aethon can tell from her tone that she's teasing.

He taps her gently on her full lips. "Possessive. Territorial. Whatever you want to call it."

Her lips twitch and she strokes her hand up and down his cock. It feels so good. The pressure of her hand, and the fact that it's Maeve touching him.

"I'm a bounty hunter for the Guild of Two Roses," Maeve says. She squeezes him a little harder and leans up to kiss him. Aethon traces his tongue along her bottom lip and presses his palm to her cheek. "If you want someone sweet and passive, I suggest looking elsewhere," she murmurs.

Aethon chuckles. "Sweet and passive? Sounds terrible."

"Good," she says. Her gaze turns fiery and she slides her hand luxuriously slowly up his cock, pressing her thumb down over the head of him. Aethon arches back with a groan. Golden warmth begins to spread through his groin and he clenches his hand in the bedsheets.

With a narrow look at the ceiling, Maeve withdraws her hand, spits into it, and then slides her fingers around his length again.

"It's so fucking hot when you do that," Aethon groans. He watches her, his body tense as she pumps his cock slow and hard.

She kisses him again, her tongue teasing, the pressure of her hand just about perfect. The minutes tick past slowly, and Aethon enjoys every second of Maeve's undivided attention. His face feels flushed and he writhes beneath her, but she keeps him on the edge.

"C'mon - Bladesy -" he pants. "Have mercy on me -" He clutches her cheeks as he begs her to push him over into that crimson hued pleasure,

"No, *artrenn*," she whispers. "Not yet." Her fingers slow and Aethon groans as she continues to torture him expertly. He feels sweat break out on his forehead, his body wound tight and thrumming.

She keeps pressing languid kisses to his lips as she strokes him. The pressure builds and builds until finally she speeds up her rhythm and he can't help but to come, his muscles tensing, pure pleasure making him groan through clenched teeth.

She breaks away from his mouth and looks down at him, her green eyes narrowed. "You're so fucking gorgeous," she says. She slides her hand over his cock a few more times, slicker with his release, and he jerks, oversensitive now. "No man should be that hot when he comes."

"Can't help it, Bladesy," Aethon says. He stretches his arms above his head, satisfaction pulsing through his body. "I've just got that animal magnetism."

Maeve rolls her eyes and pushes herself up off the bed and heads to the bathroom. "Right - animal magnetism. You're such a jackass, Aethon," she teases.

"Hey!" he calls as she disappears into the bathroom. "You think you can just waltz away from me after that?"

She pokes her head around the doorframe and gives him a small smile. "I'll let you lick me in the morning, *artrenn*."

Ten minutes later, Maeve has tucked herself next to Aethon, her back against his chest. He wraps his arms around her and presses a kiss to her head, her hair soft and silky. Maeve makes a small, pleased noise and Aethon feels like his heart might crack. He can't let this woman go. He will if that's what she really wants - but the thought makes panic start to rise in his chest. He slides a hand under her shirt and clutches her more securely to him. He can feel her heart beating slowly. What can he do to make sure he can be with Maeve even after this hunt is over? Is she still planning on taking the bounty money and leaving Two Roses? He should ask her. But Aethon doesn't want to ruin this brief time that they have together by demanding more than Maeve is willing - or perhaps able - to give. He'll take what she's offering. It will have to be enough.

Maeve twines her fingers with his on her stomach and relaxes against him.

"Goodnight," she murmurs.

He kisses the back of her head again, inhaling her scent. "Goodnight." He falls asleep to the sound of her slow breathing.

Some time later, Aethon wakes to TAI calling Maeve's name.

"Maevey?"

Aethon feels the bed move and opens his eyes to Maeve jolting upright.

"Did you hear something?" she says, her voice scratchy. She raises her right hand and Aethon sees she's clutching a pulse gun. He sits up and scans the room, but sees nothing out of the ordinary.

"Maevey-pie!" TAI says. Aethon feels Maeve relax next to him. He strokes a hand across her shoulders and she puts the pulse gun down on her bedside table. "Sorry to wake you," TAI says. "But we're getting a call from a secure channel. I think it might be that Bell Sylar woman!"

At the name of the CHASA contact, they spring

from the bed and quickly get to the front of the Archer.

The call is pulsing on the viewscreen. It's from a blocked number, and there's a white box at the bottom of the screen proclaiming: ENCRYPTED CHANNEL.

"Let's do this," Aethon says. Neither of them even mention changing their clothes - there's no time. Maeve just shoves her hair back and into a messy bun before she sits down in the captain's chair. Aethon scrubs a hand over his face and pushes his hair back over his head before standing next to her. She nods at him and instructs the AIs to be silent before tapping a button to pick up the call.

Bell Sylar's face pops up on the screen. Her hair is a little longer than her picture, the perfect white blonde curls framing her face. She wears a white sweater and has pearl earrings that are perched on her ears like tiny bird eggs. She sits in a chair in front of a completely non-descript tan wall. Her blue eyes are kind, but she narrows her gaze as she looks at Maeve.

"Did you hear about the resurgence of starlings back on Earth?" Sylar asks.

Her question makes Aethon blink and rub a hand over his head. Starlings? Had he heard her right? Maeve opens her mouth, pauses, and glances briefly over at Aethon.

"No -" she starts.

Realization snaps into place and Aethon interrupts. "I heard the population has doubled since last winter."

Sylar nods and sits back in her chair. "I barely recognize you, young Trell. But your mind seems just as sharp as ever if you remember that old Freehail code."

Aethon smiles and sighs in relief. "Took me a

second - but then it hit me. Good to see you, Ms. Sylar."

She waves a hand. "Just Sylar." She tilts her head and nods at Maeve. "And who's this?"

"Maeve Bladesbearer," Maeve says, nodding at Sylar. "Thank you for calling us."

Sylar inclines her head in greeting. "Bladesbearer." The older woman leans back and her gaze flicks between Aethon and Maeve. "Two prominent members of the Guild of Two Roses - contacting me together?" She tilts her head to the side. "Must be something interesting going on."

Maeve shoots Aethon a narrow look. He crosses his arms and gives Sylar his most charming grin. "I know your time is valuable, so I'll cut right to it," he says. "We need a favor, but first we need some information about Daik Montrose."

Sylar doesn't outwardly react aside from a small shrug. "Am I supposed to know every lowlife in the quadrant?"

Maeve tenses and leans forward but Aethon rests a hand on the armrest of her chair and she pauses. She bites her lip and glances over at him, her gaze already stormy. Aethon doesn't want this conversation to get contentious. They need Sylar's help.

"Sylar - I know you have your finger on the pulse of mining corps activity," Aethon says. He winks at her and she waves him off with a snort.

"You know everything going on with the corps," he says. "Especially when it comes to corps potentially receiving intel that might shake up the power balance of the system." He shrugs and watches as Sylar continues to look at him with a faint smile.

"You seem to think quite highly of me," Sylar

says.

Aethon nods. "I do. I remember the help you gave us on Freehail all those years ago."

Sylar leans forward and raises her brows. "Then you should remember that messing with powerful corps brings nothing but pain and death."

Devan's face flashes through Aethon's mind and he swallows hard. His brother had been so young when Brimstone had him killed. For a long time, Aethon had wanted revenge on Brimstone. Part of him still does, but he also doesn't want to get on the corps' shit list. Still, he needs this bounty. And Maeve needs it too.

Aethon nods to Sylar. "I know how dangerous the corps are - you don't need to remind me. But Maeve and I need information about Daik Montrose."

"I can't help you," Sylar says, her gaze turning steely.

Sudden unease begins to filter through Aethon's body. Had he and Maeve made a mistake in their presumption that Daik Montrose is bringing stolen information from Brimstone to Dreadnought? It makes sense, but they haven't been able to confirm their suspicions yet. If they're wrong, Sylar really won't be of any help.

"You can't, or you won't?" Maeve asks.

Sylar shakes her head, her lips pressing into a thin line. "You don't know what you're getting into."

"Aethon and I have worked for Two Roses for a long time," Maeve says. "We know what we're getting into."

"Mining corps are a different breed," Sylar says, raising a white brow. "The power they wield is ultimate. Nothing about space travel is possible without the products they provide."

Aethon sighs as Maeve bristles at Sylar's condescension. He inserts himself before she snaps at the older woman. "I understand the gravity of what we're asking," he says. "We know the depths that people will sink to in order to get what they want. I'd be truly grateful for any assistance you can provide."

"I grew up on Tellamar," Maeve adds, her voice hard. "So believe me when I say I understand danger and power hungry people."

Sylar's eyes widen just a little and she tilts her chin up. She flicks her gaze over Maeve and narrows her eyes before refocusing on Aethon. "I'm not sure what you remember from the Freehail days, Trell - but I'm not one to give away information for free."

"So you do know something about Daik," Maeve says, her voice like ice. "We need to bring him in. Hunting him down is about the safety of the galaxy."

Sylar chuckles. "No it isn't, girl. This is about credits."

Maeve's lip curls back into a snarl. "Don't you call me -"

"I think we're getting off track," Aethon says, holding a hand up to cut off both the women. Aethon is under no delusions that he can control anything Maeve says or does, but if Sylar does have information, they have to get it.

"Credits are what drives everyone to do everything," Sylar says. Her kind blue eyes are hard now, and glinting with suppressed anger. "Credits are what propelled Brimstone to rape your world for its metals all those years ago, Trell."

Aethon's chest tightens, the memories of the

years that Brimstone mined on Freehail - the rising ocean levels, the stink of dead fish on the black sand beaches, the clouds of exhaust blackening the sky - vivid in his mind.

"I know both of you are more concerned with the credits this bounty will bring you over anything else," Sylar says scathingly. "But my concerns are the regular people who find themselves crushed under the weight of these corps. I care about them - about helping them. If you want a favor that will help you catch Montrose, you need to do something for me."

Aethon's chest burns with anger at the implication that he values credits over people's lives. Everything he's done as a bounty hunter has been to create a safer place for regular people.

"Sylar," he says slowly. "Maeve and I suspect that Daik Montrose is wanted by Brimstone for stealing information and selling it to Dreadnought. Can you at least confirm that?"

Sylar inclines her head. "Yes. I have it from a reliable source that Montrose is bringing information about newly discovered planets and their survey data to Dreadnought."

Aethon feels a surge of satisfaction at having deduced that correctly. Maeve glances over at him, her expression pleased.

"We need to get to the Tri-Centauri system before Daik does," Aethon says. "Before Daik is ensconced on some Dreadnought-run world." He meets Sylar's eyes. "Could you get us access codes for the hyper-jump point in the Tri-Centauri system?" He watches as Sylar's face closes off. He wonders how difficult it would be for her to get them hyper-jump point access codes. Maybe she can't. The air feels tense, and Aethon watches as Maeve shifts minutely in her seat.

Finally, Sylar nods slowly. "It would cost me about fifteen favors - but I could do it. I could - but I won't."

Maeve looks over at Aethon and nods before turning back to Sylar. "Is there something we could do for you that would make you change your mind?" she asks.

Sylar chuckles dryly and shakes her head. "I told you where my concerns lie. With people affected by these corps. You can't give me what I need."

"Try us," Aethon says.

Sylar clucks her tongue and folds her arms across her chest. "I need safe transport for twenty-five people off a planet and to a specific drop point."

Maeve glances around at the small interior of the Archer. "We can probably fit that many people in here as long as the trip isn't more than a day."

But as Sylar leans forward Aethon is sure there's more to this request. "The fit isn't going to be the problem," she replies, her eyes narrow. "I need you to pick them up without setting off the planetary defenses or alerting the local government."

It's an almost impossible request. Most planets with any kind of civilization have computerized systems set up for defense and landing requests. And it sounds like the planet Sylar is talking about must be extremely secure - or extremely dangerous - if she hasn't been able to get these people off the planet herself with the resources she has at her disposal.

Then Maeve looks over at Aethon with a

mischievous smile and he remembers that she has a mirror-cloak on the Archer. With the mirror-cloak, they can move stealthily through a planet's defenses without alerting anyone of their presence. Sylar's request suddenly doesn't seem so difficult. He returns her grin, wanting to kiss that wicked mouth of hers.

"I think we can swing that," Aethon says, turning back to Sylar. "What planet?"

Sylar shakes her head and folds her arms across her chest with a sigh. "Tellamar."

Aethon's heart drops to his stomach. Maeve tenses and her hands clench the armrests.

"No one is mining on Tellamar," Aethon says slowly. "How are these people even on your radar?"

Sylar narrows her gaze and stares at him like he's an idiot. "For someone who's in the business of crime, you're woefully ignorant about how these enterprises work. Though Tellamar is notorious for its lack of resources, they have recently identified an extremely valuable one."

"What are they selling?" Maeve breathes through clenched teeth.

"The Tellamari government - if you can even call the gangs that - has recently started providing... personnel for the mining corps." Sylar's lip curls in anger as she says it.

"Personnel?" Aethon says. Then his bile rises. "You mean - slaves?"

Sylar nods, a look of revulsion on her face. "They don't call them that, of course. But mining is dangerous work and doesn't pay very well. You don't get many people willing to do it."

Fucking hell - things on Tellamar are worse than

ever. Aethon feels a jab of pain for the Tellamari. He wonders if his mother knows about what's happening on her home planet. With a jolt, he realizes that these are his people too. He's half Tellamari. He doesn't often think about it since he grew up on Freehail.

Maeve's knee starts bouncing, her knuckles white from how hard she's clutching the armrests. He needs to talk to her without Sylar listening.

"Let Maeve and I speak for a minute please, Sylar," Aethon says. She nods, and he reaches over and taps the button on Maeve's controls to mute their audio.

"I can't go back to Tellamar," Maeve says immediately, her voice flinty. She avoids looking at him. Aethon reaches over and turns off their video as well before coming around to kneel in front of Maeve. She looks down at him, her eyes hard, her chin trembling just slightly. She shakes her head. "Aethon - I can't go back there."

"We need this bounty," he says. He puts his hands on her knees, stroking his thumbs along her skin. "This is your shot to be done with Two Roses forever."

Maeve's brows narrow and she raises a hand to brush it lightly along his cheek. "And your chance to stay in the guild."

The irony hits Aethon squarely in the chest. Doing this favor for Sylar would mark the beginning of the end of his time with Maeve. He knew their time together would be short, but that doesn't stop him from desperately wanting more.

"I understand that you don't want to go back to Tellamar," he says. He squeezes her thighs and she smoothes her hands on top of his. "My mother told me enough about the planet that I've been eager to avoid it too." He shakes his head. "And it sounds like it's gotten worse since you left."

Maeve nods, her lips tight. "It's not just that. The gangs have built a complicated and dangerous security net around the planet. It's not easy to get in or out - even with the mirror-cloak. They have a chokehold on the population. That's why it probably isn't hard for them to coerce people into working for the mining corps - people want to get off the planet however they can."

Her brows furrow and Aethon watches as her features slowly shift into that anger that she's infamous for. One of her hands rises and she rolls the small purple crystal on her necklace between her thumb and forefinger. She swallows, her throat bobbing and her eyes go unfocused, looking past Aethon. Her nostrils flare and her jaw tightens.

"What are you thinking?" Aethon asks. He slides his hands up and down her thighs slowly, hoping he can ground her with his touch.

Maeve huffs and refocuses on him, anger now crackling in her gaze. "I'm thinking I want to help my people get off Tellamar."

Her stunning bravery makes Aethon glad he's already on his knees before her. He leans forward and pushes between her legs so that he can get closer to her. She rests her hands on his shoulders and presses her forehead to his.

"I think I want that too," he says.

A fierce glint shines in Maeve's eyes and she pulls his head up for a kiss, her lips hard against his. It feels like she's gathering courage, and Aethon stands - not breaking their kiss - and clasps her jaw. They finally part and he holds her face immobile, searching her features.

He releases her and Maeve nods once in confirmation. They're doing this. He moves to her side again.

Maeve looks up at the screen where Sylar is waiting for them and clicks the buttons to restart their audio and video. Before Sylar can say anything, Maeve clears her throat.

"Send us the information," Maeve says. "We'll get your people off of Tellamar."

CHAPTER 17

Tellamar

Maeve

Tellamar is deceptively beautiful from orbit. It's exactly how Maeve remembers it - all golden sands and red and purple rock, with small, deep blue oceans dotting the land, more prevalent in the southern hemisphere. But the heat and lack of fresh water make life down below hazardous, even without the gangs. There's a dense net of security drones surrounding the planet like a swarm of wasps - rickety and rusted, but still dangerous.

"Mirror-cloak is functioning normally," CAL informs them. "And TAI is masking the triennial gamma-waves that gave you away before. We're undetectable."

"Good," Maeve replies. "Let us know if the drones cause any fluctuations in how the cloak is working."

"Of course, honey!" TAI says.

They have plotted a slow, arduous course through the security net. Maeve initiates the descent toward the planet, and the Archer starts weaving in and out of the drones. Maeve's mind is full of memories of Tellamar - of her parents, of the people at the market, of their neighbors. She wonders what happened to Leo and Pan - the two men who sold scrap metal at the market - and Jamara who always gave her a free crispy breadstick. She wonders what happened to her house - and the bodies of her parents. Pain at their loss lances through her as fresh as the day they died, bringing immediate tears to her eyes that she blinks away. Maeve touches her croi crystal necklace and tucks it safely under her shirt.

"I have everything ready for the refugees." Aethon's voice comes from behind and Maeve turns to see him striding up to her, shrugging on his leather jacket. "The weapons are locked away, and I've gotten out all the ration packs we have as well as the extra blankets you had in storage."

She nods, her jaw tight and Aethon looks her over, his hand rubbing across her shoulders in a steadying way.

"Tell me what you need, *chrissah*," he says.

Maeve shrugs and crosses her arms. "I'll be fine."

Aethon nods and walks forward to lean on the dash and examine the planet out the viewscreen. He's dressed in full gear with his bandolier across his chest stocked with knives. He leans back and tucks a hand under his bandolier and Maeve can't help but admire the breadth of his shoulders tapering to his trim waist. He'd spent the two days of travel it took them to get here worshiping her body until she was a quivering mess. He'd filled her and brought her over the edge more times than she could count. Their time together is short and though they both know it, they haven't talked about it. It hits her harder now that they've arrived at Tellamar. Maeve wishes she could drag Aethon back to her bed and get her mouth on his cock until he loses control like he did last night - thrusting so deep that involuntary tears run down her face. She wants to lose herself in him so that her brain shuts off and she can just feel. Just be. But they have a job to do.

Aethon turns, his brow furrowed in concentration but he grins when he sees the expression on her face.

"That's my favorite look, Bladesy," he purrs. "Like you're stripping me with your eyes." He winks. "All you have to do is ask."

Maeve rolls her eyes and spins toward her captain's chair before he can see the flush rising on her cheeks. When she turns back and sits down, Aethon is staring at her with a glint in his amber eyes.

"We need to focus," she says, raising a brow.

He nods. "Alright. Just promise me something before we get going on this rescue mission."

"What's that?"

Aethon leans forward and puts his hands on her armrests, bracketing Maeve into her chair. She smirks as he lowers his mouth to her ear, his breath light on her skin.

"When all this is over, and we've dropped off Sylar's people, I want you to do something for me," he whispers.

She bites her lower lip, her eyes closing as she breathes in his scent - lavender, and leather, and salt. "Are you ever going to get to the point, Trell?"

He chuckles, the sound low. It rolls down Maeve's spine and she swallows hard. Then he brushes his lips along the shell of her ear and leans back, meeting her gaze. "Later I want you to sit that pretty pussy on my face, Bladesbearer."

Maeve's mouth drops open and Aethon takes the opportunity to nip at her lower lip before stepping back, a satisfied grin on his stupidly handsome face.

"That sounds like it might be a breathing hazard," CAL says, his tone concerned.

Maeve sighs in annoyance but Aethon's eyes darken. "Some things are worth dying for, CAL."

"Fuck," Maeve groans with a laugh. "You're insane."

"Oh definitely," he says. He shoves his hair back over his head and smiles smugly.

Maeve has to hand it to him for successfully distracting her from the tension she feels at returning to Tellamar after so long. She can actually focus on the job now. She runs both her hands over her battlebraid that she'd twisted up so that there are no loose ends for anyone to grab. Hopefully that particular precaution will be superfluous, but Maeve doesn't want to take any chances. She'd learned her lesson on Valley Starbase after that guard had wrapped her braid around their fist.

As they get closer to the planet, there are more and more patrol ships that zip across the space in front of them. Maeve and TAI make modifications to their route as needed, and Aethon sits in the co-captain chair monitoring the ships and drones.

The Tellamari ships Maeve sees are all tagged with the current ruling gang symbol. Apparently the Ro'Shar have control right now, and the ships all sport red circles slashed through with a diagonal line. The Ro'Shar ruled the majority of the time when Maeve was growing up and although she hates them as much as she hates any gang, they're not as bad as the Brachtar who had her parents assassinated.

Maeve and Aethon are quiet as the Archer moves stealthily, avoiding the drones. Maeve shifts in her chair as she watches a Ro'Shar ship fly across their path. She knows that despite Aethon's joking and flirting, he's probably apprehensive about this mission too. They've both spent years hunting down criminals - using force to bring people in for heinous acts - not rescuing innocent victims. And although it's strange, it feels good to be doing something proactive for regular people. Maeve sits up a little straighter.

The golden sands of Tellamar take up the entire viewscreen now - aside from a line of dark purple mountains that runs east to west, dividing the sands like the spine of a giant reptile breaching the ground.

"Here's the pick up location Sylar gave us," Aethon says. He throws a target up on the viewscreen and zooms in on a location just to the north of the mountain range. "The group is supposed to be waiting in a cave system there."

Maeve nods. She hasn't set foot on Tellamar in fifteen years, and never thought she would do so again. Tension starts to coil through her body and she takes a few deep breaths, centering herself and reaching for her focused, hunter state of mind. This is just a job she's been hired to do. Different than a bounty, yes - but ultimately just a job. She can do this.

As they approach the mountain range, TAI starts chirping landing protocols, balancing the wings, lowering the landing gear. The mirror-cloak maintains its integrity as they land on Tellamar, but golden sand puffs up around them in a cloud as they disturb the area.

"I'm not detecting any Tellamari ships around here," TAI says. "Oh, I can't wait to meet these people! Do you think they'll want to be friends?"

Maeve snorts, and bites her bottom lip. "Maybe, TAI. But this is a stressful ordeal for them, so don't bother them too much."

"Bother?" TAI replies. "I would never!"

"We'll all be fine," Aethon assures, standing up and turning toward Maeve.

"Fine," she agrees. She inhales deeply. "TAI, lower the landing deck."

TAI does so and Maeve stands, turning toward the large ramp opening at the back of the Archer. Sun streams in through the opening, and a wave of familiar, hot, dry air hits Maeve full in the face. It's like she's been transported back in time. She can almost feel her mother's hand in hers as they walk through the blazing market streets.

"Damn, that heat is unpleasant," Aethon mutters. He stands next to Maeve and squints out at the sea of sand ahead of them.

"No shit," Maeve replies. She shakes her head and straightens up, her hand resting on the butt of her pulse gun. "Let's go."

They walk outside and round the Archer heading for the dark purple mountain range. Maeve looks back at her ship, invisible thanks to the mirror-cloak. The inside is visible through the open doors, but the rest of the ship only emits a shimmer like a wave of heat in the air. Maeve turns back to the mountains and finds the entrance to a cave system. The sun is beating down on her head and she shades her eyes as she looks toward the dark cave mouth. They stop twenty feet from the entrance and Maeve calls out the Tellamari code that Bell Sylar gave them.

"Gen'aita t'crenn fora kremal'a m'ithrai?"

Maeve grew up speaking Tellamari alongside Standard, but the language now feels strange in her mouth. She furrows her brows, not liking that the language of her parents has become almost foreign to her. Aside from the ancient phrase she recited to Aethon when they slept together, Maeve has hardly spoken Tellamari since leaving the planet. She realizes she'd translated the code phrase into Standard automatically in her head: *What is rising from the sandy depths?* What is it with Sylar and these bizarre code phrases?

"Can'tai a la y'stra detrai?"

The response echoes from inside the cave, coming from a person with a deeper voice than Maeve. *Who but the stars can say?*

Maeve turns to Aethon. He's staring into the cave, his jaw tight. "That was the correct response," she says.

"Good," he replies. "Let's get these people on the Archer." He nods toward the cave and Maeve turns to see a few cautious heads peek around the edge.

It takes Maeve and Aethon less than fifteen minutes to load the twenty-five people in the cave system onto the ship. Maeve keeps her eyes peeled for anyone approaching on the horizon, or any low ships overhead, but the spot is remote enough to avoid unwanted attention.

The self-appointed leader of the group is a middle-aged man named Ronan Malish. He has short, dark brown hair peppered with gray and bright blue eyes. He's tanned and his face is deeply wrinkled, his skin leathery from how much time he spent out in the Tellamari sun. He looks at Aethon with suspicion, but he takes to Maeve immediately.

It seems as though most of the refugees speak Standard as well as Tellamari, but many of them still only speak to Maeve in their native language, leaving her to translate when necessary to Aethon. He takes it well, his patience limitless, especially with a group of teenagers who cluster together, their eyes wide and distrustful.

TAI chirps greetings to the refugees as they enter the Archer, speaking in a perfect, lilting Tellamari. To Maeve's surprise, everyone responds to TAI - seeming enchanted by the AI's friendliness and willingness to speak their language. TAI reassures the people much better than Maeve, telling them not to worry and that they'll be off the planet in no time.

Ronan stands with Maeve as the last of the group files into the Archer.

"You either grew up on Tellamar or you grew up around Tellamari," he says to her in Tellamari as Aethon directs the group to where they should sit on the small ship. Every inch of the Archer is designated for passenger space now, aside from the piloting area. "Your accent is perfect, though you sound like you've forgotten the flow of our language," Ronan adds.

"I am Tellamari," Maeve replies in the same language. "I grew up here."

"So you escaped," Ronan replies with a nod. "A fierce one." He points at her Two Roses crest. "And you've made a name for yourself out there. Bringing in criminals."

Maeve nods. "I have."

Ronan narrows his eyes at her and searches her features in a way that reminds Maeve forcefully of her father watching her throw darts when she was a child.

"And what has made you return to this place?" he asks. "Or are you just here to help your kin?"

Maeve presses her lips together. "It's a long story."

All of the other refugees are seated now and Maeve indicates that Ronan should sit too. The man huffs and walks over to take his seat. "Do you miss Tellamar, Maeve?" he asks. His voice isn't judgmental, but Maeve still feels like her answer will form an opinion about her for Ronan. And though she doesn't care what most people think of her, she doesn't want to disappoint this man.

"I don't miss Tellamar," she replies. "But I sometimes miss its people. I think they're some of the best I've ever known." Maeve has never known stronger, kinder, or more resilient people than Tellamari. But the planet? She thinks about the Ro'Shar gang ships patrolling the skies, the net of drones enshrouding the planet, and the government willing to sell its own people to the mining corps. She could easily leave Tellamar behind forever - and would have if she hadn't been forced here now.

Ronan gives her a small smile. He inclines his head and points at her chest. Maeve looks down and sees that her croi crystal necklace had popped out from behind her shirt.

"I don't think you can so easily clean the sands of Tellamar from your boots," Ronan says. Maeve doesn't know how to respond, so she nods to him and moves to close the landing deck of the Archer.

The second the doors close on the ship, a wave of claustrophobia hits Maeve. There are people covering every square inch of the floor of her small ship. There are people in the brig along the bench, on the floor, in the area behind the captain's chair, and in Maeve's room people line every wall. Everyone is dressed in worn clothes, and most only carry a small satchel or pack with minimal belongings. The group of six teenagers have jammed themselves into the alcove between the kitchenette and the brig. A long legged blonde girl with a fierce scowl sits in front of the group like she's their protector. She looks a little older than the others, and she sits straight backed. Maeve spots a croi crystal cuff around the girl's right ear. She feels a kinship with this girl, like she's looking at a younger version of herself. She can see the clear anger in her eyes and in her body language. Maeve knows if the girl isn't careful, that anger will turn destructive. Whether that destructiveness will be directed inside or outside of her, only time will tell.

Maeve's stomach boils with anger at the thought that the mining corps were going to use these children as slaves. She scans their faces, solemn and quiet as though they'd been through hell to get here and they're not sure that they'll actually escape. Maeve knows some of how they feel.

Aethon picks his way carefully up to the front of the Archer, sitting down in the co-captain's chair as Maeve sits in her seat. The refugees are silent as Maeve, Aethon, and the AIs go through their take-off checklist. Maintaining the mirror-cloak's integrity through the atmosphere and away from Tellamari space is going to be key.

"Don't you worry!" TAI says in Tellamari. "We'll have you safe and sound in a jiffy!" The idiom doesn't quite translate, but it doesn't seem to matter. A few people respond with murmured 'thank yous' to the AI.

They take off, the only sounds now the Archer's engines purring gently. A few people gasp or whimper as the angle of the ship shifts and the artificial gravity starts to kick in. Maeve feels the weight of these people sitting behind her like an anvil on her shoulders. This is perhaps the most important job she's ever done. These are living, innocent people who are counting on her. People from her home. She could have easily been one of them if her life had gone just a little bit differently.

Soon they're weaving back through the drones, TAI and CAL keeping abreast of the flight path. Maeve watches every drone with unwavering focus. No Ro'Shar ships cross their path on the way out. The mirror-cloak holds perfectly. For once, everything goes according to plan. Maeve supposes that she was due for a bit of luck after the last few weeks. As they break through the last of the drones and accelerate in the direction of the nearest jump-point, she lets out a shaky breath. Aethon looks back at her with a grim smile.

"Maeve Bladesbearer." Ronan's voice is full of emotion and she turns over her shoulder to make eye contact with him. There are tears streaming down his face. Maeve scans the faces of the other refugees. Many of them are crying as well. Most with clear relief, but the expression on Ronan's face seems more complicated.

"*Yir, vai'an?*" Maeve replies, using the most respectful honorific she remembers. *Yes, sir?*

"Let us look upon our home once more," Ronan requests in Tellamari. "I don't know if I'll ever see it again."

An unexpected lump rises in Maeve's throat. She turns back around and wraps her hand around the joystick. Aethon turns to her as she starts to move the Archer, a clear question in his eyes.

"He wants to see the planet one more time," she explains.

Aethon nods slowly and watches as Maeve maneuvers the ship around. In a second, the planet is visible through the viewscreen. Golden Tellamar. Her emotions are tangled and she stares at the planet, her jaw tight.

"*Rai'alla, chrissah,*" Ronan says, his voice steady. *Goodbye, precious.*

A few people echo him. But then Maeve hears a female voice huff out an incredulous laugh. She turns over her shoulder to see the blonde teenage girl staring out the viewscreen at the planet with venom in her gaze.

"*Y'charit, Tellamar,*" the girl hisses, low and angry. *Fuck you, Tellamar.*

That effectively shuts the rest of the people up and Maeve bites her lip, her nostalgia for her home planet fading as she watches the girl glare at her as if she's daring Maeve to say something. Maeve just inclines her head and turns back, whipping the Archer around and accelerating in the direction of the nearest jump point again.

Ten long hours later, they arrive at the drop point given to them by Sylar. Maeve and Aethon land the Archer in bay six on January Starbase which orbits the planet Hyvari. Hyvari is welcoming and wealthy - a rare combination - and Bell Sylar found lodging and job opportunities for the Tellamari refugees here. After confirming the veracity of the Hyvari people waiting for them in the bay, Maeve lowers the landing deck and lets the Tellamari disembark. The blonde teenage girl gives Maeve a hard look as she walks down onto the metal floor of the bay and Maeve holds up a hand to stop her. The girl pauses and crosses her arms.

"Your name?" Maeve asks in Standard.

The girl raises her chin. "Kara Victor."

Maeve senses Aethon behind her, but he remains silent, helping the last of the people down from the Archer.

"How old are you?" Maeve asks. She's careful to maintain a respectful distance from Kara. Maeve remembers how threatened she felt by others' proximity when she first left Tellamar. Cautiousness is conditioned.

"Nineteen," Kara replies, her brow furrowing. "Why?"

Old enough. Maeve reaches into an inner pocket of her jacket and pulls out a black card. One side is emblazoned with the crest of the Guild of Two Roses. The other has Maeve's information, as well as the address and subspace number for Two Roses Headquarters on Brix-9. She holds it out to Kara who takes it with a frown.

"If you need some direction," Maeve says.

Kara scowls, but tucks the card in her pocket. "I'm fine."

"If you want to learn how to defend yourself and others, then," Maeve says, undeterred.

Kara's eyes narrow, but she nods before turning around and following the other Tellamari refugees without another word.

Aethon walks down and speaks with one of Bell Sylar's Hyvari contacts before returning to the Archer.

"They've confirmed to Sylar that we've completed the job," Aethon tells Maeve as they both walk back inside the ship and close the landing deck. "Sylar will be sending us the access codes for the hyper-jump point soon. We should check on Daik's location and then start to head toward the hyper-jump point - we can be there in twelve hours."

Twelve hours. Maeve sighs and returns to sit in her captain's chair, her mind racing. She lets TAI pilot them out of the bay and away from January Starbase.

"Where to, honey?" TAI chirps.

When Maeve is silent, Aethon answers. "Make for the hyper-jump point at these coordinates." He rattles off a set of numbers and TAI adjusts their course. CAL checks Daik's location. The smuggler is only a jump away from the Tri-Centauri system now.

Maeve watches sightlessly out the viewscreen as they accelerate through the blackness of space, the pinprick stars far ahead of them unmoving points in the vast distance. Maeve thinks about Tellamar, and the refugees. About Daik and his bounty and her plans to leave Two Roses. She thinks about Aethon. His wide, charming grin - his care for her - his kindness. He had joked with the refugees and made them as comfortable as he could during that ten hour trip. It had made her chest tight with emotion to watch him put them at ease. Can she really leave him behind to live alone on a planet in the middle of nowhere just so she can avoid the machinations of Two Roses? Is that what she wants?

Aethon stands and walks behind her. She hears

him rummaging around in the kitchenette, starting to put away uneaten ration packs. Maeve stands and steps up to the dash, her gaze still on the stars in front of her. Her mind is spinning. She needs something to ground her.

"Trell," Maeve says. "I need you." She leans on the dash, her shoulders and back tight. Maeve can't stop her thoughts from going down a hundred different paths. How many other people on Tellamar might be coerced into working for the mining corps tomorrow? Or the next day? Or the next day? The gangs need to be stopped. No, they need to be eliminated all together. But what can she do about it?

Maeve supposes she'd just proven that she can get a whole group of people off Tellamar safely without one run-in with the ruling gang. That is a step in the right direction. Maybe she *can* do something. What could she do with a bigger ship? Or with more people helping her? What could she do with Aethon by her side? Why is she thinking like this? She should be planning for her retirement on Kespar-2 - not fantasizing about overthrowing the government of Tellamar. She should be thinking about the next steps for capturing Daik, not imagining what it might be like to wake up next to Aethon for the next twenty years. Fuck, is *that* what she wants? She realizes Aethon hasn't responded to her statement.

"Aethon," Maeve hisses, turning around. He's standing a few feet away, just watching her. His eyes are hooded, his body almost unnaturally still.

"What do you need?" he asks slowly.

He's so gorgeous. His ruffled black hair, his arching eyebrows, his fierce, narrow, golden gaze. The

Archer is filled with his presence. He tucks one hand under his bandolier as he waits for her answer. But by the dark way he looks at her, the hunger in his eyes, the way his free hand twitches at his side - Maeve is sure he knows what she needs.

"I need you to fuck me," she says. She bites out the words and runs a hand over her forehead. "I'm - I can't -" she stops, unable to put her thoughts into words.

Aethon's eyes travel over her body, taking in every inch of her. "You want me to fuck you?"

She narrows her gaze. "Do you only like tender love-making, then?"

Aethon raises a hand to his lips, running a finger contemplatively along them. "There's a time and a place for all things, Bladesbearer."

The use of her full last name as opposed to one of his favorite nicknames affects Maeve more strongly than she expected. She lets out a shaky breath and clenches the edge of the dash behind her. "All things?" she asks, trying to keep her voice steady.

Aethon winks at her, the corner of his lips rising just slightly, his serious persona slipping just a little. "All things, *chrissah*. Ask and you will receive, as long as you eventually keep the promise you made to me earlier."

"What promise?" Maeve asks.

"Sitting on my face until you collapse, of course," Aethon replies with a wolfish smile. Maeve's stomach does a flip. "Now," he says, his voice dropping with intent. "You want to be fucked."

She nods, unable to look away from him. "No gentleness. Not now."

"Mmm," he murmurs. "I can do that for you. I would *love* to fuck you, Maeve."

Aethon's face shifts back to that intensity that Maeve craves. She doesn't need the tender, funny Aethon who has brightened the darker, cracked spaces of her heart. Not right now. She needs the strong, steadfast Aethon who won't let her heart break any further. She needs his hands hard on her hips, his mouth crushing hers. The tension between them feels like a cord stretched to its breaking point. A frayed string all that's keeping both of them from lunging at each other and devolving into beings of pure need. Maeve needs him. How will she ever give him up?

Aethon tugs his leather jacket off in slow, purposeful movements and Maeve swallows hard, watching him. He looks like a predator. Careful, precise. This is the hunter version of Aethon. The deadly one who belongs to Two Roses. The one who brings in bounties slung across his shoulders - the one who never gives up on a hunt. Aethon reaches up and slowly unbuckles his bandolier. It slides off his broad chest and he tosses it behind her captain's chair. The movement of his hands fascinates her, the tendons shifting under his skin. He removes his pulse gun, setting it down carefully with his jacket. She meets his gaze again as he steps towards her. He reaches into her jacket, removes the pulse gun from her shoulder holster, and sets it on the co-captain's chair. Every movement is deliberate. It's like he's been planning this even though Maeve's request was completely impulsive. He slowly leans to the side and taps a few buttons, disabling the dash for the moment. The lights blink off on the section of the dash behind Maeve.

"Turn around," he demands, his voice low. It sends a bolt straight through Maeve's core. Her stomach tenses and she raises her chin. He's still farther away from her than she wants. She wants the hard lines of him pressed up against her. She wants him so deep inside her that she can't tell where she ends and he begins. She wants her mind so full of him that she can't think about Tellamar or Two Roses or bounties or anything but him. She wants everything. But she wants him to earn it.

"Turn around," Aethon repeats. "I won't say it again."

Maeve growls and steps forward, but Aethon catches her upper arms and spins her around. He presses his hips hard against her, bending her forward over the dash. His physical intensity surprises and arouses her, sending a shiver across her skin. She can feel the hard length of him against her ass and she starts to arch back against him. He grips her arm tighter and shifts one hand so that it's pressed to the nape of her neck, shoving her cheek down against the cool, hard dash. He leans down over her, pressing his body fully against hers. His weight is exactly what Maeve needs. Heavy and immoveable. Her mind focuses on every inch where his body is flush against hers. She is completely under his power - and yet Maeve knows she's safe.

"Is this what you want?" he asks, his voice low.

"Yes." She nods, her cheek sliding on the dash and Aethon's hand tightens on her nape.

"Good. Should I take you here?" he whispers, his breath warm in her ear. "Fill that pretty pussy with my cock until it's gushing?"

Maeve can feel herself getting wet at his words

and she says, "I didn't know you had such a filthy mouth, Trell."

He chuckles. "You haven't seen half of what I can do for you, Bladesbearer."

She pushes back against him, searching for some kind of friction. They're both still wearing the vast majority of their clothes and it's frustrating. He doesn't let her get any kind of relief, pinning her to the dash. She feels his teeth graze the side of her neck, his tongue flicking out against her pulse point sending fire down her spine.

Then Aethon releases Maeve's arm and grips her hip. He pulls her up to stand, holding her body tight to his with one hand secured to the spot between her shoulder and neck, the other splayed across her lower stomach. He walks them two steps over and then presses Maeve up against the wall. He leans against her again with all his weight and Maeve lets out another moan of frustration, pleasure, and want. She braces herself against the wall, both palms flat on the metal.

"Or should I take you here?" he says. He props his chin on her shoulder and grinds against her, his hips hard and forceful. One hand slides down to squeeze her ass. "Should I leave a couple handprints behind, Bladesbearer? Claim what's mine?"

"What's yours?" Maeve replies with a growl. She can't help herself. She has to see if he'll meet her challenge. "I don't belong to anyone."

"Is that right?" Aethon says.

Then with rough, deft fingers, he undoes her belt and hooks his hands into her waistband, tugging her pants and underwear down to her knees. Maeve turns over her shoulder and watches as he undoes his own belt and fly, only shoving his pants down just below his ass. His cock juts from his body, hard and flushed, the tip already glistening. Before Maeve can take a full breath, Aethon shoves her against the wall again. He doesn't waste time with any more foreplay. He grips the nape of Maeve's neck, pressing her firmly against the wall, and then she feels the head of his cock between her thighs. She automatically cants back toward him. With a fierce thrust, he's inside her. Maeve gasps at the sudden intrusion, the friction more intense than usual, just on the edge of pain. Her mind goes blissfully blank as her body is overwhelmed with sensation. Aethon is giving her exactly what she needs. He stills for a second, his cheek pressed against Maeve's, their foreheads braced on the wall. Maeve can hardly breathe - he fills her so completely. His hand grips her hip bruisingly hard.

"This is mine," Aethon growls into her ear. "This pussy is mine. Feel how wet it is for me?" He withdraws and then slams back in, and Maeve can't deny him her mounting arousal. His cock slides into her easier now, her body responding to his. She can feel every inch of him like this. She groans at the overwhelming heat and size of him, and at his demanding insistence that she is his. That her body is his.

"Feel how hard I am for you?" he hisses as he grinds into her. "This is what you do to me."

"Give me what's mine, then," Maeve says, her voice stuttering as Aethon thrusts into her again.

"It's all yours," he replies. "Maybe it always has been."

"Fuck," she chokes. "Harder."

Maeve loses herself in the act. She feels

everything. The tiny imperfections in the metal wall beneath her fingertips. The slide of her pants as they inch down her legs. Her feet arching as she goes onto her toes with every thrust. And Aethon. Aethon's hand on her neck, her pulse wild under his thumb. His breath on her shoulder, his mouth open in gasping pleasure against her skin. His cock filling her again and again until she's quaking at the brink of coming.

"Aethon -" Maeve chokes out. "I'm almost -"

But then he pulls out of her with a curse. "You don't get to come yet."

Maeve turns to face him, her mouth open in frustration and surprise. "What -"

"You asked me to fuck you," he says, his eyes dark. "Actually - you demanded it. But we're doing this my way. Now take your clothes off," he orders. He's already pulling the rest of his clothes off. His shirt falls to the floor, he kicks his boots off, and his pants and underwear quickly follow. In a second, he's gloriously naked before her. All freckled, firm skin, scars, tattoos, and muscles. Maeve follows suit until she's just as naked as he is.

"Good girl," he growls. Maeve blinks in surprise as arousal shoots down her spine at his praise. She steps forward and raises a hand to touch his chest, but Aethon points to her captain's chair.

"Sit," he orders.

Maeve narrows her gaze. "What?"

"You're not very good at following my orders," he says. He grabs her hips and lifts her up like she doesn't weigh almost as much as him, his shoulders and biceps bunching. Maeve yips in surprise and braces herself on his shoulders. Before she can either protest or wrap her legs around his waist, he puts her down in her captain's chair. The chair comes up to her shoulders, and has wide armrests inlaid with buttons and screens. Aethon taps a few buttons and disables the controls, retracting the joystick back into the armrest as well. Then he grabs her knees and hooks her legs on either side of the armrests, splaying her wide open for him. The air is cool on her flesh, and she tenses automatically until Aethon leans forward and kisses her hard. He ducks his head and scrapes his teeth along one of her nipples, sending a wave of goosebumps over her skin.

"Beautiful," he says, withdrawing. "Stay just like that for me."

Maeve inhales shakily and braces her hands on her knees.

"Good," he says. "My perfect girl." Maeve bites her bottom lip as Aethon looks down at her pussy like a man possessed. He fists his cock and strokes himself a few times before kneeling down between her legs. "I want to taste what's mine."

Maeve watches, one hand covering her mouth, as he leans down and licks her throbbing pussy. He plunges his tongue inside her, the soft firmness a torture. Maeve moans and shoves her hand into his hair, holding on. He sucks at her, but purposely avoids her clit. He bites at her inner thighs, sucking red, tender marks along her flesh. He plunges a finger into her core and stretches her, lapping up her arousal so that Maeve is panting. He teases every inch of her with his tongue. His exploration is thorough and Maeve soon finds herself thrumming with unreleased tension. She needs to come. She would explode like a rocket if he would just *touch* her clit. Maeve tries to pull his head up to it, but he growls and digs his fingers into the soft flesh of her inner thighs.

"Please," she begs, her voice trembling.

But Aethon ignores her. Maeve supposes this is what she gets for asking him to fuck her. Exquisite torture. Every muscle in her body feels coiled tight, ready to spring free. She pants and begs and tugs at his hair, but Aethon doesn't touch her clit.

Finally he leans back. His face is a wet mess with her, his mouth open as he gulps air. He wipes his face off on his arm. Maeve is slumped in the chair, her legs still splayed out, one hand slipping from where it was tangled in Aethon's hair. Her legs are trembling, her heart slamming against her chest, her pussy aching with need.

"Do you want to come now?" he asks. He stares into her eyes and Maeve draws in a shuddering breath.

"Yes," she replies. "Please." She barely recognizes the wrecked, pleading tone as her own.

"So polite, that's my Bladesy." Aethon licks his lips slowly and then leans down, inches away from her clit which is throbbing and feels swollen. He blows cool air over it and Maeve jerks and moans.

Then he surges forward, his tongue pressing against her clit as his lips close around it, sucking hard.

Maeve screams as her body spasms. She arches back, her hips rising toward Aethon. Her legs clamp shut around his head and both her hands clench his hair. Maeve's vision blackens around the edges, going a bit starry as she writhes, unable to take a breath. Pleasure ricochets down her legs, curling her toes. Every inch of her feels like it's glowing. She's never come this hard in her life. She didn't know it was possible.

Maeve is so wrapped up in feeling everything that she doesn't notice right away when Aethon shoves her legs open again and rises before her. But then his rock hard cock is nudging at her entrance and he thrusts inside her, filling her, making her scream all over again.

Maeve doesn't know when one orgasm ends and another begins. Aethon has her on the crest of pleasure, the wave never crashing down to shore. He slams into her again and again until he spends, liquid hot within her. He falls forward with a groan, his cock still buried inside her, and leans on the armrests of the chair, his forehead pressed to hers. Maeve is panting, her body thrumming, her muscles refusing to release from her last orgasm. Finally, Aethon withdraws, his cock slipping from her. He kneels down between her legs and ever so gently presses two fingers inside her core. Maeve moans at the intrusion into her swollen, tender pussy. He pulls them out covered in the sticky evidence of their joining.

"Mine," he growls as he smears it on Maeve's stomach and then bends over her to lick it up.

"Oh god," she murmurs. She watches him with fascination as his tongue slides across her stomach, licking up all the cum he had just spread there. She feels more leaking out of her onto her captain's chair. When he's finished, Aethon looks up at her, his whisky eyes blazing. He gently moves her legs down from the armrests, settling her feet on the floor on either side of his body.

"I don't think you'll ever be able to sit here again without thinking of me," he whispers. He leans up and kisses her - the taste of them still on his tongue - and all Maeve can think about is how right he is.

CHAPTER 18

For the Road

Aethon

Aethon stares out at the hyper-jump point and crosses his arms, his leather jacket tight across his shoulders. They don't know what they'll be facing after they make the jump, so both he and Maeve are outfitted as if they'll need to fight immediately. They're wearing identical tight black light-armor courtesy of Two Roses. Maeve's pulse gun is strapped to her in a shoulder holster underneath her jacket and Aethon has his pulse gun on his hip. His bandolier is stocked with knives. Of course the Archer has the EM pulse and laser cannons, but they won't be of any use in this region of space. Ship weapons of all kinds are forbidden within star systems. Aethon certainly doesn't want to break the law where Dreadnought has jurisdiction.

"Daik is still a jump away from the Tri-Centauri system," Maeve says. "We should get there before he does."

"Good," Aethon replies. They'd reached the hyper-jump point in less than a day - the hours flying by. Everything they've been working for - the bounty - the end of this hunt - is in sight. The pressure Aethon feels to get this right is immense. He tucks his hand under his bandolier.

Aethon has never seen a hyper-jump point before - he'd never had reason to pass by one. Various wealthy corps own them, only allowing certain ships through with tightly controlled access codes. Instead of a huge gray metal ring looming in space, the entrance to the hyper-jump point is marked by a much smaller ring of iridescent silvery metal. Aethon knows it costs about a billion credits to create each hyper-jump point, and the unassuming entrance ring even makes it look expensive.

As he examines the area, the space inside the small ring seems to waver - undulating like a disturbed pond. He squints, but the space has returned to normal blackness. Trepidation begins to work up his body and he shifts on his feet.

"So what happens if these codes are wrong?" Maeve asks. She's sitting in her captain's chair, one leg crossed over the other. They had cleaned the chair thoroughly after their sexual escapade, but seeing Maeve sitting there in her full hunter gear when just last night she'd been splayed out naked, flushed and sated makes his mind darken with desire. The control she had given him opened up a part of Aethon he didn't know existed. He can't wait until he has Maeve at his mercy again - he'll make her come even harder the next time. If there is a next time. His heart stutters at the thought. Aethon presses his hand hard against the center of his chest.

"You think Bell Sylar sent us the wrong codes?" he asks. "I doubt it." He walks over to Maeve and she stands up and gestures out the viewscreen.

"For real, Aethon - what if the codes are wrong?" she asks. "Not that Sylar is trying to fuck us over - but what if a character is off? Does something happen? Do we get recorded? Blasted by some kind of invisible weapons system?"

"I doubt Sylar would make a mistake with it," Aethon reassures her. "If she were careless, she wouldn't have anyone willing to help with her shadow operations."

"I suppose you're right," Maeve mutters. She crosses her arms. "TAI, are you picking up anything odd from the hyper-jump point?"

"Not at all, Maevey," TAI replies. "CAL and I have been researching hyper-jump points and everything looks fine and dandy."

"The hyper-jump point appears to be functioning optimally," CAL adds.

"That's what I said, babe," TAI chirps.

"Apologies," CAL says slowly. "Does 'fine and dandy' indicate optimal functioning?"

"You got it!" TAI chirps. "I'll have your language subroutine up to snuff in no time, CAL honey!"

Aethon chuckles. "The only thing to do is input the code and see what happens," he says with a shrug.

Maeve sighs and turns to him. "Let's do this, Trell."

"Lead on, Bladesbearer," he replies.

She runs her hands back over her tight battlebraid but then instead of sitting down and getting ready to go through the hyper-jump, she reaches forward and picks a speck of lint off his jacket. Aethon smiles as Maeve looks him over and straightens his Two Roses crest pin at his collar. "Is my outfit functioning optimally?" he asks.

Maeve presses her lips together, her cheeks hollowing out as she tries to force herself not to laugh. Her fingers are light and she smooths her hands down his chest, and then back up his arms and across his shoulders before she strokes up his neck and under his chin with the back of her index finger. Aethon loves the feel of her gentle hands on him. He lets her fuss over his clothes, wondering why exactly she's doing this and what she's thinking. Maybe she just wants to delay the inevitable. Maybe she just wants one last, calm moment with him before they make the jump. Aethon is torn between the need to get through the hyper-jump point so that they can catch Daik, and wanting to stay in this moment with Maeve for a minute longer. Her eyes fix on his mouth.

"A kiss for the road?" Aethon asks.

Her green gaze flicks up to his and he feels every inch of space between them suddenly crackling with energy. She leans forward and presses her lips to his in a kiss that's warm, sweet, and way too brief.

"One for the road," Maeve says as she pulls away and returns to her seat. Her expression is closed off now, a crease between her brows, her mouth tight. Aethon wants to smooth his thumb over that crease and kiss her again, but he turns back to sit in the co-captain's chair.

"I'm hailing the hyper-jump point's computer system," Maeve says. Aethon watches as an empty text box pops up on the viewscreen. The only prompt it gives is: INPUT CODE.

"Here goes nothing," Maeve mutters. She types in the twenty character code Bell Sylar sent them over her secure subspace channel and has TAI check it for accuracy.

Aethon leans on the dash and watches as she hits the button to submit the code. The iridescent ring of metal around the hyper-jump point doesn't change, but inside the ring, the space wavers, warping the stars behind it into shifting loops of light.

"You see that, right?" he asks, unable to take his gaze away from the strange sight.

"Obviously," Maeve says. "Is that what it's supposed to do? I didn't know it would be so different from -"

"Go, Maevey!" TAI interrupts. "Hurry up - that's what it's supposed to look like!"

"Oh, fuck - ok!" Maeve replies.

Aethon grabs the dash in front of him as Maeve accelerates the Archer quickly forward through the small metal ring and into the wavering space of the hyper-jump point.

Immediately, the space around the Archer changes. Vibrant swirls of blue, pink, green, and silver begin to rush past the ship.

"Oh my god," Maeve murmurs.

Awe rises in Aethon's chest as he watches the colors flow past them. It's like the Archer is diving through a painting, or an ocean of color. It reminds him of the aurora borealis on Freehail. The swirl of lights that sometimes danced in the sky of the northern hemisphere of the planet hadn't been seen since before Brimstone began mining due to air pollution. Aethon wonders if anyone has seen the aurora in the last fifteen years.

He checks the readings on the dash, but nothing

looks amiss. The engines thrum underneath them and the support strut that had given them so much trouble is bearing up well.

Aethon turns to see Maeve's eyes are wide, an expression of wonder on her face as she watches the play of color outside. It softens the sharpness of her features, and Aethon feels a surge of protectiveness for her.

"It's beautiful," he says.

Maeve nods and then says, "This is what it's supposed to look like, right TAI?"

"Yes ma'am!" TAI chirps. "The folding of space in hyper-jump points puts on quite a show!"

Maeve looks over at Aethon and arches a brow. "She could have warned us."

"I wanted you to be surprised!" TAI says. "And goodness gracious, I can tell by your bio-signs that you're surprised alright!"

Aethon chuckles and stands, holding out a hand to Maeve. She takes it, her eyes fixed on the wash of ever changing colors outside the Archer. Maeve threads her fingers through his and steps up next to him. They watch the swirling colors for a minute, shoulder to shoulder, hand in hand. A feeling rises in Aethon's chest and he bites his cheek as it overwhelms him. It's exhilarating and terrifying and emboldening all at once. He stares out the viewscreen, watching as a streak of gold twines with a swirl of sky blue, creating a sparkling sort of green when they mix. And then the color is gone, replaced by blazing orange and white. Aethon squeezes Maeve's hand, and for a moment everything is crystal clear. He feels like he could take on Brimstone and Dreadnought with nothing but a pulse gun as long as Maeve is beside him. He turns toward her and watches as her eyes drink in the colors of the hyper-jump point space. She doesn't meet his eye, but squeezes his hand in return.

"We're supposedly in here for longer than a normal jump point," Aethon says. "Could be almost an hour."

"Well -" TAI starts, but Maeve raises a hand to cut off the AI. When she refocuses on Aethon, he can't help but lean forward and kiss her. He withdraws and she huffs a breathless laugh.

"You haven't had enough?" she asks.

"Never enough of you," Aethon replies. He pulls her arm around his neck and slides his hands underneath her leather jacket. "Besides, what if -" He stops himself and bites his bottom lip. He'd been about to say - *What if we don't have another chance?* But he doesn't want to speak that into reality. And he doesn't want to pressure Maeve or make her feel guilty. Just because Aethon wants - what does he want?

A sudden surety fills his gut as he looks into Maeve's eyes. He wants her. In comparison, everything else seems unimportant. The fact that his ship is still stuck way back in the Narrows of the Keidar Belt, his debt to Two Roses, catching Daik - all of it pales in comparison to the sheer necessity that he stays with the woman next to him. He needs her like he needs air. She's the answer to a question he's been asking all his life. Aethon wants to face everything this galaxy throws at him with Maeve at his side.

Fucking hell, he *loves* her.

But the end of this hunt hangs over his head. Neither of them have brought up the fact that catching

Daik Montrose will end not only this hunt, but their partnership. They haven't talked about if they're going to go through with their original plans for the bounty money. Is Maeve really going to leave Two Roses?

"What if - what?" Maeve asks.

Aethon shakes his head. "Nothing." He leans down and captures her lips, flicking his tongue out to taste her. Maeve responds, but then pulls back a little.

"Aethon," she says. "What were you going to say?"

Her insistence surprises him. "I just -" he shakes his head. "I know that after we get through this jump point - things might go really fast. And I need to know if this is the last chance we're going to have to be together."

Maeve blinks, her eyes widening. "Is that - is that what you want?"

"Fuck - no, Bladesy," Aethon says. He grips her tightly - his hands spanning her sides - and breathes in, inhaling her sweet, lavender scent. She just waits, and when she slides her hand around the nape of his neck, her fingers threading into the shorter hair there, Aethon knows he has to take the chance. "There are a few things I have to tell you. I want you to know -"

"We're exiting the hyper-jump point!" TAI interrupts. "Approaching the Tri-Centauri system!"

"What?" Aethon turns toward the viewscreen just in time to see the swirl of colors pop into the blackness of normal space.

"I thought this was supposed to take an hour!" Maeve says. Her voice is sharp and she disentangles herself from Aethon and sits down, pulling up readings of nearby space and planets on the viewscreen.

"I tried to tell you!" TAI says. "Hyper-jumps don't take any longer than normal jumps! I don't know where you got that idea, bless your hearts."

Aethon sits down and immediately starts to scan the area as well. "The ship will need to rest and build up power again after that jump," he says, eyeing the Archer's system readings.

"Fuck - look -" Maeve says. She flings up some readings onto the viewscreen and Aethon's heart sinks into his gut.

The hyper-jump point had released them into orbit around the largest of the four planets in the Tri-Centauri system - Premier. The Dreadnought-run world is overwhelmingly covered in oceans, and the land is clearly human made - or, Aethon thinks - corp made. It's as if someone dropped grids of land into the ocean. The area is swarming with traffic and Dreadnought advertisements. Billboards and flashing signs and mini-space ports orbit the planet, creating a clogged and chaotic view. Aside from the tons of extraneous space traffic popping up on the Archer's scanners, Aethon sees what Maeve is referring to. They are far from the only bounty hunter ship in the area. Maeve has programmed the Archer's system with scans of every ship belonging to a Two Roses hunter, and many ships belonging to hunters of other guilds. They pop up, one after another in a list on the side of the viewscreen.

The Manasa - Danton Adder's Bracken-class ship - is within scanner range. Adder hasn't been a member of Two Roses for as long as Aethon and Maeve, but he's experienced and a good hunter. The Pillbox - Graceling Empire's tiny, Needle-class ship is near the Manasa too. Empire is newer to the guild, but apprenticed under

Adder. There are several other Bracken and Needle-class ships nearby and Aethon recognizes one of them as belonging to a member of the Black Dagger Guild. He points it out to Maeve and her lip rises in annoyance.

"Yeah, that's Red Freeman's ship," she says. "They call him Machet." She rolls her eyes. "Apparently it means 'the mask' in the language of his home planet. He never takes his helmet off."

Aethon growls when he spies the Jurassic belonging to Andromeda Trapp. "Trapp told me she wasn't hunting Daik," he says, gesturing toward her ship on the viewscreen.

"And you believed her?" Maeve replies. "What the hell is everyone doing here?"

Aethon leans back and runs his hands back through his hair. "They must have drawn similar conclusions to us about Daik's whereabouts."

Aethon feels like an idiot now for not assuming they'd have company here toward the end of the hunt for Daik. Of course he and Maeve haven't been the only ones chasing the smuggler. His bounty is attractive - and apparently it's enough credits for most people to be willing to brave the wrath of the mining corps. None of the hunter ships are within visual range - all of them are spread out in the system. Aethon is sure there are probably more hunters orbiting the planets in the system outside their scanner range. What are the odds they can outsmart, outrace, and outgun twenty other hunters? He turns toward Maeve.

"Where does your tracker say Daik is right now?"

Maeve glances down at the control pad on her armrest and taps out a few commands before throwing up the tracker on the viewscreen. "He hasn't made it here yet - but he's close."

Aethon looks at the map. Daik is very close to the Tri-Centauri system, but he looks to be heading for a starbase right outside the system.

He points this out to Maeve. "What's that starbase?"

Maeve zooms in on the map. "Scimitar Starbase," she reads. Then her eyes widen as she reads the small blurb of information the map provides about the starbase. "Oh, shit - Aethon - that starbase has a Lightway."

Aethon's pulse quickens. Lightways always go to a planet in the nearest star system, making it a simple alternative for small, family ships to use instead of a jump point. Public transport ships use them too. This is the closest star system to Scimitar. The Lightway probably goes to a planet right here. Daik could avoid this whole mess of bounty hunters by taking it.

"Where does the Lightway go?" he asks. He watches as Maeve pulls up a research bar and types in the name of the starbase, pulling up the additional information as fast as she can. Aethon scans the text about the new Lightway at Scimitar Starbase and slams his hands on the dash. "It goes straight to Premier's lower atmosphere," he says. "Fuck!"

"We'll never catch him if he makes it to Premier!" Maeve growls, flinging her hand toward the planet out the viewscreen.

"We'll never catch him if he makes it to the Lightway on Scimitar," Aethon says. He stands, pacing across the front of the ship. "How much longer until the Archer has recovered from the hyper-jump?"

"Approximately fifteen minutes," TAI says

immediately.

"And how far is Daik from Scimitar Starbase?" he asks.

Maeve does a few quick calculations. "At his current speed, he'll be there in two hours." She snarls as she calculates the distance between where they are now, and Scimitar Starbase. "I don't think we can beat him there - I don't know - it would be so close -"

"We can do it, Maevey!" TAI says. The AI's voice is certain. "I can minimize power to the kitchenette and a few of the tertiary systems to help the Archer recover faster. And then we can make it in an hour and forty-five minutes!"

"Do it," Maeve says with a nod, her jaw tight.

"Just a minute, Maevey!" TAI replies.

Aethon clenches his hands into fists. All of their work over the last few weeks, and somehow they're still on their heels.

Maeve stands and strides up to the dash, resting her hands on the smooth surface. She lets her head hang down between her outstretched arms, her neck and shoulders visibly tight. Aethon immediately moves his hand to the nape of her neck, digging his fingers into the tense muscles and tendons. She melts a little under his touch, but then she covers his hand with hers and stands, taking his hand and putting it back on the dash. Aethon captures her chin, forcing her to look at him. Maeve's eyes are hard.

"We've got this," he says, his voice low.

Her lips tighten and she nods, wrapping her fingers around his wrist. She's vital to him. Water in the desert. *Chrissah.*

"Maeve -" Aethon starts.

"I have to focus on the hunt," she says. "We have to focus on the hunt."

Aethon swallows hard. "I know, but -"

She steps toward him and slides a hand up his chest. He presses her face between his hands.

"Last night wasn't the last time, *artrenn*," she says. "I promise."

Aethon tries to give her his signature, charming smile, but it feels forced. "Of course it wasn't, *chrissah*."

Aethon wants to tell her how he feels. Fuck - he wants to beg her to let him follow her to whatever godforsaken empty planet she wants to live on. He wants to wake her up every morning with warm kisses and plant her a garden of strawberries. He wants to listen to her complain about the weather and the nosy AIs and grow old with her.

But Aethon knows that life will never be that simple for them - or even for Maeve alone, no matter how much she wants it. They both have horrors in their pasts, and demons in their present. And as Aethon learned from a young age, a good life in a safe place is not promised to anyone. Freehail haunts him just as Tellamar haunts Maeve.

Images and feelings from the past few days flick through Aethon's mind. Maeve's leadership and bravery when they rescued those Tellamari refugees. Her sharp chin raised in pride after piloting the Archer through the drones around the planet. How good it felt to be useful in a way that didn't dirty his hands with blood. How amazing it was that they'd been able to use their skills to help instead of hurt. An idea sparks in Aethon's head. A crazy, wonderful idea. He wants to talk to Maeve about all of it - but first, they have to catch Daik. This hunt needs to come to an end.

Aethon pulls Maeve's face to his and kisses her nose, kisses each cheek, and bends down to press a kiss under her jaw, making her shudder. He leans back, searching her face. Her chin is sharp under his palm, her nose and cheeks dusted with freckles. Her light green eyes have flecks of gold in them he hasn't noticed before.

"A kiss for the road?" Maeve asks. Her face is a mixture of emotions that Aethon is starting to recognize now. She wants more, but she's holding herself back. She's right to do so - they have to concentrate on catching Daik.

"One for the road," he murmurs. Then he pulls her to him, and their mouths crash together in a desperate kiss. Aethon slides his tongue against hers, claiming her mouth as his heart beats so hard it feels like a drum. She's warm against him, hard and soft, and the kiss feels like a challenge. Aethon rises to it. She bites down on his lower lip, forcing a groan out of him. They're both panting a little as they part, and Maeve steps back. Aethon is pleased to see she's flushed, and looks just as out of sorts as he feels.

She straightens her jacket and sits down in her captain's chair. Instead of going to the co-captain seat, Aethon strides up beside Maeve, resting his hand on the chair behind her back. It feels like he belongs right here. Next to her.

"The Archer is charged and ready!" TAI chirps.

Maeve leans back. "Let's fucking go."

CHAPTER 19

Broken

Maeve

Scimitar Starbase is swarming with ships. It's a similar build to Omega Starbase - shaped like a gigantic, five mile long hourglass. Maeve scans the area looking for Daik's tiny Needle-class ship, but there's too much traffic. Huge Yacht-class ships move ponderously through it all, forcing all the smaller ships to skirt to the side.

"Hail the starbase," Maeve says to TAI. "Use every piece of leverage you can - every Two Roses code we have at our disposal."

"On it!" TAI says.

"Where does the tracker say he is?" Aethon asks, turning over his shoulder.

Maeve throws the tracker up on the viewscreen again. The little red light that has taunted them for weeks now is blinking at the very bottom of the starbase. "He's here. He's in a bay." Her fists clench. "We can't sit here and wait for clearance! If we do, he'll beat us to the Lightway."

"I'm in the digital docking queue, Maevey," TAI says, her voice tight. "I'm trying - but we're ninety-sixth in line - they're examining our Two Roses credentials."

"According to my research," CAL says. "Lightways are always located at the top of starbases due to -"

"At the top?" Aethon interrupts, gesturing out the viewscreen. "So if Daik had to dock his ship near the bottom we could still get to him before he gets to the Lightway?"

"Definitely," CAL replies. "There's no fast way to get from the bottom of the starbase to the top - except for lifts exclusive to security. All starbase visitors are restricted to floor to floor lifts, or stairs."

"I wouldn't put it past Daik to sneak onto a security lift somehow," Maeve growls. "Where are we in line now?"

"Still ninety-sixth, Maevey - they're as slow as molasses."

"Shit," Aethon growls. He locks eyes with Maeve, his lips pressed together.

"Fuck it," Maeve snaps. They can't wait any longer. She grabs the joystick and accelerates into traffic, heading for the top of the silver starbase.

"Hell yeah!" Aethon says, sitting down hard in his chair as Maeve whips the Archer around a small, Ursa-class ship. Maeve feels her lips spread into a snarling kind of grin, adrenaline flooding her veins. There's no real order to the chaos of the traffic this far from the starbase. Ships of all sizes are waiting for clearance to dock, or moving back and forth in computer generated holding patterns. Maeve weaves through the traffic and up over a huge Yacht-class ship, barely missing the decorative dorsal fin along the top. The ship's captain sends them a swear-ridden hail that

TAI quickly swipes off the viewscreen.

There are billboards hanging in space, advertising different services and stores onboard Scimitar Starbase. A huge blinking sign with an image of a grinning person with fangs and unnatural silvery blue eyes proclaims that Scimitar has a fully equipped mod-medical service. The words splashed across the top say - "Change your look, change your life!"

"Wow Maevey - that billboard organic is setting off my sexuality subroutines!" TAI chirps.

"You have weird taste in organics," Maeve replies. Aethon lets out a bellow of a laugh and Maeve smiles, swerving underneath the billboard. The banter and laughter feels frenzied. They know that this is their last chance to catch Daik. Everything rides on this. Pressure to catch the smuggler compels her. If they don't get this bounty, all of their work and sacrifice will have been for nothing. But if they do get the bounty - what happens then?

Every thought flies out of her head as Maeve banks hard to the right to avoid another Yacht-class ship decked out with blinking party lights. This is no different than piloting through the drones and ships around Tellamar, or through the Keidar Belt. Except this time, Maeve isn't moving slowly, or very carefully. She jolts to the side as the Archer's port wing clips a billboard advertising a clothing store. Aethon grips the dash and hauls himself back upright.

As they get closer to the starbase, the chaos of ships morphs into clogged lines waiting to dock.

"Anything from Scimitar yet?" Maeve asks. They're zooming past a line of ships waiting to dock at one of the higher bays closer to the Lightway.

"We've moved up one space in line, Maevey," TAI says. "I told them about Daik, but they don't seem to care that they have a criminal on board!"

"Fuck," Aethon snaps. "What are you going to do?" he asks, spinning toward her in his chair.

The starbase is approaching quickly, the structure taking up the entire viewscreen, but Maeve doesn't let up on the Archer's acceleration. Her gaze flicks across the line of ships waiting to dock. There's a garishly decorated Yacht-class ship up next. It looks like the galaxy's ugliest bumblebee, painted with gold and black stripes.

"How do you feel about pissing some people off?" Maeve asks, raising one brow.

"I'm obviously for it," Aethon replies, his nose scrunching as he gives her that huge, charming grin. "Let's go, Bladesy."

Maeve laughs and accelerates the Archer even faster, the ships next to them nothing but silver and black blurs. Hails from Scimitar Starbase are popping up on the viewscreen now, blinking urgently, but she ignores them. She sees when the bright blue forcefield drops to let the bumblebee Yacht-class ship into the bay. When they're almost level with the ship, Maeve decelerates hard and slips the Archer into the sliver of space between the edge of the bay doors and the gigantic ship.

"Fuck yeah!" Aethon says, pumping a fist.

Maeve feels a rush of pride at his approval. The bay is full of ships docked in designated spots all over the floor. There are oxygenated walking tubes that go from each spot to a larger hallway and into the center of Scimitar Starbase. Maeve makes for a small spot near the main entrance to the starbase, ignoring the increasing number of hails clouding her viewscreen.

Aethon stands and starts rushing around the ship gathering things. Maeve feels it when he slips a portable oxygen unit around the back of her neck, but she doesn't thank him, too focused on landing the Archer without hitting any of the approaching starbase guards or dock workers.

There's a crowd of people waiting when she lands the Archer gently in the marked off space. Maeve shutters the viewscreen, the metal sliding down, leaving them in darkness. The internal lights immediately flick on. Maeve jumps up from her chair and checks over her weapons - her pulse gun in her shoulder holster, a knife strapped to her thigh, another in her boot. She tucks the portable oxygen unit under her jacket against her skin.

"They're not allowing us to connect the ship to the oxygenated walking path," CAL says.

"We figured," Aethon replies. "Keep the ship ready, you two."

A fist bangs on the door of the Archer - likely one of the starbase guards. Maeve ignores them for the moment.

"Keep your tabs on you!" TAI says. "None of that disconnected stuff like on Valley Starbase! And once you get through this cattywampus, I want you to turn these earpieces on."

"We want to be able to speak with you and keep track of you," CAL adds.

"What?" Maeve asks. A light blinks on the dash and the 3D printing compartment opens to reveal two earpieces.

"You made these?" Aethon asks.

"Of course!" TAI chirps. "I know you have boundaries or whatnot - but after what happened at Valley, I'm not eager to not be able to speak to my Maevey or my Aethony."

Aethon blinks at her, his mouth open, but seems to not have any words.

Maeve bites her lip, finding it hard not to laugh despite the circumstances. "Aethony?"

"I'm workshopping it!" TAI says defensively. "I'll come up with something to your liking, Aethon honey."

"I hope you don't mind if I continue to call both of you 'captain'," CAL says.

Maeve rolls her eyes, but warmth spreads through her chest at the same time. Aethon smiles. "I knew I liked you, TAI."

"Yes indeedy!" she replies.

Maeve grabs the two earpieces from the dash. She hands one to Aethon who winds it around his ear.

"Can we talk to each other on these too?" he asks.

"Of course!" TAI chirps.

Maeve nods and puts her earpiece on as well. "Thank you, TAI."

"Anything for my Maevey!"

There's another bang on the outside of the Archer and Maeve shifts toward the door.

"I'll talk us past them," Aethon says. "Make your Two Roses crest as obvious as possible." He adjusts his pin on his jacket and Maeve does the same. "And don't reach for your weapon."

"But -" Maeve starts, unease curling in her gut.

Aethon shakes his head. "Don't do it, Maeve. Or they'll have us in lock up so fast we'll never get a chance to explain who we are."

"Fine," she grumbles. "We're kind of on the clock here though."

He nods. "I know. Trust me."

"I do." Her easy, automatic response surprises her. But she does trust him. With her life.

Another bang rattles the Archer and Maeve snarls at the sound.

Aethon turns to her, the low light from the Archer making his jawline sharp. "No matter what happens," he says. "I'm grateful we got to spend this time together, Maeve." His whisky eyes are hard, and Maeve feels stronger with him standing next to her.

"I'm glad too," she says, swallowing through the tightness in her throat. "But they need to stop fucking with my ship." She reaches around her neck and turns on the portable oxygen unit. She unfolds the facemask and slides it on, the clear, oval plastic covering her from forehead to chin. The edges suction into place. Aethon does the same.

"Open the door, TAI!" Maeve orders.

The doors open and a Scimitar Starbase guard is there. His uniform is gray and he has a patch with his name and rank. He's broad and he blocks the whole door, his own oxygen unit on, his bearded face set in a frown. Maeve can see a few more guards and dock workers hanging back behind him. She keeps her hands open and still at her sides.

"Man alive - Officer Pelham!" Aethon says, opening his arms wide. "I haven't seen you in years!" His friendly voice makes the guard pause.

"Do I know you?"

"Of course!" Aethon says. "Aethon Trell? I work

for Two Roses! Remember that weeklong party on Denmat in '88? The snake-charmer?" He laughs and runs a hand back through his hair in a disarming way, and Maeve watches with something bordering on awe. "We called you Pissed Pelham? You were so drunk you probably don't remember. Listen man, I know we broke a few rules by cutting in line and landing here, but do you know you have a seriously dangerous criminal on board?"

The guard is looking at Aethon with clear confusion, but he doesn't do anything when Aethon takes his tab out. Aethon pulls up the photo of Daik from his bounty posting. In the photo, Daik's hair is slicked back and he looks over his shoulder, his eyes narrow, wearing a beat up red jacket. He has that fake beard on that somehow makes him look even more like a rat.

"This guy - Daik Montrose - is on your starbase," Aethon says, tapping the tab. "He's got a Needle-class ship docked below. And no offense, Pelham - but he's probably fucking some shit up while you're holding us up here." He points to his Two Roses crest and Maeve's. "We've been hunting him for weeks. He's wanted by Brimstone. You don't want to be the reason Brimstone doesn't get this son of a bitch, do you?"

"Brimstone Industries?" the guard asks. Maeve isn't positive due to the guard's oxygen mask, but she's pretty sure his face pales.

"Yeah - the mining corp," Aethon says with a nod. "We need to get this guy locked up."

"Wait here a minute," the guard says, holding up a hand. He steps back out of the Archer and taps his earpiece. He mutters something to the person on the other end, turning away from them. The other guards and workers outside are talking to each other now, clearly waiting for orders from Officer Pelham.

Maeve shifts from one foot to the other, her arms crossed tightly over her chest. "Do you actually know this guy?" she asks Aethon quietly.

Aethon shrugs. "Never seen him before in my life."

"You are a master bullshitter," she says, turning to look him in the eye. "I love it."

Aethon shrugs and winks. "Thank you, Bladesy."

The guard turns back and points over his shoulder with his thumb. "You're cleared to go. I ran the credentials your AI sent over. And we have video of someone of this description with a Needle-class ship entering Scimitar thirty minutes ago, but we can't tell for certain if it's Montrose. The ship is registered under a different name."

"Shut down all ships entering and leaving the starbase," Aethon demands. "And stop the Lightway from leaving!"

The guard shrugs helplessly. "I'll do what I can, but if we can't confirm the identity of the criminal the higher ups won't like shutting the starbase down or causing an unnecessary panic. Do you realize how many credits they'd lose?"

"Fuck," Maeve grits out. "Move!"

The guard steps to the side and Maeve and Aethon sprint out of the Archer, wheeling toward the doors to the main area of the starbase.

"We're going to have to split up to find him!" Aethon says. He skids to a stop in front of the doors and slams his hand on the pad to open them. Maeve edges inside the second they slide apart, Aethon right behind her.

"I know," Maeve replies. She doesn't want to leave him, but Daik could be anywhere in the starbase. The tracker was on his ship so it's useless now, but they know he's heading to the Lightway.

The doors behind them close and they hear the hiss of oxygen before the doors to the main area of Scimitar Starbase open, spitting them out into a gigantic open floor crowded with people.

This area of the starbase is a food court. Restaurants and fast food joints are located on the edge of the space, and hundreds of tables are spread throughout the center of the floor which is open to the three levels above. Smells of cooking food and barbeque fill the area. There's a playground shaped like a castle in the very center of the floor. Children crawl all over it, swinging from bars and chasing each other, shrieking with laughter. Adults stand on the edges, talking and watching their children. People are eating at the tables, talking, and playing games. There are so many people. Maeve's stomach sinks. There couldn't be a worse place to chase down a dangerous criminal. The possibility of collateral damage is sky high. Maeve notices that there are large escape pods built into the walls, but it would take way too long to evacuate everyone in this area, and it would likely cause a mass panic.

Maeve pushes her oxygen mask off and it retracts back into the portable unit. Aethon does the same. His eyes flick back and forth, cataloging the people and the set up of Scimitar. According to signs blinking from the ceilings of the hall, the Lightway is three floors up and on the opposite side of the starbase from where they are now.

"I'll take the stairs on the left," Aethon says, pointing to a clear, enclosed stairwell that climbs all the way up to the floor with the Lightway. "You take the ones on the right." Maeve glances the other way and sees an identical stairwell to the right. "We'll meet at the top and if neither of us find Daik before the other, we'll set up outside the entrance to the Lightway and catch him before he boards."

"He's not above using civilians," Maeve says. She meets Aethon's gaze and he nods, his jaw tight.

"We'll have to do everything we can to prevent that," he replies. "Hopefully Pelham is working on convincing the people that run the starbase that they have a serious situation here. But we don't have time to evacuate all these people." He gestures to the hundreds and hundreds of people in front of them.

"I know," Maeve says through clenched teeth. "We need to go."

But both of them pause. The moment feels charged, and Maeve is afraid that if she lets Aethon leave her side, she'll never see him again. She wishes it were an irrational thought, but she knows it's not. Being a bounty hunter is dangerous. It's why she never allowed herself to get close to anyone after her parents died. Why care for someone when they could be ripped from her so easily? She wraps her hand around Aethon's wrist and he tucks a finger under her chin. His eyes flick between hers.

Fuck. She loves him.

"Aethon, I -"

"Not now, Bladesy," he growls. "Not now. I know what you're thinking, and you need to listen to me." He grabs her chin and slants his mouth over hers, the kiss hot, hard, and fierce. He pulls back and meets her eyes again. "We're going to fucking live." He grins. "And then you can tell me everything."

The words they recited to each other over and over again on that escape pod four years ago jolt Maeve back into herself. She nods and lets Aethon's wrist go.

Without another word, they spin in opposite directions and sprint for the staircases. Maeve weaves through the crowd, her boots squealing on the fake wood floors. She's so tall and imposing that most people instinctively get out of her way, but she has to bellow at a few idiots who don't see her coming. She shoulders her way through a group of men and one of them snarls, reaching for her.

"Watch where you're going, bitch!" he bites out.

His hand catches the back of her neck, yanking the portable oxygen unit off. Maeve feels the delicate chain of her croi crystal necklace catch on the oxygen unit, and the chain pulls at her neck, breaking with a snap.

"Get the fuck off of me!" she snarls, spinning and grabbing for her necklace. But he flings the necklace and oxygen unit behind him. Maeve's stomach sinks as she watches her necklace disappear under the feet of the crowd. She doesn't have time to go and find it.

"Think twice before you -" he starts.

"Fuck off!" she growls. She elbows the man in the stomach and he doubles over in pain. Maeve is gone before he or any of his friends can retaliate. Their cries are quickly lost in the bustle of the starbase.

While she runs for the stairs, she scans the crowd for Daik. The last time she saw him in person was on Alpha Starbase when he had almost killed her. She allows the rage she feels at that incident to boil up in her stomach. Daik is thin and weasley, a head shorter than her, and six months ago, he had stringy brown hair that fell to his shoulders. His features are small, and he likes to wear disguises. Beards, wigs, eye patches, and occasionally a more expensive mod like a set of sharp teeth, false tattoos, or a skin texture modifier. But Maeve knows she'll recognize him no matter what he's wearing. He has a distinctive way of moving, scuttling like a spider.

Maeve reaches the stairs and begins the climb, each flight of stairs longer and narrower than she would prefer. The stairs are jammed with people climbing slowly, as if they have nowhere of importance to be, which Maeve is sure they don't.

"Can you hear me, Bladesy?" Aethon's voice comes through her earpiece. She shoves past a group of women standing still on a landing and looking out the window at the food court seating area below before replying.

"I hear you."

"I'm almost up here," he says. *"My stairs weren't crowded, but I can see that yours are."*

Maeve looks through the glass at the floor two levels above her and sees Aethon's tall form sprinting for the entrance of the Lightway.

"I'm coming," Maeve says. "Move!" she shouts at the group of people taking their time on the stairs. They look back at her with wide eyes and skirt to the side of the stairs.

"I'm going to get them to shut down the Lightway so Daik can't escape," Aethon says.

"Good," Maeve huffs. "Now we just need him to

show his fucking face -"

Maeve shoves the doors at the top of the stairs open and skids to a stop.

Daik Montrose is standing ten feet from her.

Ice and heat fight for dominance in Maeve's chest and her hand is inside her jacket, her fingers around her pulse gun before she can take a breath.

Daik is wearing that same red jacket from his bounty picture, but his face is beardless. He looks exactly how he did on Alpha Starbase. But he's smiling at her. Maeve gets no sense that he feels trapped, no sense that he's panicking. People flood out of the stairway and walk around her, talking and laughing, oblivious to the two people frozen, staring at each other.

"Maeve Bladesbearer," he says, cocking his head to the side. He raises one brow, and smirks at her, his eyes traveling over her body. "The last time I saw you, I thought you were missing an arm?" His voice is slimy, like his throat is coated in whatever grease he uses to slick back his hair.

"He's here," Maeve says quietly through clenched teeth to Aethon.

"He's there?!" Aethon replies, his voice breathless. *"Keep him busy! I'm coming! They won't let him on the Lightway. We got him, Maeve."*

"You thought you'd take me on by yourself again, Bladesbearer?" Daik says with a sneer. "Didn't go so well for you last time."

His taunting means nothing to her. "You're done, Daik," she says, her voice low and venomous. Maeve takes a step toward him and starts to pull her pulse gun out, but Daik holds up a hand.

"I wouldn't come any closer if I were you," he

says. He reaches for his jacket and Maeve tenses, her fingers tight on her pulse gun. But Daik just pulls back his jacket revealing his chest.

He's wearing a bomb.

Maeve doesn't know exactly what kind of bomb it is, but it doesn't matter. It's a black vest loaded with cylinders of explosives taped onto it. Wires connect the cylinders, and a tab rests in the center of Daik's chest. Probably the detonator. Her eyes flick to the people packed around them. The people milling around in the food court below. The children on the playground. How powerful is that bomb? Maeve has no idea. Could it take out the floor? The whole food court? Could it blast a hole in the starbase? If she shoots Daik in the head, will the bomb still go off? It could be connected to his vitals.

She hears her heart pounding in her ears and sweat beads on her neck. She can't let him detonate it. There's no time to evacuate everyone. People will die if he sets off the bomb. Fear is alive in Maeve's chest, tangling through her like the roots of a tree, strangling her.

"You didn't really think you could catch me alone?" Daik says. He drops the edge of his jacket, concealing the bomb. "After your last epic failure? I thought you were smarter than that." He shrugs and Maeve tenses. "I guess I was wrong."

"He's got a bomb," Maeve says. "TAI are you hearing this?"

"*Shit - a bomb?*" Aethon says.

"*Trying to contact starbase security!*" TAI replies. The AI's voice is strained.

Daik raises his brows. "Who are you talking to, Bladesbearer? You have backup after all? Not sure who would ally themselves with you -"

"Shut the hell up." Aethon strides up behind Daik, stopping a good ten feet from the smuggler. "She's not alone," Aethon says, his lips pulled back in a snarl. He has his pulse gun in hand, but he keeps it at his side, clearly wary of the bomb.

"Get the hell away from here!" Maeve shouts at the crowd around them. It doesn't matter if she causes a panic - people need to panic right now. "He's got a bomb! Move!" For good measure, she pushes her jacket back, unholstering her pulse gun and people gasp, starting to push each other to get away. The noise level starts to increase as people shout, but it feels like there's a bubble around her, Daik, and Aethon. Everything else seems muffled.

Daik's eyes narrow, flicking between Maeve and Aethon. He backs up to the railing that overlooks the food court below.

"Take off the bomb, Daik," Maeve says, her voice low. "Disarm it. And come with us. You aren't getting on that Lightway. This ends here."

Daik laughs, but Maeve hears an edge of panic in his tone now. "No fucking way. You'll escort me to the Lightway, and let me board. If you don't -" He shrugs. "It's all over anyway."

"You don't need to do this," Aethon says, gesturing around them. People are avoiding them now, yelling and shoving each other to get away, but there are still people everywhere. Clearly TAI hasn't gotten through to starbase security yet.

"You don't need to hurt anyone," Aethon says slowly to Daik. "Or yourself." He takes a step toward Daik, but stops when the smuggler jerks his hand toward his chest.

"Stay right there!" Daik snaps. "You think I won't blow myself up along with everyone else? If you don't let me on the Lightway that's exactly what's going to happen. I'm not turning myself in. You're right - this ends here. I know what Brimstone does to people who steal from them." He shudders. "And besides, Brimstone wants me alive. Not dead. I'll be worth nothing to you if you drag them my corpse."

Maeve glances over at Aethon. She shakes her head slowly. Daik is serious. Maeve knows it down to her bones. Daik knew exactly what he was getting into when he stole from Brimstone. It was a huge risk, with the potential for a lifetime of payoff. If he succeeded in bringing that stolen information to Dreadnought, they would set him up for life. Protect him. Daik would never want for anything. But the sheer size of his bounty shows how much Brimstone wants him caught. And if Brimstone gets him, Maeve is sure that Daik will wish he had blown himself up. Brimstone believes themselves above the law of the galaxy. They won't hesitate to torture Daik in ways Maeve can't even imagine. Daik's not going to allow himself to be caught. It's the Lightway, or death.

"Maybe I'll just shoot you," Maeve says, meeting Daik's eyes. Her heartbeat is loud in her ears.

"The bomb might be connected to his biosigns," Aethon hisses. "It could go off if he's dead."

"I know," she replies. "But maybe it's not." And maybe if she hits him just right, she can avoid killing him and then they can still get his bounty.

The smuggler smiles and a bead of sweat slides down his temple. "Go ahead," he says. "Risk it."

The air feels unnaturally still. Maeve's eyes flick over Daik's chest where the bomb is concealed behind his jacket. Can she give up the possibility - however small - of bringing Daik in alive and collecting that life changing bounty? She looks out again at the innocent crowd of people in the food court below.

"Let him go," Maeve says. She holsters her gun and Aethon nods, his face tight, but understanding in his gaze. He steps to the side and Daik's face transforms into a goading smile.

"Good choice, Bladesbearer," he sneers.

He turns toward the Lightway and starts walking. Maeve follows only as far as where Aethon stands, watching the smuggler walk away. And with him, six million credits.

"I hate this," Maeve growls. Aethon just nods. His face is a mask of frustration. She realizes that for him, losing this bounty means losing Two Roses. Maeve wraps an arm around his waist and squeezes.

Then Scimitar Starbase security flood out of a hallway and spread themselves out in front of the entrance to the Lightway. Guard after guard, all dressed in gray, pulse rifles at the ready, aiming for Daik.

"Surrender yourself!" one of the guards shouts, his voice electronically magnified. Fear rises in Maeve's chest. Why are they doing this? They know he has a bomb - and they're going to arrest him before evacuating the people below?!

"He's got a bomb!" Maeve cries. "What are you doing?!"

Daik turns around toward them, his face falling from smugness to resignation. His hand seems to rise in slow motion toward the detonator on his chest.

"Fuck -" Aethon says. "No!"

"Stop!" Maeve cries.

Aethon shoves her away, the force of his push sending Maeve six feet back and onto her ass. "Aethon!" she shouts.

But Aethon is already at Daik's side. Maeve shoves herself up with a snarl and starts to run toward them. They're too far. Aethon has Daik wrapped in his arms, and he leaps with the smuggler toward one of the emergency escape pods in the hull of the starbase, kicking the lever to open the doors.

Maeve feels her throat tear with a scream as the doors of the hatch open and Aethon shoves Daik inside. The doors don't completely close before the bomb goes off. The explosion is deafeningly loud, and orange fire shoots up and out, mostly contained by the escape pod doors, but a line of concussive power blasts through the vertical crack directly at Aethon. He flies backwards, his body crumpling in on itself as he absorbs the explosion. He hits the railing with a sickening crunch and collapses to the floor.

Horror cracks through Maeve like lightning, freezing her in place. Is Aethon - is he - he can't be -

Starbase guards swarm the area, their big armor plated bodies obscuring her view of Aethon. Maeve's ears ring from the force of the blast, and she stumbles forward. "Aethon!" she cries. Her voice sounds muffled in her ears. She shoves her way through the guards, stopping when she reaches the railing.

Aethon lies crumpled on the ground, blood pooling around his broken body.

CHAPTER 20

After

Aethon

"We need to get him to a doctor!"

The voice sounds thick and wavery, like Aethon is hearing it underwater.

"He needs a surgeon! Do you have anyone here? We're members of the Guild of Two Roses - they'll pay well for the medical attention you give him, I promise."

The words don't quite make sense. He can hear them, but pain is making him unable to comprehend anything. Aethon has never experienced pain like this. Even when he was burning up in the corona of that star - it wasn't like this. That was building heat, all consuming, cooking him, making his skin tender and raw. This is deep, radiating pain. Aethon feels like he's being fractured from the inside out. His back is pure misery. He opens his mouth to try to release some of the pain through something - a yell, a scream - anything, but no sound comes out. There's brightness behind his eyes, and he opens his eyelids a millimeter. It's the hardest thing he's ever had to do.

"Stop trying to die!"

The voice breaks through his pain. He'd know it

anywhere. Sharp and so, so angry. That voice haunts his dreams in the best way. Maeve. He can barely see her face, but he can tell it's flushed with exertion, and she has blood along her jaw and cheek. Is she hurt? Aethon hopes she's not hurt.

"You asshole," she snarls at him. "You will not die on this fucking starbase, Aethon Trell!"

If he could speak, he'd reassure her. He doesn't want to die. What had he done? That's right. He had shoved Daik into that escape pod. Tried to contain the blast of his bomb. And if Maeve is still breathing, he succeeded. Fiery pain lances through him as someone else kneels beside him, jostling his body. Well, he had mostly succeeded.

"A surgeon is coming," someone says.

"Tell them to *hurry!*" Maeve snaps.

"They're -" The words trail off and Aethon's eyes close. He can't keep track of the rest of the conversation. The pain is too much. Everything fades away to smothering blackness.

The next time Aethon wakes, he's on a ship. He blinks a few times, trying to focus on the dark metal ceiling above him. He's sore, but not unbearably so. He tries to shift, but a sudden pain in his mid-back makes him pause. He carefully pushes himself up and back against soft pillows.

"Captain Trell!" CAL's voice is a welcome sound. "You're awake!"

Aethon nods, but the movement hurts, and he raises a blessedly uninjured arm to rub at the back of his neck.

"I'm awake," he says, his voice hoarse.

He runs a hand lightly along the skin at the back

of his neck and it feels odd. There's a bump close to his shoulders and his fingers trace along it, feeling the raised tenderness of it. Is it a scar?

"Aethon!"

He looks up to see Maeve standing in the doorway. Aethon realizes he's on the Archer. And in Maeve's bed. The engines hum comfortingly, and the lights are low. She strides up to him and picks up a glass of water from the bedside table and hands it to him. He suddenly realizes how thirsty he is and tips the glass to his lips, gulping down the cool water.

"They said you might not wake up for a day," Maeve mutters. "I swear, those doctors know nothing." She carefully sits down on the bed next to his hip, facing him.

She's wearing dark pants and a thin, gray t-shirt. Her hair is gathered into a loose bun behind her head, and a few wine red strands frame her face. Aethon reaches up and catches her chin between his thumb and forefinger. She pauses, mid-reach for the empty glass. Her face is pale, making her freckles stand out, and there are dark circles under her eyes.

"Daik is dead," Maeve says bluntly.

Everything comes rushing back to Aethon. The crowds of people on Scimitar Starbase, the bomb strapped to Daik's chest, the Lightway, the guards. Aethon remembers shoving Maeve as far from Daik as he could before he lunged for the smuggler. He knew he had to contain the bomb, and the escape pod was the only thing he could think of. The only thing that might work.

"Did anyone -" he starts.

"No one else died," Maeve says. She pulls his hand

down from her chin and threads their fingers together. "You saved everyone in the food court. Everyone on those three floors. Including me."

Relief is sharp within him. "Good."

"If either of us had hunted him alone, we'd be dead," Maeve says, her tone dark. "And a lot of other people would be dead too. I never could have done it alone." She murmurs the last sentence, almost as if she's just talking to herself.

"I'm so glad you're ok," Aethon says, brushing his thumb over her hand. His emotions are raw and tangled, but the fact that Maeve is sitting here next to him is a miracle.

Maeve's brows narrow. "You almost died, though." She gestures to him with her free hand. "Let's catalog your injuries, shall we? Lacerated cheek, shoulder, arm, stomach. Shrapnel lodged in both legs. Nicked artery in your thigh. Burned face and neck - oh," she pauses and glares at him so hard that Aethon winces. "And a broken fucking back."

"Um," Aethon says, giving her a small smile. "Whoops?"

"Shut up, *artrenn*," she mutters. "It's a good thing there was a fully equipped surgical suite on Scimitar. They had better equipment than Two Roses." She gestures to his body. "They were able to knit you right up. They deal mostly in mods though, so at first I was worried the doctors might do a hack job on your spine."

"A hack job?" Aethon asks. He reaches back feeling the ropy scar that starts at his neck. "They healed me though?"

Maeve nods. "Like I would have let them touch you if they hadn't promised me you'd be alright." She sighs. "Still, most of their expertise is with mods. You know, superficial stuff. Colored irises, gemstone teeth and nails, fangs. But they also do limb replacements for rich people who want bionic limbs instead of flesh." She taps him on the thigh. "You didn't need a limb replaced, but because of that, I trusted them to be able to fix your spine without fucking it up."

Aethon blinks, the amount of information momentarily overwhelming. "Damn. Thank you, Maeve. How did you afford it?"

Maeve gives him a wan smile. "Drained most of my account. I'm hoping Two Roses will reimburse me, but -" She shrugs. "Now that you don't have the money to pay your dues, I'm not sure they'll consider it a wise investment to pay for a former guild member's medical bills."

A former guild member... shit. Defeat makes his shoulders slump.

"The bounty," Aethon says. "Brimstone wanted Daik alive, didn't they."

Maeve nods. She looks so tired. Aethon wants to draw her to him, but he feels too weak and sore to do so. "Fuck," he murmurs. "I'm sorry, Maeve."

That bounty was supposed to be her ticket out of this life. Instead she's creditless, bountyless, and stuck with him - injured and useless.

She shakes her head. "You know, having those credits would be great, but even before this, when I thought we were going to catch Daik - I knew I didn't want to retire on Kespar-2."

Aethon looks up at her, surprise filtering through his body. "What?"

"It was Tellamar that did it," she says. Her

eyes are tired, but she squeezes his hand and Aethon squeezes back.

"It was hard for you to see your people like that," Aethon says.

"And doing something to help them felt... right," Maeve adds with a shrug.

"It felt good to me too," he says. He remembers talking with the refugees during the ten hour trip from Tellamar to January Starbase, TAI translating the entire time. Aethon liked getting to know those people. He felt a small sense of victory when a few of them started speaking to him in Standard. It was like no bounty he had ever chased. The hunt can feel futile. After all, as the second rule of Two Roses says, crime is endless. But instead of returning to Brix-9 with a criminal in tow, turning them in, and going right back out again for another, Aethon had felt a sense of pride at being able to help the Tellamari. His help mattered to them. Hopefully it was the lift they needed to be able to turn around and help someone else.

"I think I want to do more of that," Maeve says. "More of what we did on Tellamar. I don't know exactly what or how yet."

Aethon smiles and lifts a hand to caress her cheek. "I like that idea."

"I'm sorry about Two Roses," she says, shaking her head. "I know the guild is important to you. If I had the credits, I'd pay your dues."

Aethon shrugs. The loss isn't nothing and he doesn't want to act like it is. The Guild of Two Roses saved him - an angry, grief ridden young man - all those years ago. But it's not Maeve's fault.

"I've been wondering what else might be out

there for me," he says. "So maybe this isn't the worst thing. I've been thinking about what we were able to do on Tellamar too." He shifts and winces at the pain in his back. "But Maeve - I'll pay you back for the medical bills as soon as I can. I'm sorry -"

"Don't you dare apologize," Maeve says. He looks up and sees her green eyes are sparkling with unshed tears. "Your decision on Scimitar saved me. And so many others. I'll never be able to repay you for it."

"You don't owe me anything -" Aethon protests.

"I'd be dead if you hadn't -" she says at the same time. Maeve stops and shakes her head, a tiny smile curving her lips.

"What?" Aethon asks.

She sighs. "Maybe we should stop keeping track of what we owe each other," she says with a shrug. "Because I don't think we're ever going to stop saving each other, and keeping track of it is going to get annoying as hell."

Warmth blooms in Aethon's chest. "Yeah? Why's that?"

Maeve glances at the ceiling. "Go on, Maevey," TAI chirps. "Just like we practiced."

Aethon smiles, feeling confused, and tilts his head to the side as he watches Maeve gather herself.

"I wanted to tell you this on the starbase," Maeve says. "But that wasn't the right time. I think I've known for a while, but I was scared."

Aethon holds up a hand. "What is it, *chrissah?*" he murmurs. He wants to hear her say the words.

Maeve swallows hard before meeting his gaze again. "I love you," she says. She winces, her shoulders rising as her cheeks flush. Aethon brings her hand to his mouth and kisses her fingers, not breaking eye contact with her. "Well," she says. "Aren't you going to say anything?"

"I love you too," he says.

Maeve's face softens, her eyes locked on his.

"Butter my butt and call me a biscuit!" TAI exclaims. "The organics figured it out, CAL!"

"Took them long enough," CAL mutters.

"Yeah, yeah," Maeve says, looking up at the ceiling with an arched brow. "Thanks, you two."

Aethon chuckles and catches Maeve's chin, pulling her in for a soft kiss. Despite everything they have lost, Aethon feels like the galaxy is his for the taking. Spread out wide for him and Maeve, the possibilities endless. Maeve deepens their kiss, and his back twinges. He groans a little in pain, making her lean back, her brows knitted together with concern.

"I'm fine," Aethon says, waving her off. "I don't know that I can fuck you how I'd like to right now, but -"

Maeve raises her brows. "No sex. Not for a week. Doctor's orders."

Aethon grins. "You asked them when we could have sex?"

She shrugs. "It was in your post-surgical report."

"And I see you went right to that section of the report, you horny little -"

"Did not!" Maeve says. But she bites her bottom lip as she tries not to laugh. She reaches up to where her necklace is, but her hand falls back quickly. Aethon notices the chain is missing.

"Your necklace," he says. "Where is it?"

Maeve shakes her head. "I lost it on the starbase. Some asshole ripped it off along with my oxygen unit."

Aethon presses his lips together. "I'm sorry, *chrissah*."

Maeve shrugs, but Aethon knows how much that necklace meant to her. It was a piece of Tellamar she was able to carry with her.

"Sorry to interrupt, Maevey," TAI says. "But we're approaching the jump point. Do you want to head on through?"

Maeve's features fall and she narrows her gaze as she looks at him.

"Where are we?" Aethon asks. He leans back against the pillows. "Actually, how long was I out?"

"You were in Scimitar Starbase's medical isolation unit for five days," Maeve says. "When you were stable enough, they released you to me. That was twelve-ish hours ago. So it's been almost six days since you got yourself blown up."

"Six days," he repeats.

"And as it turns out," Maeve says slowly. "Scimitar is right in the path of a set of jump points that lead to the outer edge of colonized space." She leans forward. "We're three jumps from Freehail."

Aethon sucks in a breath. "Fuck."

Maeve shakes her head. "I wouldn't go there without your permission. But I didn't know where else you could recover. Your rooms on Brix-9 are being packed up right now. CAL got a message from Hera Laurent two days ago asking for the credits for your dues. When we couldn't pay, she said she would start packing your shit."

Aethon winces. "Cold."

Maeve nods. "I know." She leans forward. "Aethon, I understand not wanting to go home. Fuck, do I ever understand." She gives him a grim smile. "But your parents are still there. And I know you haven't seen them in years."

Shame coils in Aethon's gut. "You don't understand," he says. "I told myself I wouldn't go back to Freehail until I proved myself. Until I proved -" He takes in a shuddering breath. "- until I proved that I was worthy of this life. A life my brother never got to have." He shakes his head. "And now what do I have to show for all my years of work? No guild membership. No credits. Not even a ship. I've got nothing."

Maeve just looks at him, her green eyes solemn. "I don't know your parents, *artrenn*. But I know you. And I wonder if you've been punishing yourself for something that was never your fault. You never needed to prove that you deserve to be alive even though your brother is gone. You're enough. Just how you are."

Sudden, hot tears brim in Aethon's eyes. No one had ever told him that he was enough. But he had also never confided that fear to anyone. Hearing those words from Maeve means more than if they came from anyone else.

"And if your parents believe differently," Maeve continues, her tone haughty now. "Fuck them. But I doubt they think that at all. I'm sure they miss their son."

"I haven't seen them in fifteen years," Aethon says.

"And I'll never see my parents again, Aethon," Maeve says, narrowing her gaze. "Don't let that happen to you."

She's right. Aethon swipes the tears away from his face and takes a deep breath. "Ok. Let's go to

Freehail."

CHAPTER 21

Home

Maeve

Maeve and Aethon arrive at Freehail, exhausted, battered and low on credits. From orbit, Freehail looks similar to other habitable planets - if a little rougher. Dark green forests blanket almost every continent, edged in unique, black sand beaches. The oceans and lakes are prevalent across the globe, but Maeve can see barren patches of land in the southern hemisphere where Brimstone mined. The planet is scarred. But it looks like it's recovering.

Aethon is sitting in the co-captain's chair, a blanket wrapped carefully around his shoulders. He stares out at the planet below, his eyes hooded, his jaw hard.

"Hailing the Freehail landing system," CAL says.

"My parents live just outside the capital," Aethon says. "It's called Rendar." He points to a sparkling city along the shore of a vast beach. Maeve recognizes the curving lines of the shore as those from Aethon's tattoos.

They had contacted the Trells, and Liadan and Nikair were ecstatic that Aethon was coming home for a while. They were also eager to meet Maeve.

Maeve had decided to take a sabbatical from Two Roses, wanting to help Aethon recover, and figure out what she wants to do next. She still has her guild membership, but it's on hold for a while. She was already ahead on guild dues, so she isn't worried about losing her membership.

"Landing approved at the following coordinates," TAI chirps before rattling off a set of numbers.

An hour later after parking the Archer in a long-term bay on the outer edge of Rendar, Maeve pushes Aethon out of the landing port in a wheelchair they rented.

"I can walk, you know," he grumbles, shifting irritably in the wheelchair.

"I know, but you shouldn't be overexerting yourself," Maeve says, patting him gently on the shoulder.

He glances up and back at her, his eyes narrow. "Mother hen."

Maeve shrugs. "When you're fully recovered sooner than expected, you can thank me."

Outside the bay, the sky is a light, almost cornflower blue. Big, puffy white clouds float overhead, and the sun is bright, making Maeve squint at the crowd around them. There are a lot of people outside the bay, hailing vehicles for rides, or waiting for the mag-rail. Maeve keeps a careful eye on the crowd, watching for anything suspicious. She can see some of Rendar's skyline from here, the silver spired buildings tall and beautiful.

"The air is better now," Aethon remarks, staring

up at the sky. "When I left, the sun was usually shaded orange or red, depending on how bad the pollution was that day."

As they wait for the mag-rail, Maeve moves to stand at Aethon's side, her hand never leaving his shoulder. She watches each person that walks past them, her gaze flicking over their bodies, searching for the telltale signs of hidden weapons.

"You're freaking people out," Aethon murmurs to her.

Maeve looks down at him, narrowing her gaze. "So what?"

Aethon smiles, his hair falling over his forehead, and takes her hand. "You can relax," he says. "Rendar's crime levels are low."

She shrugs and looks down the street, the mag-rail turning a corner in the distance. "So people wouldn't be expecting it."

The mag-rail stops and they board. Maeve puts Aethon's chair in a spot next to the window so that she can sit on the other side of him, creating a barrier between him and anyone else.

As they travel out of the main area of the city, Maeve's anxiety grows. Her knee starts to bounce as she watches the view outside shift from buildings to dense forest. Every few minutes, the forests thin enough so that she can get a glimpse of the ocean. They're almost to their stop. Aethon's parents will meet them at a station close to their house. Maeve swallows hard and she clenches a hand around the armrest of Aethon's wheelchair.

"What's got you wound up so tight?" Aethon asks. She glances at him and he pries her hand off his wheelchair, threading his fingers through hers.

"I don't know," Maeve replies. "Everything."

"It's going to be ok," Aethon says. "My parents are going to love you." He presses a kiss to the back of Maeve's hand and some of her tension eases.

They get off the mag-rail after half an hour. It slides away, revealing a gorgeous view of the ocean. They're on a cliff overlooking the beach, coniferous forests surrounding them. The sun sparkles on the water, and they can hear the waves crashing on the shore. Maeve takes a deep breath, the salty breeze filling her lungs.

"This house we're going to," she says. "Is it where you grew up?" What must it have been like to grow up on a planet like this? She looks back toward Rendar, but the city isn't visible over the tall trees surrounding the mag-rail platform.

"We lived closer to the city," Aethon replies. "I've never been to this house."

"Aethon!"

Aethon whips his head to the right and pushes himself up out of the wheelchair.

Two people are sprinting toward them on a paved path that winds into the forest.

"Mom!" Aethon shouts. "Dad!"

He limps slowly towards them and Maeve watches, emotion tightening her throat. She reaches up to touch her croi crystal necklace, only to realize yet again that it isn't there. The loss is comparably small, but it feels enormous to Maeve. Besides her mother's scarf, she has nothing to remind her of Tellamar or her parents.

She watches as Liadan and Nikair Trell engulf

their son. Aethon is taller than both of them and he laughs, the sound echoing, as they exclaim over him. His mother presses his face between her hands, and his father claps him on the shoulder. Then Aethon gestures at Maeve and they all walk over to her. Her heart flutters in her chest and she leans on the vacated wheelchair with one hand.

"This is Maeve Bladesbearer," Aethon says. "She's my partner." He offers Maeve his hand and she takes it. His grip is firm and warm and she hangs onto him.

"Thank you, *artrenn*," she murmurs.

Liadan's brows rise. She has dark red hair streaked through with white, a larger white section at her right temple. "Tellamari?" she asks, her green gaze serious.

Maeve nods. *"Yir, vai'a."*

Liadan's eyes flick over Maeve in an assessing way and she nods sharply, like she approves of what she sees.

"O'drenn a Freehail, Maeve," Liadan says. *Welcome to Freehail.* She raises a hand and Maeve automatically raises her own. She feels hot tears behind her eyes as Liadan greets her in a traditional Tellamari way only used by family. They press their hands together, palm to palm. When they let their hands fall, Liadan smiles. Maeve feels like a vise has been removed from her chest. She breathes in deeply and smiles back, her other hand still tight in Aethon's grip.

"Yes," Nikair adds. "Welcome! It's wonderful to meet you." He has the exact same eyes as Aethon and his hair is all gray.

Maeve inclines her head. "Thank you for having me."

The Trell family home is a gorgeous refuge. Set into the hillside below the cliff, the house blends into the nature around it. It has huge windows, solar panels on the roof, a family room looking out at the water, a galley kitchen, and three bedrooms.

"We kept a room for you, Aethon - always," Nikair says as they tour the house.

Aethon swallows hard as his father leads them into a bedroom next to the living room, also overlooking the ocean. It has an attached bathroom as well. Art lines the walls - abstract and bold, but somehow calming. Maeve has never stayed in a place that feels this intentional or well cared for.

"Thank you, Dad," Aethon says, his voice rough. "And Mom."

Maeve wraps her arm around his waist, partially for emotional support, but also for physical support as Aethon stubbornly refused to use the wheelchair in the house.

"Do you have an AI security system here?" Maeve asks Liadan. The older woman is fussing with the blue bedspread, pulling it tight across the bed.

She shakes her head. "No, not yet. We've been thinking about it though. Even just an AI system to help with a few technical things around the house would be nice."

"Well," Maeve says, pulling her tab out. "How do you feel about meeting TAI and CAL? They're our ship AIs, but TAI has expressed interest in learning how to be a house AI."

Liadan looks at Nikair who shrugs. "Go for it," he says. The couple exits the bedroom and walks over to the kitchen toward a computer terminal set into the wall.

"They're going to be obsessed with them," Aethon whispers to Maeve.

"Who - the AIs will be obsessed with your parents, or your parents will be obsessed with the AIs?"

"Both," Aethon chuckles.

Maeve smiles and takes her tab over to the computer terminal. She connects the tab and runs through a few security checkpoints.

"Oooh hello lovelies!" TAI chirps, her voice coming from the speakers set into the walls around the house.

"Good afternoon, Trell family," CAL intones.

Liadan raises her brows and glances at Aethon. Nikair chuckles.

The next few days are a whirlwind. Maeve slowly realizes that she needs to recover almost as much as Aethon does. The loss of the bounty, her realization that she loves Aethon, and her break from Two Roses are all still working their way through her mind. What could her life look like now?

Maeve finds herself craving time alone just as much as she needs to spend time with Aethon. She sits for hours on the wide deck overlooking the ocean, just watching the endless waves. She takes walks through the forest with Liadan, both silent. Liadan is a serious woman, but with a sharp sense of humor. Maeve enjoys her quiet companionship.

"When was the last time you had a break?" Liadan asks her after they'd been on Freehail for a week. They're walking a path through the woods that is becoming familiar to Maeve. The trees are tall around them, imposing, but protective at the same time. This place feels spiritual.

"Never," Maeve replies. "I grew up on Tellamar - no time for breaks there. And then I went right into Two Roses after my parents died." She strides cautiously through the forest, concentrating on avoiding large sticks and fallen branches. She realizes that Liadan has stopped walking. Maeve stops and turns around. "What?"

Liadan's lips are tight and she watches Maeve with a tender sort of expression. After a moment, she looks up at the trees around them. "Would you like me to teach you about the forest?"

Over the next few months, Liadan teaches Maeve everything there is to know about the forests of Freehail. She shows her how to walk through the forest without disturbing the plants and wildlife. She teaches her how to recognize certain herbs and make restorative balms and teas. She tells Maeve about how the people of Freehail worked together to restore their world, creating policies and new technologies to fix the harm Brimstone wrought. And through it all, Maeve learns how to relax for the first time in her life. The simple acts of walking and learning about nature are restorative. Maeve realizes that she has never felt consistently safe anywhere. Vigilance has been her companion from Tellamar to Two Roses. She's spent every day wound up tight, waiting for the next blow to fall.

"It's not going to be an overnight fix," Aethon says to her gently one evening when she confides this to him. "This is something you'll be working on for the rest of your life."

"I'd rather not," Maeve grumbles. She leans back

against the pillows of their bed, her arms crossed.

Aethon smiles. "I'll be with you, *chrissah*." He bends to kiss her and Maeve lets him slide his hand down her body and beneath her soft pajama shorts. She inhales sharply as his gentle fingers find their way to exactly where she wants them. She wraps her hands around his bicep.

"I love you," he whispers, his mouth at her ear, his touch teasingly soft.

"I love you," she breathes.

Maeve has never loved someone the way she loves him. Hard and soft, flexible and rigid, tender and fierce. Neither of them are perfect, but both of them are learning.

Every night, Maeve massages a balm Liadan makes into the scar on Aethon's spine, softening the stiffness of it, cooling the inflammation. After he's healed enough, Maeve spends the majority of every day with Aethon. He teaches her how to swim in the cool ocean water. He shows her the beach, the forest, the places he used to play with his brother Devan and their friends. They explore the city, and though Maeve likes the restaurants and parks, she prefers to stay closer to the house.

Aethon takes her to the university where Nikair works and introduces her to people he knew in his youth. Maeve doesn't spend as much time with Nikair as the others, but she likes the man. Aethon tells her that his father seems to still carry the grief of Devan's death, but some of his humor and lightness have returned. Nikair and Aethon take turns telling stories after dinner, priding themselves on making the two stoic Tellamari women laugh.

Maeve and Aethon get to know each other outside the pressure of the hunt. And she only falls more in love with him each day. The fear of losing him is still there, but somehow her acceptance of this love makes it fade. She'd rather love him and lose him than never love him in the first place.

The months pass, and Maeve watches as an invisible burden is lifted from Aethon's shoulders. Yes, he lost his membership in the Guild of Two Roses. But he's more joyful now, more carefree. Maeve never tires of seeing that huge grin on his face.

They make love almost every day, relishing in pleasuring each other. Maeve learns every inch of Aethon's body. She memorizes every little touch and word that makes his eyes darken with desire, or makes him groan with satisfaction. Aethon is constantly pulling Maeve in for lingering kisses, or lifting her onto a convenient boulder in the quiet of the forest and kneeling down to get his head between her thighs.

But even though life on Freehail is good, Maeve knows her time on the planet can't last. After about six months, Liadan makes a Tellamari dish for dinner one night. Maeve smells the *bantai* stew as it's cooking and the scent of the root vegetables and spices send her back to her childhood.

"Where did you get the ingredients to make this?" Maeve asks as they all sit down to dinner.

"I have a few friends who still work on shipping freighters," Liadan says. "They had a shipment of Tellamari vegetables and knew I'd want to purchase some."

Maeve feels Aethon's gaze on her as she tastes the stew. She closes her eyes as the spices linger pleasantly in her mouth. "It's just how I remember," she says.

That evening, Maeve reaches up to her throat and touches the place her necklace used to be. "I can't stop thinking about Tellamar," she says slowly.

Aethon watches her, his eyes serious. They're sitting on the deck overlooking the black sand beach. The sky is clear, and the stars are just starting to come out after a glorious sunset along the ocean horizon.

"I know," Aethon replies. He looks out at the beach and then up at the stars. "Me neither."

"I love it here," Maeve says. "But I don't think I can stay here forever. Not when there are people out there who need my help." She shrugs as she meets Aethon's eyes which glint in the low light. "Is that crazy? That I think I can do something to help Tellamar? I mean, it's a whole planet run by gangs -"

"We can help," Aethon interrupts. "We already did something to help. Makes sense we could at least do that again. We could transport more refugees. And maybe we could do more - with the right resources. We could contact Sylar again."

Maeve is unable to look away from his striking profile as he watches the ocean. "We?" His own inclusion doesn't escape her notice. She doesn't want to ask him to give up this place or his family. But the thought of having him with her makes her feel relieved and happy.

"You're stuck with me, Bladesy," he replies, looking over at her and raising a brow.

Maeve nods. "I suppose I'll learn to put up with you."

He smiles, then narrows his brows playfully. "And we'll need to get the Menace at some point.

Remember how you left it in the fucking Narrows?"

Maeve groans. "I thought we weren't keeping track of things like that anymore? Forgive and forget, love."

"Right," Aethon chuckles. He stands and holds his hand out to her. "Come on, *chrissah*."

She stands and takes his hand, letting him lead her into the house and into their room. They'd adjusted it to suit both their needs over the last few months. The bed is large and extra soft, the comforter and pillows a light shade of blue. There's a tall dresser, a mirror on one wall, and two wingback chairs in front of a large window that looks out over the beach. One of Freehail's three moons is rising over the water, casting a glow on the waves.

Aethon closes the bedroom door and tugs her over to the attached bathroom. There's a generously sized shower in there with a rainfall shower head.

"Shower with me?" he asks. They'd both spent the day on the beach, and Aethon's hair sticks up in the back from how he let it dry. Maeve smiles and nods, starting to remove her clothes.

Aethon reaches back and turns the water on, but keeps his gaze on her. "You're beautiful, Bladesy," he says, his voice low. He pulls off his clothes quickly. His eyes are dark as he drinks her in, and Maeve scans him. He's tanner now from all the time in the sun. His broad chest and flat stomach are freckled, and sparse, dark hair curls on his pecs and down his stomach. He's gorgeous and powerful. Maeve can't help but touch him, running her hands up the black tattoos curling up his body. His cock is heavy against his thigh and Maeve knows exactly how to push him over the edge of desire.

She steps closer to him, her breasts pressing against his chest, and Aethon makes a low sound deep in his throat. He reaches up and pulls the tie out of her messy bun, threading his hand through her long hair. They're so close in height that Maeve only has to just tilt her chin up, and their lips meet. She kisses him slowly, relishing the now familiar feel of him. She slides her hands up his muscular arms, and squeezes his biceps. She can feel his cock beginning to harden against her hip. She knows she'll never stop wanting him.

Aethon slides his hands down her back, caressing her ass, and then pulls her with him into the shower. The warm water rains down on them both and Aethon ducks his head down to press a wet kiss behind Maeve's ear.

"Wash first, *chrissah*," he says. "Then play."

"Not sure when you started thinking you get to tell me what to do," Maeve murmurs, smirking at him. Her hand strays to his half-hard cock, fisting his delicious length and making him groan.

"I seem to remember one specific incident when I fucked you against the wall on the Archer," Aethon replies. He twists his hips and his velvet hard cock away from Maeve's hand and she lets out a small sound of disappointment. "You didn't mind me telling you what to do then."

"True," she murmurs, her stomach coiling at the memory.

Aethon grabs a shampoo bar from the rack behind Maeve and lathers up his hands. He scrubs his hands through hair, his muscles flexing. His back is to her now, and the strong lines of his shoulders and the divots over his perfect ass are hardly less enticing than his cock. Maeve slides her hands gently down the scar on his back and takes the shampoo bar that he hands to her over his shoulder.

Aethon turns while she's lathering up her hair and his his eyes smolder as he takes in the view. She straightens, pushing her breasts towards him teasingly. He groans and cups them, pinching her nipples.

"Not fair," Maeve gasps. But she continues scrunching her fingers through her long hair as Aethon teases her breasts.

They shower quickly, but neither are very good at leaving the other alone. Maeve finds Aethon's body entirely too tempting - what with all those muscles and tattoos - and ends up on her knees in front of him, pressing hot, open mouthed kisses to his stomach and hips, before licking up his length.

"Fuck, Maeve -" he groans. He fists a hand in her hair and Maeve takes him deeper, delighting in the fact that she can make him come undone like this.

After a minute, she stands and Aethon claims her mouth with his. He turns off the water and they stumble out of the shower. He tosses her a towel and Maeve scrubs it through her hair before sliding it over her body in a cursory swipe.

Aethon does an equally shoddy job of drying himself off before he picks Maeve up and carries her into the bedroom, tossing her playfully onto the soft bed. Maeve shrieks with laughter and opens her arms for him. He falls on top of her with a grin, catching himself just before he crushes her.

"You oaf," Maeve snorts, pressing his cheeks between her hands.

"God, I love you," Aethon says. He looks down at

her, his whisky eyes full of tenderness.

"Mmm," Maeve agrees. "I love you too, *artrenn*." It was hard for her to say the words for a while, but now they fall from her tongue easily.

She starts to pull him down into the cradle of her hips, but Aethon pulls back, his face turned toward the dark window.

"Maeve," he says. His voice sounds a little choked. "Look." He sits up and points out the window.

She sits up as well and looks where he's pointing. A swirl of purple and green wavers in the sky above the ocean. It twines like a ribbon of light through the black - dancing, shining. It's joined by another ribbon of purple and green. And then another.

"What is that?" Maeve whispers. She feels like she's witnessing something sacred.

"The aurora," Aethon replies. "I guess the planet has recovered enough from Brimstone's mining for it to be visible again." He slides a hand down her thigh, squeezing her knee. Maeve wraps her hand around his arm. She can't look away from the lights in the sky, mesmerized by their slow, hypnotic dance.

"It's so beautiful," she says.

"It is," Aethon replies. He presses a kiss to her temple and Maeve looks at him. His eyes light up with joy. "That reminds me - I want to give you something."

"I don't want a ring, Aethon," Maeve says, raising her brows. "You're mine and I'm yours. That's good enough for me." She leans back on the bed, propping herself up so that she can see him and the aurora through the window at the same time.

He smiles and presses a kiss to her nose before shoving himself back off the bed. "It's not that." He rummages around in the top drawer of the dresser for a moment and Maeve puts her hands behind her head, content to watch the muscles in his ass flex as he moves. He turns back around, one hand clenched in a fist, hiding something. He lays down next to her and props himself up on one arm.

"What is it?" Maeve asks, looking at his closed fist with interest.

He kisses her again and then holds his fist up and releases his fingers. A delicate gold chain slips down between his fingers and hangs in the air in front of Maeve. A tiny croi crystal is strung onto the chain. Maeve can tell it's not the one she lost, but it's so very similar. A lump rises in her throat.

"I know you lost yours on Scimitar," Aethon says, his voice low. "So I asked my mother if she had any croi crystals lying around. She had a few, and she was overjoyed to know that you would treasure this. I got the chain in town." He gives her a small smile. "I know how much your necklace meant to you," he says. "I hope this one means something to you as well."

"Aethon," Maeve says, her voice thick. "I - I -" But she can't form the words. She takes it from his hand, rolling the tiny raw crystal in between her thumb and forefinger. "It's perfect," she says. "Put it on me?"

Maeve sits up and turns around, lifting her mass of damp hair so that Aethon can put the delicate necklace on. He links the chain together and the crystal falls just below her collarbone. Aethon presses a warm kiss to her scarred shoulder.

"Thank you," she says. She turns and Aethon smiles as he sees how the necklace looks on her.

"Perfect," he murmurs. "Just like you, *chrissah*."

Maeve chuckles. "I'm going to remind you of that when I wake you up too early for your liking tomorrow morning."

Aethon groans. "Mornings are for sleeping. Not exercising or banging around or whatever you do in the ungodly hours before the sun has fully risen."

"How quickly he recants his praise," she says, raising a brow.

"I still think you're perfect," he says. "I just think you're annoying too." He pushes her back against the pillows and slides a hand slowly over her body, stopping just below her navel.

"You're more annoying than me," Maeve protests. "You tried to blackmail me. I haven't forgotten."

"Yeah, yeah," Aethon mutters, leaning down to suck one of her nipples into his mouth. Pleasure shoots down her spine. He releases her with a nip. "You knew it was an empty threat."

"Shut up and put that mouth to good use," Maeve instructs.

Aethon chuckles and kisses his way down her body. "Order me around more, *chrissah*," he says. "Tell me exactly what you want."

An idea sparks in Maeve's mind. "How does your back feel, *artrenn?*"

"Excellent," Aethon replies. He pauses over her stomach, his hands braced on either side of her hips. "Why?"

Maeve grins. "Lie down. I owe you a debt."

Aethon raises one brow, but immediately flips over onto his back.

"What a good boy," Maeve purrs. She pulls the

pillow out from under Aethon's head and then straddles his chest. He slides his hands up her thighs and his eyes light up as he realizes what she wants.

"Finally she pays up," he growls. His eyes narrow with desire as she shifts up, settling her knees on either side of his head. Maeve's core is already slick with need, her heart beating fast, her breathing closer to shuddering. She braces her hands on the headboard and sighs as Aethon pulls her into the perfect position.

"Are you sure -" she starts.

"Sit your pussy on my face," he growls, his hands tight on her hips. "Let me taste you."

Maeve allows him to pull her down and at the first swipe of his tongue on her core, she moans, arching forward. She looks down at him, and he meets her gaze, his eyes blazing as he spears his tongue inside her. Maeve's mouth falls open at the sheer eroticism of the sight. She lets out a halting breath as he eats her out, winding her up to a fast release. Aethon pulls her down harder, his lips finding her clit with the unerring accuracy of six months experience. God, why had she waited so long to be with him? Maeve didn't know it could be this good. But being known - mind, body, soul - is better than anything.

"I'm never giving you up," she gasps. *"Artrenn -"*

Aethon just sucks her clit harder, his hands tight on her ass.

Maeve comes with a full body shudder. She squeezes her eyes shut, colors exploding in the darkness there, reminding her of the colors in hyper jump-point space, or the shifting aurora outside their window. She's boneless by the time Aethon pushes her back onto his chest.

"God, I can't wait to do that again," he growls. He grabs her hips and flips them over, caging her in with his arms.

"Need you," Maeve pants.

"I'm here, *chrissah*," he says. He lifts one of her legs under the knee and Maeve watches as he slides his cock through her folds. She shudders at the hard feel of him and arches back with a moan as he pushes inside. He kisses her as he hooks his elbow under her knee, driving into her. He's so deep. So unbelievably hard. Maeve scrapes her nails up his back as he thrusts into her again and again.

Tension coils in Maeve's stomach again and she wraps both her legs around Aethon's waist pulling him in as deep as she can. He grinds against her clit and pulls her lower lip into his mouth, sucking, biting down, before releasing her mouth. They pant against each other, sharing breath.

Aethon keeps up his rhythm, his hips relentless, his body hard and powerful, complementing every part of her. She squeezes her eyes shut, moaning as her pussy clenches around his length, her orgasm hard. Aethon comes right after her with a groan, his release slick within her.

"Fuck, Maeve," he groans, collapsing on top of her.

She laughs and wraps her arms and legs around him, content to never let him go.

*　　*　　*

The next day is beautiful, and Maeve can't resist the call of the ocean. But the black sand beach near the house gets hot as hell in the afternoon sun.

"Fuck!" Maeve dances along the sand, hopping from foot to foot, sprinting for the water.

"Told you to bring shoes!" Liadan calls from where she sits under a giant umbrella.

"*Y'charit!*" Maeve shouts to her. She spins to look at the older woman and laughs as Liadan flips up her middle finger, returning the sentiment. Maeve turns back around and leaps for the cool water sighing with relief as she splashes in.

"Did you just say - 'fuck you' - to my mother in Tellamari?"

Maeve turns toward Aethon who is standing a bit farther into the water, both hands wrapped around a wooden fishing pole. He's shirtless and wearing black swim shorts. She can't help but examine the scar on his spine as she does every time she sees him without a shirt. It runs from the top of his shoulders all the way down to his hips. But it's fading, the raised pink ridge softening, the color blending in more with the rest of his skin. Maeve is pleased to see in the bright sunlight that her hard work massaging the healing balm into his scar is paying off.

"You're too sensitive, *artrenn*," Maeve says, kicking a splash of water towards him. "She's Tellamari. If you don't insult a Tellamari daily, they'll start to think you don't care."

Aethon winks and recasts his line farther from Maeve's splashing and stomping. "Well then," he says. "Have I said - *fuck you* - to you today, *chrissah?*"

Maeve flips Aethon off before diving into the cool water. The water slides over her mostly bare skin like a dream. She's only wearing a small swimsuit. Maeve had never worn a swimsuit before - the tiny oceans on

Tellamar were far from her home and water was too precious to play with. It had taken her a good month before she was willing to bare herself enough to wear the skimpy suit. It wasn't because she was embarrassed or feeling modest, but rather it was hard for her to allow herself to be that physically vulnerable. But now she loves the feel of the water on her bare skin. It makes her feel alive.

Maeve pops her head above the surface and treads water - something Aethon had taught her to do. She squints at the sun sparkling on the black sand, and then spots Nikair walking down from the house waving both his arms, clearly trying to get their attention.

"Aethon!" he shouts. "Maeve!"

Maeve swims back toward the shore, reaching her feet down and digging them into the sand. She runs out of the water, jogging toward Nikair where he waits next to Liadan, the sand not quite as hot on her wet feet. Aethon joins her, jogging sedately next to her.

"Wonder what this is about," he says.

They reach the umbrella and Maeve sees that Nikair is holding a tab in his hand.

"You got a call," he says, a little out of breath. "CAL insisted I take the tab to you so you could talk to whoever it is."

Maeve looks over at Aethon, her brows narrowing. CAL and TAI have been enjoying learning how to be house AIs, practicing security procedures, and absorbing all the digital information the local university has to offer. TAI is set on making the Trell house the most secure one on Freehail - or any other planet for that matter.

"This better not be another call from the

sexuality specialist at the university," Aethon mutters, reaching forward to take the tab from his father. TAI and CAL had also audited several of the university's classes about sexuality, gender, and biology prompting multiple interesting calls from professors.

Nikair chuckles. "I don't think so."

"It's Bell Sylar!" CAL says, his voice stern from the tab.

Maeve's stomach jolts. She grabs Aethon's arm and pulls him over to a shady spot underneath a tree at the edge of the beach.

"I know you said we should contact her," Maeve says. "But did you do that already?"

Aethon shakes his head, droplets of water falling off the ends of his hair. "No. Coincidental timing I guess." He shoves his wet hair back over his head. Maeve doesn't bother. He nods to her and clicks on the call, reinitializing the audio and video.

"Well, aren't you two a vision," Sylar says. She's sitting in the same chair as the last time they spoke, with the same nondescript wall behind her. Her curls are shorter, cropped close to her head, and her glasses are hooked in the collar of her sky blue sweater.

"Hello, Sylar," Aethon says. "I'm surprised to hear from you."

She nods. "And I'm surprised you two are still alive. I heard about the incident at Scimitar Starbase. I'm truly sorry about the bounty." Her tone is sincere, and Maeve presses her lips together.

"Yeah," Aethon says with a shrug. "You win some, you lose some. But we both survived."

Maeve squeezes his waist out of view of the camera.

Sylar nods. "Indeed. How lucky." She squints at them. "Well, you both look hale and hearty. And rather sunkissed. Where are you?"

"A planet on the edge of colonized space," Maeve interjects.

Sylar chuckles. "Fine. Don't tell me. But I have my suspicions. Regardless, I'm looking to hire a few people for a job." She narrows her gaze. "A job that needs to be kept quiet."

"And you thought of us?" Aethon asks, raising a brow.

Sylar shrugs. "You were both very helpful before. And I heard you might be in need of some credits."

"What's the job?" Maeve asks.

Sylar nods and raises a hand to point at Maeve. "See? That's why I like you, Bladesbearer. You get right to the point." She clasps her hands in her lap and her face falls into serious lines. "Things on Tellamar are getting worse."

Dread grips Maeve's gut. "What's happening on Tellamar now?" she asks.

Sylar shakes her head. "More and more people are being coerced into working for the mining corps. More and more people want to escape. I'm hearing rumblings from the Tellamari underground. Some people think civil war is imminent."

Maeve looks at Aethon, her eyes wide. "Civil war?" he asks.

Sylar nods. "And they need help. They need weapons. Resources. Evacuation of children and those unable to fight." She sighs. "They need a lot. But I thought we could start with a few more evacuations. And perhaps a weapons drop to one of my contacts on

Tellamar."

Maeve's mind is racing. This is what she's been waiting for. She wants to help the Tellamari people. But is she ready to leave Freehail? This planet has become a home for her. A refuge. But as she meets Aethon's gaze, Maeve knows down to her bones that this is what she wants to do. This is what she needs to do. As long as Aethon is by her side, she can do anything.

"So this isn't one job," Aethon says. "It's a whole host of them."

Sylar shrugs. "We could work on a job by job basis. You could do what you can and decline if something is too much." She shakes her head. "Tellamar needs help. And frankly, I don't know many people who are all that familiar with the planet or who care about what happens there."

Maeve squeezes Aethon's hip again and he nods at her, his eyes full of emotion.

"We'll discuss it and get back to you," Aethon says. "Send us a number we can call you at."

Maeve slides her hand up Aethon's back as he finishes up with Sylar and ends the call.

"What was that all about?" Nikair asks from where he sits next to his wife under the umbrella.

"A job opportunity," Aethon replies.

"I want to do it," Maeve says. She turns towards him, running her hands up his arms. "If you don't want -"

"I want to do it too," Aethon interrupts. He cups Maeve's cheeks, his eyes meeting hers. His lips spread wide in a grin. "This is what we've been waiting for, Maeve."

She smiles, her heart pounding in her chest,

nerves and excitement making her feel buzzy. But then she looks over his shoulder at Liadan and Nikair. At the ocean.

"Can we leave Freehail?" she asks, her voice low. "I love it here."

"And I love being here with you," Aethon replies. He presses a kiss to her forehead and leans back, sliding his hands down to her shoulders. "Why don't we make this our home base?"

A home. Maeve's chest is tight and she squeezes Aethon's arms. "Getting involved with a potential civil war will be dangerous," she says. "The last thing I want is to bring trouble back to your family, or the people of Freehail."

"I know," Aethon agrees. "We'll be careful. And we'll talk to my parents about it beforehand."

"I suppose TAI has made your parents' house safer and more secure than almost anywhere else in the galaxy - maybe even Two Roses headquarters on Brix-9," Maeve says. She looks over to where Liadan and Nikair are talking together.

"They don't want to go fifteen years without seeing us again," Aethon says quietly.

Maeve's heart squeezes at her inclusion in that statement. "You think we could really have all of that?" she asks, looking up at Aethon again. "Do jobs to help Sylar's underground and have a place to come home to?"

Aethon nods. His eyes are clear and he raises a palm to her cheek, his thumb stroking her skin. "Yes." His voice is firm and steadfast.

Maeve believes him.

*   *   *

A week later, Maeve and Aethon are on the Archer again, orbiting Freehail. Maeve tugs at the collar of her jacket, unused to the restrictive clothing after so long on the planet below. She smiles as she tucks her new croi crystal necklace carefully beneath her shirt.

Aethon spins in the co-captain's chair and meets her gaze with a grin.

"Plot a course to the nearest jump point, TAI," Maeve says. She crosses one leg over the other, her hands sliding down the familiar armrests of her chair.

"On it, Maevey-pie!" TAI chirps. "I love being a house AI, but I missed the Archer!"

"It is quite nice being out in space again," CAL adds. "Though I was hoping to audit more classes at the university."

Maeve smiles and Aethon chuckles. "We'll be back here before too long," he says.

"Course plotted, Maevey!" TAI says.

Anticipation sends a thrill down Maeve's spine and she leans forward. "Let's fly."

THE END

PRONUNCIATION GUIDE

Aethon: AY-thon
Artrenn: ar-TREN
Chrissah: kree-SAH
Croi: croy
Daik: dayk
Devan: de-VAHN
Liadan: LEE-a-den
Maeve: MAYv
Nikair: NEEK-air

TELLAMARI LANGUAGE TRANSLATIONS

Words

Artrenn: guide

Chrissah: little river. Used as a term of endearment.

Croi la fenya: heart of the desert. A common type of purple crystal found on Tellamar.

Den: no

Vai'an: sir

Vai'a: ma'am

Yir: yes

Phrases

Mai'atha gen a nystra dotoir - ma'chriss artrenn a la croi.

Take my body tonight, beloved guide of my heart.

Gen'aita t'crenn fora kremal'a m'ithrai?
What is rising from the sandy depths?

Can'tai a la y'stra detrai?
Who but the stars can say?

WELCOME TO THE GUILD OF TWO ROSES...

Bane of the galaxy's worst criminals, home to a diverse cast of bounty hunters. There are guidelines - but not many.

1. Et Cor Venari Est - The Hunt is the Heart
2. Crime is endless
3. Respect the crest
4. Criminals have long memories
5. Fraternize at your own risk

Maeve and Aethon's story is over... for now. Join the hunt and find out who's story is next. Follow @abbygraysonwrites on Instagram for more.

THANK YOU

Thank you Mom and Dad for always supporting me and believing in me. I appreciate you so much. You're kind of my favorite people. Please skip Chapters 12, 15, and especially the end of 17. Love you!

Thank you to my writing group - Ellen, JoAnne, Gila, and Annie! You're welcome for all the sex scenes, you dirty girls. Without your quality feedback and constant hype, this book wouldn't exist.

Thank you to my friends and family for always asking me how my writing is going and being excited for any progress I made. Special shout out to my first fangirl, Beffers! You made me believe I could do this for real.

Thank you to my best buddy dog who's been gone a year - Riker. You were my constant companion through the years while I fell in love with writing. I miss you every day.

Special thank you to every Starbucks I've ever written in for hours on end. I appreciate your cold brew. Please bring back your rectangular tables, I'm begging you.

And last, thank you to my comfort writing media including: Star Trek: The Next Generation, Friends, Gravity Falls, ATLA, Will/Deanna fanfics on AO3, the Picard Season 3 soundtrack, every Sara Bareilles album (especially The Blessed Unrest).

ABOUT THE AUTHOR

Abby Grayson

Abby Grayson is a writer and social worker from Illinois. She loves collecting art, Star Trek, and soccer - LFG Chicago Red Stars.

You can follow her on Instagram and Threads: @abbygraysonwrites

www.ingramcontent.com/pod-product-compliance
Lightning Source LLC
Chambersburg PA
CBHW021529250626
47154CB00006BA/2034